LARRY NIVEN

RINGWORLD'S CHILDREN

LARRY NIVEN and
EDWARD M. LERNER

FLEET of WORLDS

A TOM DOHERTY ASSOCIATES BOOK • NEW YORK

This is a work of fiction. All of the characters, organizations, and events portrayed in these novels are either products of the authors' imaginations or are used fictitiously.

RINGWORLD'S CHILDREN AND FLEET OF WORLDS

Ringworld's Children copyright © 2004 by Larry Niven

Fleet of Worlds copyright © 2007 by Larry Niven and Edward M. Lerner

All rights reserved.

A Forge Book
Published by Tom Doherty Associates, LLC
175 Fifth Avenue
New York, NY 10010

www.tor-forge.com

Forge® is a registered trademark of Tom Doherty Associates, LLC.

ISBN 978-0-7653-8686-1

Our books may be purchased in bulk for promotional, educational, or business use. Please contact your local bookseller or the Macmillan Corporate and Premium Sales Department at 1-800-221-7945, extension 5442, or by e-mail at MacmillanSpecialMarkets@macmillan.com.

First Edition: March 2016

Printed in the United States of America

0 9 8 7 6 5 4 3 2 1

CONTENTS

RINGWORLD'S CHILDREN

This is for the firemen of California and neighboring
states who fought the fires of October 2003,
with particular thanks to those who saved our house
and others in Indian Falls, Chatsworth,
Los Angeles County.

PREFACE

The Ringworld is about the same mass as Jupiter. Its shape is that of a ribbon a million miles across and six hundred million miles long, which makes it a bit larger than the Earth's orbit, and a few miles thick. It circles a yellow dwarf star. Its spin, at 770 miles/second, is enough to give it about Earth's gravity of centrifugal force. Walls along both rims, standing a thousand miles high, are enough to hold an atmosphere for millions of years.

Much else derives from these basic assumptions.

The inner surface is a habitat three million times the area of planet Earth. The topography is literally a work of art, carved in by whoever built the thing, so that from underneath the Ringworld resembles the back of a mask.

An inner ring of shadow squares block the sun, giving periods of night; else it would always be noon. A system of pipes leads from the bottoms of oceans, under the Ringworld floor, up the back of the rim wall and over the edge, to recycle seabottom ooze (or *flup*) into spill mountains. Huge attitude jets stand atop the rim wall, Bussard ramjets using the solar wind of protons for their fuel, to hold the Ringworld against its inherent instability. There are spaceport ledges outside the walls. Two vast salt oceans serve as preserves for seagoing life, and as something more: maps of several worlds at one-to-one scale. The Ringworld floor is of unnaturally strong material, dubbed *scrith*, with other unusual properties.

The sun itself is involved in the Ringworld's meteor defense. A superconducting network embedded in the Ringworld floor generates a superthermal laser effect in a solar flare. The drawback: it can't fire through the Ringworld itself. Thus any meteorite that strikes the Ringworld, such as the one that made Fist-of-God Mountain, generally rams upward from underneath.

Some details become clues to the nature of the Builders.

The plethora of harbors and fjords, plus the shallow oceans (most of them), suggest a race that uses only the top of an ocean.

The nastier life forms—mosquitoes, flies, jackals, sharks, vampire bats—don't exist. Hominids have moved into some of those ecological slots. The Engineers weren't ecologists, they were gardeners.

The inhabitants are hominids in bewildering variety, some intelligent, some not. They fill ecological niches which on Earth are held by almost any mammal, but particularly the nastier life forms, jackals and wolves and vampire bats . . . as if mankind's ancestor, *Homo habilis,* had been protected until they numbered hundreds of billions, then abandoned to mutate endlessly.

You don't know the Ringworld until you've grasped its size.

After the book came out, a friend was going to build a scale model for an upcoming convention. He had a marble, a blue immy, to serve as the Earth, for scale. Turns out he'd need a ribbon five feet tall and half a mile long. The hotel wasn't big enough.

One guy who tried to map the Ringworld told me he ran out of computer space very rapidly. He ran into too many powers of ten.

David Gerrold speaks of a class of novel called "the Enormous Big Thing." Today you could fill a fair-sized shelf with them. Arthur C. Clarke's *Rendezvous with Rama* and Bob Shaw's *Orbitsville* are in that class, and so is my own *Rainbow Mars.*

But *Ringworld* came first, published in 1970.

It might have been laughed at. Too big, too improbable. Any normal structural material would be torn apart by its spin. I waited for the reviews in some fear.

James Blish wrote that he thought it would win the Hugo Award, but it *shouldn't*.

The readers gave it a Hugo Award anyway.

The writers gave it a Nebula.

I didn't have a sequel planned. I was not expecting a flood of redesigns.

During one of my speeches, a man pointed out that the Ringworld's mathematics are simple: it's a suspension bridge with no endpoints.

An academic in England pointed out that the tensile strength of the Ringworld frame must be approximately the force that holds an atomic nucleus together. (Hence, *scrith*.)

A grade school class in Florida spent a semester on the Ringworld. Their conclusion: the worst problem is that, without tectonic activity, all the topsoil would flow into the oceans in a few thousand years. (Hence, *flup* and the spillpipes.)

At the 1970 World Science Fiction Convention there were MIT students in the halls chanting, "The Ringworld is unstable! The Ringworld is unstable!" (Did the best that I was able . . . hence, *attitude jets*.)

Somebody decided that the shadow squares shed too much twilight. What's needed is five long shadow squares orbiting retrograde.

Ultimately there was too much opportunity for redesign. I had to write *The Ringworld Engineers*.

All of these readers had found something worth knowing. The Ringworld is a great, gaudy, intellectual toy, a playground with the gates left wide open.

Some readers just read a book and stop.

Others play with the characters, or the assumptions, or the environment. They make up their own homework. We

readers have been doing that for unguessable thousands
of years: demanding more data on Atlantis from Plato, inventing Purgatory to put between Hell and Heaven, redesigning Dante's Inferno, writing new Odysseys. An
amazing subculture has sprung up around Star Trek.

The Internet opens a whole new metaplayground for
such people. A number of Web sites have sprung up (well,
at least two) whose topic is Larry Niven's fiction.

In September 1999, tipped off by my lovely agent,
Eleanor Wood, I logged onto *larryniven-1@bucknell.edu*.
They were arguing about whether you can clone a protector, and whether Seeker and Teela Brown might have
left a child behind. If they'd been right I wouldn't have
seen a story, but they were off on the wrong foot, and I
could fix it. After a few months of following these discussions, rarely interrupting, I had enough material for
Ringworld's Children.

This is a playground for the mind. It's a puzzle too, a
maze. Question every turn or you'll get lost. When you've
finished the book, remember not to lock the gate.

"All this was indispensably necessary," replied the one-eyed doctor, "for private misfortunes are public benefits, so that the more private misfortunes there are, the greater is the general good."

—Pangloss, in *Candide*, by Voltaire

RINGWORLD PARAMETERS

30 hours = one Ringworld day

1 Ringworld rotation = 7½ days

75 days = 10 turns = 1 falan

Mass = 2 × 10exp30 grams

Radius = .95 × 10exp8 miles

Circumference = 6 × 10exp8 miles

Width = .997 × 10exp6 miles

Surface area = 6 × 10exp14 square miles = 3 million times the surface area of the Earth

Surface gravity = .992 *G* (spin)

Spin velocity = 770 miles/second

Rim walls rise inward, 1000 miles.

Star: G3 verging on G2, barely smaller and cooler than Sol

CAST OF CHARACTERS

Recent arrivals

Louis Wu: Earth born. First and second Ringworld expeditions.

Teela Brown: Earth born, of a line bred for luck by Pierson's puppeteer manipulation. Turned protector in *The Ringworld Engineers*, and now deceased. First Ringworld expedition.

Nessus: Pierson's puppeteer, the Hindmost's partner and mate. Led the first Ringworld expedition.

The Hindmost: Pierson's puppeteer, once Chief-in-Command of his species. Led the second Ringworld expedition.

Chmeee, once Speaker-to-Animals: Kzin. First and second Ringworld expeditions.

Roxanny Gauthier: Earth born, Detective-One in the ARM. Served aboard *Snail Darter* and *Gray Nurse*.

Oliver Forrestier: Wunderland born, Detective, ARM. Served aboard *Snail Darter* and *Gray Nurse*.

Claus Raschid: Earth born, Detective-Two, ARM. Served aboard *Snail Darter* and *Gray Nurse*.

Detective-Major Schmidt: Earth born. Served aboard *Gray Nurse*.

Wes Carlton Wu: Earth born, Flight Captain aboard *Koala*.

Tanya Haynes Wu: Earth born, Purser aboard *Koala*.

Ringworld's children

Seeker: species unknown, last seen with Teela Brown.

Acolyte: Kzin, Chmeee's exiled son.

Bram: Vampire turned protector, ruler of the Repair Center for countless aeons until killed by Tunesmith with Louis Wu's help.

Wembleth: species unknown, Ringworld-born traveler.

Tunesmith: Night Person (Ghoul) turned protector.

Kazarp: Night Person, Tunesmith's son.

Hanuman: Hanging Person turned protector.

Valavirgillin: Machine People, represents Farsight Trading.

Proserpina: surviving Pak protector.

The Penultimate: Pak protector, long dead.

Szeblinda: Hinsh. Giraffe People.

Kawaresksenjajok: City Builder.

Fortaralisplyar: City Builder.

GLOSSARY

Aerobrake: To shed velocity by passing through a planetary atmosphere.

Antispin: Direction opposite the Ringworld's direction of spin.

Arch: The Ringworld as seen from anywhere on its surface.

ARM: Once the Amalgamation of Regional Militia; for several hundred years, the United Nations armed forces. Jurisdiction was originally limited to Earth-Moon system.

Autodoc: Any system built to perform automated medical operations.

Belter: Citizen of the asteroid belt, Sol system.

Canyon: A world of human space, once Patriarchy property.

Carlos Wu's autodoc: An experimental medical system first seen in "Procrustes."

Droud: A small device that plugs into the skull of a current addict. Its purpose: to meter a current flow to the pleasure center of the user's brain.

Elbow root: A ubiquitous Ringworld plant. Grows as a kind of natural fence.

Experimentalist: A Pierson's puppeteer political faction now out of power.

Eyestorm: The pattern of winds that forms above a puncture in the Ringworld floor. A tornado on its side. (Hurricanes and tornadoes are impossible on the Ringworld's flat surface.)

Fleet of Worlds: The homeworld of the Pierson's

puppeteer species, and four more worlds sequestered for farming, all occupy a Kemplerer rosette moving at near lightspeed.

Flup: Seabottom ooze.

Flycycle: A one- or two-LE flying device.

Fringe War: All the spacegoing species of known space seem to have sent ships to Ringworld system. Bram, when he was in command of the Repair Center, shot them down if they approached too close. Tunesmith hasn't done that, and the Fringe War is currently in a cold state.

General Products: A company owned by Pierson's puppeteers that sold mostly spacecraft hulls. Dissolved two hundred years ago.

The Great Ocean: One of two salt seas on the Ringworld, measuring six hundred times the surface area of the Earth.

Grippy: An all purpose hand tool.

Home: A world of human space, unusually Earthlike.

Hot Needle of Inquiry: Second ship (of Experimentalist design) to reach the Ringworld.

Human space: The region of stars explored by humanity.

Known space: The region of the universe known to explorers who communicate with humanity.

LE (*Legal Entity*): Any entity (human or not, organic or not) legally entitled to civil rights.

Long Shot: Prototype Quantum II hyperdrive spacecraft, first ship to visit the galactic core.

Lying Bastard: First ship (of Experimentalist design) to reach the Ringworld.

Map of Earth (or *Mars, Kzin, Kdatlyno, etc.*): The Great Ocean is scattered with maps of nearby inhabited worlds at one-to-one scale, complete with local ecologies as of the time the Ringworld was built.

Meteor Defense: Ringworld systems can cause a solar flare, and a superthermal laser effect within the flare. Energy output is awesome, but the effect is slow.

N-child: Lineal descendant.

Outsider hyperdrive or *Hyperdrive:* A means of faster-than-light travel common in known space.

Patriarchy: The Kzinti interstellar empire.

Port: To the left as one looks spinward.

Quantum II hyperdrive: An advanced experimental faster-than-light system, puppeteer designed, first seen in "At the Core." One Ringworld day under QII hyperdrive = 1440 light years.

Repair Center: The ancient center of Ringworld repair, maintenance, and control, housed beneath the Map of Mars on the Great Ocean.

Rishathra (reshtra, etc.): Sexual practice outside one's own species but within the intelligent hominids.

Scrith: Ringworld structural material. Scrith underlies all the terraformed and contoured inner surface of the Ringworld. The rim walls are also of scrith. Very dense, with a tensile strength on the order of the force that holds an atomic nucleus together.

Sheathclaws: A world held by humans and Kzinti together.

Spill mountains: Mountains standing against the rim wall, the outflow of the rim spillpipes. One stage in the circulation of flup.

Spin or *Spinward:* In the direction of rotation of the Ringworld. (Against the rotation of the sky.)

Starboard: To the right as one looks spinward.

Stasis field: Human technology. An induced state in which time passes very slowly. Ratios can be as high as a billion years of real time to a few seconds in stasis. An object in stasis is very nearly invulnerable.

Stepping disks: Puppeteer technology, an advanced form of teleportation.

Stet: Leave it alone; accept as written; make no change; restore.

Tanj: An expletive, once shorthand for "There ain't no justice."

Thruster: Reactionless drive. In human space, thrusters have generally replaced fusion rockets on all spacecraft save warcraft.

Vishnishtee (Vashneesht, Vasnesht, Vasneesit, etc.*):* Wizard or protector.

Webeye: Puppeteer technology, a multisensory transmitter.

Weenie plant: Ubiquitous Ringworld plant. Edible.

2893 A.D.

1
LOUIS WU

Louis Wu woke aflame with new life, under a coffin lid.

Displays glowed above his eyes. Bone composition, blood parameters, deep reflexes, urea and potassium and zinc balance: he could identify most of these. The damage listed wasn't great. Punctures and gouges; fatigue; torn ligaments and extensive bruises; two ribs cracked; all relics of the battle with the Vampire protector, Bram. All healed now. The 'doc would have rebuilt him cell by cell. He'd felt dead and cooling when he climbed into the Intensive Care Cavity.

Eighty-four days ago, the display said.

Sixty-seven Ringworld days. Almost a falan; a falan was ten Ringworld rotations, seventy-five thirty-hour days. Twenty or thirty days should have healed him! But he'd known he was injured. What with all the general bruising from the battle with Bram, he hadn't even noticed puncture wounds in his back.

He'd been under repair for twice that long the first time he lay in this box. Then, his internal plumbing systems had been leaking into each other, and he'd eleven years without the longevity complex called *boosterspice*. He'd been dying, and *old*.

Testosterone was high, adrenaline high and rising.

Louis pushed steadily up against the lid of the 'doc. The lid wouldn't move faster, but his body craved *action*. He slid out and dropped to a stone floor, cold beneath his bare feet. *Stone?*

He was naked. He stood in a vast cavern. Where was *Needle?*

The interstellar spacecraft *Hot Needle of Inquiry* had been embedded in cooled magma when last he looked, and Carlos Wu's experimental nanotech repair system had been in the crew quarters. Now its components sat within a nest of instruments and cables on a floor of cooled lava. The 'doc had been partly pulled apart. Everything was still running.

Hubristic, massive, awesome: this was a protector's work. Tunesmith, the Ghoul protector, must have been studying the 'doc while it healed Louis.

Nearby, *Hot Needle of Inquiry* had been fileted like a finless fish. A slice of hull running almost nose to tail had been cut away, exposing housing, cargo space, docking for a Lander now destroyed, thruster plates, and the hyperdrive motor housing. More than half of the ship's volume was tanks, and of course they'd been drained. The rim of the cut had been lined with copper or bronze, and cables in the metal led to instruments and a generator.

The cut section had been pulled aside by massive machinery. The cut surface was rimmed in bronze laced with cables.

The hyperdrive motor had run the length of the ship. Now it was laid out on the lava, in a nest of instruments. Tunesmith again?

Louis wandered over to look.

It had been repaired.

Louis had stranded the Hindmost in Ringworld space by chopping the hyperdrive in half, twelve or thirteen years ago. Dismounted, it looked otherwise ready to take *Needle* between the stars at Quantum I speeds, three days to the light year.

I could go home, Louis thought, tasting the notion.

Where is everybody? Louis looked around him, feeling the adrenaline surge. He was starting to shiver with cold.

He'd be almost two hundred and forty years old by now, wouldn't he? Easy to lose track here. But the nano machines in Carlos Wu's experimental 'doc had read his DNA and repaired everything down through the cell nuclei. Louis had done this dance before. His body thought it was just past puberty.

Keep it cool, boy. Nobody's challenged you yet.

The spacecraft, the hull section, the 'doc, machines to move and repair these masses, and crude-looking instruments arrayed to study them, all formed a tight cluster within vaster spaces. The cavern was tremendous and nearly empty. Louis saw float plates like stacks of poker chips, and beyond those a tilted tower of tremendous toroids that ran through a gap in the floor right up to the roof. Cylinders lay near the gap, caged within more of Tunesmith's machinery. They were bigger than *Needle*, each a little different from the others.

He'd passed through this place once before. Louis looked up, knowing what to expect.

Five or six miles up, he thought. The Map of Mars stood forty miles high. This level would be near the roof. Louis could make out its contours. Think of it as the back of a mask . . . the mask of a shield volcano the size of Ceres.

Needle had smashed down through the crater in Mons Olympus, into the repair center that underlay the one-to-one scale Map of Mars. Teela Brown had trapped them there after she turned protector. She had moved the ship eight hundred miles through these corridors, then poured molten rock around them. They'd used stepping disks— the puppeteers' instant transport system—to reach Teela. For all these years since, the ship had been trapped.

Now Tunesmith had brought it back to the workstation under Mons Olympus.

Louis knew Tunesmith, but not well. Louis had set a trap for Tunesmith, the Night Person, the breeder, and Tunesmith had become a protector. He'd watched Tunesmith fight Bram; and that was about all he knew of Tunesmith the protector. Now Tunesmith held Louis's life in his hands, and it was Louis's own doing.

He'd be smarter than Louis. Trying to outguess a protector was . . . futz . . . was both silly and inevitable. No human culture has ever stopped trying to outguess God.

So. *Needle* was an interstellar spacecraft, if someone could remount the hyperdrive. That tremendous tilted tower—forty miles of it if it reached all the way to the Repair Center floor—was a linear accelerator, a launching system. One day Tunesmith might need a spacecraft. Meanwhile he'd leave *Needle* gutted, because Louis Wu and the Hindmost might otherwise use it to run, and the protector couldn't have that.

Louis walked until *Needle* loomed: a hundred-and-ten-foot diameter cylinder with a flattened belly. Not much of the ship was missing. The hyperdrive, the 'doc, what else? The crew housing was a cross section, its floor eighty feet up. Under the floor, all of the kitchen and recycling systems were exposed.

If he could climb that high, he'd have his breakfast, and clothing too. He didn't see any obvious route. Maybe there was a stepping disk link? But he couldn't guess where Tunesmith might place a stepping disk, or where it would lead.

The Hindmost's command deck was exposed too. It was three stories tall, with lower ceilings than a Kzin would need. Louis saw how he could climb up to the lowest floor. A protector would have no trouble at all.

Louis shook his head. What must the Hindmost be *thinking?*

Pierson's puppeteers held to a million-year-old philosophy based on cowardice. When the Hindmost built *Needle*, he had isolated his command deck from any intruders, even from his own alien crew. There were no doors at all, just stepping disks booby-trapped a thousand ways. Now . . . the puppeteer must feel as naked as Louis.

Louis crouched beneath the edge of some flat-topped

mass, maybe the breathing-air system. Leapt, pulled up, and kept climbing. The 'doc's repairs had left him thin, almost gaunt; he wasn't lifting much weight. Fifty feet up, he hung by his fingers for a moment.

This was the lowest floor of the Hindmost's cabin, his most private area. There would be defenses. Tunesmith might have turned them off . . . or not.

He pulled up and was in forbidden space.

He saw the Hindmost. Then he saw his own droud sitting on a table.

The droud was the connector between any wall socket and Louis Wu's brain. Louis had destroyed that . . . had given it to Chmeee and watched the Kzin batter it to bits.

So, a replacement. Bait for Louis Wu, the current addict, the wirehead. Louis's hand crept into the hair at the back of his head, under the queue. Plug in the droud, let it trickle electric current down into the pleasure center . . . where was the socket?

Louis laughed wildly. It wasn't there! The autodoc's nano machines had rebuilt his skull without a socket for the droud!

Louis thought it over. Then he took the droud. When confused, send a confusing message.

The Hindmost lay like a jeweled footstool, his three legs and both heads tucked protectively beneath his torso. Louis's lips curled. He stepped forward to sink his hand into the jeweled mane and shake the puppeteer out of his funk.

"Touch nothing!"

Louis flinched violently. The voice was a blast of contralto music, the Hindmost's voice with the sound turned up, and it spoke Interworld. "Whatever you desire," it said, "instruct me. Touch nothing."

The Hindmost's voice—*Needle*'s autopilot—knew him, knew his language at least, and hadn't killed him. Louis found his own voice. "Were you expecting me?"

"Yes. I give you limited freedom in this place. Find a current source next to—"

"No. Breakfast," Louis said as his belly suddenly screamed that it was empty, dying. "I need food."

"There is no kitchen for your kind here."

A shallow ramp wound round the walls to the upper floors. "I'll be back," Louis said.

He walked, then ran up the ramp. He eased around the wall above a drop of eighty feet—not difficult, just scary—and was in crew quarters.

A pit showed where the 'doc had been removed. Crew quarters were not otherwise changed. The plants were still alive. Louis went to the kitchen wall and dialed cappuccino and a fruit plate. He ate. He dressed, pants and blouse and a vest that was all pockets, the droud bulging one of the pockets. He finished the fruit, then dialed up an omelet, potatoes, another cappuccino, and a waffle.

He thought while he ate. What *was* his desire?

Wake the Hindmost? He needed the Hindmost to tell him what was going on . . . but puppeteers were manipulative and secretive, and the balance of power in the Repair Center kept changing. Best learn more first. Get a little leverage before he reached for the truth.

He dumped the breakfast dishes in the recycler toilet. He climbed around the wall, carefully. "Hindmost's Voice," he said.

"At your command. You need not risk a fall. Here is a stepping-disk link," and a cursor arrowhead showed him a spot on the floor of crew quarters.

"Show me the Meteor Defense Room."

"That term is unknown." A hologram window popped up in the portside wall. "Is this the place you mean?"

Meteor Defense beneath the Map of Mars was a vast, dark space. All the stars in the universe ran round an ellipsoidal wall thirty feet high, and the floor and ceiling. Three long swinging booms ended in chairs equipped with lap keyboards, and those stood black-on-black before the wall display.

Past the edge of the pop-up window, under a glare of light, knobby bones had been laid out for study. This was the oldest protector Louis knew of, and Louis had named him Cronus. In the far shadows stood pillars with large plates on top, mechanical mushrooms. Louis pointed into the window. "What are those?"

"Service stacks," the Hindmost's Voice said, "each made from several float plates topped by a stepping disk."

Louis nodded. The Ringworld engineers had left float plates all through the Repair Center. If you stacked them, they'd lift more. Adding a stepping disk seemed an obvious refinement . . . if you had them to spare.

Louis saw a boom swing across the starscape. It ended in a knobby, angular shadow.

All protectors look something like medieval armor.

The protector was watching a spray of stars. His cameras would be mounted on the Ringworld itself, maybe on the outside of the rim wall, looking away from the sun. He didn't seem aware that he was being spied on.

Louis knew better than to expect asteroids or worlds. Unknown engineers had cleared all that out of the Ringworld system. This drift of moving lights would be spacecraft held by several species. Now the view focused on a gauzy, fragile Outsider ship; now on a glass needle, a General Products' #2 hull, tenant unknown; now a crowbar-shaped ARM warship.

Tunesmith's concentration seemed total. He zoomed on starscape occluded by a foggy lump, a proto-comet. Tiny angular machines drifted around it, marked by blinking cursor circles. A lance of light glared much brighter: some warship's fusion drive. Here came another, zipping across the screen. No weapon fired.

The Fringe War is still cold, Louis thought. He'd wondered how long that could last. A formal truce could not hold among so many different minds.

The protector's arms jittered above the keyboard.

In the corner of Louis's eye, sunlight glared down. Louis spun around.

Above *Needle* the crater in Mons Olympus was sliding open, flooding the cavern with unfiltered light.

The linear accelerator roared; an arc of lightning ran bottom to top.

The crater began to close.

Louis turned back to the display. Looking over Tunesmith's shoulder, he watched fusion light flare from offscreen and dwindle to a bright point. Whatever Tunesmith had launched was already too far to see.

Tunesmith had joined the Fringe War!

A protector could not be expected to do nothing, even if the alternative was to bring war down on their heads. Louis scowled. Bram the protector had been crazy, even if supremely intelligent. Louis must eventually decide if Tunesmith was crazy too, and what to do about it.

Meanwhile this latest maneuver should keep the protector busy. Now, how much freedom had Louis been allotted? Louis said, "Hindmost's Voice, show me the locations of all stepping disks."

The Hindmost's Voice popped up three hundred and sixty degrees of Map Room. The Ringworld surrounded Louis, a ring six hundred million miles around and a million miles wide, banded in blue for day and black for night and broad fuzzy edges for dusk and dawn. Winking orange cursor lights were displayed across its face. Some were shaped like arrowheads.

This pattern had changed greatly since Louis had last seen it. "How many?"

"Ninety-five stepping disks are now in use. Two failed. Three were dropped into deep space and probes launched through them. The fleets shot them down. Ten are held in reserve."

The Hindmost had stocked stepping disks aboard *Hot Needle of Inquiry*, but not a hundred and ten! "Is the Hindmost building more stepping disks?"

"With his help Tunesmith has built a stepping-disk factory. Work proceeds slowly."

The blinking orange lights that marked stepping disks were thick along the near side of the Ringworld, the Great Ocean arc. The far side looked sparse. Two blinking orange arrowheads had nearly reached the edge of the Other Ocean. Others were moving in that direction.

The Other Ocean was a diamond shape sprawling across most of the width of the Ringworld, one hundred eighty degrees around from the Great Ocean. Two such masses of water must counterbalance each other. The Hindmost's crew had not explored the Other Ocean. *High time*, Louis thought.

Most of the stepping disks were clustered around the Great Ocean, and of those, most were in a tight cluster that must be the Map of Mars. Louis pointed at one offshore from Mars. "What is that?"

"That is *Hot Needle of Inquiry*'s lander."

Teela the protector had blasted the lander during their last duel. "It's functional?"

"The stepping-disk link is functional."

"What about the lander?"

"Life support is marginal. Drive systems and weaponry have failed."

"Can some of these service stacks be locked out of the system?"

"That has been done." Lines spread across the map to link the blinking lights. Some had crossed-circle *verboten* marks on them: *closed*. The maze was complicated, and Louis didn't try to understand it. "My Master has override codes," the Voice said.

"May I have those?"

"No."

"Number these stepping-disk sites for me. Then print out a map."

As the Ringworld was vast, the scale was extreme. His naked eye would never get any detail out of it. When the map extruded, he folded it and stuffed it in a pocket anyway.

He broke for lunch and came back.

He set two service stacks moving and changed a number of links. The Hindmost's Voice printed another map with his changes added. He pocketed that too. Better keep both. Now, with luck, he'd have avenues of travel unknown to Tunesmith.

Or it might be wasted effort. The Hindmost, when he woke, could change it all back in a moment.

The Voice refused to make weapons. Of course the kitchen in *Needle*'s crew quarters hadn't done that either.

Tunesmith was still at the end of a boom, still tracking whatever he'd launched.

"Where are the rest of us?" Louis asked the Voice.

"Who do you seek?"

"Acolyte."

"I do not have that name—"

"The Kzin we shared this ship with. Chmeee's child."

"I list that LE as—" blood-curdling howl. Louis had to pry his fingers loose from a table edge. "Rename him Acolyte?"

"Please."

The map was back, and a blinking point next to Fist-of-God . . . a hundred thousand miles port-and-antispin from Fist-of-God—four times the circumference of the Earth—and twice that far to spinward of the Map of Mars. The hugeness of the Ringworld had to be learned over and over. The Voice said, "Here we set Acolyte, with a service stack, thirty-one days ago. He has since moved by eleven hundred miles." The point jumped minutely. "Tunesmith has altered the setting for the stepping disk. It sends to an observation point on the Map of Earth."

Home to Acolyte's father. "Has he used it?"

"No."

"Where are the City Builders?"

"Do you mean the librarians? Kawaresksenjajok and Fortaralisplyar and three children were returned to their origin—"

"Good!" He'd meant to do that himself.

"To the library in the floating city. I note your approval. Who else shall I track?"

Who else had been his companions? Two protectors. Bram the Vampire protector was dead. Tunesmith was . . . still busy, it seemed. In the Meteor Defense Room the protector's telescope screen was following a receding point, the vehicle he'd launched earlier. Its drive was off . . . flared brilliantly and blinked off again.

That was a warship. Reaction motors were still needed for war; modern thrusters couldn't switch on and off as fast.

Louis asked, "Have you kept track of Valavirgillin?"

The map jumped. "Here, near the floating city and a local center of Machine People culture."

Good, and she was well away from vampires. They had not met in twelve years. "*Why* did you track her, Hindmost's Voice?"

"Orders."

Carefully, "Who do you take orders from?"

"From you and Tunesmith and—" a blast of orchestral chaos, piercingly sweet. Louis recognized the Hindmost's true name. "But all such may be countermanded by—" the Hindmost's name again.

"Is Tunesmith restricted from any interesting levels of this ship?"

"Not currently."

The Hindmost was still in wrapped-around-himself catatonia. "How long since he's eaten?" Louis asked.

"Two local days. He wakes to eat."

"Wake him up."

"How shall I wake him without trauma?"

"I saw him in a dance once. Turn that on. Prepare food for him."

2

THE HINDMOST

The Hindmost dreamed *of perfect safety.*

He did not dream that he was Hindmost again, ruler of a trillion of his own kind. He'd been mad to be so ambitious. Always he had known that that was no stable state, that his Experimentalist faction could lose power in a moment. As it had.

He dreamed that he was young again. That was so long ago that all detail had been smoothed from his mind, and he only remembered a generic sense of being little and protected and unique.

He dreamed that no tool would ever bite his hand.

And then the dance began—

The illusion was marvelous.

Louis stood in a vast hall. The floor was all broad, shallow steps. A thousand aliens moved around him; two thousand throats uttered orchestral music that was also conversation, unbearably complex. Wolfgang Amadeus Mozart would have gone crazy. The Beatles . . . started out crazy, but futz, so did Mozart.

Kick, slide, left heads brush fingerlips; hind leg kicks, partner shies. The Hindmost kicked. A flat one-eyed head emerged from beneath his torso. *Spin, kick;* the Hindmost lurched to his forefeet and tried to turn. Was this a dance or a martial art?

The Hindmost whistled. The dance dissipated. "Louis," the puppeteer said.

"How long were you out?"

"I sleep much. Where is Tunesmith?"

"Fighting a war, I think."

A head turned to the display of the Meteor Defense Room. "I watched him build that vehicle. The Fringe War grows ever hotter. Have they invaded the Ringworld?"

"I have no idea. Hindmost, how did *Needle* come to be in this state?"

"Recall that Tunesmith accepted me as his teacher, on your advice."

Tunesmith, the Ghoul musician, had been newborn as a protector and thirsty for learning. "He needed training, and fast," Louis said. "I thought that the more he learned from us, the more we could guess what he'd do. Did you try to keep secrets?"

"Yes."

"And you barred him from the flight deck, of course."

"I did," the puppeteer acknowledged. "I taught using your displays in crew quarters. I taught well, but he learned faster, always faster. He demanded access to my tools. I refused. Six days after you entered the 'doc, I woke to find him standing over me *here* where I thought he could not reach. I gave him everything."

"When did he chop up your ship?"

"Some time afterward. I was in fear-coma for eleven days. I woke and found this. Little has changed since. Louis, he has repaired the hyperdrive!"

"A fat lot of good—"

"He will reassemble the ship. When he does, I flee. Be aboard."

"When?"

The puppeteer's eyes looked at each other.

That meant confusion, or amusement, or any form of internal conflict. Louis asked, "What's he been doing? Building a warship—"

"Yes, and tracking the Fringe War, delving the secrets of my machinery—he wouldn't trust me to teach him—and ridding himself of my allies and yours. The Machine People are sent home. Acolyte is sent to spy on nothing at all. You, he kept safely asleep in the Intensive Care Cavity, and did extensive experiments there too. Louis, I must instruct you. You shall know everything you might need."

Louis asked, "Why?"

"We are allies!"

"Why?" The droud was gone from its place, a bulge in Louis's pocket. Would the Hindmost mention it?

"Tunesmith has us enslaved! Can't you see what he plans for you?"

"I think so. He'll make me a protector."

Protector was the adult form of the human species.

Child, breeder, protector. At middle age—younger for some species of hominid, older for a few, around forty-five for humans—a breeder can become a protector. His/her skin thickens and wrinkles to armor. The brain case expands. A second two-chamber heart grows where the femoral arteries run into the legs. Joints grow bulky, giving a greater momentum for greater leverage in muscles and tendons.

There are psychological changes too. A protector loses the attributes of gender. A protector will protect his/her progeny, identifying them by scent. Mutations are left to die. A protector with no surviving children usually stops eating and dies . . . but some may choose to protect and nurture their entire species. That can work, if there is a perceived threat.

But none of it happens without the virus that lives in tree-of-life to trigger the change.

Tree-of-life did not grow properly on Earth. On the Ringworld it had been found only in chambers beneath the Map of Mars. The hominids of Earth, and of the Ring-world too, had evolved as breeders, an unfinished form, like axolotls.

Too young a hominid does not react to the smell of tree-of-life root. The root will poison an elderly hominid. Louis Wu had been too old until Carlos Wu's autodoc changed him, and now he was too young.

"I'm safe for at least a quarter century," he said.

The puppeteer said, "Longer than that, if you use Carlos Wu's autodoc in time. The 'doc rejuvenates you. Tunesmith will stop you from doing that."

Good point. Louis said, "And what if he waits that long before he puts *Needle* back together?"

The puppeteer spoke in mournful music. "Then I am lost. Severed from my family, my home. Slave to a creature shaped by his evolution to hold nothing of worth beyond his own bloodline. Louis, you face the same. You are not of Tunesmith's species."

"On the Ringworld I'm not of any species."

"Yes, Louis, *yes*," in crescendo, "don't you see the implication? He will feed you tree-of-life. You will be a protector. He will not give you power over *him*. You are to be only a prisoner and advisor, a talking head, the protector who has no descendants to guard. You will be the Voice that speaks for the safety of the Ringworld itself!"

"Yes," Louis said patiently, "but not for twenty-five years. I've been rebuilt young. I don't react to the smell of the root. I'm not old enough to make the change."

"But do you want that?"

"No. Nonono. What can you do for me? I've been studying your placement of stepping disks. I made a few changes."

The Hindmost whistled up the Map Room display, the Ringworld and stepping disks, and vectors and all. He turned a complete circle, heads held wide apart for extreme binocular vision. "Good."

"I expect you could reset everything. Understand though, Hindmost, if a service stack isn't where I expect to find it, that could kill me. You should give me access codes."

"Yes."

"By now Tunesmith must know everything about the 'doc. What don't I know?"

"You would not have the mental capacity."

Louis was silent.

"Carlos Wu built an experimental nanotech-based medical system more than two hundred years ago. The United Nations considered him a proprietary genius. They claimed his work too. He took the 'doc when he disappeared. Carlos Wu was never found. The 'doc reappeared six years later on Shasht-Fafnir. My agent, Nessus, was able to buy it. My research team modified it to accommodate Kzinti and Pierson's puppeteer physiology and to make it more versatile and dependable.

"Now Tunesmith has rebuilt the machine. I expect it will accommodate Night People too. He's mastered this form of nanotechnology and is using nanomachines to make more stepping disks. What else must you know? The 'doc is set to rebuild certain life forms from their genetic codes."

"Let's talk about *Needle*. Has he added weapons?"

"Yes, and mastered mine, and boosted my thrusters beyond sane safety limits—"

"What's he doing now?"

In the pop-up window, the black silhouette of Tunesmith wasn't doing anything. All the action was in deep space, where a point was moving away from the Ringworld at high speed. The ships of the Fringe War hadn't found it yet.

"A very agile ship with a miniature cabin. A small Hanging People protector is the pilot," the Hindmost said. "Little fuel, large thruster and reaction motors, weapons not from my library. As you saw, launched via linear accelerator. Onboard fuel is used only to dodge and decelerate. Tunesmith names it *Probe One*."

Probe One was hard to see when its motor was off, but the motor was sputtering now as it dodged plasma weapons and missiles and, somehow, even lasers. Tunesmith's instruments followed it out toward interstellar space.

The Ringworld system retained its outer comets. All the near masses—planets, moons, asteroids—had been stripped from Ringworld system long ago, but comets must have been judged no threat to the Ringworld. After all, there were no big masses to change their orbits and hurl them inward.

Ships of half a dozen species had been hiding among the comets ever since Chmeee and Louis revealed the Ringworld's existence nearly forty years ago.

Now ARM ships—human-built, the police and military branch of the United Nations—streaked in from off-screen. They looked more like tethers than ships, some with smaller ships attached. *Probe One* lit like a flash-bulb—*guessed wrong about a laser!*—and vanished.

Tunesmith's screen swung wide, following nothing obvious.

Louis hadn't seen any debris.

"Hanging People" was a generic designation for hominids who lived a monkey lifestyle. Some weren't sapient. A Hanging People protector would still gain human intelligence or better. Hastily trained for spaceflight, it might outguess ARM defenses, but Tunesmith would still outthink it, would still keep control. Being a protector was all about control.

Tunesmith's telescope swung half around the sky, a hundred and eighty degrees, or nearly that. Tunesmith's viewpoint focused on a fuzzy object . . . a comet, loosely packed ice drifting apart. Then on a spacecraft emerging from within the cloud.

It was lens shaped, painted black with vivid orange markings in the dots-and-commas of Kzinti script.

"Markings name this ship *Diplomat*," the Hindmost told Louis. "We've observed. *Diplomat* seems well armed, but it never comes close to the Ringworld star. Always it lurks among the comets. Always it can flee in hyperdrive."

"That doesn't sound like Kzinti."

"They learn. I deem *Diplomat* the command ship for the Patriarchy fleet."

Probe One was back. It had circled halfway around Ringworld's sun through hyperspace in less than thirty minutes. Its huge intrinsic velocity had pointed away from the sun; now it carried the ship inward, straight toward *Diplomat.*

Word from the other side of the sky would not have reached *Diplomat* yet. Minutes passed before the ship's Kzinti crew reacted to the intruder. Then threads of interplanetary dust glowed a bit in *Diplomat*'s laser fire, and a handful of small ships zipped out of the ice cloud.

Probe One began dodging. A laser: *Probe One* flared brilliantly. Louis squinted against the glare. Tunesmith's screen wasn't built to protect viewers from blindness. *Probe One* dodged out of the beam and into a scintillation of impacts and was still going.

Louis asked, "General Products' hull?"

"That, under a layer of Ringworld floor material."

Another ship popped out nearby, just long enough for Louis to get a good view. It was much larger than *Diplomat*, a transparent sphere with complex machinery packed tightly inside the hull . . . gone now, like the soap bubble it resembled.

"*Long Shot*," Louis said, anger rising.

"I saw it," the Hindmost said.

"They ran. Kzinti don't do that."

"*Long Shot* is being used for courier service. It's too valuable to risk, and the Patriarchy will not have found room for armaments."

"ARM and Patriarchy were supposed to *share* that ship. Chmeee and I gave it to them with that understanding."

Probe One was too near the lens ship, accelerating sideways to get around it while fighting energy displays and lesser ships. Suddenly there was actinic light. Louis blinked hard. When he could see again, *Probe One* was gone.

"What the futz was that?" he demanded.

"Antimatter bullet. The newer ARM ships are all powered by antimatter, but we had not seen it used by the Patriarchy. They must manufacture their own in a particle accelerator somewhere. The ARM has a source, an antimatter solar system."

"Antimatter. Hindmost, that makes the Fringe War a *lot* more dangerous. The Ringworld is too fragile for this."

"Agreed."

"What's he doing now?"

The shadow of a protector leapt from its chair, arced like a ballet superstar across the view of comets and warships, touched down at one focus of the elliptical room, and was gone.

A hand like a sackful of ball bearings closed on Louis's forearm. He spasmed like a man electrocuted. "Louis! Good, you're awake," Tunesmith said briskly. "Without you this would have been difficult. Hindmost, come out of there. Danger does not await our convenience. Louis, are you all right? Your heartbeat sounds funny."

3

RECRUITING

Tunesmith was a *young* protector.

A Night People male of middle age had been lured into a cavern that grew tree-of-life. Tunesmith had emerged from his cocoon state a hundred and ten days ago: a tremendous mind demanding to be trained, in a hominid body hardened for endless war.

At first he must have satisfied himself with the Librarians' incomplete knowledge, and Acolyte's, and with what came in niggardly driblets from the Hindmost.

Tunesmith would not have begun his intrusions in any tentative fashion, Louis thought. The Hindmost might block that. Tunesmith must have built this heavy equipment and programmed it at his leisure, then set it moving all at once, after he'd picked the Hindmost's locks.

Fait accompli: suddenly he's standing over the puppeteer in his own living quarters. Suddenly he's filleted the Hindmost's spacecraft and is removing components as a fisher guts a trout.

Protectors of any species would be manipulative. Intelligence *was* manipulative, wasn't it? A superior intelligence would want to *control* his teachers. Knock them off balance from time to time. The differences between ally, servant, slave, and sled dog blur when the difference in intelligence is great enough.

A moment ago Louis had been spying on a protector. Suddenly the protector was beside him, gripping his wrist.

Louis said, "I'm fine. Much too young to have a heart attack."

The puppeteer's heads and legs were buried under him.

"Work on him," Tunesmith said. "I'm going to be busy."

"Two questions," Louis said, but the protector was gone.

The Hindmost eased a head into the open. No part of the neck showed, only eye and mouth.

Tunesmith could be seen sprinting about outside *Hot Needle of Inquiry*, working controls, then shouting into thin air. Heavy machinery began to move. The rebuilt hyperdrive motor was in motion. Unequal halves of the ship's hull began to close. The top of the linear accelerator began to track across the underside of Mons Olympus.

The Hindmost whistled. "I was right! He's—" The head ducked back under him. Tunesmith was back.

He stooped to work controls on the hidden stepping

disk. Then he picked up the curled-up puppeteer, evading the hind leg as it lashed out. They weighed about the same, Louis guessed. "Louis, follow," he barked, and stepped forward and was gone.

Just for an instant, Louis Wu rebelled.

It was a test, of course. Would Louis Wu follow him without question? This was all just too familiar.

An alien mastermind bursts into Louis Wu's life, assembles a crew, and hares off on a mission known only to the master. First Nessus, then the Hindmost, then the protector Teela Brown, then Bram, now Tunesmith, each chooses Louis Wu for reasons of convenience, drops him into the middle of a situation he doesn't understand, and runs him like a marionette. By the time Louis finishes playing catch-up, he's committed to something on the far side of sanity.

Pierson's puppeteers were control freaks. A true coward never turns his back on danger.

Being a protector was all about control.

Where would he be, what would Louis Wu have done, by the time he knew anything?

The instant passed. If he didn't follow, he'd be out of the action entirely. Louis stepped forward, onto a stepping disk that looked like the rest of the floor, and flicked out.

A flood of sunlight made him squint.

He stood on a high peak, on a stack of six float plates and a stepping disk. Tunesmith and the Hindmost stood below him on a translucent gray surface. Louis looked first for the Arch, to orient himself.

The Arch—the far side of the Ringworld—arced from horizon to horizon, broad above the haze at the spinward and antispin horizons, narrowing toward noon where it passed behind the sun. Louis hadn't seen the Arch in some time.

Fist-of-God Mountain loomed to port like a lost moon, poking far out of the atmosphere. Around its foot the land was more moonscape than desert, hundreds of millions of square miles of lifeless pitted rock. Fist-of-God was an inverted crater. A meteoroid had punched up through the Ringworld floor from underneath, hundreds of years ago. The blast had flayed soil from the high places, even this far away. Naked scrith was dramatically slippery.

Closer were silver threads of river and silver patches of sea, and the dark green tint of life gradually encroaching. The land below the hill was a broad jungle, and cutting through it, a river miles across.

"Watch your footing," Tunesmith said. Louis lowered himself carefully onto naked scrith.

It was worth remembering: beneath this shell of landscape was nothing but stars and vacuum. There would be no springs hereabouts, no groundwater, nothing to support life. No busybody to wander by, to fiddle with the controls on an abandoned service stack. Exposed as it was, this was an excellent hiding place for high-tech tools such as these.

Louis asked, "Are you going to explain what's going on?"

Tunesmith said, "Briefly. As a breeder I knew little but remembered a great deal. Coming out of my transition from breeder to protector, the first thing I was sure of was that the Ringworld is terribly fragile. I knew that I was reborn to protect the Ringworld and all its species.

"That has come in steps. I whiffed Bram, of course, and knew I had to kill him. I spent some time learning from the Hindmost and his library, and watching the Fringe War develop. Then for a time it seemed best to work alone or with a few Hanging People protectors. Now I must assemble a team."

"To do what?"

Tunesmith touched controls. The service stack lifted. Four float plates detached from the bottom and eased apart. Tunesmith boarded a stack of two, leaving one each for the puppeteer and the man.

The puppeteer was looking about him. He said, "Downslope, one could survive. Ringworld folk are generally hospitable to strangers. Tunesmith, you never accept my word when you can test it. Why do you involve *me*?"

"And for *what*?" Louis demanded.

Tunesmith floated off downslope. Louis and the puppeteer boarded and followed. The protector's voice carried easily. He spoke Interworld with no trace of accent, projecting his voice from deep in his belly, fearing no interruption, like a king.

"The Fringe War grows more intense. The ARM is using antimatter instead of hydrogen fusion to power their motors and weapons. Louis, the Ringworld cannot survive this. Something must be done."

"See if you can describe it!"

"Louis, to shape a *plan* I need to learn more. Did the Hindmost tell you of a courier ship? Of puppeteer manufacture, with an experimental drive—"

"*Long Shot*. I've flown it. The warcats have it!" He hadn't called a Kzin a warcat in a very long time.

"We're going to take it back. We have time to recruit Acolyte," Tunesmith said.

They were nearing the edge of the jungle.

"Why would Acolyte join you?"

"I expect you will tell him to. Acolyte's father sent him to you 'to learn wisdom.'"

"Joining you on a piracy expedition, is that wisdom?"

The puppeteer asked, "Do you need us? Do you trust us? Could you fight alone?"

The protector said, "I must leave someone to fly *Hot Needle of Inquiry*, or else leave *Needle* abandoned and adrift among the comets."

The Hindmost immediately said, "I can fly *Needle*."

"Hindmost, you would run."

"Louis and I will be pleased to—"

"Louis flew *Long Shot* once before. He will again. You and Acolyte will fly *Needle*."

"As you will," the Hindmost said.

Tunesmith said, "Louis, you swore an oath. You must protect the Ringworld."

In a mad moment Louis Wu had sworn to *save* the Ringworld. He'd done that, twelve years ago, when the Ringworld had drifted off center . . . but Louis only said, "I won't force Acolyte."

"Then I must await developments."

There were long-tailed Hanging People in the jungle. They threw sticks and dung. Louis and the Hindmost rose above the treetops, but Tunesmith's float plates dropped near the forest floor. They heard him whoop and saw him flinging missiles. Stones and sticks flew faster and more accurately than Hanging People could dodge. In less than a minute they'd vanished.

Tunesmith rose to join them. "Tell me again why Ringworld species are always hospitable!"

"Tunesmith, those were apes," Louis said. "Hominids aren't always sapient, you know. Is this what you picked to pilot your probe?"

"Yes, made into protectors. Sapience is relative."

Louis wondered if a protector really didn't see the difference between these apes and Louis Wu. A protector's lips and gums hardened into something like a beak; he could not frown, or smile, or sneer, or grin.

It was jungle all the way, trees and vines that Louis couldn't name, and a species of elbow root growing in chains at sixty-degree angles, big enough to match sequoias.

Louis switched his faceplate display to infrared. Now lights on the ground wove about each other, lurked, charged, merged. Thousands of tiny lights above him must be birds. Larger lights in the trees would be sloth and Hanging People and—Louis swerved to dodge a fifty-pound flying squirrel with a head that was all ears and fangs. It cursed luridly as it passed under him.

Hominid?

Nice day for a float.

Tunesmith settled in a circle of elbow trees. The ground was uneven, humped here and there, and overgrown with a tangle of grass. The Hindmost descended and Louis followed, still seeing nothing . . . and then an abandoned float plate. How had that gotten here?

His own disk settled. Louis stepped off, and they were surrounded. Weird little men stepped out of the elbow trees and women popped out of the ground. All were armed with short blades. They only stood heart-high. Louis, wearing impact armor, did not feel threatened.

Tunesmith hailed them and began talking rapidly. Louis's translator device had never heard this language; it and he could only listen. But he could see through torn grass into a burrow that ran deep underground. The grass was torn just so in fifty places.

He was standing on a city.

Hominids—descended from the Pak who must have built the Ringworld—had occupied every possible ecological niche, starting half a million years ago with a population already in the trillions (though the numbers were pretty much guesswork). This group were burrowers. They wore only their own straight brown body hair, and carried animal-skin pouches. They had a streamlined look, like ferrets.

They were looking less defensive now. Some were laughing. Tunesmith spoke and more laughed. One stepped to a rise of ground and pointed.

Tunesmith bowed. He said, "Acolyte is hunting a daywalk or three to spin of port. Louis, what shall I tell them? They offer rishathra."

He was tempted for an instant, then embarrassed. "Louis isn't in season."

Tunesmith barked. The Burrowing People laughed hysterically, looking at Louis with myopic eyes.

Louis asked, "What was your excuse?"

"I've been here. They know about protectors. Board your disk."

4

ACOLYTE

The smells were *stunningly rich. Hundreds of varieties of plants, scores of animals. Kzinti could survive in style here, until their numbers grew too great. Acolyte, millions of miles from the nearest Kzinti, did not miss their company; but Acolyte resolved to tell his father about this place.*

He sniffed, seeking an elusive smell: anything large or lethal.

It wasn't there. Only the smell of brachiating hominids.

His father's hunting park had been more dangerous. The danger level of father's park was as carefully measured as the placement of each bush. Kzinti needed a threat to bring them alive, and to keep their numbers down too.

Pak protectors didn't think like that.

Louis Wu had explained it thus: protectors had spread life across this land in imitation of the life patterns that evolved on Ball Worlds, but they had left out anything that harmed or annoyed Pak breeders, from carnivores down to parasites and bacteria. Whatever attacked today's bewildering variety of hominids had evolved over the million years, the four million falans, that followed.

Of course Louis was guessing. He'd said that too.

So, here was a safe place to play. One day Tunesmith would call, or Louis, and Acolyte would find danger enough. The lights in the night sky were not all stars.

A blotch in infrared, bigger than other blotches, went from perfect stillness to a blur of speed, leapt into a tree, merged with a smaller glow, paused—

Tunesmith yowled.

A returning yowl seemed muffled. Louis's dawdling translator caught up; it said, "Acolyte!" "Here. Wait." Then: "Louis!"

"Hello, Acolyte!" called Louis.

"Louis! I was worried! How are you?"

"Young. Hungry, antsy, not quite sane."

"You were forever in the healing box!"

Tunesmith said, "Acolyte kept bothering me for updates until I had to find work for him elsewhere."

Louis was touched. Acolyte had worried . . . thinking that Louis remained in the 'doc because there was more to be done for him. More likely Tunesmith was just keeping Louis out of the way; or he might have been refining the rejuvenation process, or using Louis as a test subject to study nanotechnology, tanj him. A twelve-year-old should not be forced to such cynical thinking, even a twelve-year-old Kzin.

The massive cat was halfway up a tree trunk, eating, while Hanging People threw hard fruit from a distance. Tunesmith separated his float plates and hovered one next to Acolyte.

Chmeee was a Kzin chosen by the puppeteer Nessus to join his exploration team, decades ago. Acolyte was Chmeee's eldest son, cast out by his father and sent to "learn wisdom" from Louis Wu. He stood seven feet tall, shorter than his father, furred in orange and dark chocolate: dark ears, dark stripes down his back, a smaller chocolate comma down his tail and leg. Three parallel ridges ran down his belly, possibly his father's legacy; Louis had never asked.

On a huge tilted trunk under green-black foliage, he looked utterly at home.

He asked, "Are we finally ready?"

"Yes," said Tunesmith.

Acolyte judged the distance above a drop of fifty feet. He had to make a twisting leap. He hit the disk on all fours. The disk dropped under his weight, and Acolyte slid, scrambled, and had his grip.

A Kzin's hands were good, but with his claws extended his fingers would have slid off. Anger might have killed him. It was a jest, or a test—and Tunesmith had been dropping past him, ready to catch him.

"I should reclaim my float plate," Acolyte said. He dropped toward the forest floor and took off through tilted trunks along a path Louis couldn't find.

A float plate floated above a display of huge, gorgeous orange flowers. Acolyte eased the disk he was riding down over the other float plate, and with a magnetic *click* they locked.

"I left one with the Underpeople, their toy until I need it," the Kzin said. "I mass too much. I have to be too careful when it's just one floater."

The double disk took off, Tunesmith followed, and they were racing.

Louis tried to keep up, but it was a hairy ride. They were leaving the Hindmost far behind. Tunesmith called, "What have you learned?"

The Kzin bellowed, "Nothing since we spoke. Teela's path ends with the Mechanics, two months after she left Louis and my father. I have dwelt among five civilizations, six species—interesting symbiotic culture, Mechanics, and a variety of Hanging People. None tell any tale of Teela Brown, or Seeker, or weapons that throw light, advanced medicine, famine averted, a flycycle— Whatever I thought of, they never heard of it."

"Were you lied to?"

"Who would dare? Who would care? Teela's path is discontinuous. I never tracked her through the sky! I only found places where she and Seeker landed. The Mechanics remember her from two or three falans after a floating building passed over, a hundred and fifty falans ago. Have you sought rumors of flying devices? Or assessed conflicting reports?"

"Yes."

"Louis—" Acolyte looked back, then slowed. Tunesmith slowed too: the race was over.

"Louis, I was asked to track Seeker and Teela Brown. I found little. They disappeared for seventy or eighty falans. Then the Vampire protector Bram tells us they entered the Repair Center as breeders. The man died of tree-of-life—too old—and Teela woke from coma as a protector."

Tunesmith said, "I want to know how breeders could find their way into the Map of Mars. I want to know why Bram let Teela wake. It would have been so easy to study her in her coma, then kill her. They may be trivial questions, but I wonder."

Louis shrugged. He'd wondered too. Bram had had little respect for human life, breeder or protector.

Acolyte asked, "Are you caught up with what's happening?"

"Tanj, no. Tunesmith is driving me crazy with his secrets."

The protector said, "I'll talk as we go.

"Louis, you made me. You saw that a Vampire protector was unfit to decide the Ringworld's fate, or else that Bram himself was unfit. You thought a Ghoul would serve. You lured me into the Repair Center. A tree-of-life garden made me a protector. You expected me to kill Bram, and I did. I assume you considered implications." No anger, no bitterness showed. A protector's face was like hardened leather.

"Consider this implication: no protector ever evolved to stand aside when his descendents are in danger. You

saw that a Ghoul's children must benefit where other hominids survive well, but did you see that too? We must act,
sensibly or not. The Fringe War was bad enough when
you entered the 'doc, Louis. Now the ARM has brought
antimatter-powered ships, twenty and counting. Now it
seems the Kzinti have stolen the puppeteers' Quantum II
hyperdrive ship. To use it for courier service tells us interesting secrets, doesn't it?"

Louis agreed. "They don't dare endanger it. They don't
know how to duplicate the drive. There's still only one
ship."

Tunesmith asked, "Hindmost, could *you* build another
Long Shot?"

"No. My research team could, but trial and error played
a large part, and the cost . . . broke my power, drove me
into exile, as much as any of my other mistakes."

They circled Tunesmith's service stack, then landed.
Tunesmith said, "I can't do nothing. If I can understand
Long Shot— Here, let me reset our destination. Acolyte,
this setting would take you to your father. Were you
tempted?"

"I have nothing to offer him yet."

"Follow me through." Tunesmith stepped from his float
plate and was gone.

They came out underground, where float plates waited.
The air smelled of the caverns beneath the Map of
Mars. Tunesmith showed off his toys as they drifted through
tunnels and caverns.

A dozen float plates carried a huge laser cannon at a
walking pace. "I made this from specs in the Hindmost's
records," the protector said, "with a few improvements.
I'll mount it on Mons Olympus. I've heliographed the design to protectors along the rim wall. Soon we won't have
to depend on the sun to let us talk. I should mount one on
Fist-of-God too.

"Here—" He reached out and down to snatch up a nest

of tubing. He put one end to his mouth and wild music emerged. "What do you think?" He blew again, and what the futz, Louis danced on the float plate with an imaginary partner.

Tunesmith stopped to examine massive machinery, then reworked some superconducting circuitry with a spray gun. The mass crept away on sixty or seventy float plates. "Meteor repair kit," he said. "Finished, but now it's got to be moved to the launcher."

Stepping disks were growing in a vat while instruments monitored the metal content of the fluid. Tunesmith used a finished stepping disk to flick them into the Meteor Defense Room.

Louis had no idea where he'd been.

No idea what they were doing.

It seemed to Louis that the protector's mind was like a vast maze, and Louis lost within it. Working with Bram had been no different. The Vampire protector had committed an intolerable crime, and Louis had found him out. Louis had taken steps to replace him with a Ghoul, a Night People. Well and good, but had he expected to suddenly attain freedom?

Protectors themselves didn't have freedom. If Tunesmith could always see the right answer, why would he ever choose otherwise? And all that a poor stupid breeder could do was ride along. But if Louis didn't get some answers soon—

The Fringe War was all laid out on the floor-to-ceiling screen circling the Meteor Defense Room. Ships and bases were marked with blinking cursors in neon colors. Kzinti and human ships were numerous. Others manifested a presence: puppeteers, Outsiders, Trinocs, ships and probes Tunesmith hadn't identified. The Ringworld was of interest to any entity who learned of it.

A Kzinti ship fell through the inner system, rounding the sun without a challenge.

Tunesmith said, "An ARM attempted to talk to me, but I choose not to answer. No other faction has. There were early attempts to invade. The meteor defense stops everything but microprobes, but those must be everywhere. I've intercepted what must be messages between ships, too well encrypted even for me. By *Needle*'s database I can identify ships and habitats in the inner comets belonging to ARM, Patriarchy, Trinocs, an Outsider ship, and three Pierson's puppeteers all hanging well outside the system, and thousands of probes of unidentified origin. I had best assume that everyone knows everything that anyone is doing. Even for me, keeping a secret will be tricky."

He zoomed the display. "Louis, what is this?"

A dot was light-amplified to a blurred view of a ghostly torus made of black lace, all intertwining threads, a tiny point-source of yellow-white light at the center, no obvious spacecraft drive. "Thirty-two Ringworld radii distant—"

Louis said, "Another Outsider. They don't always use light sails. We bought hyperdrive technology from them, but they've got something even better. The good news is, they've got no use for liquid water and high gravity, so they've no interest in human worlds."

"And this?" A battered cylinder, flared at the tail, windows glinting about its waist.

"Mmm? The design looks like United Nations work of a long time ago. Maybe a slowboat retrofitted with hyperdrive. It might be from Sheathclaws. Would they try to deal themselves in? That planet was settled by Kzinti telepaths and humans."

"Sheathclaws. A threat?"

"No. They couldn't afford serious weapons."

"Good. Hindmost, did you show him *Diplomat*?"

"Yes. We watched your *Probe One* break up a rendezvous between *Diplomat* and *Long Shot*. *Long Shot* retreated to hyperspace."

"Louis, Acolyte, Hindmost, I need a sanity check," Tunesmith said. "Is this a story you can believe? My *Probe One* frightens *Long Shot* away from a scheduled rendezvous. *Long Shot* jumps in hyperdrive, not far, then observes from a safe distance, a few light minutes away, until the pilot sees no further threat. Now he returns to exchange data and packages with *Diplomat*, but he's late.

"He returns to the Patriarchy still behind schedule and trying to catch up. *Long Shot* must report directly, because who else could? Every other ship is too slow. The Kzinti homeworld is two hundred thirty light years from here. That's three hundred minutes each way. We start with ten hours to play with before *Long Shot*'s pilot can return to Ringworld space, and he will still make his next rendezvous in haste. Yes?"

"Kzinti would do that anyway," Louis said. "Charge right in."

Acolyte bristled. "We do not worship clocks and calendars, Tunesmith. This ship *Diplomat* was attacked. They will be wary."

Louis said, "Spaceborn always worship clocks and calendars. Orbits are like that."

"Hindmost?"

The puppeteer asked, "What are you risking on this guesswork?"

"Too much," Tunesmith said, "but I must gamble. Fringe War activity accelerates toward a singularity. My worst move is no move."

"What do you intend?"

"I will capture *Long Shot*."

Louis saw that he'd been right: a crazy mission. He pointed out, "*Long Shot* is three thousand times as fast as us in hyperdrive, and never enters the Ringworld singularity."

"They can't use hyperdrive if they're docked with another ship. Follow me." Tunesmith strode forward and was gone. And again, Louis followed.

5

HANUMAN

As best he *could tell*, Probe Two *was a perfect machine. Hanuman continued working on it anyway. Of all the fascinating machines in Tunesmith's domain, this was the one he felt justified in making his own. His own life would ride this ship.*

He had watched Tunesmith at work on the Meteor Reweaving System.

Tunesmith talked while he worked. Hanuman almost felt he understood it. Inside a Ringworld puncture, vast numbers of minimally tiny components would weave strands of scrith out of lesser matter, pulling the vast structure back together, closing the holes. Something else would be going on while the nanomachines worked. Similarly tiny components would weave magnetic cables thinner than the hair on Hanuman's body, following superconducting cables already in place inside the torn floor of the Ringworld.

A protector's nature was to act. It was all Hanuman could do, to stand away from the Meteor Reweaving System, to keep his hands off machines that could save the Ringworld and every species on it, including Hanuman's own. He dared not touch what he didn't understand.

For fifteen hundred turns of the sky, Hanuman had lived in trees with others of his kind. He had loved; had sired children; had grown old. Then a knotted creature sheathed in leather armor had given Hanuman a root to eat.

Hanuman had only been intelligent for a falan or so. He knew this much: Tunesmith was a superior intellect. Hanuman's touch on Tunesmith's machines could only ruin them unless he were explicitly directed and guided.

But he could work on Probe Two. *This was the machine that might kill him. He was hoping to understand it better. Tunesmith—as much Hanuman's superior as he was superior to his species' breeders—didn't quite understand it either.*

Hanuman heard a puff of air and turned around. Tunesmith had arrived, with visitors.

They were in the cavern beneath Mons Olympus. Tunesmith strode toward an individual half his height. He said, "Hanuman, these are friends. Folk, this is Hanuman, pilot for *Probe Two*."

The stranger's voice was high-pitched but not childish. "Acolyte, Louis Wu, Hindmost. Hello."

Louis said, "A pleasure. *Hanuman*?" Still trying to decide what he was seeing. The stranger wouldn't weigh more than fifty pounds. Three feet tall, with two feet of tail, swollen joints and swollen skull and skin like cured leather pleated in folds. "You'd be a Hanging People protector?"

"Yes. Tunesmith made me and named me. 'Hanuman' is a literary reference from the library in *Hot Needle of Inquiry*." Hanuman switched to another language: Ghoulish, spoken far too fast. As he and Tunesmith chattered, Louis's translator caught a word here and there.

"—haste—"

"—lower that into place."

"A single theory to be tested. If your vehicle survives—"

A cylinder waited beside the linear accelerator. It looked too small for a passenger, but the nose was fully transparent, and the magnet coils behind it—the linear accelerator—were more than a mile across.

Machines had already mounted the rebuilt hyperdrive motor in *Needle*'s belly. Now *Needle*'s missing hull section crawled forward to rejoin *Needle*.

Needle's sliced-off wall had been breeched. A drum-shaped cylinder ran into and through it. The outer, hull side of the intrusion was opaque, painted with more of that bronze stuff. As the hull section moved to join *Hot Needle of Inquiry*, the intrusion eased into what had once been the garage for *Needle*'s lander.

The intrusion was an airlock, Louis saw. A big one, big enough to transfer a dozen humans at a time.

The bronze edges matched. Then the bronze edging oozed away, coiling on the lava like a snake. The bronze splotch on the airlock remained in place.

Louis said, "I can't stand it. What is that bronze stuff?"

Hanuman said, "Glue."

Louis waited.

Tunesmith spoke with a touch of reluctance. "It's more complex than that. Do you know about General Products' hulls? Each variation is a molecule with its interatomic bonding artificially enhanced. It's very strong, but if the molecule is cut, it comes apart. I've engineered a substance to replace the interatomic bonds. It does more than allow me to slice up a hull. I can bond one General Products ship's hull to another. Hanuman, are you ready?"

"Yes."

"Only fulfill your mission, then save yourself if you can. Go."

Hanuman scampered across the stone floor, climbed into the tiny missile, and closed the transparent nose. His ship dropped below floor level.

Hanuman spared a *moment to wonder about Tunesmith's companions. One was a breeder, species unknown, but all three showed their alien state. Starborn, alien to the Ringworld. Hanuman knew a little about them from* Needle *and its computer files.*

Where did they stand with regard to Hanuman?

"Glue," Hanuman had said, to see if Louis Wu would extrapolate the rest. He didn't. Not that bright.

Hanuman was brighter than a Hanging People, but he couldn't see what Tunesmith saw: the right answer, every time. Louis Wu had chosen Tunesmith. Did that make him bright enough to trust? The big hairy alien was a youth; he'd have little to say. The two-headed one was as old as seas and mountains. . . .

Probe Two was ready to launch, and Hanuman had his instructions. But if he survived, he must come to know who to trust.

Hydrogen fuel flooded into *Needle*'s tanks.

Tunesmith waved at the tower of rings. "Bram built this to launch meteor defense and repair systems. I've altered it. It will give us higher initial velocity than our fuel and thrusters would buy. Board *Needle* now, don pressure suits, strap down. Hindmost, up front with me. We should launch behind *Probe Two*."

Now *Hot Needle of Inquiry* was sliding across the lava. Louis wondered if they'd have to run after the ship, but Tunesmith led them to a stepping disk that flicked them aboard. The Hindmost and Tunesmith moved to the control room; Acolyte and Louis stayed in crew quarters.

While Louis was getting into his suit, *Probe Two* launched in a flare of lightning and was gone into the sky. The launch system was inefficient, Louis thought. Bad for the environment. Tunesmith must have power to throw away.

Needle sank toward the base of the launcher.

Tunesmith was suited up much faster than the others. "Eat before you close your helmets!" he shouted. "There's time." He raced through some diagnostic programs, then began using stepping disks to flick through the ship, stopping to observe, to fiddle. In two or three minutes he was back.

Needle's control cabin had been given place for a co-pilot. Tunesmith's bolted-in seat was a layer of plates that moved to accommodate him. He glanced around at his crew—in place, webbed down, the Hindmost beside him—and launched.

6

THE BLIND SPOT

"Another one!" Forrestier *shouted.*

'*Tec Roxanny Gauthier looked. In the wall display, what was rising past the edge of the Ringworld was no more than a blurred point.* Gray Nurse *was on patrol among the inner comets, far, far away from any Ringworld action.*

Roxanny asked, "Did you see where it came from?"

"Same as the other. One of the big salt oceans, an island cluster."

The fighter-recon crews didn't actually know anything. They were watching a wall display relayed from Control. The officers in Control could feed them any data they liked. That didn't stop crewfolk from speculating.

Roxanny said, "The first one was too small. So's this one. They're not ships, they're just probes."

"Fast, though. 'Tec Gauthier, what's that?"

That, rising from the same Great Ocean island, was a larger dot, elongated, moving with the same amazing speed as the probe.

"That's a ship," *Roxanny said.* Headquarters would have to respond to that! Gray Nurse *herself would not fight. She was a carrier. She was long and slender, built for spin gravity in emergencies, and she carried twenty fighter-recon ships. Roxanny belonged to the crew of the fighter* Snail Darter.

Crewfolk numbered about two men for every woman, all between forty and eighty years old. Younger than forty, Command wouldn't trust your reflexes. Older than eighty, why hadn't you been promoted? In Sol system they'd been the best. Here, in this strange place, some were startled to find themselves average.

Roxanny Gauthier was fifty-one, and still one of the best. Lack of action didn't bother her. For two years she'd enjoyed Gray Nurse's *modest rec facilities, kept herself in shape, competed ferociously in war simulations, and worked on her education. She enjoyed dominance games. Some of the fighter crew found her intimidating.*

The Fringe War couldn't last forever. The forces involved controlled energies that were too powerful. If the Ringworld itself was getting involved, nothing would last much longer.

Gray Nurse came under power. Her nose swung around. The voice of Command—placid, not quite soothing—said, "All fighter-recon crews, we will be passing through the inner system in fifty to sixty hours. You're on down time until then. Eat, sleep, wash. After you launch, you'll wish you had."

One or two crewfolk blew raspberries. Gray Nurse *hadn't launched a fighter since their arrival ten months ago.*

Launch was ferocious. Louis heard a whine from the cabin gravity generators, and a planet's mass settled on him and squeezed out all the air. That wasn't supposed to happen! Then

discontinuity

the view jumped, navy blue masked by flame colors around a black disk. The flames died, leaving the sun a deeper black disk on black sky.

He could breathe again.

The ship's wall protected them from unfiltered sunlight by imposing a black patch on the sun. As Louis's eyes adjusted, he could make out stars, and here and there a spear of fusion light. A sudden starship zipped past, an advanced ARM design, too close.

Tunesmith said, "Sorry. I reworked the stasis field generator. The stasis effect was holding for too long. It would have left us vulnerable, but now it doesn't become active fast enough. I'll fix it. Is everyone all right?"

"We could have been crushed!" the Hindmost whimpered.

"Where is Hanuman?" Acolyte asked.

A virtual window appeared, and zoomed. "There, ahead of us."

The Fringe War was starting to notice Hanuman's tiny ship and the larger craft following four minutes behind. Tunesmith jigged and jogged to avoid dangers unseen. Ahead of them, Hanuman's *Probe Two* was jittering all over the sky. The black patch that covered the sun was expanding.

Tunesmith used the thrusters for a sustained surge; veered in the midst of the burn. The forward view went black, then cleared.

Probe Two was gone.

Louis had never had a chance to know the little protector. He asked, "Now, what did that accomplish, Tunesmith?"

Pyrotechnics sought them out, Fringe War weapons following *Needle*'s jittery path. Tunesmith ignored all that. "What you've seen buys us nothing yet—"

Probe Two was *back*. It had moved, pulled ahead by a crazy quarter of a million miles. *Tanj dammit, what has Hanuman done?*

Tunesmith said, "We are constantly testing each other, aren't we, Louis? Let me *show* you what I have learned."

The puppeteer's orchestral scream drowned out Louis's, "Wait!" Tunesmith's hands moved.

* * *

There was color and flow. Shapes weren't there, just flow patterns of light and a few tiny dark comma shapes.

In the Blind Spot, in hyperdrive, Louis had never been able to see anything.

To go into hyperdrive this close to a sun was insane, but Hanuman's *Probe Two* had done it anyway. And somehow popped out again. And Tunesmith was about to do that too! They screamed at him but he did it. He went into hyperdrive while too close to a sun.

Born and raised on the Map of Earth, Acolyte hadn't even guessed the danger. Launch must have been scary enough. In this nightmare of scrambled light and dark darting commas, he was only drawing breath to roar when they were out again.

Stars. The singularity hadn't eaten them, it had spit them out. Louis looked around, savoring his ability to see. Close behind him was a black half-moon rimmed in fire: the sun chopped in half.

Hyperdrive gone wrong might, in theory, take them anywhere. Louis had not expected to see a black arc of Ringworld eclipsing half the sun—out of all the quintillions of suns in the universe, he had not thought he would still be next to *this* one—but it was there.

Tunesmith said, "Hindmost . . . no? Louis, then. Will you tell me if that was the Blind Spot your histories speak of?"

Louis said, "The Blind Spot is what you don't see in hyperspace. If you try to look through a window, you're blind. You can only see what's inside the cabin. It's why most pilots use paint and curtains to cover up a General Products' hull. There are freaks, though, people and other LEs who can at least use a mass detector without going nuts. I can do that. Hindmost?" The puppeteer was in footstool mode. "Acolyte?"

The Kzin said, "Tunesmith, if you can't see while flying in hyperspace, this will be a fun ride."

"But that's not the point!" Louis tried to explain the

obvious. "Ships just disappear if they drop into hyperspace too near a big mass. The space is too warped. What happened? We should be dead, or somewhere else in the universe, or in some other universe. Why aren't we? We're still in Ringworld system!"

Tunesmith said, "I found no convincing theory anywhere in the records. I must evolve one. 'Hyperspace' is a false term, Louis. The universe accessed through the Outsider drive corresponds to our own Einstein universe, point-to-point, but there are fixed velocities, quantized.

"You're aware that you can map any part of a mathematical domain onto the whole domain? For every point in one domain, you can place a unique point in the other. I thought the relationship here might be point-to-point except that space warped by nearby masses isn't represented. A ship that tried what Hanuman tried would go nowhere. Then I thought of an alternate model. We'll have to look at the recordings to know if I'm right, but after all, Hanuman *did* get in and back out— Excuse me," Tunesmith said, and turned to his controls.

Hot Needle of Inquiry began to dodge.

The war wasn't letting them through. Thermonuclear fireworks bloomed outside the ship. The ship surged, and protective blackness washed across the walls.

Louis's inclination was to beat Tunesmith over the head with something heavy until he talked, but that would not be prudent while he was flying them through a firestorm.

Tunesmith said, "Notice that we didn't travel far in hyperdrive. Hanuman didn't either. A light year in three days is characteristic of mass-free space. This close to a star's mass, space isn't flat. I'm not sure we even exceeded lightspeed.

"We launched at point one C. We'll be among the comets in a few hours. We can safely use hyperdrive then. Hindmost, will you take the controls?"

One head poked above the jeweled mane. "No."

"Then get into ship's memory and summon up what information we collected."

A mass pointer can't record, because the user's mind is a necessary component. Tunesmith had built something better, something that took pictures in hyperdrive.

A virtual screen showed the streaming colors Louis remembered, and a deep violet dot expanding into a tadpole shape. Tunesmith said, "This explains why we didn't travel far. Too close to the sun's mass—"

"Inside the singularity," Louis said.

"Louis, I don't think there's a mathematical singularity here at all. I found reference to a mass pointer in the Hindmost's library. Have you used a mass pointer?"

"There's one in front of you. It only works in hyperdrive."

"This?" A crystal sphere, inert now. "What do you think you see with it?"

"Stars."

"Starlight?"

". . . No. A mass pointer is a psionics device. You perceive, but it's not with your usual senses. Stars look bigger than they should, as if you're seeing a whole solar system."

"You've been perceiving *this*." Tunesmith waved into a recorded view of neon paint streaming through oil. "Dark matter. The missing mass. Instruments in Einstein space can't find it, but it huddles close around suns in this other domain you've been calling hyperspace. Dark matter makes galaxies more massive, changes their spin—"

"We rammed through that?"

"Wrong picture, Louis. My instruments didn't record *any* resistance. We'll test that later. It might have been different if *this* had reached us." A deep violet comma-shaped shadow. "We find life everywhere we look in this universe. Would it be surprising if an ecology has grown up within dark matter? And predators?"

Maybe Tunesmith *was* mad. Louis asked, "Are you suggesting that ships that use hyperdrive near a star are *eaten*?"

Tunesmith said, "Yes."

Crazy. But . . . the Hindmost continued his work with the recordings and *Needle*'s instruments. He hadn't flinched at the notion of predators eating spacecraft.

The puppeteer already knew.

"I only held us in hyperdrive for a moment," Tunesmith said, "but these hypothetical predators only have one speed, Louis, and it's *fast*. 'Singularity' is a mathematical term. Certainly there are mathematics involved, but they may be more complex than just places where an equation gives infinities. Inside this morass of dark matter, the characteristic speed may be drastically lowered. The proof is that we live."

"We are being observed," the Hindmost said. "I sense ranging beams from ARM and Patriarchy telescopes and neutrino detectors. Ships begin to accelerate inward. The ship from Sheathclaws houses telepaths of both species, though they can't reach us yet. I've found the comet cluster that hides the Kzinti flagship *Diplomat*. It's across the solar system, seven light-hours away and receding behind us. Tunesmith, do you have a plan?"

The Ghoul protector said, "I have the simple part. We will observe the Fringe War as we coast outward. Let our velocity carry us beyond the danger zone, the dark matter zone where predators lurk. Then swing around the system in hyperdrive. Approach *Diplomat* from the other side of the system. Await developments."

Hours passed. The Fringe War made no further test of *Needle*'s defenses. When the sun was only a bright point and the Ringworld was barely more than that, Tunesmith asked, "Hindmost, can you perceive hyperspace directly?"

"Yes."

"I can't. But if you can't fly for terror, I must fly *Needle*."

The puppeteer uncoiled. He took *Needle*'s controls. "Where shall I fly?"

"Take us ten light-minutes outward from *Diplomat*'s last position."

Human beings can't look into the Blind Spot. Most would go mad. Some can use a mass pointer to steer through hyperspace and keep their sanity too. Some Kzinti can perceive hyperspace directly; their female kin have mated into the family of the Patriarch for half a thousand years.

This time there was nothing. Not darkness, not featureless gray, not even the memory of sight. Louis fumbled until he could opaque the hull in crew quarters.

Acolyte said, "I don't know enough to ask intelligent questions, Louis."

"We're okay. I understand this. This is hyperdrive the way I'm used to seeing it. We're outside the . . . borderline," Louis said. "Even if I have to unlearn everything I know."

All his life he'd thought in terms of a mathematical singularity. In such a system, the realm of heavy masses—suns and planets—would be undefined in hyperspace. Ships couldn't go there.

"What we're doing is a standard maneuver. We have a velocity, right? We were flung up from the Ringworld, toward the sun and past it and outward. We still have that huge velocity, straight out from the sun.

"But the Hindmost is taking us halfway around the system in hyperdrive. When he comes out, we'll have the same velocity we started with, but pointed back toward the sun and the Ringworld."

"We're out," the Hindmost said. They were in black space with one overbright star. They'd been in hyperdrive about five minutes.

The Hindmost said, "The Fringe War doesn't normally reach this far out. We're safe for the moment. Our velocity vector is inward, toward *Diplomat*. We should act within ten minutes, before *Diplomat* can see our neutrino wake and Cherenkov radiation."

"Get me a view," Tunesmith ordered.

Ten light-minutes is further than the distance between Earth and Sol. The virtual window popped up, and zoomed, and wiggled a loose-packed comet out of the starscape, and zoomed . . .

A lens of steel and glass was the Kzinti command ship *Diplomat* emerging from its cometary nest.

That larger sphere just popping into view was *Long Shot*, close and closing.

Tunesmith barely glanced at the view. "They'll be a few minutes matching. We have time. Hindmost, show us what we recorded in this last hyperdrive jump."

The hypercamera's record was blank. Louis snickered.

Tunesmith reproved him. "Louis, there's nothing to see. We're outside the envelope of dark matter that collects around our star. Where there almost isn't any dark matter, there almost isn't space either! This is why we can travel faster than light does in vacuum, because distance in this domain is drastically contracted.

"Now I need only learn why there is more than one characteristic velocity. I'll get that by studying *Long Shot*. Hindmost, take us in range of *Diplomat*."

"Two fighting ships guard the near side of the comet."

"I see them. Use hyperdrive. We'll beat our own light."

The Blind Spot flashed for only an instant.

Their target was still too far away to see, but the virtual window nailed it: a loose dark fluffy comet, icy puffball satellites drifting around it, and four ships, two linked. Tunesmith's knotty hands danced. *Needle* surged: the cabin gravity motors were whining again. The larger ships, *Diplomat* and *Long Shot* locked together at the airlocks, were coming up fast. Slowing. Slowing.

"I'm taking the controls," Tunesmith said.

Diplomat fired lasers: crew quarters went black.

The virtual window was looking at something other than light. A flock of dim points was coming at them. *Needle* didn't have rocket motors; Tunesmith was using only the sluggish thrusters. Now the virtual window disappeared, and the hull was slapped sideways, then backward.

Louis just had time to realize that they were mated. Then *Needle*'s cabin gravity surged uneasily while the generators whined. Three ships, locked together, tried to turn round their common center of mass.

Diplomat ripped loose, tumbling, dwindling.

Hot Needle of Inquiry was using full thrust to push *Long Shot*. *Needle*'s overbuilt thrusters against *Long Shot*'s sizeable mass would give, what, around ten gravities? And *Long Shot* hadn't had cabin gravity when Louis flew it. In all that packed space there hadn't been room for extra machinery, or so he had assumed. Ten gravities would flatten any Kzinti aboard, knock them out or kill them.

Diplomat, the Kzinti command ship, fired a cloud of missiles, then disappeared in a black-cored fireball.

The missiles twinkled. Tunesmith was exercising his marksmanship. The warrior ships didn't fire—for fear of harming *Long Shot*? Tunesmith exploded the ship that tried to take up escort. The other fell behind.

A ship carrying antimatter is very vulnerable, Louis thought. Was that reassuring, or just scary?

Needle's thrust died. Tunesmith was out of his seat shouting, "Lander bay!" He reached a stepping disk and was gone.

Acolyte followed before Louis could quite get moving. The wall had become a window again, and *Long Shot* was a planet jammed against *Needle*'s hull, with the cabin right up against *Needle*'s new airlock, the view blocked by bronze "glue." Louis was out of his web, weapon in hand, running for the stepping disk. He saw Tunesmith race through the hangar, dive into the airlock, look, open the second door, leap, with Acolyte right behind. Then Louis flicked into the hangar.

He was ten feet behind Acolyte, moving at a dead run, leaning forward because he was about to enter free fall, a laser weapon in one hand. *Pirate!* he thought, elated, expecting no real resistance.

But light sputtered where Tunesmith disappeared. Acolyte stopped suddenly, then leapt out of sight.

In free fall now, Louis dug his feet into the wall and jumped behind his extended weapon.

Generated gravity slammed him to the floor.

That was confusing, if he'd had time to think about it. *Long Shot* hadn't had gravity generators.

Long Shot's life support system was only the pilot's cramped cabin and a cramped sleep-and-rec room above it, now occupied by Tunesmith and three Kzinti. Two Kzinti were sprawled in pools of orange blood, chopped and seared and dead. A third was fluffed out like a yellow-and-black cloud with teeth. Louis held his aim on that one until he was sure it was Acolyte.

Tunesmith's voice spoke in Louis's helmet. "Time presses. Louis, take your place as pilot. Acolyte, return to *Needle*. Hindmost, go with him. You have your instructions."

Louis wriggled past Acolyte and took the pilot's chair.

Acolyte pushed the dead Patriarchy warriors into the recreation space. He sprang toward the airlock. The puppeteer had gone ahead of him.

Tunesmith's communicator voice followed them. "Hindmost, what does it mean if we found cabin gravity aboard *Long Shot*?"

Silence.

"Hindmost!"

The puppeteer was reluctant, but he spoke. "It suggests that the Patriarchy has solved some of our secrets. Some of what we packed *Long Shot* with was data-collecting instruments. Some was mere misdirection. The Patriarch's science team must have learned how much superfluous space is there. They've used it to install a cabin gravity generator and who knows what else. What would human or Kzinti warriors do with so fast a ship if they knew there was extra space for thrusters, fighter ships, and weapons? Tunesmith, if you can't imagine that, ask Louis."

"Louis?"

"Just be glad this ship is ours again," Louis said. He studied *Long Shot*'s control system. A crude second control panel had been set beside the first. All the indicators had been reworked in Kzinti dots-and-commas.

Gravity rolled uneasily. They were in motion, and *Long Shot*'s cabin gravity generator wasn't happy with the unbalanced configuration.

Tunesmith was behind Louis's shoulder, his jaw against Louis's neck. "Can you fly it?"

"Yah," Louis said. "I may have to close my eyes—"

"Do you read the Heroes' Tongue?"

"No."

"I do. Make room. Join your companions aboard *Needle*."

"I can fly *Long Shot*. I remember the controls."

"They've been changed. Go!"

"Can you fly this ship?"

"I must try. Go."

When Louis entered *Needle*'s hangar, Acolyte was already gone.

Louis took a moment to contain his fury. Typical of a protector, to bet his own life and everybody else's on his own not-yet-formed abilities, on nebulous theories, on risks Louis wouldn't have taken even in his teens and twenties. But that wasn't enough. He'd bet Louis Wu's life because he might need him . . . and now he didn't. What the futz, just another gamble that hadn't paid off.

Inhale through the nose, hold it, flatten that abdomen,

exhale . . . it felt remarkably good to be back in his teens and twenties. Lovely if he could live through it.

Needle lurched and separated from *Long Shot*.

Louis found the hidden stepping disk and flicked to crew quarters. Acolyte was there. The Hindmost was on the flight deck, his back to them. He said, "We must make our way separately. Louis, Acolyte, strap down."

Acolyte said, "I was to be copilot."

"Plans change," the Hindmost said without turning around.

Louis didn't even wonder how the Hindmost had gained control of the bronze "glue" that linked the hulls. Tunesmith didn't hesitate either. From *Long Shot* he said, "As you will, Hindmost. Your enemies in this part of space include every ARM and Patriarchy ship and very likely all strangers. I've sheathed *Needle*'s hull in scrith, giving two layers of defense, but antimatter is still a danger. Make your way to the Map of Mars as best you can."

The Hindmost didn't answer. *Hot Needle of Inquiry* turned toward interstellar space.

7

END RUN

Acolyte asked, "Louis, are we pointed the wrong way?"

Four fusion rocket motors glowed blue on *Long Shot*, grown tiny now. The great ship didn't have much acceleration, and that was all fusion flame, conspicuous against a sky full of enemies.

Would the ARM, would the Patriarchy, try to destroy *Long Shot*? Not while there was a ghost of a hope of capturing it. The Quantum II hyperdrive was just too valuable, Louis thought. Unless another faction looked ready to make a capture. Then what?

How could the protector expect to hide the great ship? A mile in diameter . . . but that was tiny against the scale of deep space.

But none of Tunesmith's problems had any relevance to what the Hindmost was doing: turning toward interstellar space, toward his home.

Louis hadn't answered at once. Acolyte said, "My father often assumes that I know things I don't. He learned them too early. They must seem obvious. Spherical geometry, centrifugal force, seasons, the way light falls across a Ball World—"

"He's trying to escape," Louis said.

"Escape?"

The Hindmost was certainly able to listen, and Tunesmith might hear this too, but what did Louis have to hide? "The Hindmost has an intact spacecraft now," he said. "He sees the Ringworld as fragile. It makes him feel trapped. Now he's out. He'll run for the Fleet of Worlds . . . the Ball Worlds where the puppeteers live."

"Then I am kidnapped! *Hindmost!*"

The puppeteer didn't answer.

"I'm kidnapped too. Relax," Louis said. "We have time. This ship couldn't reach human space in less than two years. Even the Fleet of Worlds is months away. We've got time to think."

"Louis, what will you do when you finish teaching me patience?"

Louis smiled. "Mount you as a statue in your father's palace." It was their private joke.

So, the Fleet of Worlds might be the Hindmost's target. Then again, Fleet of Worlds politics had ousted him from the supreme position . . . years ago, but puppeteers thought in much greater time spans. The Hindmost might not be welcome among his own kind.

One could hope.

As for Louis Wu, the United Nations wanted him for holding proprietary knowledge . . . for the crime of knowing too much. The UN held great power among the worlds of human space. Still, they didn't rule everywhere. Their rule only included the Earth and Moon—and all targets which might threaten that domain.

The Hindmost had found Louis Wu on Canyon and snatched him away, some fifteen years ago. The local government or the ARM would have claimed his possessions there. His homes on Earth were forfeit. So. Where? There *had* to be a place of safety.

He hadn't really seen this day coming.

Louis said, "I'll have to be persuasive. Maybe I can get the Hindmost to drop us somewhere in human space. Then I'll find a way to get you home. I'll show you some of human space first. Could be fun."

"Why human space? Take us to the Patriarchy! Let *me* guide *you*."

Louis had been an interspecies hero, briefly, when they brought back *Long Shot*. He said, "I've been in the Patriarch's palace and hunting park. Have you?"

"Guide me then. Show me where my father grew up."

"I'm afraid to go there. I could show you recordings I made, if I could get to Earth or Canyon . . . but even that's too risky." Even in a daydream, the ARM would have claimed his possessions. "But I could read up on the Fringe War before we come back here. Tunesmith doesn't know enough. Maybe nobody does. It'll be like the War of the Roses, or the Vietnam War, or Avenge Mecca: it could last forever. Nobody knows how to turn off a war."

"Stet, take me to human space. Will they grant me my place, my rights?"

Louis laughed. "No. Stick to Interspeak, the way Chmeee and I taught it to you. We'll claim you're from Sheathclaws or Fafnir, grown up in a Kzin-and-human community. They'd *expect* you to be a little strange. Tanj, why haven't we moved? *Hindmost*!"

Long Shot was lost in starscape and sunglare, and *Needle* wasn't doing anything at all.

Louis shouted, "Do *something*, Hindmost!"

The puppeteer squawked. Then, tonelessly, "Louis. Acolyte. The carrion eater has disabled my hyperdrive motor."

Louis had nothing to say.

The puppeteer said, "I could have circled in hyperspace to hide my point of return into Ringworld system! Now every telescope in the system will be watching while I try to reach safety. We'll be under fire for . . . two days as a most optimistic estimate. Tunesmith has much to answer for."

"You would have run," Louis said.

The puppeteer snorted an orchestral dischord. *Needle* swung about.

Clouds of missiles and a score of ships began drifting in from the comets an hour after the Hindmost started his run. They watched it all coming while *Needle* accelerated toward the sun.

The Hindmost remained on the flight deck. Acolyte and Louis were sealed in their own quarters. They talked of this, voices low, as if they couldn't be heard that way.

Louis watched the Fringe War coming.

The faster missiles weren't a danger. Nothing with high thrust would carry antimatter. You couldn't risk antimatter jarring against its containment. Some ships, particularly those elongated ARM ships, might carry antimatter bullets and a linear motor to fire them, but those ships would be slow, too slow to catch *Needle*.

Tracking *Long Shot* gave the invaders no problem at all. The mile-wide sphere was conspicuous and undefended.

On the second day missiles began to arrive. Most of them gathered in a cloud around *Long Shot*.

Tunesmith had added a laser turret to *Needle*. The Hindmost shot down the few scores of missiles that sought *Needle* out. The sun grew large. Louis wondered if more ships waited in the inner system.

"Shouldn't we be making turnaround, Hindmost?"

"That's just what they'll be expecting," the puppeteer said.

Louis wondered what the puppeteer intended. Then, looking ahead, he knew.

How dangerous could it be? Puppeteers are cowards, right? Louis Wu couldn't show fear before a Kzin. Better if he could persuade himself that he was having fun. *It's a ride!*

But the Hindmost was more afraid of his pursuers than of what he was doing.

Louis took a moment to consider his words. Then, "Hindmost, everything new about *Needle*, even the hyperdrive, has been built or rebuilt by Tunesmith and never tested afterward. Do you still trust it all? Even the stasis field?"

"I must," the Hindmost said. "Out here I'm prey. Any creature with a telescope might have seen our attack on *Long Shot*. Are we a mere diversion? Will Tunesmith throw our lives away for misdirection? Louis, he is your kind more than mine!"

Being asked for his opinion of Tunesmith, Louis gave it. "Don't trust him. Take your best shot. Assume he reacts very fast."

"Even if we can reach the Ringworld, I'm still his prisoner," the Hindmost said. "But I will not accept that. I will not. I tire of being put at risk for purposes I don't understand."

"*Tell* me about it."

Hot Needle of Inquiry had picked up considerable velocity and was still accelerating as it passed the rim wall. As it did, ships lifted from the Ringworld's black underside. Then *Needle* was inside the Ringworld's arc in a glare of sunlight and a halo of thousands of tiny probes.

Louis heard a howl to melt bones and a rhythmic thudding sound, but he didn't walk around the kitchen wall to see. It was just Acolyte attacking a wall, getting some exercise.

The ship was jigging and jogging across the sky, but only the jittery starscape showed that. *Needle* had tremendous acceleration, but its cabin gravity was up to the challenge. Then again, so were the probes. Nothing was attacking *Needle*, but every species wanted to look.

What would they see? A #3 General Products hull, puppeteer made, and a puppeteer in the command section. *Needle* should be safe. Most LEs wanted to avoid frightening a puppeteer.

The black spot that hid the sun was growing larger.

It was going to be a hell of a ride.

A sudden glare blinked white-black. Acolyte asked, sarcastically, "Missiles don't carry antimatter?"

"Maybe it's a ship hit by an antimatter bullet. The light looked right. I'm guessing, of course. Hindmost, keep dodging."

The puppeteer's voice sang, "As opposed to *what*? Distract yourself. What if they kill Tunesmith? Will you choose another protector? Or choose none?"

"How's he doing?"

The Hindmost popped up a virtual window.

Shoals of missiles and ships were converging in a shell around the mile-wide crystal sphere. Lasers and bombs sparkled among them. Against all sense, a ship had fired on *Long Shot*, and now others were firing too. The sphere turned, bright-dark-bright in laser light, its four archaic rocket motors flaring.

Then *Long Shot* was gone.

"Dodged into hyperspace," Louis said. "Crazy bastard. He'll lose them if he didn't get himself eaten."

"What will you do if Tunesmith is dead?" the Hindmost persisted.

"There's too much tree-of-life around. I have to do something," Louis said. "Otherwise the protectors on the rim wall will take over everything. *That's* no good. They're evolved too far out of the mainstream of hominid development, and they don't know enough. Hindmost, a Ghoul is still the best choice. They live a jackal lifestyle. Whatever lives is theirs eventually. They do best for their own kind by making life better and safer for everyone. Aside from that, their heliograph system is wonderful. We need it."

The Hindmost said, "Tunesmith is arrogant and manipulative."

The black blotch covering the sun expanded and swallowed them.

discontinuity

8

TRY AN ANTIMATTER BOMB

For two days Gray Nurse *had been accelerating, then merely falling toward the sun and the Ringworld. The carrier would whip past the rim wall in a few hours. In that moment there would be an option. A linear motor ran the length of* Gray Nurse*'s hull. Fighter-lurker ships could be backfired into range of the Ringworld itself.*

The crews waited.

Whatever had gone on in that Kzinti-held patch of comets and vacuum, it took place far above Gray Nurse, *half-hidden in a fog of ice crystals. Fighter crews could speculate, of course. Explorer probes were on their way to do forensic work. Meanwhile the attackers were in view and running.*

"The little one is a GP hull," 'Tec-Two Claus Raschid said. "Might be anyone."

"Anyone but puppeteers," Roxanny said. "They'd never have the nerve."

"But the big, slow one, that's Long Shot."

The rest of the Fringe War had taken notice. Both ships were now surrounded by probes from half a dozen civilizations. Feeds were shown on the common-room monitors. A Pierson's puppeteer was at the helm of the GP#3 ship. Long Shot's *pilot looked like a man.*

*"*Long Shot's *ours," Claus said. "This might be our chance to get it back."*

The crewfolk watched the feeds. A sudden burst of fire-power surrounded Long Shot—*threatening an experimental ship of inestimable value—and Roxanny smiled at their cursing. Her smile slipped and the cursing stopped when the crystal sphere simply disappeared.*

The voice of Command spoke at last. "Board your ships! All fighter crews board your ships now!"

Gone like a soap bubble, *Roxanny thought.* How? But *she was scurrying along the corridor toward her station, flinching from burly hot shots who thought they could fly in these narrow confines.*

Her station was Snail Darter. *She crawled through the lock and took her assigned seat. Claus Raschid followed her through. The third crewman—"Where's Forrestier?" she rapped.*

'Tec Oliver Forrestier swung in and took his place. The three were back to back, looking into their wall displays. Oliver asked, "Think they'll launch us this time?"

Roxanny Gauthier grinned. She liked this: herself and two males in an environment that couldn't possibly rid the air of all pheromones, in conditions too cramped to do anything beyond flirting. Claus and Oliver already found her intimidating. "We'll launch," she said. "Depending on what those ships do, we could see the Ringworld close up. We might even get down to the surface. Gird up thy loins, Legal Entities! We are going in."

The ship jerked, and Louis jerked too, as everything around them shifted. *Needle* was out of stasis.

Views to the side showed fearsome coronas above a

black horizon of blocked-out sun. Aft was only black: the sun, receding.

Louis couldn't see what the Hindmost's cabin displays saw. *Good.* If he could see graphs and false-color representations, he would *feel* the hull temperature rising. There was that about Pierson's puppeteers: they never ignored danger, never pretended it wasn't there. Never turned their backs on a threat except to kick.

Ahead, arcs of glowing coronal gas streamed past. The stars were hidden in a ruby glare that might actually be *Needle*'s invisible hull giving off black body radiation.

The ships of the Fringe War . . . were not to be seen. The puppeteer had lost their pursuers by aerobraking his ship through the sun.

They were already nearing the ring of huge rectangles that cast shadows of night across the Ringworld. The Hindmost drifted his ship behind a shadow square, then boosted to some ferocious acceleration and ran for it.

Louis wondered idly if Tunesmith had turned off the meteor defense. Once before, the meteor defense had fired on Louis. *Lying Bastard* in stasis had smashed into the Ringworld floor and plowed a furrow across the land. They'd survived without a bruise . . . but this time Tunesmith had futzed the timing on their stasis field.

This time the Ringworld's sun-powered superthermal laser didn't fire, or didn't fire quick enough to catch *Needle*.

But the Fringe War found them. "We're being followed," Acolyte said.

The Hindmost sang, "I'll lose them. Don't distract me."

The Ringworld came up like a vast fly swatter. *Needle* dove straight toward a long strip of nightbound land. Louis could see the Other Ocean almost below, a vast diamond dotted with clusters of islands, easing off to the side as *Needle* came down. The Hindmost aimed at lightning-lit cloud laid out like a flattened hourglass in a pattern several times larger than the Earth.

* * *

An eyestorm is the visible sign of a puncture in the Ringworld floor.

It's the Ringworld equivalent of the hurricanes and tornados that form on planets. Air draining through the puncture produces a partial vacuum. Air flowing from spinward slows against its spin velocity; it weighs less; it wants to rise. Air from antispinward speeds up, grows heavier, wants to sink. From overhead the pattern is a sketchy flattened hourglass with a puncture at the throat. From port or starboard the storm takes the appearance of an eye, upper lid and lower lid and a horizontal tornado whorl in the center, and perhaps an eyebrow of high cirrus.

A Ringworld protector, Tunesmith or Bram before him, would have filled in any large puncture by now. Lost air is hard to replace. The meteor crater at the heart of this storm would be a small one, and old: these storms took generations to form.

The Hindmost dove toward the whirling throat of the hourglass, slowing hard, with one large and two smaller ships still in his wake. Then *Needle* plunged into the black whirlwind as if in suicidal frenzy, and out. Out through the meteor crater into black interstellar space, looping hard around and up. The Hindmost fired a laser at the Ringworld's black underside. A ruby glare lit an array of spillpipes broken by another ancient meteor.

Have to tell Tunesmith, Louis thought. *The Ringworld is wearing out. It's losing air and water. Everything needs repairs, underside, rim walls, landscape. Yah, in our copious free time.*

They were driving through a plume of ice crystals now. A block of frozen seawater was being boiled away. Acolyte suddenly demanded, "Louis, stop saying that!"

"Sorry."

"I know what 'It's a ride' means. Billions of your kind pay a sum for the privilege of being scared out of their wits under conditions of assured safety. A hero must risk real danger!"

"You did that when we fought Bram. *Here* we go," as *Needle* surged upward. *It's not a death trap. It's a ride.*

The foamy black sea ice was nearly boiled away. *Needle* rammed up through a smashed drainhole, through a last barrier of ice, and into the sea above.

Hot Needle of Inquiry settled through black water and came to rest.

"And here the ship may stay," the Hindmost said. He popped up the lip of a stepping disk and went to work on its controls.

Louis asked, "How much of this were you expecting?"

"Contingencies," the Hindmost said. "If Tunesmith ever gave me a chance to move *Needle*, I'd need a place to hide it. Here, Louis, this link leads to the Repair Center. The stepping disk network is open to us."

Acolyte's ears were up. He watched them like a tennis match.

Louis thought it through. The ocean around them would drain until an ice plug formed. Tunesmith could find them by the plume of water vapor, if he had the leisure. But *Long Shot* was slow in normal space, and if hyperdrive near a star was no longer sure death, it was still tanj dangerous. Tunesmith and *Long Shot* would be hunted across the sky for days yet.

So *Hot Needle of Inquiry* was . . . "Hindmost, you can't *hide* the ship."

"I have."

"We need access to *Needle* for food, beds, showers, pressure suits. We need a stepping-disk link, and that's all Tunesmith needs too."

"I can hide its location, Louis."

The Hindmost was searching for the illusion of control. It seemed futile, but hey, Louis was doing the same. "Think now," Louis said. "While Tunesmith is watching *Hot Needle of Inquiry*, why don't we steal *Long Shot*?"

"How?"

"I have no idea. But I'm tired of being run around like

a marionette *by him or you*, Hindmost. There has to be some way out of this box!"

"While Tunesmith is occupied, we might yet have a day or two to accomplish something."

They flicked to the Meteor Defense Room.

Daylight had swept across the eyestorm. Louis was looking across a hundred and ninety million miles, past the rim of the sun and the black edges of shadow squares.

Silver knots and threads still marked rivers, lakes, seas; but time and a puncture wound had desiccated this land. Three ships dodged and weaved in and out of a flattened hourglass made of storm. These must be the ships that had followed *Needle* down. The big ship was Kzinti, and the smallest was an ARM fighter, and the third was ARM too. They'd be able to detect each other through cloud, as anyone could given deep-radar.

Lightning flickered sporadically in the constriction, but a sudden sputter was too bright to be lightning.

"The trouble with an antimatter bullet," Louis surmised, "is that the crew will use any excuse to get it off the ship."

Both ARM ships were chasing the Kzin ship. The Kzin dove back into cloud. Louis could track its deep-radar shadow through the axis of the eyestorm, one ARM ship in its wake, one darting ahead through open air. Then the Kzin ship was gone, down through the drainhole and out.

Two ARM ships now commanded perhaps a trillion square miles of Ringworld. They spent the next several hours quartering the area, returning every so often to the eyestorm.

"Guarding the puncture against entry," the Hindmost suggested. "You and Chmeee blurted that secret to all of known space, didn't you, Louis? Enter and leave the Ringworld through any meteor puncture. Otherwise face a solar-pumped superthermal laser meteor defense."

"If they find *Needle*," Louis said, "they'll have access

to the stepping-disk network. Hindmost, is that technology easy to copy? The United Nations never had the chance. It's a lot more advanced than transfer booths."

The Hindmost didn't answer, of course.

Louis found himself staring at the display of the Other Ocean. The vast expanse of water and land looked like tapestry on a castle wall. Clusters of islands . . . continents; they'd be that big, as big as the maps in the Great Ocean, one of which was a one-to-one scale map of Earth. These were more thickly clustered, and they seemed all identical.

"Hindmost, was the Ringworld built by Pak?"

"I don't know, Louis."

"I thought you might, by now. I wondered if there might be real Pak, somewhere among all these variant hominids. We've never seen anything of Pak but old bones."

The puppeteer said, "We can deduce a good deal about Pak breeders. They slept or hid during the day and night. They hunted and did their business at twilight. They lived above a shoreline."

Louis was startled. "How can you know all that?"

"Your partial baldness suggests that your ancestors swam regularly, and I've watched you in the water, too. As for twilight, this Ringworld gets far more twilight than a planet would, and it's wholly unnecessary. Let me show you."

The Hindmost boarded a chair, clumsily. His questing mouth found controls. The wall display jumped, became a featureless blue. The Hindmost began to draw in white lines. A blob of white: the sun. A circle: the Ringworld. A much smaller ring, concentric: thirty-odd shadow squares moving a little faster than orbit, held in a net of cables. "This is the way the Ringworld was designed," the Hindmost said. "A thirty hour day with ten hours blacked out, and more than an hour of a sun partly blocked. Instead—"

He sketched in five long shadow squares sliding retro-

grade, against the Ringworld's spin. "This model would
avoid the long, long twilight period and give equal day
and night. The builders didn't want that. Whoever built
the Ringworld must have wanted endless summers and
long twilights. We surmise they were Pak protectors, and
we surmise that the Pak world was like that."

Louis studied the picture. *Or else*, he thought, *they built
an advanced model somewhere else.*

The Hindmost said, "I'm hungry. Will you keep
watch?"

"Hungry," the Kzin agreed. "Hurry."

Time had slid by unnoticed. Louis realized he was half
starved.

A puppeteer must eat more often than a carnivore. The
Hindmost was gone for most of an hour. He returned with
jewels sparkling in a newly coifed mane. A float plate
heaped with fodder followed him.

"We'll regret the time we're wasting," he said. "Our last
hours free from Tunesmith, but what can we do with
them? My plans didn't reach far enough. Look, more warships."

Three Kzinti, then an unfamiliar larger craft, then three
more ARM ships danced around the inner ring of shadow
squares, not firing yet.

Louis said, "Acolyte, go feed yourself." Who wants to
be around a hungry Kzin?

Louis and the Hindmost watched the warships at play.
"They won't all have stasis fields," Louis speculated. "Stasis fields are expensive and not too dependable, and of
course they take a ship out of the action. So they'll be
leery of the Ringworld's meteor defense, but Tunesmith
turned that off, and they're starting to realize that. So,"
as three Kzinti ships began a long dive toward the Ringworld surface, "here come Kzinti to stop the first ARM
ships, and more ARMs to stop *them*—tanj dammit!" A
brilliant streak inside the atmosphere ended in a flash
against desert.

"That was an antimatter bullet," said the puppeteer.

"And now it's a little eyestorm. Tanj, this isn't even the main event! What they want is *Long Shot. Needle* is nothing."

"A *Needle* in a haystack? What you describe is mostly your imagination," said the Hindmost. "Much of a war goes unseen. That larger ship, I have identified it. Lure of Far Lands Limited, the Kdatlyno and Jinx business alliance. They won't fight, they will only observe. Here is Acolyte. Louis, go eat. Bathe."

Louis jerked awake. Something had disturbed him . . . a flash of light from the screen?

Acolyte and the Hindmost were asleep, sprawled far apart on the hard floor beneath the Meteor Defense Room walls. It was good to be clean; he'd eaten like an army; sleeping plates would be good too. But anyone who slept aboard *Needle* would miss something.

Louis sat up. Nothing hurt! He grinned, remembering what an older woman had told him at his two hundreth birthday party. "Dearest, if you can wake in the morning with no pain in your joints and muscles, it's a sure sign that you have died in the night."

The Hindmost had reset the wraparound screen. It showed a skyscape with windows in it, views of an eyestorm and the Other Ocean. Around the windows stars moved uneasily: ships of the Fringe War. All views were quiet now.

It did bother him, that he couldn't think of anything to do except watch. He was trying to outthink a protector. What chance would he have later if he couldn't find an angle now, while Tunesmith was being hunted across the system?

On the Ringworld were millions of seas. Louis couldn't guess where the Hindmost had put *Hot Needle of Inquiry*. He could get there by a stepping-disk setting. The first pair of ARM ships hadn't found it, and now they were too busy maneuvering. The war above the eyestorm had been quiet for hours, but ships continued to shift position.

Sudden light splashed around the Farland ship: antimatter bullets intercepted in transit. The Farland ship was accelerating away from the action. Its new course would miss the Ringworld. A ruby laser lit it brilliantly, but diffused, its attacker already deep in atmosphere. Ships tens of millions of miles apart had some chance to defend themselves.

But the war above the eyestorm was getting too tight.

Fire burst into the clouds where two ARM ships were hiding. Louis cried, "Wake up! Wake up! You're missing action!"

The others stirred.

Tunesmith's deep-radar window showed one ARM ship diving through the puncture hole—leaving hard-won turf abandoned, but safeguarding data from its explorations, unless some ambush waited beneath the Ringworld floor. The other accelerated hard, running down the storm's axis in a channel of clear air, the pupil of the eye.

Kzinti had deep-radar too. Two lens ships were diving. Fire followed them down.

The eyestorm flashed to a blue-white glare.

The Hindmost killed the zoom window before it could blind them. On a less expanded view—Tunesmith must have a camera on one of the shadow squares—a star glared near the Other Ocean, as big as . . . too big . . . far too big.

The puppeteer said, "I believe one of the ARM ships exploded. Antimatter. We'll have a hole the size of . . ." The Hindmost thought it through, then folded into himself and was silent.

The eyestorm was gone, blasted apart. Cloud patterns showed an expanding ring of shock wave crossing seas and gray-green land. A hemisphere of cloud enveloped a dimming fireball.

"What has happened here?"

Tunesmith and the little chimp-protector were on the stepping disk: a sorcerer confronting wayward apprentices, demanding explanations. Louis's throat closed on him. It felt like he should have stopped this. It felt like Tunesmith would, *should* blame him.

"Antimatter explosion," Acolyte said.

"Is there a hole under that cloud?"

The question was already silly: the dome of cloud was dimpled in the center. It was being sucked into interstellar space. When Acolyte didn't answer, Louis said, "There was already a hole—"

"Of course. We have to move fast," Tunesmith said. "Come." He had the lip of the stepping disk up and was redirecting it.

Louis found his voice. "Sure, *now's* a good time to move fast. You've brought the war home! And now the air's draining out of the Ringworld!"

What had been a fireball was nearly gone. The Ringworld floor was naked scrith within a slowly expanding ring of cloud. Clouds streamed toward the hole.

And Tunesmith had Louis by the forearm. He walked them to a stepping disk.

Hanuman's eyes took *it all in in one sweep:*

He'd bent the laws that governed this universe and a hypothetical other. His mission was a total success. And none of it mattered. The Ringworld held everything worth saving, and the Ringworld floor was ripped open.

The puncture was on the far side of the arch. That was both good and ill. Death would be a long time marching around the curve to reach them here; but Tunesmith's countermeasures would have to cross that same gap.

The aliens saw it too. The most alien was the eldest, the most experienced, perhaps the wisest, and that one had shut down his mind. The hominid had lost hope. The youngest, the nothing-like-a-big-cat, was—like Hanuman— waiting for someone to solve it.

Tunesmith?

Tunesmith was in motion while Hanuman was still catching up. The Ghoul protector showed no doubts. When Tunesmith and Louis Wu vanished, the little protector followed. Tunesmith would fix it.

Machinery on a Brobdingnagian scale had been moved into the workstation under Mons Olympus.

Tunesmith dropped Louis's arm and moved among his instruments at a sprint. The little protector, Hanuman, scampered after.

Acolyte popped up next to Louis. "Louis, what's happening?"

"The air's draining out of the Ringworld."

"That would be . . . the end of everything?"

"Yah. Starting on the far side. We might have days, but only because the Ringworld is so endlessly *big*. I have no idea what Tunesmith thinks he's doing."

"What is that massive structure? I've seen it—"

Hanuman rejoined them. "That is a meteor plug, largest version. Of course it was never tested."

It was the shape of an aspirin tablet and roughly the size of the Twin Peaks arcology or a small mountain, still small compared to the puncture in the Ringworld. Louis said, "I remember. It was in one of the caverns. He set it moving here on big stacks of float plates."

They watched it slide into the hole in the floor and fall, guided by magnetic fields toward the base of the linear launcher. Tunesmith was at the edge, watching. Louis and Acolyte went to join him.

Forty miles from the roof to the floor of the Repair Center ran the loops of the linear launcher. It was way overbuilt for something as small as *Hot Needle of Inquiry*. It would better accommodate something like this half-mile-wide package of Tunesmith's. The launcher's bottom sat on an array of float plates, and that was moving to adjust its aim.

The package was near the bottom now, still falling, but slowing.

Tunesmith saw them watching. Immediately he hustled them away from the hole in the floor.

Lightning roared at their backs. Louis turned to see something tremendous flash past, out through the crater in Mons Olympus and gone.

Acolyte's ears were curled into tight knots. Hanuman lifted his hands from his ears and said something inaudible. Louis couldn't hear anything. His ears still held the roar and agony of that lightning blast.

Louis didn't lose his deafness for some time. Acolyte recovered much faster. Louis could see the Kzin discussing . . . whatever . . . with Tunesmith and Hanuman while they all followed the action in a wall display of the Meteor Defense Room. The Hindmost remained in footstool mode.

Louis could only watch.

Tunesmith's meteor-plug package drifted toward the sun. *Needle* had been launched at a tenth of lightspeed; the launch system was capable of that. But over such a distance the package's fall seemed sluggish.

In a zoom window the puncture showed as a black dot on landscape that looked lunar: clear and sharp and barren of water's silver or the dark gray-green of life. Louis guessed the puncture was sixty to seventy miles across. A ring of fog surrounded it, bigger than the Earth and still growing.

The Ringworld was not yet aware of its death. Air and water would flow into the hole and out into vacuum, but first it all had to move . . . from up to three hundred million miles around each arc before the shock could reach the Ringworld's far side, the Great Ocean, *here*. Not much would be lost in a hundred and sixty minutes, while Tunesmith's package crossed the Ringworld's diameter. Even the Other Ocean wouldn't have begun to boil yet.

Hanuman wandered over. He said—loudly, spitting his consonants; it was fun to watch his lips—"I have been in this state for less than a falan. I still cannot grasp the scale of things. I did not grow up in a universe fifty billion falans old, on a ring spinning around one fleck of light among ten-to-the-twentieth of flecks. There were not that many of anything! My world was small, cozy, easily grasped."

"You get used to it," Louis said. He could barely hear himself. "Hanuman, what is that? What can it do? We're losing our atmosphere!"

"I know little."

"Share it with me," Louis demanded.

"Two bright minds with similar goals will solve problems in similar ways. The Vampire protector Bram saw a need to plug meteor holes. His first meteor plugs were small, but his mass driver under Mons Olympus is hundreds of falans old and hugely overbuilt. The Fist-of-God meteoroid impact must have frightened Bram witless.

"Tunesmith builds bigger yet. That package is his biggest effort." Hanuman was constantly in motion, bouncing around Louis as he spoke, arms swinging. "We shall see it in action. Tunesmith wants us to observe on site. If there is partial failure, then we must see what must be redesigned."

"This double-X-large meteor patch, how does it work?"

"I would be guessing."

"It's never been tested?"

"Tested when? You were stored in the 'doc for less than a falan. Tunesmith made and trained four Hanging People protectors, built a nanotech factory to make bigger meteor plugs, monitored the Fringe War, designed several probe ships, built a stepping-disk factory, redesigned your *Hot Needle of*—"

"He's been busy?"

"He's been crazy as a stingbug hive city! And if the plug doesn't work, it's all for nothing."

"Do you have children?"

"Yes, and they have children. Since Tunesmith made me, I've not had the chance to count them, nor even to sniff them. Of course they are all forfeit to Tunesmith's schemes and the Fringe War."

"Aren't we all. Should Tunesmith have taken such a risk?"

"How should I judge?" Hanuman's frantic dance, the hands pounding his chest, would have been an uncontrollable rage in any human. "Tunesmith implies that the greatest risk was not to act. Louis, how can you remain so still?"

"Fifty years . . . two hundred falans of yoga. I'll teach you."

"I *must* act," Hanuman said, "but not because to be still is wrong. It may be that way with Tunesmith. How can I know? I am enraged with no target."

The sun's gravity was bending the package's course minutely.

Tunesmith and Acolyte walked over. Tunesmith asked, "Louis, do you have your hearing back? Have you rested?"

"I slept. Where did you land *Long Shot*?"

"Why would I tell you that?" Tunesmith waved it off. "You and Acolyte and Hanuman must observe my plug in action. Has Hanuman told you anything?"

"It's a double-X-large-size meteor plug."

"Good. I have a stepping disk in place—"

"You saw this coming," Louis said.

"I did."

"Could you have stopped it?"

"How?"

"Don't steal *Long Shot*?"

"I need to understand the Quantum II hyperdrive. Louis, you must *see* that the Fringe War would never have stayed in the comets. These Ball World species covet the technology that made the Ringworld. It isn't the Ringworld they want to preserve. They want the knowledge, and to keep it from each other."

Louis nodded. It wasn't a new thought. "Scrith armor. Cheap fusion plants."

"Trivia," Tunesmith said. "The Ringworld engineers needed motors to spin this structure up. They must have confined a hydrogen mass equivalent to a dozen gas giant Ball Worlds, then fed it all through force fields arrayed to act as hydrogen fusion motors. Your Ball World bandits don't have decent magnetic control, and what they have won't scale up. They might learn something by studying our motors on the rim wall. They would study the Ringworld. They need not preserve it. Am I talking sense?"

"Maybe."

"Louis, I want you in place to observe the meteor patch as it deploys."

"Tunesmith, it bothers me to be expendable."

"I don't use the word, Louis. I don't use the concept. All life dies, all life resists dying. I would not put you in unneeded danger."

"Interesting word."

"I have a stepping disk in place from which you may observe. A sight not to be missed. Hanuman will go. Will you? Acolyte, will you go? Or will you rest here in comfort to learn if all we know has been destroyed?"

Acolyte looked to Louis.

Louis threw up his hands. "Stet. You want us in pressure suits?"

"With all my heart," Tunesmith said. "Use full gear."

9

VIEW FROM A HEIGHT

They geared up in *Needle* and flicked from there. The Hindmost wasn't with them. They'd left the puppeteer in a depressed and uncommunicative state.

At lightspeed via stepping disks, they'd arrive ahead of Tunesmith's plug package.

Acolyte wore Chmeee's spare pressure suit, retrieved from *Needle*'s stores. He looked like a bunch of grapes. Hanuman, in a skintight suit with a fishbowl helmet, went first. Louis stepped onto the plate.

The bottom dropped out.

Louis hadn't expected free fall. He hadn't expected to be thousands of miles up, either. He snatched at something: Hanuman's hand. Hanuman pulled him to the stepping disk.

The Ringworld, two or three thousand miles below, skimmed past at ferocious speed. It looked infinite in all directions. The rim walls were too distant to show as more than sharp lines.

Acolyte yowled.

Louis didn't dare reach for the thrashing, terrified Kzin. Acolyte's father's spare pressure suit was all balloons, but there were waldo claws on all four limbs. It would have been like reaching into a threshing machine.

"It's all right. You have attitude jets," Louis shouted. "Use them when you feel like it."

The yowling stopped.

Louis's magnetic soles held him down. Hanuman had turned the stepping disk off. Otherwise they'd be back aboard *Needle*.

"Plenty of time, Acolyte," Louis said. "We're orbiting the sun." Louis held his voice calm, soothing. *He's only twelve.* "Essentially we're standing still, and the Ring-world goes at the usual seven hundred and seventy miles per second, so we'll see the whole thing go under us in seven and a half days. Hanuman—?"

"Eight," Hanuman said. "Eight stepping disks are now in orbit. Tunesmith intended more. This was the nearest. I've committed the stepping-disk system to memory. If we need to reach the surface, there's a service stack not too far, but meanwhile we can see it all. Can you pick out the puncture?"

"I don't see it yet."

"Look antispin."

"It's *behind* us? Stet, I have it. It looks like a target." Airless moonscape rimmed with cloud, scored with lines pointing inward toward a black dot.

The land racing below them still had river networks lined with the dark green of life. Through the land a white streak ran to antispin. Louis thought he knew what that was, but it was less urgent than the puncture. "Acolyte—?"

"I see the wound. I do not see the plug package."

"I haven't found that either," Hanuman said. "Too small. Tunesmith, are you with us?"

"Half hour delay," Louis reminded him. "Sixteen minutes each way, lightspeed." This was a *protector*? But upgraded from an animal. You didn't expect a protector to forget things . . . and Hanuman must be very accustomed to Tunesmith's guidance.

Acolyte bounced against the stepping disk. Magnetic boots clung. He stood uncertainly. "My father tried to tell me about free fall," he said. "I don't think he ever feared it."

Tunesmith spoke from sixteen minutes in the past. "I've sent the signal to deploy the double-X-large meteor plug. Tell me what you see, all three of you. Be free to interrupt each other, I can sort your voices."

A lamp lit above the target.

It didn't look much brighter than a street lamp, but its

size . . . Louis squinted past the glare. "Something unfold-ing. Tunesmith, it looks like fire salamanders mating . . . or a balloon inflating . . . it's bulking up into a shape like a sailing ship's life preserver. Jets firing at fusion temper-atures. What have you got there, Tunesmith?"

Acolyte: "It's settling. Slowing. A torus. It's much wider than the puncture, a thousand to two thousand klicks across. Was this what you wanted to hear?"

Hanuman: "The scrith foundation that holds the Ring together demonstrates tremendous tensile strength. I've done the numbers. The forces that hold scrith together would generate showers of quarks if pulled apart. A bag made of such material would be strong enough to confine a hydrogen fusion explosion. There's risk, Tunesmith, but it seems to be holding."

Acolyte: "It's settling—"

Louis: "—enclosing the puncture. Leaving the punc-ture exposed like a bull's-eye on a target. I'm guessing your balloon stands fifty miles tall, so it'll confine the at-mosphere as long as it holds."

Hanuman: "Tunesmith, how good an insulator is a scrith balloon? We wouldn't see it if it weren't leaking en-ergy. When it cools enough, it'll collapse. Tunesmith, it will leak air. The ground beneath will be uneven."

Answer came there none. Tunesmith's reaction was a Ringworld diameter away.

So he must have spoken sixteen minutes ago. "Watch for the second package," the protector said. "Tell me if it settles inside the ring."

Acolyte: "I don't see anything. Louis? Hanuman?"

Louis: "There won't be a meteor trail—"

Acolyte: "Rocket! I see it. Fusion, by its color. Settling slowly at the edge of the hole. It's down."

Louis: "We're drifting too far. I can't see the puncture any more."

Hanuman bent over the rim of the stepping disk. "I'll

fix that. The next stepping disk is thirty degrees around
the Ringworld arc. Ready?"

They flicked.

The Ringworld flowed beneath them. They'd jumped
thirty degrees, about fifty million miles. Louis, looking
ahead of him, found a line of white several worlds wide,
and a brighter line peeping above its center. Acolyte said,
"There it is. We can't see detail, Tunesmith. We won't be
over it for half a day."

Louis: "There's a zoom function in our faceplates.
Tunesmith, I don't see any change. Your balloon plug is
still inflated. Everything outside the balloon is fog. We've
lost a . . . few percent of the Ringworld already."

Around the edges of the fog, the land would be ravaged
by shock waves running through air, sea, earth, and the
scrith foundation. Weather patterns would be shattered. . . .
Louis realized he was being optimistic. He was assuming that Tunesmith would plug the hole, stop the loss.

He had once estimated the Ringworld's population at
thirty trillion, with hominid species in every possible ecological niche. That vast plain of fog would be water drop-
lets condensed by a drop in pressure. Ecologies under that
fog blanket would be dehydrated and suffocating. Around
it they'd soon be ravaged by climate change.

But only if Tunesmith made a miracle.

"I think a ship in stasis crashed to antispin of the puncture," Louis said. "I can't see it from here."

Hanuman said, "We won't be over it for half a day. I'm
going to flick us home."

A moment later—plus a quarter hour—they were
aboard *Needle*.

Moments afterward, so was Tunesmith. "Hanuman, report," he said.

"Your device deployed. It will hold for days, but it will
leak. What are you expecting?"

"I sent a reweaving system to make more scrith. I based

my design on nanotechnology from the 'doc aboard *Needle*. A complicated matter, this. The system must replace not only the scrith floor but the superconductor grid within."

Hanuman said, "There are species whose breeders evolved intelligent. Their protectors would be bright enough to help you with such problems."

"Bright enough to quarrel, too, and to hold the Ringworld hostage for the advantage of their own gene pool. Louis, tell me what you saw of a downed spacecraft."

"Just a streak," Louis said

"Different from other streaks?"

He spoke too patiently. Louis flushed. "We saw it from a long way away, but—I reached the Ringworld aboard a ship in stasis. *Lying Bastard* came down with a horizontal velocity of seven hundred and seventy miles per second, like anything that brushes the Ringworld. We left a streak of molten lava and bare scrith. Now I've seen one just like it. I think when one ship exploded, another got knocked down."

"We'll have to find it."

"That's easy, but not now," Louis pleaded. "Your orbiting stepping disk won't be in view of the puncture for twelve hours anyway. Let us get some sleep." He was ready to weep, exhausted physically and emotionally.

"Sleep, then."

They slept aboard *Needle*. Louis shared sleeping plates with Hanuman. The little protector just had to try it.

10
A TALE TO TELL

They woke, they breakfasted, they returned to the work-station under Olympus where Tunesmith was waiting.

Tunesmith had added to their gear. The new gear included two flycycles.

Nessus and his motley crew had carried four flycycles: flying structures built something like a dumbbell with a seat mounted between the weights. They'd all been ruined on that first voyage. These two must have been modeled on the wreckage; but they were longer, each with two seats and a big luggage rack.

Louis inspected one of the vehicles. The kitchen converter would store in the luggage rack or swing out. Mounts on the dash carried a flashlight laser and some other tools. Nessus's team had reached the Ringworld with gear similar to this, some of puppeteer make, some purchased off shelves in human space.

"I reworked the sonic fold too," Tunesmith said. "Orbiting Stepping-Disk Eight will be almost in place, Hanuman. You can take it from here."

"Stet." To Acolyte and Louis, Hanuman said, "Get into your pressure gear, then stow your baggage. We'll push the flycycles through first."

"Where's the Hindmost?" Louis asked.

"He's still in a depressed state," said Tunesmith. "That worries me. He may be suffering a chemical imbalance. I'll put him in the 'doc after you're gone."

Louis didn't comment. They geared up and went.

And out into free fall with the Ringworld blazing below. The Kzin, the protector, Louis, and two flycycles drifted apart. Riding lights flashed on the flycycles.

Orbiting Stepping-Disk Eight had drifted in the night, twenty degrees, thirty-three million miles. Louis was looking almost straight down into a black hole with a glitter at the rim, in a quasi-lunar landscape marked with radial streamlines and glittering threads of frozen riverbed. A torus the size of a mountain range, glowing ruby from within and beginning to sag, was its border. It looked like God had dropped one of his toys. A plane of white cloud surrounded the torus, bigger than worlds.

To antispin, where cloud cover became patchy, a white scratch ran across the land.

Louis pointed it out. "A ship dug that gouge. We'll find it at the antispin end, the far end. I don't see it yet, so it'll be small. Hanuman, shall we start decelerating?"

"Yes. Board a flycycle, I'll take the other, Acolyte rides with whom he will. Acolyte?"

"With you," Acolyte said.

"Stet. Keep your altitude until your relative velocity is low, Louis. The sonic fold won't take more than a few times sonic speed. I'll keep you in sight. Guide us down to the ship."

A grid of superconducting material ran beneath the Ringworld floor. Nessus's flycycles had flown by magnetic levitation. With maglev for lift, thrusters didn't have to be powerful . . . but these redesigned machines did deliver some serious push. When his velocity relative to the landscape had decreased to something reasonable, Louis eased down into atmosphere until he could hear a thin whine in the sonic fold. He could see a lacework of water vapor around the other flycycle. His own shock waves were barely visible.

Tunesmith spoke suddenly in his earphones. "Your mission is to seek out a crashed ship. Louis, guide them. Report to me at every step. Watch for more than one ship down. The crash grooves they carve would be close together and parallel.

"I want to know the species and what to expect of them.

Don't throw your life away to find out. Don't kill any LE if you can avoid it, but if you must, leave no sign. If possible, negotiate. I'll make any guests glad they met me.

"I worry for what I might forget to tell you.

"Louis, remember that information storage is easy. All of human knowledge is probably stored aboard every ARM spacecraft, with blocks to restrict secrets. The right officer will know the right passwords. Acolyte, if you find a Patriarchy ship instead, give up. The knowledge may be there, but no hero will give it to you—"

Louis said, "A telepath might," but Tunesmith's monologue droned on.

I worry for what I might forget to tell you . . . that it's a three hundred million mile walk home, and the stepping disk is orbiting beyond your reach, and the Hindmost will be in the 'doc. So you can't count on him for an ally, and you can't use the 'doc to rejuvenate, Louis. In the fullness of time, I'll make you a protector. . . . Not likely that Tunesmith would say any of that. Louis concentrated on flying.

Far behind them was the low wall of fog. The ship they were tracking had skipped across a sea, a river, another river. A ridge showed a glittering notch of bare scrith where the ship must have bounced aloft. The arrow-straight canyon resumed further on, scrith rimmed with splashed lava. Following it was easy. It ran across forest, a white sand beach, a long, long stretch of veldt . . . there . . .

So small a thing to have wrought so much damage.

Against another ridge lay an elegantly contoured half-cylinder, flat along one side, no cabins, no windows, no breaks in the reflective surface, except near one end. Louis zoomed his faceplate.

"Is that an ARM ship?" Acolyte asked. "Or Patriarchy? Smooth as it is, it might be puppeteer. But they'd use a General Products' hull, wouldn't they?"

Closing now at several mach. The protrusion at one end looked like a bee's stinger.

"It's a drop tank," Louis said.

"Explain," Hanuman rapped.

"It's not a spacecraft. It's part of a spacecraft, the part that carries extra fuel, the part you can throw away." He was furious with himself, and then, suddenly, elated. "The ship whapped down in stasis. After the stasis field collapsed, they still had a working spacecraft."

Working spacecraft!

Keep talking. Somehow he held his voice steady. "They drop the tank when they want agility or longer range. I'd say they were getting ready for a dogfight."

But a working spacecraft!

Hanuman said, "Flup. We have to find that ship. Were you expecting this?"

"No. *Lying Bastard* was a different design. After we hit, we were grounded. Now what?"

"Possibilities suggest themselves," Hanuman said. "First, I'm linked to Tunesmith. Tunesmith, you have Louis's assessment. Shall we wait for the ship to return for its fuel? Is it ARM or Kzinti or something else? Must we negotiate or challenge?"

Louis said, "ARM." Kzinti would have marked their property. Pierin or Kdat or Trinocs wouldn't challenge Kzinti or men; Kzinti had owned them. Puppeteers wouldn't directly challenge anything. Outsiders wouldn't get this close to a star. "Might be some other human branch, or Kzinti bandits, or Trinocs . . . but call it ARM.

"That's a little tank, so we're looking for a little ship. A fighter won't carry antimatter fuel. Energy stored in a battery. Water for reaction mass because it's easy to store and pump. They might have antimatter weapons. It's surprising that a little ship would have a stasis field. Maybe the UN is getting better at building them."

Any part of a warcraft would have dot-sized cameras

all over it. "If they're not watching us, they might still record us," Louis said. "So what shall we be?"

The little hologram heads of his companions looked blank.

Louis explained. "We're operatives working for a superintelligent protector who used to be an eater of the dead. That's too scary. Any military LE who heard *that* might shoot us out of hand. An ARM ship will have records of what a protector is. That'll scare them too.

"So, what do we want to be? We're a Kzin and a man and a Hanging People protector. We don't want to be Patriarchy. They're scary too. We can't show ARM identification—"

"Ah," Hanuman said. "You want to lie."

"Hanuman? A new concept?"

Acolyte rumbled in dissatisfaction. Hanuman said, "My species' breeders aren't sapient. I've been able to think and speak for less than a falan. Who would I lie to? Tunesmith?"

A dog will try to lie to its human master, Louis thought, *but getting away with it*—"Stet, but we *do not* want to confront them with a protector. Hanuman, do you remember how you behaved as a breeder? Can you do it again?"

"You would make me a *pet monkey*?"

"Yah."

"Stet. If I can't talk, I can't be caught in a lie. Acolyte's pet, I assume. What of you?"

Louis said, "I think Tunesmith saw this coming. Our gear is pretty close to what Nessus brought aboard *Lying Bastard*. Let's be the Hindmost's new crew. With the puppeteer leading from wayyy behind, as usual. It would explain flycycles. Hanuman, any thoughts?"

"We're telling a story. Better if they do not learn that Louis Wu made a protector and set him in charge of the Ringworld. You would seem too powerful and too undefended. Best if we do not mention an experimental medical system using nanotechnology, either. That was stolen from the United Nations, even if eight hundred falans ago. They'd want it back."

"I hadn't even *thought* of that. Stet, let's keep working on this. Acolyte—"

"I am proud of what I am! And I was not taught to lie. We serve a powerful master. Why not simply demand what we want?"

"Maybe this is why Chmeee sent you to me. Acolyte, it's only a fighter, but their mother ship would carry *anti-matter fuel.* Hanuman, how many double-X-large plugs does Tunesmith have?"

"One partly completed."

Worse than he'd thought. The Ringworld couldn't afford another antimatter explosion! "Acolyte, you're Chmeee's son. Stick with the truth, as much as you can. Just don't talk about the Repair Center or Tunesmith or Carlos Wu's nanotech autodoc. Your father, Chmeee, rules a chunk of the Map of Earth. The Hindmost made you an offer, and you went off with him rather than fight your father again. You're his hostage, but you don't know it."

"And how did I meet Louis Wu?" the Kzin demanded.

"I . . . hadn't got that far."

"Land," ordered Hanuman. "We'll fill our kitchen slots while we wait for the ship's return. Louis, how long does a dogfight take?"

"Not long. Hours."

They landed among trees like redwood-sized dandelions. Louis had seen these elsewhere.

Light and noise would alert them if a ship returned. Meanwhile they dismounted, stretched, removed their pressure suits. As soon as Acolyte sniffed the air, he bounded away with a howl, hot in pursuit of something the others never saw.

Louis swung his kitchen converter out on its boom. He loaded grass and small plants into the hopper. Hanuman was doing the same. If the kitchen box was based on what they'd used thirty-odd years ago, it would process local vegetation or animal flesh, make handmeal bricks he could eat, and discard the dross. He'd have to catch something meaty, soon.

It extruded a brick.

"Wrong setting," Hanuman said. "Here." He turned a dial on Louis's kitchen. "That was for me. Fruit eater."

Louis broke a chunk off the protector's brick and tasted it. "Good, though. We eat fruit too."

It hit him without warning, a rush of nostalgia. He'd been here before, on unknown landscape in all this Ringworld *hugeness*, sharing a handmeal brick with Teela. He turned away from Hanuman as his eyes filled with tears.

He remembered Teela Brown.

She was tall and slender and walked with the confidence of a centenarian, though she was only in her thirties. He'd first seen her wearing silver net on blue skin; hair scarlet and orange and black, like bonfire flames and smoke, streaming upward. Later she'd put aside flatlander style. Nordik-pale skin, oval face, big brown eyes, and a small, serious mouth; dark and wavy hair cut short to fit into a pressure suit helmet.

She had never stumbled, never had a bad love affair, never been sick or hurt, never been caught in scandal or a public gaffe, until she attended Louis Wu's birthday party. Louis still believed that was a statistical fluke. Among a population in the tens of billions, someone like Teela Brown could surely be found.

But the Experimentalist Party among Pierson's puppeteers believed that they had been breeding the human race for luck. Teela was the descendant of six generations of Birthright Lottery winners. Whatever happened to Teela could be interpreted as lucky:

Falling in love with Louis Wu. Following him here.

Losing her way, in a domain three million times the surface area of the Earth. Finding Seeker, the brawny explorer who could show her so much of the Ringworld's secrets.

Finding the Repair Center beneath the Map of Mars. Finding a cache of tree-of-life root. Falling into a coma while her joints and brain case expanded, gender disappeared, gums and lips fused to horseshoes of sharp bone, skin thickened and wrinkled into armor . . . while she became a protector.

Nessus led us, and I led Teela, to the biggest, gaudiest toy in the universe. How could she not want to make it her own? But only a protector's intelligence could hold the Ringworld safe. And when the Ringworld was endangered, Teela Brown the protector saw that she must die.

Death isn't bad luck to a protector. It's just another tool.

Acolyte returned with his mouth bloody. "Good hunting here. My father is missing another fine adventure."

Hanuman asked, "Louis, can you pass for crew on an ARM ship?"

"*There's* a notion." Louis thought about it. Did he really remember enough . . . ? "What I can't pass for is a local. I'm Homo sapiens, Earth origin. Why do I want to be a crewman, Hanuman? Crew of what?"

Hanuman said, "We must not be servants of a protector. So, I must be a tree-dwelling animal, and you must be a wanderer unless you serve some greater force. If you serve, it must be some aspect of the Fringe War—"

"The ARM, of course. But I don't know ARM protocol, and I'm not in their records."

"Isn't there a way you could have been missed?"

". . . No. Let's try something else."

He munched on a handmeal while he thought. Drop the

previous story; start over. Tell something simple. Something Louis Wu can keep straight, and Acolyte also.

He said, "Let's try to guess what a random ARM fighter has in its computer records.

"They know that we came home—that Chmeee and Louis Wu came home with Nessus injured and no Teela Brown. Suppose Teela lived? She never finds the Repair Center and tree-of-life.

"They might know that the Hindmost landed on Canyon twenty-three years later, and Louis Wu disappeared then. They might have tracked Chmeee too, from one of the Kzin worlds up to where the Hindmost collected *him*.

"So the Hindmost brings us both back to the Ringworld as crew. That's the way it happened, but let's say he planned to rendezvous with Teela. She and Louis Wu have been living together ever since." It could have been that way. Should have been! Even though the Ringworld would have been torn apart a year later. Still daydreaming, Louis said, "They had a child after her implant wore off, and that's me."

Hanuman said, "Hypothesis diverges from ARM records."

Tanj! "How?"

"When would these events take place? Louis Wu returned here thirteen years ago. Does the ARM know that?"

". . . Yes, they do. ARM found me on Canyon just before the Hindmost collected me." Louis had killed two agents. "Tanj! That would make Louis Wu's son twelve years old at best."

"Can you pass for twelve?" Hanuman asked.

"Hah hah."

"Could you, Louis Eldest, have left Teela with a child? The child would be aged a hundred and sixty falans."

"Almost forty years old. Couldn't happen. Teela must have had her five-year infertility shots. They'd have had to wear off. We never had the time."

Acolyte asked, "Can you be a child of Teela and Seeker?"

"Hah! No. Different species."

Hanuman and Acolyte waited.

Start over. "At the end of the first expedition, thirty-eight years ago, Chmeee and I came back to known space and the Patriarchy. We turned over *Long Shot* and some information about the Ringworld. We were debriefed by a joint commission, then the ARM asked me a lot more questions. They didn't learn much, because we didn't explore much. Our second expedition was twenty-three years later. What if there was an expedition in between?"

Hanuman asked, "Who sent it?"

"The Hindmost sent it. Expedition number one-and-a-half. I can fake that. I met a puppeteer named Chiron on the Fleet of Worlds. He was pure white, perfectly coiffed with a wonderful array of classic gems, and a little smaller than Nessus—" His companions had never met Nessus. "Thirty pounds lighter than the Hindmost. He sounded just like the Hindmost; I suppose they all had the same training.

"So now we can all describe him, stet? The Hindmost puts Chiron in charge. Chiron leaves not long after Chmeee, and I came back to human space. That brings him here . . . mmm . . . at least thirty years ago. He finds Teela. Her infertility shot has worn off. Teela takes up living with one of Chiron's crew. I'm the child."

"What is your name, child?"

"Luis." Acolyte might forget, but he'd still sound right: *Loo-iss, Luis.* "Luis Tamasan," the first Oriental name he could think of, to account for the epicanthic folds in his eyes. "Chiron had his records erased. The ARM already knows that puppeteers meddle with their records. There's no Fertility Board record either, because my father . . . mmm. *Horace* Tamasan was born to a freemother, an illegal birth. Lots of bastards go to space."

Hanuman said, "A consistent tale. Have we the acting knack to tell it?"

* * *

Tunesmith's voice broke in without warning. "Hanuman, you surmise that an ARM fighter has dropped its add-on tank and gone off to battle. I scan an area bigger than worlds, and I find nothing to fight. My neutrino scan shows no power sources. Battery-powered ships would not register, I assume. Must I watch until they fire lasers or antimatter bullets?"

Louis said, "That half hour delay is going to drive us nuts sooner or later."

"Small ships might escape Tunesmith's instruments, but he wouldn't miss a weapons laser or antimatter flash," said Hanuman. "Would they fight while refusing to use such weapons? No. I surmise there is no fight at all, Luis."

Louis mulled that. If the ARMs hadn't been expecting a fight, where had the ARM ship gone? Why had they dropped their tank first?

"The tank might be empty," Hanuman suggested. "They wanted greater range. They won't be back."

Louis said, "All right, let's rethink. Spinward of us, there's a lot of fog to hide in. Ships could be hunting each other. Ah, flup, never mind." Both aliens were looking at him. "If there's nothing to fight, they've gone off to look at the puncture! What else is there? The Ringworld is dying. They need to tell their mother ship what's happening here, and they might want to run away fast, so they dropped their tank."

Hanuman thought it over; nodded. "Don your pressure suits."

11

THE WOUNDED LAND

Most of the *Mouse Eaters were dozing underground after a morning meal.*

This wasn't Wembleth's custom. Wembleth was a traveler; he adapted his behavior to his hosts. He'd been living with these nocturnal hunters for several turns of the sky, sharing their meals and their women, teaching them how to make and use tools he'd learned of elsewhere.

Most of the villagers were inside their burrow houses. Older children and elders were cleaning up after the feast, with Wembleth's help, while shadow withdrew from the sun. For him it was a good choice; he needed some sunlight to stay healthy. In a minute they'd all go in—

And the day lit up.

Children began screaming.

Mouse Eaters couldn't deal with mere daylight; what would this glare do to them? His own eyes squinted to teary slits. Wembleth scooped up two small children, hugged their faces against his chest, and shouted at the rest. "Get inside!" He darted into the nearest house. The others would have to follow, or find their own houses.

Windows were mere slits in Mouse Eater houses. Wembleth dropped his load of children into the dark, wiggled past more frightened children and out again.

In the horrid light children and elders were running blind. Elder Mouse Eaters tended to lose their sight anyway; it let them move around in daylight. Through squinted eyes Wembleth could still see. They could not. Adults were bigger than he was. Somehow he wrestled them into doorways.

He couldn't guess how much time passed. The light

faded. A hot fierce wind blasted across the plaza, scattering coals from the commonfire, and died. Presently a softer wind was blowing the other way. When he couldn't find anyone, couldn't see anyway, he crawled indoors. Indoors was perfect blackness; his night sight had faded, and the horrid light had faded too. Wembleth lay down and gasped for air.

Something would change. Something always did, when things went bad. You had to watch for the opportunity that would follow.

Presently Wembleth realized that he was suffocating.

The blast spit Snail Darter, *in stasis, into a rocky cliff above a vast forest. When time resumed, the ship had become part of an immense landslide of shattered shale.*

Far, far to spinward, a sea of mist ran all across the horizon, hiding everything up to the base of the Arch. Worlds away, the mist domed upward. The near edge of the mist was a shock wave still moving sluggishly toward Snail Darter.

"It looks like the end of the world. Any world. Lots of worlds," *Oliver said.*

"See who's around," *Roxanny ordered.*

Detective Oliver Forrestier busied himself with various sensors. Right Whale, *the big ARM cruiser, had gone up against a nameless Kzinti juggernaut, just before the fireball and blackout. There had been other ships too . . . but now there was nothing.* "No obvious contrails," *Oliver said.* "The cloud is spitting neutrinos . . . last traces of antimatter, I guess, and diminishing. No point sources. No big ships."

"The fireball is collapsing. Like it's being sucked down," *Claus said uneasily.*

"Well," *Roxanny said,* "let's go look. We've run out of enemies, right, 'Tec Forrestier? The blast must have smashed them all. Friends too. So our mission is to collect data. Lift us, Claus."

Snail Darter *lifted.* 'Tec-Two Claus Raschid asked, *"Just go straight on in, Roxanny?"*

"Stay low, take our time. Look around. Claus, there's a hole *at the center of all this. A hole in the Ringworld is a way home."*

"Roxanny, what has you so cheerful?"

Roxanny Gauthier laughed boisterously. "We're alive! Isn't that enough? Look at the trail we left! We can follow it right back to the explosion. Claus, Oliver, for all we know about stasis fields, did you really believe it? Does it make sense that you can stop time and restart it? When I saw the light, I knew I was in an antimatter explosion. I thought we were dead!"

"This was a city," Oliver said. He played his instruments along the grid of streets and buildings. *"Big one. Spread out, like Sydney."*

"Claus, slow us down," Roxanny said. *"I don't see much in the way of corpses. Where are the dead?"*

Oliver guessed. *"Inside, taking cover from the shock wave. Look at your displays, Roxanny. Air pressure is down and dropping. They hid from the shock wave and then—"*

"Suffocated? The air's draining out." Claus wasn't stupid; he was only coming out of denial. *"We've killed the whole Ringworld. Hey—"*

"We'll be ten thousand years investigating the structure, learning its secrets," Roxanny said. *"What are you doing, Claus?"*

"Landing. I can see a survivor."

Underground,Wembleth was *suffocating.*

He clawed his way into the light, but the air wasn't any better.

The light was no more than broad daylight, but there was a weirdness to spinward as if half the world had been taken away, leaving only fog and chaos. Wembleth made his way to the commons, his chest heaving.

An hour ago they'd been feasting. Now there was no-
body. The fires had gone out. Mouse Eaters wouldn't
come outside in an emergency, and Wembleth didn't have
a better answer than they did.

Something shaped vaguely like a silver vinch's egg was
dropping out of the sky.

Wembleth stood up, though he nearly fainted, and
waved both arms. When in doubt, ask for help. It was his
normal instinct, but his fading intellect backed him up:

Here were folk with the power to fly! Tales told of such
power, but these were flying in the winds of a major di-
saster. Anyone who could do that must know something.

News of this disaster must be carried to other peoples.

Wembleth was on his hands and knees, his vision
blacking out, when two men of unknown species de-
scended to him. They wore hard armor, like the mythical
Vashneesht. They offered him a bag to crawl into.

Wembleth did.

Air hissed into the bag. He could breathe.

He didn't know how to tell the Vashneesht that oth-
ers needed rescuing. It never occurred to him that
Vashneesht—wizards—might be the cause of a world-
destroying disaster.

Gravity near a Ball World follows an inverse square law.
In contrast, the Ringworld is a plane surface. Gravity does
not dwindle as you rise, nor does spin gravity nor magnetic
force, until the Ringworld looks less like a plane than a
ribbon, from hundreds of thousands of miles high.

The Ringworld engineers embedded a lacework of
superconducting cable in the Ringworld floor. The grid
allows magnetic manipulation of solar flares to cause
a superthermal laser effect, the Ringworld meteor defense; but it also opens the entire Ringworld to magnetic
levitation.

Magnetically powered vehicles could rise to any height.
It was night when the skycycles lifted. Sixty miles high,

effectively out of the atmosphere, they followed the gouge spinward. Verdant landscape became stormy, in ripples and streams of lightning-lit cloud rather than in whorl patterns. Then it was all unbroken clouds.

The terminator, the shadow of the edge of a shadow square, swept over them. A growing sliver of sun became a noonday glare. How long had it been since Louis saw a sunrise?

They crossed above a tremendous, sagging, faintly glowing tube. Horsetails of mist were flowing over the tube's flaccidities and disappearing into vacuum. Tunesmith's plug wouldn't hold forever.

Soil and rock still clung to the scrith floor. There were pools and ribbons of foamy ice, all ravaged in a radial pattern. They followed it inward toward the puncture.

The rim of the hole glittered. Maybe, maybe Tunesmith's "reweaving" system was working.

"Spacecraft," Acolyte said. "Above the hole."

There was no exhaust. The ship hovered on thrusters: a cylinder with a flattened belly, a little bigger than the tank it had left behind, but with a bulb of transparent canopy for a nose.

"That's an ARM design, Kittycatcher Class," Louis said. "A fighter. Three crew. They'll have seen us by now."

"Will they fire on us?"

"We must look harmless enough." Louis was trying to persuade himself.

Hologram miniatures of his two allies blurred, then became two views of a dark-skinned woman in ARM uniform. A contralto voice blared from his speaker. "Intruders, answer at once or be destroyed! You have entered a war zone!"

"I'm Luis Tamasan," Louis Wu answered. "Can you hear me?"

"We hear you, Luis Tamasan. Please approach *Snail Darter.*"

"What are your intentions?"

"We are observers for the United Nations," the woman said. "What do you know of events in this region?"

"We came to observe a puncture in the Ringworld floor."

"Your associate is a Kzin."

Louis laughed. "Acolyte is local, a Ringworld native. I'm local too."

She peered at his hologram. "You look human."

"I'm human. Born here. Acolyte was too, and he's Kzin."

"There are Kzinti here?"

"Archaic Kzinti, in the Great Ocean." That should rouse their curiosity.

The ARM woman sounded peevish. "We tried every reasonable frequency. Why are you communicating in a mode used by the Fleet of Worlds?"

"Puppeteers found the Ringworld and puppeteers explored it first," Louis said with a trace of chill in his voice. "My parents and Acolyte's father came here with Pierson's puppeteers."

"Land there at the edge."

"We came to examine the puncture. May we circle above it?"

"Land *now*, Ringworld's children."

Louis said, "Down, Acolyte." He let his flycycle sink.

The ARM asked, "Acolyte, do you speak Interworld?"

"Madam LE, I do," the Kzin rumbled.

"While I serve the United Nations you may address me by my rank, as Copilot or 'Tec, not as Legal Entity. How may I call you?"

"Acolyte, until I earn a more worthy name."

"What is your connection to the Patriarchy?"

"I hear of them from my father. We see the lights of the Fringe War."

The skycycles settled on bare scrith.

Snail Darter descended with evident caution, and touched down. An airlock opened below its rounded tip. A human shape emerged, then a second pulling a bulb of some kind through a door that was too narrow. It got through anyway.

One ARM flew to meet the flycycles while the other lowered the bulb to the desiccated turf. The bulb was a rescue pod, an inflated balloon with a few opaque bulges of life-support gear. The shadow of a walking man showed in the bulb as it rolled toward the flycycles.

'Tec-First Gauthier—easily recognized through her fishbowl helmet—must have had a clear view of Hanuman riding alert in Acolyte's lap. Acolyte attached a line to Hanuman's pressure suit, as if the Hanging Person might scamper away and have to be caught. The pair debarked and joined Louis. Gauthier settled before them.

"I feel small," Acolyte said uneasily.

This close to the puncture, the floor was polished by the antimatter blast: featureless scrith, translucent and smooth, artificial and infinite. Louis and his companions were tiny. Louis hadn't felt it until the Kzin spoke.

"LE Acolyte, LE Luis," said Gauthier—courtesy, because Acolyte couldn't ever have been registered as a Legal Entity, nor could Luis Tamasan. "—meet 'Tec Oliver Forrestier and LE Wembleth. I'm 'Tec Roxanny Gauthier." Her manner had softened.

'Tec Forrestier, the second flyer, was large and pale, perhaps a Belter raised in low G. Like Gauthier's his rust-colored curly hair was cut close to his scalp. He smiled and touched gloves with the man, then the Kzin. "We're glad to find you," he said.

Gauthier asked, "Can you take Wembleth for us? We don't have room for him."

"It's a three man ship," Forrestier explained.

"What's Wembleth, then?" Louis asked. "Local?"

Wembleth had lagged behind. Rolling a balloon by walking on its bottom didn't seem to bother him, but it was slow going. When he tried to stop, the balloon kept moving; he fell over, and got up without embarrassment.

Could Wembleth hear their communicators? He wasn't speaking.

Forrestier said, "We found him where the air was disappearing. Corpses and smashed burrows all around him. Do you recognize his type?"

"His species?" Louis studied Wembleth.

Wembleth blinked back as if light hurt his eyes, but they met Louis's without a flinch. He was eight inches shorter than Louis, five feet six or a little more. He was dressed in woven cloth, trousers and a loose shirt with patch pockets, all the color of sand. His feet were bare, large, and horny, with toenails like jagged weapons. His skin was darker than Louis's, paler than Roxanny Gauthier's, and his hands and face and neck were wrinkled. Thick hair, black and white, hid most of his face. Blue scrollwork on his brow and cheeks might have been ritual tattooing, or might have been naturally evolved camouflage. He was smiling, interested, where any normal man might have cowered in terror.

"I don't know this exact species." Louis hadn't met any locals within hundreds of millions of miles, but he didn't say that. He hadn't decided how far "Luis Tamasan" had traveled. He said, "There are thousands of hominid species on the Ringworld, maybe tens of thousands, and most of them are sapient. Wembleth is about average size. Dark skin's pretty common too. Teeth—" Wembleth smiled; Louis winced.

Wembleth's teeth were crooked and discolored. Four were missing, leaving black gaps. Louis could *feel* what that must be like. Wouldn't he be constantly chewing up his tongue?

Wembleth still had three canines, though. Louis asked, "Meat eater?"

'Tec Gauthier shrugged. "We gave him a standard dole brick. There's a setting for raw meat, of course, in case we get a Kzinti prisoner. He ate some of that."

"We can feed Wembleth, then. Even if his whole ecology is dead," Louis said.

"Good! Another matter. Tell me anything you can," Oliver Forrestier said, "about *that*." His arm swept a circle.

"The sudden mountain range." Obvious first question, yet Louis hadn't planned an answer. He improvised: "We saw it come down. Things of this scale, Ringworld scale, even my parents never have much to say. Chiron sent us to learn more."

"Chiron?"

"He brought my father to this place. A puppeteer."

"Stet. Come here, Luis." Forrestier walked toward the puncture seventy feet away. Louis followed.

Forrestier stopped. His toes were too near the edge. From this viewpoint it was still a bottomless pit ten or fifteen miles across. Shrinking, it was shrinking. The edge was hard to focus on; it blurred and shimmered when Louis moved his head.

Forrestier asked, "Is this normal?"

"I've never looked into a rip in the floor of the world," Louis said. "It's scary." It was barely a lie. He'd seen Fist-of-God crater . . . but "Luis" hadn't.

Gauthier said, "Well, it looks like it's repairing itself. Does it always do that? Over the years we've seen some of those hourglass storms die out. We think those are punctures and air leakage."

Louis frowned, projecting *Don't understand*. He remembered a word from far away, used as if it meant *magicians*, but it meant *protector*. "Vashneesht," he said. "There are secrets we never learn."

'Tec-One Gauthier said, "Oliver, get back from there! Luis, Acolyte, shall we set up a tent?"

Roxanny and Oliver lifted a bulky package out of the ship's lock. They set it on the scrith and moored it with stick-strip edges. The tent inflated itself, writhing and trying to bounce, because of course the stickstrip wouldn't hold on scrith. Roxanny left Oliver to deal with that while she went back for the kitchen 'doc.

Oliver saw what she was doing and exploded. "LE Gauthier, are you schitzy? We can't lose that!"

"We can live without for a few hours."

"Why did you try to give away Wembleth? A Ringworld native! He's a wonderful find!"

"Wembleth is a prize, all right. I wish we could take them both, but he's still just a local. He doesn't know enough. I want Luis Tamasan! I'd take the Kzin if I could fit him in the ship, but I can't, so we'll question him first."

"Roxanny, he's still a Kzin!"

"You're afraid? He's a kid. They're both teen children. Both their parents were on the Ringworld before the Fleet, and the kids must have been hearing about it all their lives."

Oliver considered. "What would their parents do to get them back?"

"Maybe we'll find that out too, after we know everything they do." She grinned. "Ollie, did you see the look on Luis's face? Like—"

Oliver had, and his voice showed his resentment. "Like he never saw a woman before. All right, Roxanny, have it your way. We'll crawl into the tent with a Kzin, and by Finagle he's the first that gets fed! But we've got way more data than we were sent for, and the trick now is to get home with it!"

The ARMs were involved with erecting the tent. Nobody was looking at Louis when Tunesmith's miniature bust popped up on his dash.

The protector said, "I urgently need to know whether my reweaving system is working. Is the hole getting smaller? How drastically must I act to save *something*? I need hardly warn you not to fall into the puncture."

Was *Snail Darter* or its mother ship eavesdropping?

Even if this line were private, little glowing hologram heads would be seen. Louis said quickly, "The hole is closing. *It's closing.* We have company." He turned the holoscreen off.

Now Tunesmith could do no more than listen.

The tent had inflated into a tube with a big airlock, an alcove for vacuum gear, a living space, and silver walls that must hide a toilet. Gauthier inside, and Forrestier outside, assisted the rest to enter.

Acolyte carried Hanuman, but left him in his pressure suit. "The suit takes care of sanitary matters," Acolyte said. Hanuman ooked.

Gauthier had thrown back her helmet, though she didn't move to strip off her suit. Oliver had done the same. The ARMs didn't seem to be excessively distrustful. Louis and Acolyte opened their own helmets. The varying species settled themselves around a small kitchen box.

Wembleth spoke syllables Louis had never heard. A translator voice spoke from one of his pockets: "Good, this is much more room." The hairy man zipped his rescue pod open and wriggled out with a sigh of contentment.

"Wembleth makes number four in a three man ship," Forrestier explained. "We found him surrounded by the dead of some larger, hairier species, gasping like a beached fish, but on his feet and pulling himself toward us by any ruined wall the storm hadn't flung away. We had to stuff him in Mission and Weapons and shut it all off. We've questioned him—he knows things we need—but we can't fly like that, LE Luis. We need to defend ourselves."

"We'll take him someplace he can live," Louis said.

"We'll find a way to moor his rescue pod to your flying thing. We don't have a suit that'll fit him."

'Tec Gauthier was handing out dole bricks from the little kitchen. She made adjustments to give Acolyte a brick of drippy red, then something fruity for Hanuman. "It's the only kitchen we've got, and it's the 'doc too. In flight, in peacetime, this tent buds out from the hull. If we can't deploy it, we barely have room to wiggle. War is hell," she said lightly. "Can I give you something to drink?"

"Surprise me," Louis said. "Tea? Juice?"

"Beer?"

"Better not. And Acolyte's too young."

Acolyte growled.

Roxanny laughed. "So're you, Luis!"

She thought he was a child! He said, "Yes, LE."

She passed out squeezebulbs: something cranberry-flavored for Louis, boullion for Acolyte and Wembleth. "You both grew up on the Ringworld. Did your fathers tell you about planets?"

"We learned physics that way," Acolyte said. "Father—Chmeee—tried to show me what a Coriolis storm is, a hurricane. I'm not sure I understand."

"I'd love to see Earth," Louis said. A working space-craft! His first chance to defect since the abominable Bram had found him . . . no, since before that. Since he'd sliced up *Needle*'s hyperdrive motor!

There had to be a way to speak to Roxanny Gauthier alone.

Her suit wasn't quite a skintight: it only hinted at a shape that made his heart turn over. A strong woman, an athlete. Her face was severe, with a square chin and a straight-edged nose. She'd be in her fifties, Louis judged, based on body language and the way Forrestier deferred to her . . . unless she ranked him. Her hair was a sparse black puffball; she must depilate or shave her scalp periodically.

It took Louis by surprise, after all the hominids he'd met, how much he longed for the sight of a woman.

But she was asking something. "Do you know anything about a big transparent ship?"

Louis shook his head. Acolyte was less cautious. "Like a General Products ship? What would we see, a glass bubble?"

"Yah, a big glass bubble. What do you know about General Products hulls?"

"Luis's father came here in a Number Two," Acolyte said. He was giving too much detail. He'd be caught in inconsistencies, Louis feared . . . but Chmeee must have described *Liar*, which had been a Number Two, when he told his son of the first expedition.

And Acolyte was enjoying himself.

"A huge glass bubble filled with gear. Massive machines inside," Gauthier said.

Forrestier said, "Or four flames moving across the sky. It's got four fusion motors. It was stolen, maybe by your Chiron."

Louis said, "Chiron doesn't tell us everything. Or anything."

Roxanny said, "Actually it was stolen twice, first by the Kzinti, then from the Kzinti. We didn't see it reach the Ringworld, but we think it's here. We want it back."

"Tell us about the Chiron expedition," Oliver ordered.

Louis improvised. "Dad says it took two years, and it was way cramped." Stick to what you know where possible—"My mother came on the first expedition. She says *Lying Bastard* started as a Number Two and just grew out of all proportion, bigger every time a puppeteer thought of another safety feature. In the end *Lying Bastard* was a big flying wing with the General Products cylinder stuck into it. The stasis field enclosed the cylinder, but they lost everything that was on the wing." All of that would be in ARM records, including Louis Wu's own speculations. They'd find Louis's description of Chiron there too.

"So when Chiron built *his* ship, he wedged everything inside the hull. I've been in it, but not since I was *this* high, and it was already cramped—"

"We would like to talk to Chiron," Oliver said. "Where may we find him?"

Acolyte said, "Chiron has told us most explicitly that we must not tell anyone how to find him."

To Roxanny Oliver said, "*Long Shot* was in the hands of Kzinti. Puppeteers might find that distressing, don't you think? A puppeteer might act to get it back." He asked Louis, "Did Chiron's ship have a name?"

"*Paranoia*," Louis said without cracking a smile.

"How is it armed?"

"*Paranoia* has no armaments at all," Louis said, "barring tools which may be turned to that end. We're not to speak of those."

"Where on the Ringworld did your *Paranoia* land? Was it near the Great Ocean, where the first expedition left Teela Brown?"

Louis hadn't decided that either. "Can't say."

"Boy, you don't seem to have anything at all to trade," Roxanny Gauthier said. "What would you like to know from us? Did Chiron tell you what questions to ask?"

"He wants to know if the Ringworld is going to heal. I can see that the rupture's sealing itself. Even so, what can you tell us about the Fringe War? Is it about to go away?"

"I doubt it," Roxanny said.

"Or is it going to get so big and violent that it shatters everything?"

"That doesn't have to happen," she said firmly.

Oliver laughed. Roxanny looked around in annoyance, and Oliver said, "Just a passing thought. How old are you, Luis?"

Louis had planned to be in his thirties, but both ARMs seemed to think he was just past puberty. For some reason this delighted him. Tanj, why not? He said, "Eighty falans and a bit."

"And a falan would be?"

"Ten rotations of the sky."

"About seventy-five days? Thirty-hour Ringworld days?" Oliver was whispering to a pocket computer, bigger than a civilian version. "You're about twenty years old, Earth time. I'm forty-six. Roxanny?"

"I'm fifty-one," she said without hesitation.

"We take boosterspice, of course. It keeps us from getting old. What crossed my mind," Oliver Forrestier said, "is that this is the first human woman you've ever seen other than your mother, Luis."

Roxanny was smiling, a reluctant smile. And Louis was flushing, suddenly aware that his eyes had lingered too long on Roxanny Gauthier; that he'd edged closer to her than the cramped quarters demanded; that he couldn't look at her and talk coherently. The close air must be alive with pheromones . . . Roxanny's and Oliver's too. And as Oliver was the first human male he'd seen or sniffed in twenty-odd years—and no room for a shower aboard *Snail Darter*—it wasn't surprising if Louis felt both horny and threatened.

"Sorry," he said, and eased back by an inch.

It crossed his mind that intimidation could take many forms. They wanted something from Luis: information Louis Wu would have to make up, but still—

Roxanny laughed lightly. "Never mind. Luis, would you like to see *Snail Darter*? Acolyte, we can't take you aboard. It's too cramped. Luis can tell you about it afterward."

Hanuman's eyes met Louis's, but he said nothing. Wembleth and Acolyte had begun a halting conversation. Wembleth found the Kzin fascinating. Louis closed his faceplate and followed the ARMs out.

The ship was awesomely cramped.

Three seats faced away from each other around a central pillar. One seat was occupied. There was a pucker next to the airlock door for the now-detached tent. A hole in the floor led to a cavity the size of a man: the Weapons and Mission Room.

Roxanny entered first. She slid into the second seat. "LE Luis Tamasan, meet 'Tec-Two Claus Raschid. Claus, Luis," she said. "Not quite a native."

Claus turned around and offered a hand. He was darker

than Roxanny, taller than Oliver, and his arm had a long reach. "Luis, I'm the pilot. Sit there."

Louis had hoped to talk to Roxanny alone, or even Oliver alone. They'd both come along, a little too closely agreed for Louis's comfort, leaving Acolyte and Wembleth (and Hanuman) alone in the tent.

Louis slid into the third seat. He felt planes shifting, adjusting to his height and weight and the bulk of his pressure suit. Basic seating: it fit him imperfectly.

Roxanny Gauthier tapped an instruction into her chair arms, using both hands. A crash web held Louis before he could move.

The force field in a crash web would protect a passenger in a collision; it was also useful for police work.

Louis didn't react right away. How would *Luis* react? Frozen in panic, at least long enough for Louis to *think*. And then what?

"For your protection. You did say you wanted to see Earth," Roxanny said, smiling like a cat.

Oliver slid in through the airlock and then down through the hatch, into the fourth chair. The Mission and Weapons Room fitted Oliver like a tight suit.

Louis wriggled a bit; the field permitted that much. He asked, "Are we going to Earth?"

"Back to *Gray Nurse*, anyway," the third crewman said. "We'll be there in an hour. We'd better be. Roxanny, you left the kitchen 'doc behind."

"We had to," she said.

"Stet, but if anything goes wrong—stet. Luis, the carrier *Gray Nurse* is our first stop, and people other than us will decide where you go from there. I expect that's Earth, or at least Sol system. And hey, you can tell us some things while we're en route. Chiron can't stop you now. You'll be the second Ringworlder to reach human space."

"Don't go through this hole," Louis said.

All three ARMs turned their heads to look at him. Roxanny asked, "Why not?"

That was a tough one. Louis Wu was certain that Tune-smith wouldn't allow an ARM spacecraft to escape this easily. Something would block them . . . but why would *Luis Tamasan* say something so out of character?

He said, "Chmeee says he left the world through Fist-of-God. My father came through a different puncture. Neither of them saw anything like this . . . shimmer. Fist-of-God Mountain isn't repairing itself, is it? But this hole is."

Claus said, "So is Fist-of-God. The crater closed itself weeks ago, before we noticed. We were hoping you could tell us about that."

Tunesmith must have tested his reweaving system, Louis guessed. Luis said nothing.

Claus Raschid had something on a virtual screen. "Here we are. Luis, try to follow this. The nearest punc-ture we know of is a million miles away. Too far. They'll track us across the surface. Every tanj species in the Fringe War will want us as bad as we want you, because of what we might know. But we might escape if we go through *immediately*, *right here*, and with our motors *off*." The ship lifted. "Here is where *Gray Nurse* is wait-ing, our mother ship, in the dark, up against the Ring-world floor—"

Below them Oliver was yelling, "Raschid! What are you playing at?"

Louis tried to yell louder. Being immobilized was driv-ing him frantic. "Drop something first! See what hap-pens to it!"

"I'm getting us home," Raschid told Oliver. The ship eased sideways. Now it was above the puncture. "All power sources *off*. Luis, if we had the auxiliary fuel tank I'd drop that, but I don't."

They were falling. Louis glimpsed the tent sitting alone on the scrith. They'd be all right, he told himself; they had Hanuman to guide them. The hole expanded. It was full of stars.

Snail Darter smashed down into something that gave.

Crash webs caught his captors recoiling upward. Louis felt his brain bounce in his skull. Already in a crash web, he recovered first . . . still immobilized. He could hear Oliver screaming below him.

Claus shouted, "What did we hit?"

"Get us *out*! Get us *out*!" Roxanny screamed.

Reweaving system, Tunesmith had said. How strong would threads made of scrith be? Strong enough to stop a falling spacecraft? But they'd cut through the hull. The hole must be laced with them.

"The thrusters are dead," Claus said.

"Where are they?" Louis demanded.

Claus craned around to snarl at him. Louis asked, "They're on the bottom, aren't they?" It was ancient habit: shipbuilders tended to put thruster motors where they would have put rockets. "Whatever's in that hole, *mending* that hole, it's cutting the thrusters apart. We'll sink into it. How long before it reaches the power source? What do you use for a power source? Where is it?" Babbling, he was babbling. Why hadn't the stasis field been triggered? But if that happened, they might be here forever.

Claus was slow catching up. Roxanny Gauthier said, "Midship. It's a battery. If anything cuts into it—"

The ship was indeed sinking inch by inch into the puncture. Worse, it was beginning to tip over.

Claus was staring at them, not getting it. When he did, he yelled in terror. His hands danced above the controls.

Roxanny shouted, "Wait!"

The hatch in the floor closed. Oliver's yell chopped off.

A rocket motor bellowed. The cabin section detached and rose fast, wobbled, then steadied. Claus took over manually; the cabin tilted far over, fell, tilted upright again.

"You *killed* him!" Roxanny said. "Oliver!"

"He was sitting in the wrong place." Claus glared at

Louis Wu, who was in Oliver's chair; then at Roxanny. "Wasn't that you yelling, 'Get us out'?"

The tent billowed in the exhaust as the escape pod thumped down. Recoil threw Roxanny and Claus several inches before their crash webs caught them.

Through the wall of the tent Louis could just see that Acolyte and Hanuman were spreading the rescue pod open for Wembleth to enter.

A brilliant light flared from the direction of the puncture. Then that side of the cabin blackened. Louis yelled, "Roxanny, *let me loose!*"

"Wait it out, Luis."

A shock wave slammed the cabin.

"They're dying out there! Let me loose! Claus!"

Claus said, "Here." His hand moved, and Louis was free. He rolled out of his chair and into the tiny airlock.

The tent was splayed out in fragments like an exploded balloon. The blast had scattered its contents. Wembleth and his rescue pod rolled gently past, Wembleth tumbling like clothes in an Oil Age dryer, as Louis wiggled out of the airlock.

Acolyte was trying to find his feet, falling over, trying again. Hanuman was not in sight. Wembleth must have regained his senses: he was curled in a tight ball now, still tumbling.

"Acolyte? Are you all right? Pressure okay?"

"My suit is holding pressure. Do you see Hanuman?"

"No."

Wembleth was nearest. Louis flashed his attitude jets, dropped ahead of him, and ran alongside the balloon, pushing to stop its spin. The Ringworlder tried to help. They got it stopped, though Wembleth was unbalanced . . . off balance because Hanuman was clinging tight to him, face to chest. Hanuman still wore his pressure suit.

"Acolyte, I've got them both."

They walked back toward the ruined tent. Acolyte,

Claus, and Roxanny joined them. Roxanny was carrying something heavy, an oblong brick she hugged to her breast.

The kitchen 'doc hadn't been moved. It looked unharmed.

They moored it to Louis's flycycle, and moored Wembleth's rescue pod to Acolyte's. The ARMs gave orders as if they were superior officers. Louis asked at one point, "Any reason to take your escape vehicle? I don't think flycycle motors are up to that."

"Leave it," Roxanny said. "It's dead."

The explosion of the fighter ship's battery might have damaged Tunesmith's reweaving system, Louis thought. Tunesmith should be told . . . but he *was* being told, by voice and camera feeds. He just couldn't answer, and that was fine with Louis.

12

THE GIRAFFE PEOPLE

The glow in the XXL plug was dimmed. The tube sagged, leaking broad white rivers of tropospheric storm. It didn't matter. They'd left the puncture nearly closed.

The party flew to spinward, directly away from where they had left their fuel tank. "Leave it as bait. We don't want to be near it," Roxanny Gauthier ordered. "Whatever dropped that inflatable mountain range might take an interest. Vashneesht, you said? What do you know of Vashneesht?"

Louis said, "Vashneesht is just what we say when nobody knows anything. Wizards. Magic." Interworld words Luis would know from his parents.

She was riding the front saddle of Louis's flycycle. She'd tried to operate the controls, and turned icy when they didn't work. Louis flew from the aft saddle. Neither

Roxanny nor Claus had said so, but it seemed clear they'd been drafted into the ARM.

The other flycycle seemed in good shape. Acolyte rode the front seat; Claus was hidden behind him. The native seemed comfortable enough, slung below the flycycle in his inflated rescue pod, until he began gasping.

"Acolyte!"

"Here, Louis."

"The rescue pod has run out of air. Wembleth is in trouble."

Claus said, "Tanj, it must have been faulty."

"We descend?"

They landed. Wembleth had fainted.

They kept their suits on. The air was thin fog and hurricane wind; it dimmed their headphone voices. Louis shouted, "I don't think opening the rescue pod—"

Acolyte: "Better idea?"

"Get the tree swinger to open his helmet. His suit has a recycling feature."

The little anthropoid was quick to respond to Acolyte's gestures. He threw back his helmet, sneezed at the stink, but left it open. Concerned, he pushed his face close to Wembleth's and sniffed. Wembleth stirred and presently sat up.

They flew above fallen trees that had grown as puffy tops on tall, slender trunks. The antimatter blast had flattened them with their tops pointing spinward. Further away, the wind from the pressure drop felled them to antispin and left lower growth alive.

Falling pressure was a wave still expanding across this land. The flycycles followed the shock wave, catching up slowly. They crossed tens of thousands of miles of disaster and storm. Now there were standing trees among the fallen in the pufftop forest. The forest ran on, cleaving to the lowlands, mingling with other ecologies.

Louis took them down into a break in the pufftop forest, in a meadow alongside a rushing stream.

Air! They pulled Wembleth out of his bubble before they stripped off their own suits. Wembleth whooped; he danced, though stiffly. He plunged into the water, stripped off his coarse-woven shirt and pants, and began scrubbing himself with them.

Water! Running water, ankle deep, ran down to a deep pool. The ARMs looked at each other; then they stripped off their skintights too and dove in. In midair, Roxanny's laughing eyes brushed Luis Tamasan's. Louis couldn't breathe.

Acolyte plunged in with a mighty splash. With his fur plastered flat he looked wonderfully funny. It broke the spell. Louis laughed.

Hanuman was wrestling with the fittings of his suit. Louis helped him out. Hanuman, the affectionate anthropoid, hugged him and whispered, "The ARMs have hand weapons hidden."

"Surprise," Louis murmured.

"Ook ook ook. Get naked?"

"My problem—"

"They know. Go in like Wembleth." Hanuman eeled out of his arms and, four-legged, ran for the water. He dove in without a splash. Louis yelled and chased him, leaping into a cannonball dive.

Cold! He pulled his skintight off in deep water. He made an attempt to rub it clean against himself, then balled it up and threw it onto the rocky shore to drain.

There now. All concerned could pretend not to know that Luis Tamasan was in a state of arousal.

He stayed clear of the ARMs, who were—getting friendly, he'd thought, but Claus was backing off, and Roxanny was talking fast and inaudibly. Quarrel? They'd still want privacy.

Acolyte didn't swim well, but the stream wasn't deep.

He scooped up Hanuman and waded up to Louis, who was treading water.

Hanuman spoke briskly. "I saw a meteorite descend near the puncture. Tunesmith would spot another ship."

"He can't tell us. I turned him off. I—"

"Good. I will continue riding with Acolyte. Let me lead. I can take us to a service stack."

A service stack would take them home to the Map of Mars. Louis asked, "How far away?"

"Orbiting. Tunesmith can direct it toward us."

"Do we want the ARMs to see a service stack?"

"We'll ask Tunesmith later, when we ask if he's seen other intruders. Your opinion?"

Louis thought about it. "They'll want to rejoin their ship. We don't mind that, right? As long as they don't learn too much first."

Hanuman's voice was a whipcrack, barely audible. "Gauthier rescued their library! I want it! I want to watch them use it before we let them loose. But these ARMs are dangerous companions. No need to risk us all. Louis, what if Acolyte and I escape? We can rendezvous with a service stack. You stay and observe."

It seemed an astonishing suggestion. "Why would I?"

"Across the entire Ringworld Roxanny Gauthier is your only possible mate. You don't have a plan of your own, do you?"

Louis shrugged.

Acolyte asked, "Have you noticed that we have an audience?"

Louis looked around.

The ARMs, upstream, were waist deep and still talking, their body language gone conspiratorial. Louis had to pull his gaze away from her breasts. Wembleth was onshore, on his back on a warm flat rock, soaking up sunlight. Black birds whirled above the puffball forest, and a pair of horn-bearing quadrupeds were watching it all suspiciously.

"I don't see anything human."

Acolyte said, "Seven hominids. Three men, four women. I found them by smell. We should decide—"

Something had Wembleth's attention. Wembleth stood up. He shouted into the woods.

A man stepped forth. He walked past the horned beasts; the beasts didn't run. The man stopped a dozen yards from Wembleth. He spoke. His hands were at his sides, conspicuous. So were Wembleth's.

They were both naked. The man towered over Wembleth. He'd be taller than Acolyte, eight feet or a little less, and as slender as the trees around them. Every part of him was elongated . . . but not his head. His jaw was strong and square. The hair on his head was the same color as the forest's puffball tops.

Naked in running water, the ARMs seemed at a loss. They waded upstream toward Louis and Acolyte.

"They haven't drawn their weapons," Hanuman murmured. "Louis, will they stay calm?"

He meant the ARMs, of course. Louis said, "Don't know. Someone has to tell them about rishathra."

Wembleth and the stranger were talking freely now.

Claus came in earshot. He asked, "Any suggestions?"

"Wembleth is doing fine," Louis said. "Let him talk for us. There are more locals."

"Where?"

Acolyte said, "In the trees." He pointed. "There, all six."

"He looks like a giraffe," Claus laughed.

Roxanny said, "Or a lunie." It was a rebuff.

Luis Tamasan would never have seen a citizen of Luna. Louis said, "They'll be peaceful. Look at the jaw: he's an herbivore. Probably picks fruit from these trees. We have to decide—"

"Tanj that. Our translators have to hear them." Claus waded out. The others trailed after him. Claus picked up his skintight to wipe himself dry, then dropped it, and picked up his backpouch. If nakedness was good enough for the strangers, then Claus didn't need clothes; but the pouch held his translator, and maybe a weapon too.

Six tall, slender humanoids emerged from the tall, slender trees. *Rishathra? We still have to tell the ARMs.*

Wembleth talked rapidly, waving at Acolyte and Hanuman. The tall hominids bowed deeply, and went on talking to Wembleth. Louis and Roxanny fished out their translators and joined the group.

The ARM translators were picking up some speech. It was close to what they'd learned from Wembleth, though this local language would be a long way separated from any speech heard near the Great Ocean.

Wembleth suddenly turned to Roxanny. His speech sounded no different, but the translators all reacted. "They want to know what your kind does about—" something that didn't translate. "What shall I tell them?"

Roxanny asked, "What is it?"

Wembleth tried to explain. The activity that makes women bear children? But between different kinds it doesn't? Claus and Roxanny listened, then turned to Luis for help.

Louis said, "He's using a different word, but it means rishathra. Rishathra is sex practiced outside your species but between intelligent hominids. Not a word you'd need—"

"Smart-ass boy." Claus was not amused.

It dawned on Louis that he was afraid of Claus. "No joke, Claus. It's the first thing you need to know about a new species. Look, you can always say you're mated. Monogamous."

Claus was looking at the four women. They were as tall as the men, eight feet or just under. Not lunies, not giraffes: *Elves*. They were staring as frankly as the men; but the men were looking at Roxanny, who was blushing. Louis realized he'd blushed too.

He said, "Wembleth, tell them Acolyte is not our kind at all. He doesn't rish."

Wembleth talked. One of the women laughed. Louis's translator picked up her "Think not!"

Louis said, "But we need to decide. Claus? Roxanny?"

Claus demanded, "Luis, have *you* done this?"

"Sure!" What would *Luis* say? An adolescent wouldn't admit to being a virgin! He'd exaggerate—"With more than one species—nothing like these—but I've heard more than that. Why not?" He couldn't quite look at Roxanny, or Claus either. "It's friendly, it's safe, you can't get pregnant. Infections don't usually cross the species boundary. And who else is there for me? Human women were just rumors, as far away as the stars."

Wembleth exclaimed, "Same for me! I was a lost one too. Claus, why are you having trouble with this thought? When folk meet, they always ask this question first. Some kinds use reshtra for birth control. Water dwellers—well, to them it is a joke, unless you can hold your breath far too long. Some species can't resh, or mate with any but a life partner. Some oddly shaped ones don't expect reshtra—rishathra?—only ask for politeness. Some insist. Roxanny, can't you see the Hinsh are puzzled? It's because you haven't answered."

Louis said, "Luis" being wistful, "I'd like to meet a City Builder. They're supposed to be really good at it. They built trading empires around rishathra. They even tried to go interstellar."

Claus was grinning. "What if we say no?"

"I can do that for you," Wembleth said immediately. He began to speak Hinsh.

Claus said, "Hold up, Wembleth. I'll *do* it," his eyes flicking toward Roxanny, then away.

Wembleth asked, "In company, or only two?"

Claus was startled. "Um. Company. I wouldn't know what to say to just, just one."

Roxanny Gauthier stepped close to Wembleth. She spoke fast and low. Wembleth nodded. He changed language. Now the translators were picking up a few words of Hinsh speech.

One of the women bent far over. Her long fingers wrapped around a cantaloupe-sized yellow fruit. She bit into it, rind and all, then broke it and offered pieces to Wembleth, then Claus, then the other Hinsh. Wembleth broke his further and offered fruit to Louis and Roxanny. Louis realized that they were labeling themselves. Claus and Wembleth would rish with the women, Louis and Roxanny would not. Hanuman was getting his own fruit: he would not rish.

Do they rish with carnivores? Not by offering melon. But this ritual would eliminate Ghouls, and maybe they want that.

The fruit was red inside. It tasted a little like berries.

The others took it as a signal when the strangers ate: they feasted. There was fruit all around them. They were herbivores, all right: they needed to eat a lot. They fed Wembleth and Claus, and moved into more intimate contact.

Roxanny turned her back and walked away.

Louis picked up a melon, broke it on his knee—tanj, why not?—and followed her. He had hoped to court Roxanny's attention.

She turned and waited; looked down, grinned up at him, and said, "I told Wembleth to tell them we're courting." She took half the melon and ate.

Then she stepped into him, on tiptoe, half a head taller than he, and slid the length of her down his body until she was kneeling.

With a hoarse shout, Louis pushed her into the grass and entered her.

It was not the way he would ever have treated a woman. Roxanny was astonished. She wasn't quite ready, either, but she wrapped her arms and legs around him and made him prisoner again. Louis Wu's mind went away.

When he came to himself again, he was babbling, and he wondered if he had blurted secrets. Roxanny, still holding him prisoner in the grip of her legs, was laughing. "Boy, you are eager!"

And the Hinsh had moved to surround them.

The women knelt to rish. When they mated with their men, both knelt. The men watched the strangers with their women and made graphic half-translated commentary. They found short men funny. Wembleth, the shortest, was funniest. They learned he was ticklish.

"I'm sorry, Roxanny. I lost control of myself," Louis said. It felt like he'd mated with one of the Ringworld bloodsuckers: it was that mindless, that intense. He dared not tell her about that!

She patted his cheek. "Refreshing. Nine years to go on my implant, and it's a tanj good thing."

"I'm fertile," Louis said.

"Course you are." She stood up, her back to him, fists on hips. "I didn't buy it. Rishathra? You haven't told me every last bit of the truth, Luis. But . . . shall we join them?"

What? "We're mated! You'd shock them!"

Roxanny picked up a melon, broke it in half, and offered it to an elf.

The elf was shocked. Then he laughed, knelt, and swept her against him. Louis flushed . . . and picked up a melon.

By dusklight—too dark to tell which fruits were perfectly ripe—the Hinsh broke off eating and rishing and mating to introduce themselves: an odd reversal of order. Their names were long and formidable.

Wembleth took Louis aside and said, "The Hinsh are like others where I have traveled. If strangers plan to stay a short time, they use short names, quick to learn. This can mean, *go away soon*. But do you see all this fruit? The wind shook hundreds of manweights of fruit to the ground. Every stranger eating means less fruit left to rot. We are welcome."

Louis *felt* welcome. But rishathra was not sex. His body knew. His body wanted Roxanny.

And Claus wanted his blood.

Night on the Ringworld was rarely too dark to see. The Hinsh didn't want sleep; they conversed. The ARMs mostly listened.

Louis asked about the horned beasts. "The grass eaters? They don't bother us, we don't bother them," a man said. Of the sky he said, "The stars used to hold their course. We could use them to tell time, if we wished. Now they're loose, wandering across the sky. Only the Vashneesht know why." They spoke of the crops they'd left behind, and of the weather. Dull people, really.

They talked about the sudden wild winds.

"The climate will change," Louis told his lady companion, whose name he'd memorized as Szeblinda. His translator would fish out all eight syllables. "You may have to follow the pufftop forests as they die off to antispin. Carry melons and drop the seeds where you want more. Other folk may be running away from the disaster. You'll have to deal with them when they get here."

"Will you stay with us, to advise?"

"We have to move faster than that. We're trying to solve it *all*," Louis told her.

13

GRAY NURSE

In the morning Louis found himself on a grassy hill. He stood to look about him.

The flycycles hadn't been moved from their place on the river's shore. Acolyte slept between them. Hanuman and the Earth folk were nowhere visible. The Hinsh had departed. Downslope toward the river were melon trees and broken melon shells. A puddle of orange-and-chocolate fur beside the pool had to be Acolyte.

He walked on down.

He expected the Kzin to wake as he approached, but Acolyte didn't move. His sides moved. Good: the Kzin was breathing. Now, what mischief were the ARMs up to?

Louis took a flycycle aloft.

Claus and Roxanny were on the other side of the creek, behind a hill. They were working with the heavy oblong brick she'd stowed in Louis's baggage compartment. It unfolded into something like a holoscreen keypad: the library from their little spacecraft.

Wembleth and Hanuman were peering past them into the hologram display. Roxanny saw Louis and waved. He waved back.

That didn't look like they were keeping secrets. Louis returned to the pool.

Acolyte was sitting up, stretching. He looked around him. "Where is everyone?"

"Across the river. Are you all right?"

"Well fed and well slept out. I found a small deer or something. Louis, nobody told me not to gorge. We should have arranged to stand watch."

Louis stretched. "I wondered if they'd stunned you. Hey, I slept as well as you did. The ARMs are doing something tricky, I think, but Hanuman's watching them. Shall we see?"

They took a flycycle across.

Claus awaited their descent. He said, "Luis, Acolyte, I want to interview both of you as to what you saw at the puncture. Any objection?"

Louis thought of objections, but none that Luis could back up. "Show us how it works," he said.

"Just the Kzin first," Claus said.

"We'll help each other," Louis said, and Acolyte rumbled agreement. Then Wembleth too wanted to participate. That allowed the three to play off each other in an interview that became an animated conversation.

Louis gambled that the ARMs didn't have equipment to detect lies in the tremor of a voice. *Gray Nurse* or another in the ARM fleet might.

As to what "Luis" had seen, Louis stuck close to the truth. They had been indoors: they'd missed the explosion (and Luis knew nothing of industrial antimatter). As he and Acolyte arrived from . . . somewhere . . . a great light had appeared, not much brighter than the sun, but huge. Then a glare-yellow doughnut the size of a mountain range lay blocking the region they had come to see.

He was asked about his background. He invented, but kept it terse. A twenty-year-old wouldn't have centuries of memories; he wouldn't tell stories well, and he'd be a bit shy around elders. Acolyte, who really was only twelve, was able to stick to his own memories, because Chiron (Luis said) had never confronted the half-grown Kzin. Luis speculated aloud whether the puppeteer was afraid.

And the library fascinated all three interviewees.

Protector—1 Adult stage of the Pak species, where the line runs from child to breeder to adult. **2** Hominids in general are descended from Pak. They too have a breeder stage, at which they usually spend their lives, and an adult stage rarely achieved. **3** Archaic—

If Claus or Roxanny looked up a reference, Wembleth, Luis, and Acolyte crowded in to look. So did Hanuman, though he was generally ignored. Roxanny didn't like to be near him; he favored Claus, and Claus treated him as a pet.

There were hot buttons everywhere in the text.

Pierson's puppeteers—A species of great industrial power and sophistication, once common through *known space* and beyond, now thought to be fleeing the galactic *core explosion*. See *General Products company*. Physiology . . .

Core explosion—Thought to be a rash of supernovae . . . due to reach Earth in twenty thousand years. Inadequately studied.

General Products—A company once owned and run by Pierson's puppeteers. In human space they sold almost nothing but spacecraft hulls.

Known space—Those regions of the galaxy's Major Arm thought to be explored and understood by known sapient species.

Ringworld life forms are little understood. Ecologies tend to familiar patterns, but no trained biologist has had opportunity to investigate.

Mammals—

Hominids—Related to the genus Hominidae on Earth. Probably all such species derive from Pak breeders imported from the galactic core, subsequently evolved in many directions.

Louis Wu—{rotating hologram}

"Now give us some privacy," Roxanny said without looking up.

Louis and Acolyte backed away. Hanuman climbed into Claus's lap. Claus scratched the anthropoid's head, and didn't seem to notice its high cranial capacity or the ridge on top. The interview had lasted nearly two hours.

Louis and Acolyte settled beside the flycycle. Louis deployed the kitchen. Acolyte said, "Hanuman wants the library."

"Tunesmith will too." Louis passed the Kzin a squeeze of broth.

"One flycycle would hold all three of us if Hanuman rides my lap or yours," Acolyte said. "Hanuman learns fast. He might already know all he needs to run the library. Then we go, unless you truly want the ARM woman as mate."

"Good plan. We go when Hanuman's ready," Louis said. He sucked at a squeeze of green tea. He was not nearly so sure as he sounded.

The library codes might not be easy to crack.

The ARM might not let them go easily.

Anything could happen. The ARMs were in a shouting match, though Louis and Acolyte were too far away to make it out. Then Claus was back at work with the library, Wembleth and Hanuman were peering over his shoulder, and Roxanny strode briskly toward the flycycles. "Luis!" she said with a whip in her voice.

Louis offered her a squeezebulb. Roxanny looked startled. "Oh! Thank you. We've been in touch with *Gray Nurse*."

"And?"

She glanced at Acolyte. "Let's go somewhere," she said.

She led them across the river on stepping stones, then behind some low bushes. Sitting, they were hidden. Louis kissed her. She accepted the kiss without response, then asked, "Do you still want rescue? Do you want to visit Earth?"

"Last time I didn't have a choice."

Shrug. "You'd be very valuable. I could try to get you citizenship—"

"Roxanny, my father was an illegal birth." He wanted that established, *Luis Tamasan isn't registered*, before she tried to look up an imaginary man. "Citizenship in what? What does it mean?"

He listened carefully to her answers. There would be changes in civilization since his departure. It sounded like there were more laws, more restrictions. Maybe only in Sol system.

Luis wouldn't know—"Birthright? Roxanny, what is a birthright?"

"I'll find it for you in the library. Basically, you're born with one or two birthrights depending on—tanj—mostly on your genetic pattern. If you're healthy, you probably have two birthrights. You can lose it, or get more. Two birthrights make a child."

Louis Wu had used up his birthrights. Faking his ID would involve faking *that*, and the penalties were draconian. He said, "It doesn't sound like I want to settle on Earth."

"No, given a bastard father. It's the most interesting world, though."

It was just possible, he thought, that Luis Tamasan could become a whole new person. If he settled We Made It or Home, why would anyone ever try to connect his gene pattern to a Louis Wu? He could pay taxes. Learn a new profession. Marry— "What are our odds of getting to space?"

"We know where a puncture is, if the whoever—the wizard—hasn't closed it."

"The Phantom Weaver."

She shrugged. "Whatever you like. *Gray Nurse* can fire projectiles at a puncture from underneath. That'll tell us if it's been closed. Beyond that, who knows? Will Acolyte go along with this?"

"I suppose."

"Would he come?"

"You can't get *him* citizenship. He's a Kzin. You're fighting Kzinti, aren't you?"

"There hasn't been a formal war in, oh, four hundred years." She tapped her sleeve and read what appeared. "In sixteen hundred falans. He'd be all right. There are hundreds of thousands of Kzinti citizens in human space."

"I wouldn't tell him to come. He's younger than me, you know."

"Let's get back."

Louis didn't move. "What about Wembleth? Do we want him?"

"Yah. He's a real native, after all. He must know wonderful things, and there are people who would kill to read his genetic pattern." Roxanny stood and semaphored her arms at Claus. "Let's get back."

A shadow square had blocked all but a sliver of sun. Acolyte was squatting before the library, Claus standing behind him. Nearby, Hanuman picked imaginary parasites, looking solemn. The little protector looked up at Louis and made an urgent twirling motion.

Claus raised his hand, holding something L-shaped.

Close behind him Roxanny snapped, "Luis, don't!" Hanuman *eeked* at the sound. She had one too: a slender flat object like the butt of a handgun, clearly a weapon. Old yogatsu training told Louis she was outside his extreme reach.

Behind Roxanny, sunrise glowed on the edge of a ridge.

The light should have grabbed his attention. But Louis was facing Roxanny and Claus and two guns. His mind caught up too slowly. Hidden or not, the sun is always at noon. That *couldn't* be the sun.

The ground trembled.

Acolyte hadn't moved; he must have been warned not to.

"I think we'll do better alone," Claus told them, smiling, victorious. "We only need one flycycle, but we need you to tell us how to fly it. You both know how. We only need one of you."

Louis turned away from the fireball rising above the ridge.

The flare must have half-blinded Claus. The ground lurched, Louis lurched, Claus lurched, and Hanuman jumped into Claus's arms. Claus tried to move him aside. Acolyte turned as he rose. His claw swept across Claus and hooked him under the throat.

Louis whipped around and ran two steps. His fist took Roxanny under the jaw. He gave it plenty of follow through. She went down, rolling, and Louis leapt after her, afraid he'd hit her too hard, but he had to have that gun. In his peripheral vision, Acolyte hurled Claus into the ground in a spray of blood.

Louis's foot landed on her gun hand, and he had the gun. "Don't," he said.

She did. Her foot lashed out and caught him in the gut. Louis moved his hand: the gun missed her when it went off. Dust blasted out of the turf. A sonic weapon. He was still on his feet, trying to back away. Her other foot hooked his knee. He disengaged. She was up. The heel of her hand caught his cheek, and he was sprawling, still trying to avoid firing. Then she had his gun hand, and twisted, and had his gun. She aimed at a rising flycycle. He kicked her off balance. She fired as she fell.

He was on the ground, screaming. It felt like all the bones of his left hip and leg had shattered. Roxanny fired into the sky, lowered her arm and cursed.

When his eyes could focus, she was pointing the gun straight at him from four feet away.

The fireball was dying above the ridge. A spacecraft came out of the glare and began to settle.

One flycycle was still on the ground. The other wasn't in sight. Hanuman and Acolyte and Wembleth weren't either. Claus lay on his back, his head torn nearly off, his entrails displayed.

Roxanny had him under the gun. "Why don't I just shoot you?" she asked.

"Roxanny, don't," said Louis Wu, master of sarcasm. He dared not move and he couldn't think. Just as well. A twenty-year-old would break under the fury in her eyes. "Don't shoot me," Luis said. "I'll fly you anywhere you like. Only I can't move."

Wembleth appeared from behind a tree, saw the gun in Roxanny's hand, and ducked back.

"I don't need your flycycle," Roxanny said. "We've got a ship. Wembleth! Get aboard and take a seat. Luis, can you stand up?"

"Futz, no!" Louis said.

She stooped above him and picked him up in her arms. His leg and hip sagged as if boneless. She nearly dropped him when he screamed. The pain blasted his mind away and he missed the rest.

Louis was on his back. Some kind of talk show was running on the ceiling, but the voices didn't match. Aha: the sound was turned off. The voices had been speaking for some time, against a noisy background Louis took for a ship of war.

"I had brothers once." Wembleth sounded drugged. Wembleth's translator device sounded crisp and alert. "Stayed with their home turf when Father and I moved to . . ."

". . . Move often?" A male voice of command, one Louis had never heard.

Wembleth: "Yes."

Roxanny had shot him.

Louis couldn't believe it. How badly was he hurt? His mind was muzzy; he'd have trouble keeping a story

straight. If they questioned Luis Tamasan, they'd hear far
too much. Louis tried to move.

He couldn't feel much. There was a tickle behind the
back of his neck. His eyes could move, and his head, a
little. He could just see that he was naked, on his back,
immobilized in something like a stretch rack . . . or the
Intensive Care Cavity of a military autodoc. The noisy
background suggested a ship of war. He listened to the
voices, trying to make them out.

Male officer: ". . . brothers?"

"Chosen brothers. Grew up faster than me . . . stayed
with their own, to find mates."

"Seen many kinds of human . . . ?"

Wembleth: "Twenty, thirty species . . . reshed with . . ."

He thought he could guess what had happened up there.

A ship beneath the Ringworld floor had fired antimatter bullets upward. No need to find an eyestorm already
in place. One bullet to tear away the foamed scrith meteor insulation. The next to blast a hole through the scrith
floor and the landscape above, big enough for a small
troop transport to pass through.

It was crazy, vicious, simple, and direct. He should have
seen it coming instead of making elaborate long-range
travel plans.

Wembleth: "Can't get anywhere if you don't know . . .
reshtra . . . don't try to guess—"

Roxanny's voice. "War? Do you ever fight—"

"Seen carnivores fight plant eaters . . . eaten me too.
That what you mean?"

"Ook."

Mmm? Turning his head wasn't easy: Louis was restrained in a nest of attachments, and he'd lost all sensation below his neck. But there was Hanuman, in a cage
big enough to hold a Kzin. They locked eyes in mutual
sympathy. Then something blocked Louis's view.

Roxanny Gauthier hung back behind a burly man,
maybe a Jinxian, both wearing falling jumpers with ARM

insignia. The man loomed over Louis, judging. He said, "You'd be Luis Tamasan."

"Yah," said Louis Wu.

"You attacked one of my people."

I lived to regret it. "Sorry."

"I'm 'Tec-Major Schmidt. You're a civilian prisoner. That gives you certain rights, but you're in futzy poor shape to exercise them. These stunners only stun if you're far enough away, but you were right up against 'Tec-First Gauthier. You've got bones broken into shrapnel from your hip to your knee. The 'doc can heal you if you don't move for a while. Five days."

"Tanj." Better make nice— "Thank you, sir. I suppose I'd be crippled for life without your help."

The officer grinned. "*Oh* yah. Now, can I free your arms? It would mean you can eat. Otherwise you're on tubes."

"I won't try to pull loose," Louis said.

"You could hurt yourself pretty bad if you did. Stet." The tickle behind his neck moved down his spine—his arms came back to life, the left very tender, bruised from elbow to fingertips—and further, until—"Hiii!"—and back up an inch. Louis could still feel bruises along his ribs, but not that awful shattered shriek of agony that started with his left hip.

Schmidt's hands manipulated a video remote in Louis's peripheral vision. The talk show disappeared; Ringworld jumped into being, spilling off the ceiling, and down the rectangular walls. Schmidt asked, "Where do you come from?"

"Rotate it. More. Stet. Sir, that's the Great Ocean. Look along the spinward edge. . . ." Louis began describing the Weaver village he'd lived in last year. People, houses, the river, visiting Fishers, the webeye camera the Hindmost ("Chiron") had sprayed across the stone face of a gorge. These ARMs had no way of checking. If they could,

Weavers would tell stories of Louis Wu and the Hindmost as Vashneesht having some kind of quarrel.

But his mind was turning foggy. Louis hadn't been drunk in a long time, but it was like this.

Schmidt zoomed on the Great Ocean region. "You live there? And your parents? Who else? A Kzin family? This puppeteer you told us about?"

"No, not Chiron. Finagle knows where Chiron lives," with a laugh he wished he could suppress. His tongue was curling out of control. "Kzinti don't live in the village, they're from somewhere on the Great Ocean." If they pushed him, he'd reveal another partial truth: that Chmeee lived among Kzinti who had taken over the Map of Earth, natives and all.

'Tec-Major Schmidt said, "A lot of Kzintosh call themselves Chmeee. He was some kind of legendary hero. What do you mean, Map of Earth?"

Louis realized he'd been babbling, thinking out loud.

Schmidt repeated, "Map of Earth?" with steel in his voice.

"Sir. There." Louis pointed into the ceiling, into the Great Ocean, where the continents of Earth were arrayed around its north pole, a hundred thousand miles spinward of the Map of Mars. He knew now that he couldn't keep secrets. Maybe they'd drugged him, maybe it was just painkillers. He'd last as long as he could, and then tell them his name and watch Roxanny explode in his face.

Roxanny said, "Futz. They keep human slaves?"

Luis: "Homo habilis. Pak breeders."

Schmidt: "Unchanged? Like the skeletons in the Olduvai Gorge?"

Luis: "I never saw one. Like to see their noses."

"Maybe they're a little skewed?" Schmidt said, clearly speaking for a recorder. "From what we already know, a trillion Pak breeders had a quarter million years to evolve without protectors to cull the mutants. The Kzinti would have done some selective breeding. Anyway, these animals wouldn't have evolved into actual human beings, right, Luis?"

Louis's words came slowly. "They could have evolved intelligence. We did. Did you want to invade?" He laughed. "Rescue? These archaic Kzinti built the bigges' sea ship in history, and that was a thousand years ago. They're not using jus' spears and clubs."

"We can beat seagoing ships. Now, what kind of tech has the puppeteer got? Anything weird?"

Whump.

Louis said, as Luis, "How do I know what's weird?"

But he heard himself continue, "Cameras like copper spiderwebs? Out of a spray gun?" his voice lost in a recorded bellow. The ceiling was flashing an unfamiliar distress symbol. *Hull breach*in*aft portside consumables tank. Power*lost in*sections two*and*three.* Schmidt and Roxanny drew weapons and turned away, stooping to get through a small oval doorway. Louis spoke to nobody: "He's got stepping disks too. What was that sound?"

Gray Nurse shook herself. Gravity went away.

Hanuman said, "Invaders. We'll either be rescued or killed. Expect surprises. No protector would leave us in alien hands."

"Why not?" Louis heard the whine in his voice. "Why the futz can't they jus' leave us alone?"

He didn't hear Hanuman's answer. It had become too noisy. A spacecraft being boarded made a fearful echo chamber.

Roxanny Gauthier ducked back through the oval door and around out of Louis's sight. A moment later Wembleth drifted loose, too drugged to act. Roxanny touched points on Hanuman's cage, and it opened.

She was talking in a hysterical whisper. "I don't know what they are. Not Kzinti. Nightmares." She looked at Louis, immobile in his medical cage, and said, "Sorry."

"Wha's happening?" Louis asked. She touched his lips

with a forefinger. She braced herself behind Louis's medical cage. Only her projectile weapon showed, aimed at
the doorway.

A voice spoke from somewhere, 'Tec Schmidt's voice
sounding much too calm. "All hands, we're fighting from
the radiation refuge. I can see invaders on the hull and in
four, five, six, and ten. Our motors are burned out, but
we're under acceleration anyway. We don't know where
it's coming from. We're also facing friendly fire, ARM
missiles incoming, sixty and counting, no alien attackers
yet. 'Tec-Admiral Wrayne doesn't want us captured, I
guess."

"Why didn't we see it coming?" she whispered. "They've
got an invisible ship! Shh."

Schmidt's voice—"The missiles are veering away!"—
died in a roar of static.

A shadow blinked past the little door. Roxanny fired,
and cursed. What came through then looked like a small
man filmed fast-forward. It was behind Roxanny before
she could turn, and Louis couldn't see the rest.

Three bulkier man-shapes zipped through the door,
moving more slowly. They sealed it behind them. They
were wearing skintight pressure suits. They deployed a
balloon with inflatable tubes around it: a big nonstandard
rescue pod. They didn't wait for it to inflate.

Spill mountain people come in a variety of species, but
they all look more or less alike: burly bodies and short
thick arms and legs, large lung capacity, thick fur for insulation, hairless faces. These three had been spill mountain people. Now they weren't. They wore pressure suits
and big globular helmets, but their faces gave them away:
mouths hard and toothless, like flattened beaks; big Roman
noses; hairless skin wrinkled into leather armor. A mum-
mified look, and an uncanny grace. They'd eaten tree-
of-life. They were protectors.

The fourth came around into view towing an uncon-
scious Roxanny. It was a protector, but not of the spill

mountain people. Smaller, more slender. A dead-looking face with no more nose than an ape. Louis didn't recognize the species, but it wasn't a Hanging Person. Louis had thought Tunesmith was involved in this. He was less sure now.

They pushed Wembleth into the rescue pod, then Roxanny. Hanuman crawled in without a struggle. Then the protectors turned to Louis.

"I'm injured," he said. No reaction.

They studied the machinery around him, talking tersely in a language Louis's translator didn't have. Then they switched things off. When one reached behind Louis's back, pain came as if he'd been hit by a truck.

He fought to keep from fainting, holding his attention on his breathing. Later he remembered a good deal. The feel of their hands, large, with blunt fingers and knobby knuckles. Brown eyes with epicanthic folds. The slender odd-man-out protector gave orders in monosyllables. The others detached Louis from the ICC, pushed him into the rescue pod, and sealed it. A framework still held his leg and hip immobile. Two studied the machinery that had held him while another cut a wide hole in the hull.

Air puffed the rescue pod into space.

14

THE SPILL MOUNTAIN PEOPLE

Gray Nurse was an ARM warcraft, built more like a spear than a ship, with a few smaller ships along its length. An intruder had attached itself like a remora near the fore end. It was lighter than *Gray Nurse*, built like the skeleton of a sunfish: a cabin, then an extensive grid of cross-hatching girders like those found on a Belt mining ship meant to carry rocks and ore. Louis couldn't immediately see anything like a motor.

The protectors followed the rescue bubble into space. Others, all spill mountain protectors, emerged from further aft in *Gray Nurse*. Some towed the rescue bubble to the sunfish ship and moored it to the grid. Then they spurted away on rocket plumes, leaving their prisoners exposed to open space.

Maybe it was the drugs, maybe it was his body's defenses: the pain had gone out like a tide. Louis looked around him at the universe.

A dusting of light motes, motionless a moment ago, were swept away in an eyeblink. Spy probes dismissed as by a sweep of God's hand, but how?

Roxanny was stirring, trying to wake up. Hanuman was just watching. Wembleth was very jittery. He spoke; saw that he was not understood; switched languages. His translator said, "I don't understand."

Louis said, "Talk to me, Wembleth."

"Where am I, Looeess?"

"Under the Ringworld."

Wembleth looked up at the black wall that blocked half the sky. "We are falling."

"There's nothing to hit. You get used to this—"

The protectors were back. Two were pushing a fair-sized mass: the medical cage. They moored it to the cargo grid next to the rescue bubble. There was other cargo to be attached. Then they swarmed away to the cabin, leaving one still on the grid.

Gray Nurse was whipped away.

Louis felt no acceleration beyond a kind of flutter, but he felt his hair writhe about him. They must be doing hundreds of gravities. *Gray Nurse* was just *gone*. He'd seen nothing like a rocket motor, nor even a thruster.

Wembleth had his arms over his face.

The sunfish ship followed the thread of a spillpipe beneath the Ringworld's black underside. A slow hour later, by the watch face in the back of Louis's hand, the spillpipe led them around the rim and up into a glare of sunlight.

Louis looked down along the inside of the rim wall, a thousand miles down toward a few tiny cones along its base. Beyond was a wide shore—twenty to thirty thousand miles of shore, it must be, given how high they were—and then an infinity of blue water seen from high enough to show the texture of sea bottom, and a few sparse clusters of big flat islands.

The clustered islands were peculiar. They all looked alike, and there was something else too. Louis had never seen anything like it, and that alone meant that he was looking at the Other Ocean.

They were dropping toward the rim wall. They'd been in flight for less than an hour.

"Wembleth?"

"Roxanny! Can you talk?"

She blinked. "Luis? They took you too. Where are we? Who are these—?"

"Spill mountain people," Louis said. "There are lots of species. Do you ARMs know about—?"

"Down there below us, *those* are spill mountains," she said. "They're bigger than they look. Do you know what they are?"

"They're just the mountains," Louis said, secretly amused.

The spill mountains had grown larger. Each of the little cones had a few silver threads of river running from its base.

"Pipes run under the Ringworld floor. They pump sea-bottom slush up over the rim. Otherwise all the fertile soil would wind up in the sea bottoms and nothing would grow."

They were dropping toward one of the peaks. Roxanny said, "Those mountains are waste heaps leaning against the rim wall, forty to fifty klicks high. People live on them. We've seen balloons going between the peaks. But, Luis, I think the ones who attacked us were protectors. Do you know about protectors?"

"Same thing as Vashneesht? Magicians. Very smart, very fierce, and they're born in armor. We wondered if they were myths. There are some artifacts."

"Oh, they're real. One of those looked different from the rest," Roxanny said. "A primitive protector got as far as Sol system, seven hundred years ago, all the way from the galactic core. Its face looked like that one's."

"The joker. That's the one in charge," Louis said.

"How do you know that?"

Bram and Anne, both Vampire protectors, had found it easy to enslave spill mountain protectors. Spill mountain people couldn't live on the flats. In every case their entire species was isolated on some single mountain, held hostage with nowhere to flee. A spill mountain protector was born trapped.

Luis wouldn't know that, so Louis said, "I heard him giving orders."

They were crawling down the sky toward one of the spill mountains. Louis could hear a thin whining and feel a tremor in the rescue bubble. The sunfish ship had no kind of streamlining. They sank past an icy peak. Green showed much lower down. The sunfish ship moved close and slid sideways along a staircase of ledges, and now Louis could see trees and tiered fields and glimpse snow heaped in regular cones. Miles below was a breathtaking view of an endlessly rolling land, intricately detailed in tiny seas, rivers, ridges of hills.

There was a thump. Louis drifted against the bubble wall. Then the gravity generator went off and he slumped against the curve of wall in full gravity. Pain lashed up his leg and hip.

He didn't quite pass out. Roxanny whispered to him, "Things happen in war, Luis. Don't hold it against me," while the protectors moved around on the ice and rock, detaching treasure from *Gray Nurse* and carrying it away. Several were working on *Gray Nurse*'s 'doc.

The joker protector opened the rescue balloon. Warm air puffed out; thin cold air blew in. The joker stepped in, sniffed, looked at each of the occupants in turn. Roxanny was wary; Wembleth cringed in terror. Hanuman's eyes met the other protector's. They didn't try to speak, but they knew each other for what they were.

The joker touched Louis's leg and its brace, using great care.

Wembleth bolted for the opening. The joker swiped at him and missed . . . or else changed his mind. Wembleth bolted along the ledge, past conical houses, and was out of sight.

Wembleth was suffocating again. There wasn't enough air. The folk around him didn't seem to be having trouble. A few children watched him curiously.

He'd snatched up the translator device Roxanny had given him. Learning their language would be easier now . . . but it would still take hours. Strangers were always well treated, but the Vashneesht was a stranger too. Wembleth knew he'd have to hide *now*, and without help.

The houses were tall heaps of snow with a single small hole for a door. He'd be found quick in one of those, and only one way out. He considered hiding in a snowdrift, but only for an instant. He'd freeze. He wasn't wearing enough clothing. And he was leaving footprints!

A ridge of naked rock gave him the chance to backtrack. He followed it to where he could jump across snow onto the angled trunk of a huge elbow tree. His knees betrayed him as he jumped; he landed on the slope, slid, caught himself, and clawed his way up sixty feet of naked trunk. The top was a dense green tuft. Wembleth burrowed into it.

He could see out, a little.

* * *

Four spill mountain protectors, naked in the cold and their own thick white fur, wedged *Gray Nurse*'s 'doc through the opening into the rescue bubble.

Louis moaned when they moved him. The protectors were fiercely strong and surprisingly gentle, but it hurt. They lowered him into the Intensive Care Cavity and one reached around behind him. All sensation went away below the small of his back.

Though the military 'doc was severed from *Gray Nurse*, somehow they'd got it running.

The joker turned when Roxanny spoke. "You are in violation of several dozen laws enforced by the ARM and related governments."

The joker answered in unknown speech.

Roxanny's translator would pick up the language. Good, and Louis's would catch it too. Immobilized as he was, there was no more he could accomplish here. Louis went to sleep.

Through the greenery Wembleth watched the protector leave the rescue bubble. Roxanny followed. A dozen children followed her. The protector tracked his footprints for a time, then jumped across to the ridge of rock, examined it with her nose to the ground, then came straight toward him. She ran lightly up the trunk. She reached into the tuft and pulled Wembleth out into empty air.

She let him dangle from one hand as she climbed down. He was frozen with fear and cold.

A dozen children crowded the rescue bubble, and more swarmed outside. Hanuman was clowning for them. They shied back when Louis stirred and woke.

He smiled at a wall of white fur and two dozen eyes. "Hello," he said. A few voices answered. His translator did not.

Most of the pain above his waist—left arm, ribs—had eased off. He wondered how long he was going to be like this. If Roxanny and the joker had taught each other their speech, then the joker hadn't been speaking local dialect, and that meant Louis couldn't even talk to these kids.

But Roxanny and the joker were coming back, and Roxanny was holding Wembleth's hand.

They couldn't get through the crowd to reach the rescue bubble. They didn't try. The joker began to lecture, pointing occasionally at the humans and Wembleth. The kids inside couldn't hear, so they went out. Presently the joker sent Wembleth and Roxanny in, and gestured four remaining kids out, and closed the bubble.

Roxanny glared after the joker, who was hopping away on the struts of the cargo grid. "She won't talk," Roxanny said bitterly.

"Translator won't work?"

"The translator's fine, but it doesn't have anything to say."

Louis asked, "Are you keeping ARM secrets?"

"So's she! Yes, *she*, she told me that much. She said her name was Proserpina."

Wembleth's teeth chattered as he spoke. His translator said, "We're going for another ride."

Louis asked, "Are you up for that?"

The man shivered violently. "I pissed my clothing last time. Thank you for not noticing."

Louis sniffed. The air in the bubble had never ceased to smell clean and fresh. "Protectors build good machines," he said. "We'll be fine." He saw the joker enter the ship's cabin.

Gravity went away. "We'll be fine," he repeated.

The sunfish ship floated away from the cliff, then straight up. Blue sky darkened to black.

Louis said, "I've figured out this ship. Gravity control—"

"Magnetic," Roxanny said crisply. "They must use the grid. Luis, there's a superconductor grid in the Ringworld floor. If this ship is using a magnetic drive, then it can thrust against the Ringworld. It's like leaving your motor at home. I felt my hair stand up. Didn't you?"

"Stet, but I meant the cabin gravity. Powerful, but it flutters. Why wouldn't Vashneesht fix that? I think they're too arrogant to test what they build. They do it all in one shot."

"Got it all figured out, do you, kid?"

Louis flushed. He said, "Stet, it's magnetic. You'd have near infinite range and huge acceleration as long as you stay near the superconductor net. You could use it as a weapon too. Push away missiles and ships. It could even be seen as a message."

"Message?"

" 'I can't invade you. I'm purely defensive.' Like a fort."

"Mmm. Or just 'Keep out.' "

"We're falling again!" Wembleth burst out. "Roxanny, where are we going?"

Roxanny shook her head.

They crossed a wonderfully fractal shoreline, all curlicues of bay and beach, and were over the ocean. Ocean and sprinklings of islands. If you thought of them as islands, you didn't see that much speed, but they'd be one-to-one maps of a world.

Near the shore of the Other Ocean the clusters were a bit foreshortened. Otherwise they were all maps of the same world. One sprawling continent with a spine of mountain; four smaller bodies and an archipelago of scattered tiny islands, all to antispin of the mainland; all showed a grainy texture. If you had to tell someone where you were—say, Tunesmith, if you could get hold of any kind of communicator—how would you?

But the shadows were different. Bands and flecks and patches of shadow on only a few of the islands.

Roxanny said, "This is Ocean Two! Do you suppose we're going to one of the maps?"

"Sure. What do you make of the shadows, Roxanny?"

"We're too high to tell."

Louis didn't answer. What should "Luis Tamasan" know about this? But shadows just didn't happen in a place where it was always noon, and Louis Wu found it freaky.

Roxanny said, "Luis, Wembleth, there's two oceans on the Ringworld, you know? There are all those *billions* of little shallow seas with corrugated shorelines to give the locals lots of convenient bays and harbors, and all the trillions of klicks of twisty rivers. But then there are two big counterbalanced oceans, the one with all the inhabited worlds in known space on it—that's yours, Luis—and this, this endlessly repeated map. It's probably one-to-one scale of *something*, but it's no world known to the ARM."

Louis started to laugh.

Roxanny glared at him. She said, "There are thirty-two of these maps, all of the same world! So after we land, we *still* won't know where we are. Is that what has you amused?"

"Yah. Does the ARM have any idea what the Pak home-world looked like?"

"A permanent war zone. Every Pak protector wants his gene line to rule the world. I'm just repeating the brief-ings," Roxanny said, "and we got all that from a stray Pak protector via Jack Brennan, and *he* was a Belter turned protector who couldn't be trusted worth tanj. So, no, we don't know the shapes of the Pak continents. Maybe they change. These creatures are *powerful*.

"The joker—she looks like Pak breeder skeletons we're still finding in Asia and Africa. So where's the joker from? The Pak homeworld? But maybe it's the Map of Earth. Luis, you said the Map of Earth was originally Pak breeders."

The sunfish ship was descending toward an island clus-ter near the Other Ocean's antispinward shore . . . fifty thousand miles near, maybe. Any distortion was lost in detail as the land rose up to meet them. There were cres-cents and pools of shadow on the land . . . but how could they be shadows, with the sun just overhead? They looked almost like pictograms, or writing. A lone mountain near the continent's midpoint glittered. Dwellings? With windows?

The grainy look of the land became interlocking dots of all sizes, circular features, as if the land had been battered by meteors. They skimmed a forest, slowing now. Louis recognized chains of elbow trees and other familiar vegetation.

He said, "Most of what's on the Ringworld must have evolved as Pak plants and animals."

"Good, Luis." A verbal pat on the head.

Something about these patterns—

"It's a garden," Roxanny said.

"Roxanny? This *big*?" They were still miles high.

Still, she was right. The landscape wasn't croplands, but it was just as certainly *shaped*. Variety and color: rainbow ripples that must be thousands of square miles of flower beds; varied stands of trees in all the colors of autumn and more, still seeming no larger than hairs in a dandy's beard. A veldt shadowed with black arcs. Ponds, lakes, seas like silver plates with little central dots of island.

Roxanny said, "Formal gardens are all rectangles, unless they're supposed to look like wilderness. What kind of garden is all circles, and no two the same size? This is like . . . right."

Like the Moon, Louis thought. "Like a war?" All circles, all craters. The Pak homeworld.

"Vashneesht," Wembleth said positively.

"Yah, the joker is trying to impress us," Roxanny said. Louis laughed.

He glimpsed rectilinear outlines peeping through the wild colors. They dropped. There was a thump. Gravity ceased its flutter.

15

PROSERPINA

She brought the mag ship down in the garden, six miles downhill from the Penultimate's mainland habitat. As soon as she'd safed the motors, Proserpina rolled out of the cabin and ran aft. A sense of order might help the aliens adjust, but she'd learn less if she gave them too much time.

Isolated, shorn of her senses, imprisoned in the Isolation Zone for all of these millions of falans—Proserpina had still been able to infer general details of Ringworld history: infighting, dominance games, reshaping of world-sized stretches of topography, shifting alliances, changing genetic patterns . . .

There was only one Repair Center, set halfway around the Ringworld from this, the Isolation Zone. The Repair Center could be seen as the Ringworld's natural throne room. A Ghoul was in power now, and that was good. He was short of experience, and reckless (not good), and probably male. Males wandered further. Where tree-of-life was scarce, a male would find it first.

Control was what this was all about. In earlier ages she had seen conspiracy after conspiracy, and had always found a way to stay neutral without being destroyed. There was always a master of creation, and—after one awful early experiment—it was never Proserpina.

She hop-stepped over the struts of the cargo grid and slid into the rescue bubble.

The woman spoke. "We need to talk."

Proserpina perceived 'Tec-First Gauthier's impatience and was amused. The woman was young, though not young for a breeder. Her stance suggested a different gravity; her speech was a bit altered from what Proserpina had heard while eavesdropping on the Ghoul's retinue. Gauthier was one of the invaders. She'd have much to tell, once she stopped refusing to tell it.

Proserpina's silence made the woman uneasy. "We need to talk to make the translators work," she added.

Proserpina didn't smile. She couldn't. They'd talked while they hunted Wembleth in the spill mountain village, but they'd said nothing. Nouns, verbs: not enough to cue 'Tec Gauthier's speaking device. Gauthier was keeping secrets.

So was Proserpina. When she needed to talk, she would.

The brachiator watched her and did nothing. She'd been expecting subservience. The little protector must serve another, perhaps the Ghoul.

One of the males made a soft-voiced request. Proserpina didn't know his speech. She'd work it out presently. He stood like a local, a little stooped, but at home with Ringworld spin gravity. He wouldn't have much to tell. What he wanted was clear: he was hungry.

The other male was injured and immobilized, naked and helpless. He watched. Proserpina was struck by his patience. Though no protector, he was an elder, of the same species as the woman. This would be the Ghoul's breeder servant, Louis Wu of the Ball Worlds.

"You're all hungry," Proserpina said in Interworld. The men were unsurprised, but Gauthier jumped. "You can all tolerate fruit. We'll work out details of your diet presently. We're all omnivores, I think, except you," looking at the little one. "How are you called?"

The woman recovered her aplomb. She gestured: "Luis Tamasan. Wembleth. Roxanny Gauthier. Proserpina? How did you learn our language?"

"I've hacked into a library," Proserpina said. She saw the woman bristle: Gray Nurse's *computer! Stolen!* "I chose my name from your literature," speaking now to Luis/Louis. Wu and the little protector were keeping secrets too.

She clapped her hands. "Let's feed you. There's fruit outside, and a stream."

"I'll have to feed Luis," Roxanny said.

"You must learn what's edible. Come. Luis, we'll be back soon. Your device is giving you nutrient, but it's best if your digestive systems are exercised."

"Thank you," he said.

Roxanny looked dubious, but she went.

Roxanny followed the protector. Wembleth followed Roxanny, holding Hanuman's hand. The ape scrambled along faster than his little legs were up to.

From the back the joker looked like a small, scrawny, bald woman. She stood a meter and a half tall. All of her joints were swollen; her back was a column of pebbles. Roxanny knew that she should be afraid of the creature, but she couldn't *feel* intimidated.

Proserpina was talking to Wembleth in Interspeak. Wembleth chattered in his own language, and Roxanny listened to his translator with half her attention.

"Mother abandoned us. I never asked Father about it; he was touchy there, but I listened. They both used to go exploring. One day she was just gone. Some species do that, turn vicious and solitary, like the Swamp Folk. Friendly and curious when they're young, *great* rishathra, then something triggers, and they bulk up and change attitude and go off into the swamp. I was afraid I'd do the same. Interbreeding is rare, and you don't know what you'll get."

"Have you rished with Swamp People?"

"With a Swamp Girl until she mated, and afterward we were friends. Then she got pregnant, and she went off alone to raise the children."

There were low buildings in the forest. Trees masked them. Trees grew from the roofs, or up the side of a minaret. A huge tree grew through the hollow core of a ring two stories high.

Shadows ticked at the corners of her vision. Tree shadows wouldn't move in this weird place where it was always noon or night. Roxanny became sure that there were animals in the forest, watching them.

Proserpina was fast, darting among the trees, plucking and gathering plants in varied colors and shapes. "Try this," she said to Luis's long-armed pet, setting a purple blob in his hands. It resembled an eggplant, but it sprayed red juice when Hanuman bit into it. Hanuman buried his face in it.

"Here. Here." Proserpina distributed other fruits, and watched for reactions. Roxanny's yellow globe was bitter. She dropped it. A handful of green cherries was edible, but sour around the seeds. Wembleth liked the inner rim of a mottled yellow ring—he had to fit his head inside it—and Hanuman's purple blob.

"Roxanny, is this place very different from your Ball Worlds?"

"Very."

"How?"

"I haven't been here long. I'm still looking." Roxanny was reluctant to speak. Sooner or later the protector would be asking questions she shouldn't answer. Still—weren't there things she could learn from a protector?

So she temporized. "We learned a lot before any ship landed. It's always noon here. I expect that could drive a person nuts. If you ever saw a sunset, it would be the end of the world."

"And a mining system would hit vacuum. That's not all bad. Industries can sometimes use vacuum."

"A year ago you were shooting down every ship that came near the Ringworld. Why did you do that? Why did you stop?"

"There was a protector Vampire in the Repair Center. He did the shooting. Another replaced him."

"And now it's a kinder, gentler time?"

"Not while you're playing with antimatter, dear one! That will have to stop! You could destroy us all, and yourselves too. I think you must be schitz. Roxanny, you flinched."

"Did I?"

"Are you schitz? Were you schitz? Were. How were you cured?"

Roxanny snarled, "I stopped taking the stuff!"

"Stuff?"

"The Amalgamated Regional Militia used to draft schitzes for the lower echelons. We've tried to breed that trait out of ourselves, so it's hard to find a real schitz, but there are biochemicals that can imitate the schitz state. You see things, think thoughts, hear voices that a citizen never dreams. I took the stuff during training. I can get a shot during a mission, it makes things easier, but I try to stay off it. I'm not schitz, Proserpina. My genes are clean." Roxanny clamped her lips closed. This was far more personal than anything she'd intended to reveal.

"Lower echelons? Do any of the top ranks go schitz? No, never mind. Do warriors such as yourselves have children, Roxanny?"

"No. I can't. I've had my shot."

Proserpina stared at her. Then she turned away to gather more fruit. "I'll feed your injured one," she said. "Eat. Explore. Enjoy," waving vaguely at the forest and its hidden buildings. "The stream is that way. Follow it back. We'll talk soon."

Roxanny watched her go. Had she really been left to explore unsupervised? The prospect was terrifying and irresistible. She was in the Garden of Eden. God walked here. Nothing was otherwise harmful.

The building—

It was a toroid. One door, no windows. A sequoia-sized tree in the center lifted it two meters off its foundations. While Roxanny hesitated, Wembleth jumped to reach a doorsill, lifted himself, and was in. Roxanny waited a beat, then followed. She wished she had better armaments than the needler in the small of her back.

Roxanny jogged around the perimeter. It was all one big tubular room, a few degrees tilted. She found nothing worth seeing or stealing. The floor was deep in dirt and rotting leaves. No obvious lighting, barring the transparent roof. No offices. No toilets.

She asked Wembleth, "Do you know this style of building?"

"Vashneesht work. Very old. These walls cannot be harmed, but many lifetimes of wind made these corners round. I think servants of the Vashneesht lived here. Look, this was bed."

The vegetable trash? Roxanny was used to float plates.

The next building over looked like a pump house nested in a forest of pipes. It was, but it also held toilets, a huge tub for bathing, and dust heaps that must have been towels. Wembleth understood: he knew more primitive means for using wastes for fertilizer. Sewage and wash water flowed into a sprinkler system. It was all powered from the roof, from converted sunlight. Roxanny and Wembleth spent an hour bathing and then investigating the system. The remarkable thing was that it still worked.

Roxanny led them along the river, in the direction of flow of the shadow squares, antispinward. They came to a wide, white sand beach. Huge combers rolled in from an endless ocean.

Roxanny tried her mag specs. She knew what she ought to see, but the horizon was a line of haze; the specs only magnified it, or picked out currents of heat. She'd be peering through hundreds of miles of that, to see subcontinents belonging to this same little map. How long would it take to get used to the Ringworld's scale?

She'd get a better view from the roof of the arcology; but that was not walking distance.

Proserpina paused at the edge of the garden long enough to instruct her servants. Aliens were not to see them.

Aliens were not to be interfered with. Aliens were not barred from the Penultimate's long-abandoned buildings.

Hanuman was eating and watching her from far up a tall tree. Proserpina gestured him down.

"Who do you serve?" she asked.

The brachiator spoke a musical phrase, then translated into Interworld. "Tunesmith. He derives from one of the Night People varieties. His secrets are not mine to give."

"Why do you conceal your nature from the ARM? Why should I?"

"A ship of the ARM exploded three days ago. It tore a hole in the world's floor that would have destroyed us all." Hanuman described the location quickly and precisely. "Tunesmith repaired it—"

"How?"

"Secret, but his means are limited. Another such event would end everything. You and Tunesmith and I have this in common. To hold ARM ships away from the world is our only hope. Kzinti also must be kept distant. Puppeteers would rule us to make us dependable. They would make the Ringworld safe to a point beyond habitability. Who knows what Outsiders might do? There are other factions. Question 'Tec Gauthier or scan any ARM ship's library. Giving information to any of these invaders would only lure them all here to learn more. To tell them of protectors might scare them witless. Rewarding invaders with valuable data—"

"Enough of your chatter, I understand you. What of Luis Tamasan?"

"What sources have you been scanning?"

"Scan is too large a word. I've barely had time to browse in the libraries of *Gray Nurse* and *Hot Needle of Inquiry*."

"Seek 'Louis Wu.'"

"*Gray Nurse* has the report he made to the United Nations following the *Lying Bastard* expedition. Should I hide his identity too?"

"Please yourself. He plays a frivolous game of mate-and-dominate with the ARM woman."

"Stet, we will leave all as it is for this little time."

Hanuman asked, "What is this place? Are my charges endangered?"

"No, but guard them if you will. This was the domain of the last rebel but one, the Penultimate," Proserpina said. "Will you serve me?"

"No." No ambiguity, no hesitation.

"I want to talk to Tunesmith. How may I do this?"

"Tell me what you want said. Give me a vehicle."

"I have all of the history of this structure and its regents, all for barter. The Repair Center is not the Ringworld's only secret. Do you dare withhold my knowledge from Tunesmith?"

"No. Tunesmith is more intelligent than you or me, but he cannot act without data."

"Where is he?"

"Some distance up the arc."

"You came to investigate the antimatter explosion. You left your vehicle behind when the ARM ship took you." Hanuman didn't react. Proserpina said, "You have no transport. I have only this one mag ship. To make another would delay us for days. Can we spare the time?"

"I must guide you to Tunesmith."

Proserpina thought about this. Could she find a way to guard herself? Or was it time to die, if Tunesmith chose to make it so?

"I'll make things secure here first," she said. "Wait until tomorrow night."

Louis Wu was not unhappy. He was getting a long rest, prone in the Intensive Care Cavity. Nobody expected anything of him. Let others deal with the Fringe War, antimatter fuel tanks, the dance of protectors. He dozed, and thought, and dozed. . . .

And he fell asleep, or was put to sleep. He woke under high, dark trees. His massive ARM autodoc was no longer attached to the sunfish ship. The joker stood above him.

He tried not to be dismayed that she'd come back alone. Hanuman must be with the others: he'd protect them.

She asked, "Are you well?"

"Check the readouts," Louis said.

She took him at his word. "You're healing. You're getting nourishment and something to calm you." She tapped at a screen. "You wouldn't be getting *these* inputs if you didn't have internal injuries. They're still healing. This other concoction seems to be brewed from tree-of-life root, or some synthetic analogue, but the machine isn't feeding that to you either."

"Really? Tree-of-life? The stuff that—"

"Here, this tube."

Louis tried to sit up. "I can't see it."

She sketched a mark in the air. Louis knew that symbol, a trademark half a thousand years old. "Booster-spice."

"Intended to restore a breeder's age-raddled body? And you don't need it. You're an old man made young. Is boosterspice one of Tunesmith's secrets?"

Louis blinked. "No. It might be an ARM secret." He'd been told as a child that boosterspice had been made via genetic engineering done on ragweed. It now struck him that the longevity treatment had been introduced, and allegedly changed human nature forever, about two hundred years after an alien ramship reached Sol system. It could fit.

"You are fertile. I can smell it. Roxanny spoke of shots to make a person sterile."

Louis smiled. How would a genderless protector ever understand that?

He said, "I was chasing a woman named Paula Cherenkov. I knew she wanted children. I had the habit of bugging out of human space from time to time. I always thought I'd smuggle something some day . . . never did. This time I went to Jinx.

"Some worlds think just like flatlanders when it comes to the population explosion. Some worlds don't have much habitable territory. Not Jinx! When they need more room, they expand the terraformed regions. I got them to reconnect my vas deferens.

"Then Paula left Earth because she wanted a *large* family.

"A few years later I brought a new intelligent species into known space. The UN wanted to give me a birthright for finding the Trinocs and serving as their first ambassador. Now the doctors were waiting to fix what shouldn't have been already fixed. When Nessus made *his* offer, I went to the Ringworld."

Proserpina set her hands on Louis's belly and moved them around. Pressure above his left hip. "Old damage to the gut?"

"Yah."

"There's barely a trace. This floating rib is newly cracked—"

"Agh!"

Hands like a score of walnuts palpated his numb hips, then ran down his legs. "Six breaks, maybe more, all on the left. It doesn't matter, they can all heal at the same time. In four days you'll walk, in seven you'll run. Would you try solid food?"

Louis pointed: "That one's good. The Hinsh gave it to us." She broke a canteloupe-sized yellow fruit for him, and fed him, and ate some herself.

He asked, "Who are you?"

"I'm the oldest protector, the last of the rebels," she said. "Tell me who you are. The woman doesn't know. She didn't perceive Hanuman either. What does she think *he* is?"

"We let her think Hanuman is a tame monkey. She

thinks I'm the son of an ARM who got himself stranded. Can we keep it that way? Roxanny is an ARM detective. There are things they shouldn't know."

"ARM is one of the factions—"

"Amalgamated Regional Militia. From Earth, the United Nations police since eight hundred years ago. There are a few hundred ARM ships in the Fringe War. How much do you know, Proserpina? Have you been hacking into *Needle*?"

"Yah. Puppeteer civilization is too fascinating. I could become lost in it. Still, this Hindmost has extensive records of human civilization. Do you know the name 'Proserpina'?"

"Pluto's wife, the Lady who rules Hell. Greek myth, Elizabethan pronunciation. Is this Hell to you?"

"In a loose sense. Tell me about Tunesmith."

"Not yet. I want to know about you. Who you are."

He had the impression she was grinning. She said, "Your muscle cues aren't easy to read, flat on your back, hips and legs inert, and the rest hooked to all these pumps and sensors. Still, I sense something proprietary. Do you own Tunesmith?"

Louis laughed. "He thinks he owns me."

"You don't agree, but you don't hate him. You'd free yourself if you could. Will you serve me? No. For a time, then? Perhaps if you knew me better? I'm not prone to rages or bouts of frantic activity or megalomania, Louis. I don't suck blood, though you served a bloodsucker. I've been passive for millions of falans while the rest of my kind burned themselves out. Of course you must know me first, if we have time. My tale is complicated. I helped build the Ringworld."

"I've heard that before," Louis said.

"From some braggart breeder? They've become hugely various, haven't they? My telescopes won't penetrate atmosphere well enough, and I dare not travel to see more, but I've dealt with spill mountain species. Louis or Luis, I'm the real one. I broke promises before the work was finished, so it was finished without me, but I believe I'm the last builder. Would you like your legs back?"

What did she mean? She bent over him, reached around behind him. Pain surged.

"Can you tolerate it? It's better if you can feel what's going on."

"That's pretty fierce," he gasped.

"I'll cut the input by half—" (The pain receded.) "—and change your chemical balance a little." The pain fuzzed. "There. Will you try to urinate and evacuate? The 'doc system is equipped to handle that."

"In privacy, please."

"Stet." She turned away. "Then you can tell me about the people of the Ringworld. Who have you met? What are they like? I have the right. Our children became their ancestors."

Louis considered keeping silence. It was not his nature. He couldn't hide anything from a protector anyway. He did wonder if Proserpina had set ARM truth drugs dripping into him.

But the vampire nest wasn't a secret to be kept. It was a futzy good story. Breeders—Ringworld hominids—had evolved into an ecological slot elsewhere occupied by vampire bats. Louis Wu had interfered with the weather over a world-sized area. His intentions had been good—he'd ruined the environment for some dangerous plants—but over the next few years, vampires moved under the permanent cloud deck established by Louis Wu, and took over a floating industrial park.

That happened far around the Ringworld's arc from where Louis was dwelling with a Weaver species. He'd watched through the Hindmost's webeye camera. Louis described it for Proserpina, and the Weaver village, and that led him back and back. Floating buildings gathered to form a city, and the shadow farm beneath, that grew a hundred kinds of fungus. The Ringworld slid off center, near to brushing against its sun. Back and back, until he was telling her how he'd come to the Ringworld, lured into an expedition to explore something strange beyond the worlds he knew.

She knew what questions to ask, when to keep silent, when to break and feed him fruit. "Here, this machine makes a nutrient fluid too. Would you eat that?"

He tried it. It was basic stuff to feed an injured soldier. "Not bad."

"You eat meat too, don't you? Fresh killed? I'll hunt you up a sampling tomorrow. I'm more of a scavenger than you are, I think. How did you return to the stars? Through an eyestorm?"

"Something like that."

He spoke of Halrloprillalar, the City Builder who claimed that her kind had built the Ringworld. "She was joking with me, but she had it backward. She and her species nearly destroyed it."

"How?"

"They dismounted the attitude jets on the rim wall and built them into their spacecraft. Proserpina, why did you let that happen?"

Poker face. "We made attitude jets to be easily dismounted so that they can be easily replaced. We expected them to wear out in time. Was this a part of the Fringe War?"

"No. Earlier."

"We'll speak of this again. When did the Fringe War start?"

"Tanj, I don't know. The first ships may have got here ahead of the Hindmost, a hundred falans ago. You stole *Gray Nurse*'s library, didn't you? Have you got it running? See if it's got footage of *Needle* coming in."

"I'll do that," said the protector.

Louis called after her. "Check on the others, will you?"

"They're safe here, but I will. Sleep."

It was night, and he'd talked himself hoarse. He slept.

He woke to find Roxanny and Wembleth asleep on the plastic sheeting. He didn't disturb them. In an hour they woke, found the store of fruit, and ate.

Roxanny fed him delicately. Perhaps she'd raised a child once.

She and Wembleth had spent yesterday exploring while Louis lay in his ICC. "These elbow trees are easy to climb. It's even somewhat safe, once I found some rope. We got a wonderful view. It's all flat, the horizon never curves out of sight, and I had these." Mag specs. "Luis, did you notice one big central mountain, coming in?"

"Yah, inland."

"It's windows top to bottom, but there are only a few picture windows. The rest looks like a spray of glitter everywhere. I'd call that structure an arcology, but *big*, and built by military, or maybe paranoid crazies. Straight highways with towers at the end, wonderful fields of fire. Big helipads. I didn't see any guns; I just saw where they should be mounted.

"There's only that one huge palace. Over the rest of the island—I keep saying island, just because I can see so much of it, even though most of it dwindles into what looks like fog. *Continent.* The buildings nearby are all very basic, and there's nothing big further out. Wembleth thinks it's all housing for breeders, *Homo habilis.* We didn't see any, they could all have died off, but Luis, if this was a protector's home, there'd be defenses and research labs and libraries, wouldn't there?"

"Well, there's the arcology," Louis said.

She grinned at him. "Do you even know what *arcology* means?"

"Big building."

"Well . . . yah. I don't think she's using it. It was left by the previous tenant. I think Proserpina has a base, maybe on the little continents, maybe on another Map. She wouldn't have turned us loose where she works. This place is . . . remember I said 'garden'? Suppose you had to turn the whole Earth into a garden? Earth *is* a closed ecology, but it changes. It drifts." She looked deep into his eyes, seeking understanding. "Gardeners don't like weeds. They'd do something about deserts . . . wouldn't have to worry about tundra because there's no winter . . . but a gardener might have to control the weather."

"Weather's chaotic. It can't be controlled," Louis said.

"What if you had *huge* air masses to work with? An area of a thousand Earths, and no hurricane patterns to foul you up because you're not on a spinning ball. Air masses wouldn't move *fast*—"

Louis laughed. "Stet. Maybe."

"We won't actually see other maps," she said, suddenly depressed. "No boats for guests. What do you think, Luis? One whole supercontinent for a garden, and breeders are an integral part of the garden. Defenses on the islands. Telescopes and research facilities. Mines . . . you don't get mines on the Ringworld, do you?"

"If you could reach the spill mountains," Louis said. "Materials might layer out according to density. Otherwise, no mining rights. You dig for oil, you hit scrith, then vacuum."

"Proserpina *can* reach the spill mountains."

Louis shrugged. "I can't help you explore. Be cautious. Every culture has fairy tales about someone finding something he shouldn't."

"Even so," Roxanny said, "I'd like to get into that building."

Wembleth and Roxanny went out again after breakfast.

Proserpina was back at midday. She asked, "What are stepping disks?"

"Where did you find those?"

"Your own report to the ARM, Louis Wu. You didn't

tell enough. What if I had to *make* stepping disks? Is the Ghoul protector doing that?"

"You first. How are my companions?"

"Exploring. Hanuman went off alone, Wembleth and Roxanny are together. They'll learn little in this place. The last rebel to die lived here. I took charge of his habitat, but the Penultimate's palace is trapped. I leave it alone."

She hoisted a miniature deer nearly her own weight. It dangled, its neck broken. Big insects buzzed it. "I use this animal for food myself. Can you eat it?"

"Maybe—"

"Treat it with heat?"

"Yah. Clean out the body cavity. Shall I—?"

"You may exercise your upper body, but otherwise rest. Your bones are pinned together, but let them knit. I will cook. I can research this."

Barbecue smells made him hungry. In an hour she was back with a roasted carcass. She stripped off pieces of meat for him. He found it pleasant to be waited on.

" 'But always at my back I hear Time's winged foot-steps hurrying near,' " she said. "No, eat. I need to know how urgent this matter of the Fringe War is. Does Tune-smith have it under control?"

"More or less," he said.

"Eat. Is it more, or less?" She scowled at what she saw in his face. "Less. Hanuman tells me of the blast that tore a hole into space. I saw it from a distance, and knew I must act. Antimatter. Could it have killed all life? Did Tune-smith really prevent that?"

"Yes."

"What did you see?"

"Wembleth and Roxanny would eat some of that," Louis said.

The protector met his eyes for a long heartbeat. "I'll fetch them," she said. She set a great slab of meat in his reach, and departed.

* * *

Daylight was fading when they returned. Proserpina and the others cooked dinner outside. Louis smelled wood smoke and roasting meat. What Roxanny brought to Louis included vegetables: green-and-yellow leafy plants, and roasted yams.

Proserpina was becoming a skilled chef. She ate with them, but what she ate was raw meat and raw yams. When they had finished eating, she said, "I want your trust."

The ancient protector's eyes locked with theirs, skipping past Hanuman as if he were a dumb animal. "Wembleth, Roxanny, Luis, you'd be demented to trust me knowing no more than you do."

"Tell us a story," Louis said. Proserpina was keeping Hanuman's secrets, and Louis's, and perhaps Roxanny's too. There was no reason to trust her, and every reason to listen.

"These events all took place near the galactic core. We who held our world were ten to a hundred million protectors of the Pak species," the protector said. "The number varied wildly in the endless war.

"Something more than four million falans ago—I've lost track of time to some extent—ten thousand of us built a carrier ship and some fighter scouts. Eighty years later, six hundred were left to ride them." Proserpina spoke slowly, reaching far back into her memory. Interworld was a flexible language, but it wasn't built for these concepts.

"This land is a good map of the Pak world. Did you see its shape? Circles everywhere," Proserpina said. "Blast craters, new and ancient, from an endless variety of weapons. These maps were identical when we built them, but they've changed since. On the Pak world and here, we fought for any advantage for our blood line. Luis, *what*?"

"Well, it's strange," Louis Wu said. "One world, over and over? The Pak world was in the galactic core. Suns are packed close together there. You came *here*, thirty thousand light years in one leap. Why didn't you use worlds closer in?"

"Yes, our worlds were much closer together than yours. Endless room, endlessly coveted. We saw no way to reach them in a spacecraft carrying breeders, because we would fight for advantage of the breeders. If we solved that, we'd face another problem. Any world would require reshaping for periods of thousands of years. Before the work was complete, each would be snatched away by armies of other protectors. We could see that this had happened. Worlds near Pak were shaped to a Pak ideal, then blasted back to barren waste long before I was born. We saw no way to take other worlds unless we could change the circumstances that shaped us.

"This is what we did, we six hundred. First, we gave up nearby worlds. If another ship could reach us, that world was too close. We found records of a voyage into the galactic arms, a route already tested by an earlier colony ship. The colony failed, but we knew no intervening danger had stopped it from reaching its target world.

"Second, we segregated ourselves from our breeders. We housed them in a cylinder topographed like a rolled-up landscape. Their food would grow there too, water and air and wastes recycled, a locked ecology. No pheromones from breeder housing would reach the flight control complex. The breeders were not to love us; they would not be aware of us at all. Any protector violating the ban must die.

"Of course there was natural selection at work. Many breeders would die, did die without the company of protectors." Proserpina's eyes sought theirs. "Even now, four million falans evolved, don't you Ball Worlders sometimes need the companionship of something greater than yourselves?"

Roxanny said, "No."

"I find records of scores of religions."

"We've outgrown them," Roxanny said.

After a moment's pause, Proserpina said, "Stet. Many breeders died for lack of our company, but less every generation. Again, many protectors found we *must* smell or touch our own kind. Many found ways to enter breeder housing, and died when they were caught. Others stopped eating. In the first thousand years we lost half our number. Replacing them from breeder stock was a chancy thing. Natural selection took its toll.

"What emerged at the end of three hundred and fifty thousand falans of travel was a race that can live without the smell of our own blood line constantly in our nostrils.

"We veered away from the target world. A colony there had failed, but we could not know how badly. We might find protectors already in place, and our ship was a fragile bubble. We believed— Yes, Roxanny?"

"Earth?"

"Yes, your world, Earth. We could have had Earth. Your tree-of-life plants weren't growing right. Your protectors died. Their descendants were mutating in many directions. We didn't know that. I learned too little of the Earth colony before your evolved breeders began blasting radio waves at the stars. By then—"

Proserpina blinked at them; started over. "We arrived in the local neighborhood. We found worlds we might take, but our ambitions were greater than that. We chose a system with a gas giant planet huddled close up against its star. We surmise it formed far out in the disk that became the planets. Then it was drawn in over the billions of years, eating lesser worlds as it came. Thus we found a planetary system already cleared out for our convenience, and most of the mass gathered in a single body, a mass of almost twenty Jupiters, Roxanny.

"So we built. We met difficulties working that close to a sun, but we could use the sun's magnetic fields to confine the masses we worked with, particularly the hydrogen we needed for fusion motors to spin up the ring.

"Stars that can generate extensive planetary systems form in clusters. There were stars with planets around us where we stopped, and some were Pak-like or close to it.

We identified those that might evolve dangerous enemies. We collected local ecologies and settled them on maps of their worlds.

"We never approached Earth, Roxanny. We were afraid. We studied the system intensively at long range. The Map of Earth became home to our own breeders. We needed fifty thousand falans to build an ecology into the Ringworld's inner surface, but we started there, with the Map of Earth as a test bed."

"Whales," Louis said. "There are whales in the Great Ocean. *Some* protector must have gone to Earth."

"It may have happened after I was isolated," Proserpina said. "Wembleth, are you keeping up with this?" Proserpina changed languages and spoke rapidly. She switched back: "Later I'll show Wembleth maps of the sky, and diagrams. You two should try to tell him what a Ball World is. Roxanny, these maps of our world are prisons. We knew some of us would break the one law. We built the prisons first, to warn each other. Any felon would be isolated with a world to rule and a population all of her own kind, just as if they'd each conquered the Pak homeworld, but all made hostage to the majority.

"I was one of those."

"Why?"

"Oh, Roxanny." Proserpina's body language suggested impatience and bitter laughter. "We thought we would win! Eleven of us thought we could take the Repair Center. We'd breed our descendants to all of the lines, and cull to keep our traits dominant. In a thousand years we'd be safe, even if the power balance changed, even if an insurgence should kill us. We planned it all in an afternoon, and collected our resources as fast as ever we could. Even so, we were a little slow.

"They confined me on one of the Maps, not this one. They collected a hundred of my line and scattered them in pairs through this land. I must build a land they could live in. I must guide the breeders myself so that ultimately they meet and interbreed, or else inbreeding would destroy them. While I did all that, time passed me by. I was out of the loop. Others of my descendants lived among the Ringworld's expanding population, and their genes were hostage too."

Proserpina fell silent. Louis asked, "How long did it last? What stopped it?"

"A few hundred thousand falans—I'm guessing, Luis. Wembleth, Roxanny, you don't understand? On the Ringworld we built, a breeder population expanded to a trillion. At some point they became a chaos of mutations. Mutations are of no use to a protector; they don't smell right. Luis asks me when the protectors stopped culling their tribes, and why. I witnessed too little. I don't know why. I'm guessing even at when.

"I was a prisoner. I spent long periods in depression, noticing nothing. I never quite starved myself. When I was myself, I made telescopes but not probes. We were barred from intrusive investigations. With telescopes I could see nothing nearby, but I could study what was happening far up the arc. Meteors continued to be intercepted. An eye-storm formed; I guessed at the dynamics; I saw the storm dissipate. It meant that protectors were still doing repairs. Luis, what?"

"Depression. Sorry, I don't mean to interrupt—"

"How can I not notice when you want to speak?"

"These bouts of depression, do they make you miss things? I'm wondering about the rim-wall attitude jets, and Fist-of-God Mountain."

"Where is it?"

"Near the far ocean. It was a giant meteoroid impact, from underneath. It didn't leak much because the land was pushed up."

"I would not have acted. This is work for the resident protector."

"There was a *fight* for who would be resident protector."

Roxanny and Proserpina stared at Louis. Then Proserpina moaned. "I've been remiss."

Louis asked, "Did your jailers give you tree-of-life?"

"Yes, but neutered. A virus causes the gene flip that makes a breeder a protector. The virus lives in tree-of-life root. Neutered tree-of-life will still feed me, will feed any protector, but it won't change a breeder. What made you ask that, Luis?"

"Just a thought." Tree-of-life only grew in the Repair Center, as far as Louis knew. Apparently it had died out elsewhere. "Is it easy to get rid of the protector virus?"

"Yes."

"But you got more?"

"How did you know that? Yes, I filtered it from the air when it grew thick enough and scattered far enough, four hundred thousand falans after creation. I cultured the virus and grew it in my plants. I made a few servants then, not enough to be noticed, and sent them on errands. But they revolted, and I had to kill them, Luis, and the next time I tried it, it didn't work. My plants had been neutered again. I know not by what means, and the virus wasn't in the air any more. You ate tree-of-life tonight."

Roxanny gasped. Louis gulped. He said, "Tasted like a yam. I think it probably is a yam, Roxanny. Proserpina, when did it happen?"

"Something more than a million falans after creation. You know what happened, don't you, Luis? Tell me."

Louis shook his head. "The protectors are gone. That's all we know."

Proserpina said, "I understand now. Species differentiation has been extreme in the past two million falans. I can see how far *your* species has veered, Roxanny, under pressures that favor intelligence, hairlessness, swimming talent, and a two-legged run. My telescopes can observe the spill mountains. I went to visit them when I dared, when I was sure I was the last protector in these lands.

"Their people fission into incompatible species under nearly identical conditions. I've tapped the heliograph communication network formed by the Night People. Eaters of the dead, aren't they? And that intelligent, and as breeders! Some half-intelligent protector ruled the Repair Center for a very long time. I can't guess how many other variations there are."

Roxanny said, "Thousands."

"But on the Map of Earth there isn't room for mutations to settle in and compete and shape each other to strangeness. My servants settled my breeders among the Pak of the Map of Earth. My line may thrive there. Luis, *what are you hiding*?"

"I'm sorry."

She loomed over him, small and dangerous. "Talk to me."

Prone in his casket, he said, "I have a friend on the Map of Earth. I want him protected."

"Tunesmith wouldn't let another protector near the Map of Earth. *I* haven't survived by challenging the resident. What are you hiding?"

Roxanny spoke. "There are Kzinti on the Map of Earth. He said so. His friend Acolyte comes from there."

"Archaic Kzinti," Louis said. "Not the same as the armies of the Fringe War. They sailed across the Great Ocean and formed a colony on the Map of Earth, not that long ago."

"While I was in depression," Proserpina said. "I left too much to the resident. Stet. I'll research Kzinti, archaic and modern. Maybe we can deal. But I must confront the resident.

"Tonight I must go away. Tunesmith must be dealt with one way or another. I may be gone for days. 'Tec Gauthier, you must care for Luis. Luis, shall I give you back your sensation?"

"Try it."

When pain came, Louis wondered if Proserpina was

taking revenge on a bearer of bad news. But there was no more than an ache, though it ran from hip to heel.

"Wriggle around if you feel like it, but carefully. Don't detach anything." Proserpina stroked the tree swinger's head. "Little Hanuman, would you like to come with me?"

Hanuman considered, then jumped into her arms. She looked around at them. "I make one proscription. All of what you can reach is open to you, save only the big building to spin and starboard, and the continent nearest to antispinward. I'm sure the big building is trapped. I haven't dared it myself. The little continent is where the Penultimate kept the dangerous species from Pak. Analogues of wolves, tigers, lice, mosquitoes, needle cactus, and poison mushrooms, the plants and creatures we never wanted among our breeders. Most of them were extinct when we left the core stars, but we saved a few. We might have released them, had we known that our breeders would evolve into their ecological slots."

She turned and was gone so quietly and easily that it was as if a ghost had evaporated.

16

MEETING OF MINDS

She would let him fly!

Hanuman prepared. The chair was wrong for him; he reshaped it. Proserpina watched.

They stepped into the forest to collect a store of fruit. Sudden as lightning, Proserpina snatched a weasel-like animal out of a bush and broke its neck. She tossed it aboard with the fruit and the water.

She took her place on a horseshoe of couch and improvised a crash web. Hanuman studied the ring of telltales and controls for some seconds before he dared touch them.

They had a half-random look: fitted in whenever there was something new to be monitored.

The vehicle was nothing like an airplane.

Relaxed as if poured into her couch, Proserpina watched him lift and swoop and spin and dip almost low enough to shatter a tree and minaret, lift too fast, slow until the wind-induced tremor went away, then rise sedately into the vacuum where he could build up some *speed*.

The mag ship was as much a wonder as any of Tunesmith's ships. Its brute strength was startling: it could easily have torn itself into shreds of foil. Its motor was the Ringworld floor itself, powered by sunlight falling on trillions of square miles of shadow squares. Sailing lines of magnetic force, it moved less like an airplane than like an undersea vessel.

These controls weren't all involved with flying. Hanuman was aloft for some time before he tried anything esoteric. Proserpina watched but did not interfere as he manipulated magnetic fields beneath the landscape. Soil lifted and shifted. In his wake, a stream began to change its course.

He'd seen Tunesmith manipulating such forces in a command post in the Repair Center. This wasn't just a spacecraft. It was an entire Ringworld defense system.

Under guidance from the mag ship, the superconductor cables below the landscape could attract, repel, or shift anything metallic: incoming meteoroids, alien ships and missiles, even the occasional solar storm or lethal surge of cosmic rays. Hanuman might be good enough to orchestrate such a defense. He had watched Tunesmith at work.

The land below Hanuman was only a mask over vacuum. Knowing that in his gut, *seeing* it in the Ringworld's underside, ridges that were canyons and riverbeds, creases that were mountain ranges, had almost destroyed the newly created protector. Hanuman had never grown used to it. Only now did he begin to feel that he was its master.

Its master, barring the presence of a greater protector. Proserpina was greater than Hanuman. As a breeder, she'd evolved closer to intelligence; the tree-of-life virus had done its work on a bigger brain. She had more experience too. But Tunesmith was brighter than she.

It was a bribe, letting him fly. Hanuman understood that well. He understood, too, that he was telling secrets with every move he made. *Hanuman is a master pilot, and expendable. What has he flown?* How much did she see? How much did she already know? She reclined, and watched.

He circled above land scoured bare and half-hidden beneath tiers of cloud. The hole had closed, but even now the atmosphere had not flowed in to fill the partial vacuum. He told Proserpina, "This would have spewed all the Ringworld's air to the stars. Tunesmith stopped it."

"How?"

"I may not tell."

"Good enough that he has a way. How did you come here? I saw no ship large enough for my sensing devices."

"I may not tell."

"Stepping disk. Louis Wu described them for the ARM. We must find one. Show me that wreckage."

Hanuman skimmed over the vast deflated balloon that had been Tunesmith's meteor plug—she'd have found it without his help, of course—then hovered above the ruin of an ARM pressure tent. "Set down?"

"Yes."

They donned pressure suits and walked through the wreckage. He saw no reason not to answer her questions. What she asked told him a little of her thoughts and purposes, though Proserpina was learning more than Hanuman was.

They moored the heavy ARM kitchen 'doc to the cargo grid, and lifted again.

The battlefield had been disturbed. Proserpina walked through it, observing first, then asking questions. Hanuman tried to see what she saw. The sonic hadn't left splashed projectiles or scorch marks. There was the ant-covered splash where Claus had died. Hoof prints: small herdbeasts had run through this place afterward. Prints of big hands and feet: scavengers had come to the smell of blood, and found nothing. The ARM lander had taken Claus's corpse.

The flycycle was upside down, resting on its rack and seat backs. There were more scavenger prints around it and on it. Ghouls had tried to fly it; Tunesmith's locks had held; they'd turned it into a joke.

Hanuman said, "Tunesmith is smarter than you. Why not let him play? You've done that for ages."

"I must still be satisfied as to his fitness. I must speak to him."

The flycycle was too heavy for the strength of two protectors. Hanuman crawled under it. The vehicle lifted and righted itself. He turned the holoscreen on. Louis must have turned reception off and left the sender going. Now, how to hide the lightspeed delay, to conceal Tunesmith's location?

Hanuman saw no way. He said openly, "Now you may speak to Tunesmith. He cannot see us yet. Expect a delay of half an hour."

"He's on the far side of the Arch? Conversation will be painful. Stet, I'll begin. Tunesmith!" and she howled what Hanuman had given as his true name. "You have been meddling with the basic design of the Ringworld. You must have surmised my existence. Call me—" followed by a decidedly unmusical sound. "I reside in the Isolation Zone. Louis Wu and your pilot are both safe. Louis Wu is injured and healing. We hold 'Tec Roxanny Gauthier, an ARM, of the Ball People. The Kzin Acolyte is missing. I presume he's with you.

"I want to trade secrets and promises with you. What I have to offer is some knowledge of the Ringworld's construction and history plus whatever I can get from Roxanny Gauthier. We all want to protect the structure from what Louis calls the Fringe War. Haste seems called for. I beg you to reassure me that you can plug a hole if another antimatter explosion happens. Reassure me that you can outfly these intruders. Hanuman seems skilled and apt, but he is no better than his vehicles. Also my direct lineal descent—"

Proserpina paused, then said, "I must inquire as to the state of the Map of Earth. Tell me what you can. I give speech over to Hanuman."

Hanuman chattered at length. Meticulous descriptions of Proserpina, Roxanny, *Gray Nurse*, and ARM warriors, the sunfish ship, the flight from the rim wall, the continent on the Map of Pak, local vegetation probably imported from Pak, Proserpina's not-quite-hidden servants . . . Concise as the Ghoulish language was, he spoke for a long time.

When he stopped, it was not because Proserpina forced him to. He had given away every secret he knew, and Proserpina had not killed him to stop his mouth.

Proserpina climbed from the flycycle saddle. "How shall we occupy our time?"

"Lunch."

"Good."

They spread fruit on the grass and added a weasel carcass. Proserpina asked, "How do you suppose our guests are getting on?"

Hanuman ate a dwarf apple. He quoted something he'd found in *Needle*'s library. " 'When the cat's away, the mice will play.' Did you leave them a boat? Anything that flies? No? Then they'll try to reach the Penultimate's palace."

"There's no access," Proserpina said.

"Not even for you?"

"I have mapped hypothetical routes, but I deem the risk unacceptable. The Penultimate's inventions are nothing I can't evolve for myself. Hanuman, they are only breeders."

"They will search."

"Hello. Bored?"

"Yah."

"How are you entertaining yourself?"

"Counting up mistakes," Louis said. *There's another one. Youths don't remember enough mistakes.* Did they? He didn't really recall. It had been too long.

"Are we still friends?"

"Sure, why not?"

She cocked her head, studying him for signs of sarcasm. "Luis, I want you to forgive me for shooting you."

"Okay."

"Tanj, you're easy. You could ask me to forgive you for Claus."

"Claus pretty much killed himself," Louis said.

"Your friend killed him."

"First chance he got. Stet, why not? It's a prisoner's duty to escape. Why in the name of sanity would Claus hold a Kzin at gunpoint?"

"That's war."

"Who declared war? Roxanny, who decided to imprison me? I could have been conned into going for a ride. Done that way, maybe you could have had Acolyte too."

"What if you said no?"

He asked, genuinely curious, "Are you schitz?"

"What? . . . Not right now."

The ARM was manned by schizophrenics and paranoids. Everyone knew it. In real life, any 'doc could provide chemicals that would keep a schitz sane, but in the ARM, they did without chemicals at least some of the time.

Louis didn't comment. Roxanny glared at him. "This is pretty personal, isn't it, Luis? I've been diagnosed not schitz. I didn't join the ARM because I was schitz, I did it for the adventure."

"Ah."

"But I can fly on psychomimetics. I'm not getting them any more, but they were used in training." She shrugged it off. "Want to go for a walk?"

"I don't climb out of this thing for another two days."

"You're going to love it. This place is the Garden of Eden. There's nothing harmful, and God walks. She's just gone away for a bit."

"Any idea where she went?"

"Nope. Why did she take the little ape? I thought it might be a pet. Then I thought, maybe it smells like a relative. What do you think?"

"Not a relative. No more than you or me."

There was silence. Then, "Luis, are we lovers?"

He smiled. "In this condition?"

"I saw her turn off the nerve block. Does it hurt much?"

"Not much. Aches." He watched her take her clothes off. His own must be back aboard *Gray Nurse*. Suddenly he felt helpless. He wondered what she would do if he said "No."

She ran her hands over his feet. "Feel that?"

"Yah."

Her hands moved upward, part massage, part caress. Where he winced in pain, her touch grew lighter.

The thrill never went away. Among the Giraffe People he'd been too flustered and in too much of a hurry. When she climbed onto the ICC, he said, "You drop all your weight on me, I'll scream my head off."

"Nobody'll hear, my poor boy. I sent Wembleth to look for anything that flies. Let's see if I can get you interested. Luis, how old are you?"

"Two hundred and—"

"Seriously." She squeezed him intimately. "Sometimes

you seem older. You know things you shouldn't." Breast
tips brushed against his chest hairs as she hovered above
him. "How do you know there are whales in the Great
Ocean?"

"My father told me. You can see huge levels of detail
underwater from high enough up."

"Oh."

"You've been treating me like a kid, Roxanny. I'm not
sure I like it. I'm not sure I don't. But hey, you're definitely
in charge now."

"Oh, yah. So let's see how agile I am." With a certain
dexterity, she fitted them together. "I'm over fifty, Luis.
This 'doc is my boosterspice supply for the foreseeable future."

"Well, don't bounce too hard or you'll wreck it."

She laughed. He felt the ripple in her powerful belly
muscles.

"Roxanny. Did you know . . . boosterspice is made
from tree-of-life?"

"What? No! Who told you that?"

"Proserpina. Look at the . . . implications. If the United
Nations was playing with tree-of-life . . . half a thousand
years ago . . . what else have they done with it? Maybe
there's a protector running the ARM."

Her eyes got big. "I don't believe it. Luis, the ARM's
top rank is all paranoid schizophrenics! And they don't
take their shots! Can't you—"

"Keep moving. I thought that was just rumor."

"Well, everybody says so. They'd never let a protector
rule them. It might take over the Earth!"

"But if they did let a protector get loose, he'd run the
ARM. And he'd think like a paranoid schizophrenic,
wouldn't he? Roxanny, I should stop distracting you."

"Tanj right you should. Thinking about the ARM is no
fun at all. This feel good?"

"Yah."

"You're not ticklish?"

"Used to be."

"Not at all?"

He giggled. "No. Nope." He'd got his tickle reflex under control, long ago.

Wrong.

The holoscreen view of Tunesmith matched Proserpina's imagination: elongated jaws, a face bare of beard, knobs at the jaw hinges, flat nostrils, sharp-edged cheekbones: a Ghoul turned protector.

Tunesmith spoke the Ghoul tongue. Proserpina was only confused for a moment. The heliographs had spread a common language. She knew written Ghoulish, and a version spoken near the spill mountains. She had listened to Hanuman while he spoke into the holoscreen. It was only a matter of pronunciation. "Omnivore plains runner? I have long wondered about you. Your species survives on the Map of Earth, but not unaltered—"

Proserpina yowled. Hanuman was up a tree and hidden in its puffball top, before his mind quite caught up. But Proserpina was still at the holoscreen, and Tunesmith was still speaking—

"Local carnivores, transplanted Kzinti, have been selecting among the local hominids for such traits as please them. The exception is an invader who came with the first expedition. Chmeee tends hominids in his little sector of the Map, lets them run wild, and does not eat their meat or allow his servants to harm them. We might solve your problem most easily by giving the Map of Earth to Chmeee. We could deal with him through his son or through his ally Louis Wu.

"The Fringe War is a more difficult problem. I believe we must meet. You must view the Repair Center, and I must not leave you unwatched.

"What I know of you leads me to believe that you

have learned not to act. Such a degree of self-control is rare in one of our kind. I believe I would be safe in your presence if I can offer reasonable guarantees for your own safety.

"A guarantee you might accept is your knowledge of what I am. We evolved as intelligent breeders. My own several species survive as eaters of the dead. Thus we normally see harm to any race as bad. Where other hominids survive well, so do we. Wars are not good for us; a battle is a glut followed by famine. Drought is not good, so we guide locals in water and canal management. Deserts are not good; we guide locals in replanting. We teach flood control and farming. We keep local religions, but we guide them away from messy practices, jihads and human sacrifice and cremation. We keep track through heliographs managed by the people of the rim walls. We control our numbers.

"If I see no reason to harm you, I will not. If I desire your good will, I will act to your benefit. Learn what you can of me, and decide whether you will come to meet me. I will send a service stack to rendezvous with Hanuman's flycycle."

The face of Tunesmith went away. The picture remained: a background of interstellar space, skeletal black structures in the foreground. Proserpina shouted, "Hanuman!"

Hanuman climbed down.

Proserpina's grip had bent the armrests of the skycycle's forward chair. She said, "My descendants are being eaten by large orange carnivores."

"Did you know before last night?"

"I knew that most of the Ringworld was out of my control and barred to me. This was not nearly the worst of what I imagined, but I knew with my forebrain, Hanuman, not with my glands. Well, what is a 'service stack'?"

"Float plates topped by a stepping disk. I can guide us through the stepping-disk system."

"We should look to our guests first. You take the fly-cycle. I'll take the mag ship home. I have an errand."

Evening.

"It isn't the same as rishathra," Louis said. "Can't you feel the difference?"

"Kid, you've had more experience than I have at that," Roxanny said, "so you say. What are we doing for dinner?"

"You could go hunting."

"I feel lazy."

"Will this system make dole bricks?"

Roxanny looked it over. "Just soup."

"Draw me a mug."

She dialed for two. "Luis, how would you get into the mountain?"

"I haven't even seen it. My daydreams have mostly involved walking erect, not climbing around in an artificial mountain. What are you thinking?"

Roxanny said, "We'd need transportation. Even on Earth, arcologies are too big to explore on foot. Then I'd worry about security. Protectors were very territorial, it's said."

"This is good stuff."

Roxanny sipped. It was a heavy, grainy soup. "You get tired of it fast."

"Think about breeders."

"What?"

"Breeders. Pak who haven't turned protector. Plains apes, adults, and children. They can run alongside an antelope whacking it on the head with a knobbed bone, and not fall over. Keeping their balance may be what got them the big, complicated brain. But they can still climb. If there are booby traps in that futzy great building, they'll be set to leave breeders alone."

"Well, unless the breeders are kept out by something like, I don't know, a *fence*?"

"We should look for a fence," he agreed. "Roxanny? Don't go alone, stet?"

"What's that?" Light outside.

"Flycycle riding lights."

Roxanny went out to look. She came back holding hands with Hanuman. "That protector sent the flycycle home on automatic."

"It's got an autopilot. She might have fiddled with it. Where is she?"

Roxanny shrugged. "Nobody was aboard but the Beast."

17

THE PENULTIMATE'S CITADEL

On the fourth day Roxanny told him to walk.

"It'll be another day yet," he told her.

"I know, but the diagnostics say you're nearly cured. Benefits of youth, I guess. Luis, soldiers turn out of the 'doc when they have to fight, and futz the diagnostics. It doesn't hurt them."

Louis was tempted, but—"What's the hurry, Roxanny?"

"Wembleth says he's found a way in."

"Ah."

"We've got a flycycle. It won't fly without you. Proserpina seems to have got it to fly itself, but I can't. Proserpina hasn't come back—"

"Where's Hanuman?"

"Somewhere in the forest gorging on fruit, I think. Why?"

"He needs taking care of."

"No, he doesn't. Luis, I don't know what she's doing, but the joker won't stay away forever!"

So Louis climbed out of the ICC. He limped with one hand on Roxanny's muscular shoulder, out to the flycycle where Wembleth was waiting. There were little sharp pains all through his left leg, hip, ribs.

Roxanny asked, "Will this thing hold three?"

"Sure, Wembleth can perch in the middle. Give me the front seat." Louis took his seat, wriggled carefully into a position of minimum pain. Wembleth crawled up between him and Roxanny. It was crowded, and the native's wild pelt brushed Louis's neck and ears.

He asked, "What did you find, Wembleth?"

"A path into the fortress," the wrinkled man said.

"Stet. Point me." Louis took off.

It wasn't symmetrical, or self-consciously artistic. It looked like a mountain—like the Matterhorn, all tilted planes done in dark stone, with a pervasive glitter from thousands of windows. A broad veldt surrounded the base, ending in a vertical cliff.

The veldt was a tilted plain of gold and black: lines and arcs of black grass on a field of gold. Louis asked, "What do you make of that?"

Wembleth said, "The black is dying back."

"Black isn't unreasonable for a plant," Roxanny said. "Chlorophyll throws away all the green light. What if a plant could use it all? There are some that do, in known space."

"Yah, but Wembleth's right too. This looks like . . . writing that's been eroded, partly erased. How about this? Genetic engineering. The Penultimate planted it for decoration. It's just not as hardy as the hay, wheat, whatever."

From a height, the cliff did look artificial. Louis steered the flycycle close, then skimmed along the edge.

"This would stop plains apes," Roxanny said. "Not a flycycle."

"Nope. Do you feel lucky? Protectors are—"

"Territorial, yes, Luis. Wembleth, are we close?"

"Go more slow. Go up."

Louis took them up. "Here," Wembleth said when they were flying along the rim of the cliff. "Go left, starboard."

The tilted plain of grass might have been a lawn if it weren't so big. Patterns shifted restlessly on its vast expanse. Wind? Louis borrowed Roxanny's mag specs. With their aid he could make out thousands of creatures resembling yellow sheep.

Ahead, the rock barrier had fallen. Soil above had spilled after it. "Quake? Wembleth, what makes quakes on the Ringworld?"

Wembleth shrugged. Roxanny said, "Meteors?"

"I don't see a crater."

"Then try this, Junior. We have here a protector stronghold. What if some other protector wanted in?"

"Long, long ago," Louis said. A whole ecology, several varieties of grass and a puffball forest, had invaded the fallen rock and earth. "But that track is new."

It began as a series of scorched craters in the trees below the overgrown slope that had been a wall. The scattered dots became a dashed line of freshly chewed, carbonized earth as it rose up across the lawn and higher, into the curved walls of the Citadel itself.

"We weren't wrong about defenses," Louis said. "Something climbed this slope, and weaponry fired on it all the way. Wembleth, how did you find this?"

"Roxanny sent me out to look around. The slope looked dangerous. *Something* must have done all this damage. I climbed a tree for a better look. Look, it goes all the way through those holes in the wall."

Roxanny said, "Follow that path and we'll be safe. All the booby traps are already triggered."

"You sure? Good, then I won't turn on the sonic shield."

"You've got a shield of some kind? Stet, turn it on!"

"I was being sarcastic. Roxanny, it's crazy to go in there. That's a protector's castle. There's no telling what games he's—what did she call him?"

"Penultimate. The next-to-last protector on this sea of maps. There could be a million years of miracles in there. Louis, we can't turn back now."

It's easy to be a coward when you can't fight and can't run. Louis looked behind him, seeking an ally. Wembleth's posture urged him forward, as eager and impatient as Roxanny.

Louis flipped the sonic fold on. He couldn't see it working; they weren't moving at anywhere near sonic speed.

Dark animals had been circling the yellow sheep, hidden beneath the grass. Now they streamed straight toward the flycycle, snarling crazily. They looked like dire wolves.

They'd certainly stop Homo habilis who got this far. Louis skimmed above them, through cratered grass, following the path.

It was a time of surprises after ages of predictability. Proserpina brought the mag ship down at her base, and found:

No flycycle.

Everybody gone.

She found Hanuman among the fruit trees. He hadn't known that the flycycle was missing, but his guess was the same as Proserpina's. They ran for the mag ship and set it floating toward the Penultimate's Citadel.

On the path of destruction Louis was following, they found places where the Penultimate's own defenses had blasted away thick rock wall and left windows standing or fallen intact. The windows were hexagons about the size of a man. They were stronger than the stone. Diamond?

Louis could feel mechanical senses watching him.

He took the flycycle through a gap the size of a sailing yacht.

Sound struck at them. It was almost speech, a million angry voices yelling incomprehensibly, all muffled by the sonic fold. Light blazed at them, dimmed by the mag specs Louis had forgotten to take off. Behind him Wembleth and Roxanny both had heads bowed, tears running from their eyes. Louis looked for the nearest cover: a melted hole in a second wall. It looked too small for the sonic fold. He turned it off, screamed against the sound, went through, flipped it back on.

The roar eased, the light eased.

They were in a jumble of machinery, in a corridor twenty meters across and much higher. Some of the machines were tall and skeletal, like construction machinery. Many looked half-finished. The place looked like Tunesmith's workshop, or Bram's, but more crowded.

Roxanny said, "I was hoping whatever went through here shot out the defenses." She was rubbing her eyes. Wembleth seemed okay. But—

"That *stench*!" Roxanny said. "Like a circus!"

She was right, though "Luis" would never have seen a circus. Wembleth said, "It smells like Blond Carnivores running a troll drive. I don't understand."

It was bad enough with the sonic fold keeping some of it out. Louis asked, "Pak planet panthers? That might drive away breeders, that and the lights and noise. I wonder what this smells like to a protector? That unwashed crowd stench could be someone else's children, millions of them. Maybe a thousand angry protectors smell like this. That's it, it's a warning for protectors."

Roxanny said, "Us too. Time to q—"

Wembleth jumped from the flycycle, dropped a meter, and landed with bent knees. He ran, weaving between machines and parts of machines, following the dashed line of melted floor. He looked back at the flycycle and happily waved them on.

"I was about to say, 'Time to quit,'" Roxanny said. "But let's follow Wembleth. *Right* behind him, Luis. No short cuts. I think he's right; we shouldn't get high enough to be shot at either. And don't get too close."

"Stet," Louis muttered. "No point in being right there when something cremates the poor bastard."

The scars of blasting led Wembleth around the curve of the corridor, then rose up a wall. He couldn't follow on foot. He waved the flycycle down and climbed up between them. He pointed past Louis's ear. "There, high up."

The blast trail had broken through, high up. Louis looked around Wembleth at Roxanny. She shrugged.

There wasn't any cover. Louis took the flycycle straight up and through and let it fall. A beam—not a laser, a jet of plasma—fired at the hole after they'd dropped below it, and followed them all the way down to cower in a maze of ramps. The wall collapsed under its fury, a dozen meters too high to harm the flycycle.

They were deep inside the faux mountain. This interior cavity was mostly empty space laced with a maze of ramps of Brobdingnagian size. Louis wondered if it had been intended as a training ground for warriors. If that, it was other things too. As Roxanny had guessed, there were wonders. Here was a line of crude machines floating by magnetic or gravitic levitation. There, light rays in a haze of dust bent through a scintillating focus. There were guns or instrument packages mounted where ramps crossed. They all looked ruined by heat.

Louis was tempted to stray off the path of destruction. Roxanny was right, a lot of guns had been shot to pieces here . . . but he could still feel sensors seeking him. *Later?*

He floated across a broken ramp to a blackened flight of steps. It was fatuous to suppose that a death trap wouldn't repeat, yet Roxanny's optimism seemed to be working. A projectile weapon rained bits of metal on them, but the sonic shield diverted them all until Louis could drift

the flycycle under a ramp. He left the path to veer around
a fallen wall. Something exploded in a glare of light; the
sound barely reached them.

"Wait," Wembleth said. "What's that?"

It was a war zone lit up like a holoflick ad. Rubble like
a stack of pancakes slumped in the glare, soggy but not
quite molten. It had been one of Tunesmith's service
stacks. An attack laser on a wall high above them bathed
the rubble in pearl-white light. As they approached, it
burned out.

The stack still glowed white hot, and black at the
top. Those float plates wouldn't fly after treatment like that.
The stepping disk at its tip—

Hold that thought. "End of the trail," Louis said.

Roxanny said, "Yah. I'd say this is what we've been following, and I'd say it was armed. Down there—" She
pointed at the foot of the stack. "What do you see?"

"More melted machinery." A glitter of lenses. "Laser
cannon?"

"A weapons and shield package. It sat like a cap on that,
that tower. It must have shot up everything that attacked
it—"

"All but one, Roxanny. That last weapon got it."

"That last weapon just burned out ten seconds ago! Everything that's tried to hurt us is *damaged*. Luis, Wembleth, we have here a perfect chance to go exploring!"

That seemed a little too fortuitous to be credible. "You
say burned out. What if it's just sputtering?"

"Your point?"

"Go home now. Stick to the path, but photograph everything. Work our way back. Study what we've got. Show
it to Proserpina if we can't solve it ourselves—"

"Luis, what does any of that get us?"

"Might get us another way in," Louis said. "Roxanny,
have you got a better idea?"

"Get out and look around. Luis, if we're on foot, we'll
look like breeders. We *are* breeders. I don't think the de-

fenses will fire at a breeder on foot," Roxanny Gauthier said.

"Breeders are naked. Get naked?"

"You're already naked."

"And you're already schitz." Louis turned the flycycle and started back. That last plasma beam had burned a nice big hole in the wall. It ran to floor level. They'd be safer leaving than they'd been coming in.

Wembleth gripped his shoulder. "Look. Plants."

Far above their heads, greenery dripped over the edges of a ramp. It did seem a funny place for a garden.

"We know a way out," Louis insisted. "One."

Roxanny too was gripping his arm. Her voice was soothing. "What's biting you, Luis? Look, this ramp is as wide as a racing freeway. Just take us straight up. If something attacks, we fall back to here, and that's back on the safe path. Stet? Go straight up."

The ramps had no railings. Louis didn't say so. Roxanny saw him as a coward, and somehow he couldn't stand that. He lifted the flycycle straight up.

Nothing fired on them.

A green jungle spilled over both sides of the upper ramp.

Roxanny said, "The guns won't fire on crops either. This was the Penultimate's food supply."

"You don't know any of that. You're betting three lives!"

"ARM detectives do that, Luis. This is our last chance to learn anything without Proserpina learning it too. And Proserpina is not my superior officer! Take us there, Luis."

"The jungle?"

"Yah."

He started to turn, and something found them.

The sonic fold rang like a great bell, and kept ringing. Louis shouted against the sound. He turned off the lift motor, and Roxanny had better be right! The flycycle dropped. In midair he passed out.

* * *

From the moment it came in view of the Citadel, the mag ship was observed. Proserpina worked to muffle the wavelengths reflecting from the ship. As they neared the mountain, something got through: projectiles stuttered toward the mag ship, then veered away. Light blasted up at them and also veered. Hanuman kept flying. It was all he could do while Proserpina fought the ship.

His path wasn't in doubt. He hoped 'Tec Gauthier had followed the chain of chewed landscape. Even if she had, she could still be dead in a hundred ways, and her companions too.

He asked. "Do they live?"

Proserpina didn't answer. Her fields delicately plucked a section of wall away. There was an inner wall, and she plucked that away too. Light flared and was gone. Hanuman was looking at something like a beehive. Proserpina took them in.

There were strong arms around Louis, easing him down to a flat surface. Everything hurt.

He was familiar with this pain: the injuries he'd been healing from, plus a whack on his jaw and a ringing in his ears. He opened his eyes. Roxanny was lifting Wembleth into the forward seat. Blood ran from Wembleth's nose and ears.

She shouted. "You awake?" He could barely hear her. "Here, help me with this." She lifted him into position. She was trying to hook Wembleth into the medical systems. "We had crash fields," she said, "but he didn't. He might have broken his back or his neck. Look, he's got a nosebleed."

"So do you," he shouted.

She looked at him. "So do you. I guess that's the sonics. Tanj, is he dead?"

Louis, with Roxanny supporting him, finished mating Wembleth to the medical system. Readouts flickered on.

"He's alive," Louis said. "Trauma all the futz over his body. He'll feel like me when he wakes up."

"It's feeding him boosterspice, isn't it?"

That ancient trademark— "Yah. He's never had boosterspice before. I think he's old, Roxanny. He'll eat up the whole supply."

"Tanj. That would have been *my* boosterspice supply. All right, Luis, put your hands on the controls."

"We can't fly in this position. We should get into seats."

"I know." She set his hands on the flight stick and the keypad. She turned on the lift. Then she pushed him hard in the chest. He flew backward into space.

He fell two meters onto rock. A sea of pain washed over him. He couldn't breathe. He saw the flycycle lift, and pause.

"You're Louis Wu," Roxanny said, leaning over from the aft seat to meet his eyes. "You're a quarter of a thousand years old. You were the servant of a Pierson's puppeteer until you changed masters, and what you serve now I wouldn't care to describe—"

Groaning, Louis rolled to his knees, then managed to stand. He stretched up, but the flycycle was floating out of reach. The controls shouldn't have served other hands than his. Maybe Proserpina had hacked the security system so she could use it herself.

Louis asked again. "What *is* this?"

"I made Proserpina tell me, but I guessed first, Louis. There's just too much wrong with the way you act. You played me for a fool—"

"No, Roxanny, no. I liked being treated like a kid, being young again. No responsibility! Roxanny—" Louis Wu was fleeing from the ARM. He couldn't tell her that. There were other things she couldn't know and still run loose. He said, "I love you."

She pointed at a mass that was still red hot. "What is that?"

"A service stack. Float plates from . . . elsewhere on the Ring."

"What about the weapons? Those."

"Don't know." He could guess. Tunesmith must have lost a service stack exploring the Citadel. He'd armed the next one and invaded again, and got this far.

"And that silver cap?"

He couldn't answer.

"That's a puppeteer stepping disk, isn't it? And it's pumping light and bullets and whatever else falls on it into some other space. That means it's still working, and that's *why* it's still working—"

"Dangerous! Roxanny, you have no idea where it leads!"

"All the things you lied about! I am not a child." Roxanny studied him. "I didn't believe her. You didn't make love like an older man. So I tried you out, and you *do*."

"How could you—"

"There was a teacher."

"Roxanny—"

"Well, we seem to be a target here. I think I'll just try it." The flycycle lifted, slid sideways.

The pile of ruined lift plates glowed dull red. The plate at the top was dull silver. Roxanny dropped the flycycle onto it and was gone.

She was upside down and falling. Roxanny's breath streamed out in a long silent scream. She fell along smooth, vertical, red rock toward ochre sand a long way down. Past her feet was navy blue sky touched with pink.

Then the flycycle righted itself and began to rise again—but her scream remained. The flycycle had emerged on Mars with the sonic fold off. In a vacuum you scream, or else your lungs rupture.

Mars. Ridiculous. Insane. But she knew this place, she'd trained on Mars. Her spinning senses found the Arch, the Ringworld rising over itself. So she wasn't quite crazy, it was the Map of Mars on the Great Ocean halfway round the Ringworld. Even so, she and Wembleth would be dead in minutes, in an atmosphere that would be poison if it weren't too thin to matter.

The blood that still streamed from her nose was foaming. Wembleth's mouth was open in a long scream; he clutched the flycycle controls as if throttling them.

The flycycle eased up above a single silver plate like the one they'd come through: an inverted stepping disk.

Wembleth reached out, pulling at the umbilicals that attached him to the flycycle's 'doc. He swung a fist at the edge of the stepping disk. The rim popped up on a hardware keyboard. His fist pounded the buttons. He twisted flycycle controls, and the vehicle dropped, twisted, and rose to touch the stepping disk's undersurface.

There was air and baby blue sky.

Roxanny sucked air, gasped, gasped. She said, "Perfect," her throat a raw whisper. She hugged Wembleth. "Perfect. You saved us. That *thing* would have come after us. Proserpina. And Luis. Louis Wu." After a long moment she lifted her head. "You just slammed touch points at random, didn't you? I wonder where we are."

She could see everything there was of it. They were on a tiny island in the midst of a flat, calm sea. Nothing but scrub was growing here. It seemed a safe place to leave a stepping disk and its stack of lift plates.

Roxanny popped the cover and tapped touch points. "There," she said. "Let's see them find us now."

Louis tottered toward the service stack. He'd do better with a walking stick or a crutch. He stopped where the heat was too much. He *had* to follow her . . . but he couldn't get close. He sat down to think.

Jump to the stepping disk from a higher ramp? Yah, stet.

The service stack wouldn't be red hot forever . . . but it would take a long time to cool down. A day, two? He'd have to feed himself while he waited.

In a minute he'd start climbing toward the hanging garden.

Sputtering light woke him. He'd dozed, or fainted. He watched without surprise as Proserpina's ship descended. Lasers stuttered from a dozen directions. The sunfish ship flickered. Then all the lasers died in fiery puffballs, and the big sunfish ship hovered above him.

Hanuman, in full pressure gear, emerged from the opening hatch.

"They went through there," Louis called. "I have to catch them, but it's too hot. *Wait*!"

Hanuman jumped. He landed on the stepping disk and was gone.

What had turned it on, anyway? Plasma heat? A random bullet? Must have been something like that. Why would Tunesmith send a service stack in here with the stepping disk running? Louis saw Proserpina in the hatch, wearing a pressure suit. He called, "Watch out, it's still going!"

She dropped onto the stepping disk and was gone.

The sunfish ship turned, questing blindly. It lifted toward the hole in the wall, outside and gone.

Louis wondered how much trouble he was in.

Everyone had left him. He hadn't felt this alone since . . . he couldn't remember. Roxanny had left him. How would he ever explain . . . or did she understand too well?

He'd thought of her as his woman, decreed by fate, the only Homo sapiens woman in a vastness of three million worlds.

She'd taken the flycycle. Proserpina had programmed the sunfish ship to take itself home. Louis was on foot. That was good news and bad. It was a futz of a long way to a food source, but it was all downhill. Hunger wouldn't kill him. The Penultimate's defenses wouldn't kill him, if he believed Roxanny's analysis: he would be seen as a wandering Homo habilis. He was nearly naked already.

But he had to find water sooner than that.

There'd be water to feed that vast green veldt. Even so, there was water closer: not far above his head. His eye could follow ramps around and up and over to the hanging gardens.

Louis began to walk. Nothing shot at him. Maybe Proserpina had shut down the rest of the Penultimate's defenses.

He rested more and more frequently. Presently he was crawling. A walking stick sounded really good. Maybe he'd find a sapling in the hanging garden. Then, walk home to Proserpina's base. Climb into the ARM 'doc and finish healing. Figure out what to do next.

He knew that smell.

He'd found the Penultimate's tree-of-life supply!

It was a futzy good thing, he thought dizzily, that he hadn't landed the flycycle in the garden. Roxanny would have eaten. She was . . . maybe past the age, maybe not, given decades of boosterspice. She'd be a protector, or dead. Wembleth might have eaten too, he thought. The native's elegant black-and-white hair could be a sign of age.

Water welled up, pooled on the ramp, and ran into the plants. Louis waded into it on hands and knees. It rose to his belly. He only stopped once, when he realized he was kneeling on bright cloth: on a woman's skirt with a hologram running round it. Wild horses ran below Wyoming buttes, around and around.

No telling how long it had been here at the bottom of the pool. Good cloth didn't rot. Teela had owned a skirt like this, bought at a shop in Phoenix. And Louis was crawling again.

He crawled into the garden, dripping, pulling the skirt behind him. There were trees: he could pull himself to his feet. There was more than tree-of-life here. He saw fruit, snap beans, fist-sized ears of corn. . . . He knelt and began to dig.

He pulled up a yellow root, shook off some dirt, and bit into it. It was like chewing wood.

This was twice insane. He was too young. Carlos Wu's nanotech 'doc had made him too young. There was no reason for him to be interested in tree-of-life. It might kill him. He went on eating.

18

THE RINGWORLD FLOOR

Hanuman caught the rim of the stepping disk with a hand and a foot. Rocks like rust-colored teeth waited far below him. For millions of falans his kind had known what to do about *falling*.

Proserpina flicked through. Hanuman caught her belt, but he wasn't needed: she had the rim of the stepping disk. "Trap," she said. She pulled herself onto an ochre rock. "Crude. Aliens?"

Hanuman said, "Tunesmith is careful. Anything might come through from the Penultimate's home. Proserpina, we were told to wait. He's sent us a service stack."

"Follow," said Proserpina. She swung around from the rim and thumped soundly against the stepping disk. Nothing happened. "Gauthier's changed the link."

"I know the protocols." Hanuman popped the controls open, freed a hand, and tapped rapidly. "We'll lose Gauthier's link. Do you care where the detective and the native went?"

"She'll change the settings again. They're lost in the network. Go."

Hanuman swung himself down and was elsewhere.

* * *

Under a hemisphere of artificial sky, a sun burned low, red, and flattened. Veldt stretched out around Hanuman, with a lake and a low forest in the distance.

Proserpina flicked in behind him. She gaped at the lowering sun. "Was there a planet-born protector?"

"Yes. I don't know details," Hanuman said.

"I am suddenly very hungry." Proserpina loped toward the trees.

"I surmise," Hanuman said, "that protectors lose their hunger when they have too little to protect. Were you idle for a very long time?"

They were running through yellow grain, and Hanuman was falling behind. He recognized the trees ahead.

His memories as a breeder were murky. He was old, slowing down, joints starting to hurt. The troop had fought an intruder. Hanuman, fiercest of the males, got close enough to inhale a scent that sparked a rage of hunger. He'd eaten himself stupid, then estivated, then . . . woke like this, in a pocket of forest transplanted deep underground, with its own wandering sun. His own forest to keep him sane, and puzzles to train his newly expanded mind.

The trees were fruit trees. Lower plants grew at the edges. Ringworld life was Pak life, and all these were edible crops. Proserpina's hands plunged into the dark soil. She tore a yellow root out of the ground and ate, and gave another to Hanuman.

Presently she asked, "Where's Tunesmith?"

"I can't call him." The pressure suit Proserpina had worked up for him was a quick fix. It didn't fit well, and it didn't have a communication link to Tunesmith. "He'll find us," Hanuman said.

"I was trapped on a single map for more than a million falans," she said. "When my Pak brethren ceased to supervise the Ringworld landscape, I continued to test for protectors in the Repair Center. The Repair Center has remained active, and I have remained passive. I'm the last defense. One day I will be needed. Even now that day may not have come, but we must see. I should explore. Where can you take me?"

"Your interest is in the massing of alien craft near our sun, isn't it?"

"Yes."

Hanuman rewrote settings. "Come."

They were in a vast, dark, ellipsoidal space.

Stars glared unimpeded, light-enhanced, in walls and floor and ceiling. Spacecraft were harder to see. Tunesmith had set blinking circles round the ones he'd found; he might have missed others. Thousands of ships. Hundreds of thousands of tiny blinking points: probes.

Only Proserpina's head turned.

Three long swinging booms ended in chairs equipped with lap keyboards. All three were empty. Hanuman asked, "Would you like—?"

"Shush," she said, and continued to take it all in. Stepping disks: one visible. She couldn't see the one she was standing on. Weapons and cameras: she couldn't see those either. The star projections could mask anything.

If Tunesmith attacked, it would be from above, and Hanuman would attack too. She was ready—but that was instinct speaking. Practically speaking, if Tunesmith wanted her life, it was his. She asked, "Do you know these ships?"

"Some of them." Hanuman pointed out a few: Puppeteer, Trinoc, Outsider, Kzinti, ARM, Sheathclaws.

"Some are only observers," Proserpina said. "Some are arrayed for war. Badly. The ARM would win if they struck there and there . . ." Her voice wandered off. "And wreckage from this ship or this one might strike the Ringworld. That tail design confines antimatter fuel, doesn't it? Has Tunesmith considered destroying all of these fleets?"

"Tunesmith considers everything."

"But I don't know his tools. He must be at work on something! Something besides mere defensive meteor control. I won't know anything until I know what we can fight with. Or run with."

Hanuman said, "Run?"

"I speculate." Proserpina walked around the curve of the glowing wall. Under a glare of light were the bones of an ancient protector, laid out with some of his tools. The joints were swollen into knobs. Vertebrae in the back were fused.

"They had already begun to mutate," she said. "Do you know that we kill mutants? Do you still do that?"

"Of course, if they smell wrong, or behave wrong."

"This one was very good at what he did. Look at the state of the bones, the scarring from mere age. He must have survived tens of thousands of falans. Hanuman, should we have loosed our predators?"

"No."

"But these who were our own shape have occupied every ecological niche we didn't fill." She looked hard at Hanuman. She'd almost managed to ignore his mutant smell. "I see your point. Not just scavengers like this one, but brachiators like you. Mutations and evolution are good, if only you can stop it *now*, always *now*, so that your own kind need not change."

Hanuman didn't answer. She was only stating the obvious.

But Tunesmith spoke. "Your kind, your original Pak, *did not* survive. That's what mutations and evolution are for, Proserpina. Something almost of your shape has multiplied into the tens of trillions. You don't like some of us? When did you ever like all of your neighbors?"

He was standing atop a chair on a boom just above her head. He could have nailed her in an instant. Too clever, too quick.

Proserpina said, "Bet. Even odds we'll be dead in

nineteen falans, if I read these patterns right. You've studied them longer. Hello, Tunesmith."

Tunesmith leapt down. "Hello, Proserpina, revered ancestor. Are your guests safe?"

"I see this as more urgent than their lives. You have been meddling with our basic design!"

"Yes, but not quickly enough. I need all the help I can get."

"What design changes have you made? What changes do you contemplate?"

"What would be your approach to dealing with the Fringe War?"

"I might have tried . . . can you give me a way to make pictures?"

Tunesmith set his chair swinging near the elliptical wall. Now the starscape was gone, and the wall was deep blue. Tunesmith waved at the wall: white lines appeared.

Proserpina jumped to another chair. She waved shapes to life. Sun. Shadow squares. Ringworld. They were white lines and curves, and then they were photographically realistic views. Proserpina's arms moved like a concert master's. The sun took on detail: magnetic fields cradled the interior. The fields changed: *squeezed*. The sun's south magnetic pole curdled, churned, then sprayed light.

"I might have tried this," Proserpina said. "When we built the Ringworld, we set a superconductor network within the foundation structure. We can manipulate magnetic fields." The sun's south pole jetted X-ray-colored flame. Slowly the sun moved north, leaving the Ringworld behind. Its gravity pulled, faint lines on the blue wall, and the Ringworld followed.

"We use the sun for thrust, up to a few meters per second squared by Interworld measurement. Beyond that—" Streamlines formed. The Ringworld moved on alone, the sun lost. "Flux of interstellar matter through the Ringworld can be steered to the axis to undergo fusion. The jet from the sun gives more fuel. A fusion exhaust confined by magnetic fields replaces the sun, bathes the Ringworld in light, and serves as a ramjet too. The Ringworld survives. We can continue to accelerate."

"Drawbacks?"

"Deceleration would be difficult but not impossible. Fields could be adjusted to thrust forward. Tides would shift."

Tunesmith waited.

"When we stopped, there would be no sun." Proserpina shrugged; the picture distorted. "It doesn't matter. We can't even begin. The sun grows too hot if we try to accelerate it. The shadow-square ring can be pulled almost closed, for shielding, but if the shadow squares fell behind or were pulled ahead, landscape would be charred.

"Worst, it's too slow," Proserpina said. "The sun's gravitational pull isn't enough. I can manipulate the sun's magnetic fields to pull harder on the Ringworld, and it still isn't enough. Alien intruders still follow. I can't think of a way to leave them behind."

"It's the wrong principle," Tunesmith said. "You didn't know. You lack information. Did Louis Wu speak of Carlos Wu's medical system? Or the spacecraft we stole from the Kzinti?"

"No."

"I'll give you details when I need to. Meanwhile— those protectors vicious enough to hold the Repair Center have not always been diligent. They've allowed meteor impacts, eyestorms, erosion, and sometimes an exposed sea bottom. That fool bloodsucker left thousands of places where the Ringworld's foundation shows through. I need you and your allies and servants to find these places and shake a dust into them. I have been working with others of my own kind, with the Ringworld-wide network of Ghoul species; but I haven't been able to reach enough of these breaches. We move too slowly."

"What is this dust? What does it do?"

"You need only know—"

"I must judge for myself!"

"I don't want an equal partner, Proserpina! The dust spreads itself through scrith, but first the scrith must touch it. How can we put more of it in contact with the Ring-world floor?"

"My servants in the spill mountains," Proserpina said, "are useless on the flats. They suffocate. They'll spread dust along the spill mountain edges, on the rim wall, if you can get the dust to them. They'll travel by balloon from peak to peak."

"Good. My own spill mountain protectors have been doing that. What else?"

"Water folk," Proserpina said. "We'll use them. We need to reach the spill pipe system that circulates sea bottom sediment—"

"Flup."

"Yes, flup. We use that word too. Flup accumulates in the bottoms of the seas. Without our tending, it would stay there. Topsoil all through the Ringworld would be lost under the seas in a few thousand years. We've set in place a circulation system of spillpipes that runs under the scrith floor and up the outside of the rim wall, to fall over the edge. It becomes spill mountains. Ultimately it replenishes the earth. If your dust can be introduced into the seabottoms, can it spread into the scrith from there?"

"Yes."

"How long will it take?"

"If we begin now, less than two falans."

19

WAKENING

He ate, and he hid.

Louis crawled among the plants, working his way deep into the jungle. He lived on his belly, reaching out of the shadows to dig for the yellow roots. The hanging garden was too exposed. He couldn't do anything about that; he couldn't leave his food source. Every hominid species on Earth and the Ringworld must have kept at least this one trait: a breeder turning into a protector would hide lest other protectors find him.

Shadow and light: days flickered by.

Nothing seemed to be looking for him. He wondered about that. A loose protector ought to be a matter of concern. It suggested that the Ringworld's protectors had other concerns: they were all involved in the Fringe War problem, ignoring the usual lethal dominance games. It must be bad. He should be helping.

Changing body, restless mind. Why was he eating tree-of-life at an effective age of twenty or so? That had an obvious answer, but the implications were serious.

The 'doc had given him the symptoms, but hadn't really made him an adolescent. Why not?

Tunesmith had opened Carlos Wu's experimental autodoc and spread it out like an autopsy patient, to solve all its puzzles. He'd kept Louis Wu in there much longer than Louis needed, to test his notions, and for another reason. The 'doc's nanotechnology had rewritten Louis Wu's genetics, possibly over and over, until he was ready to become a protector at any time Tunesmith chose.

If Tunesmith had studied nanotechnology in such detail, by now he'd know that subject better than any mind in known space. What was he doing with it?

And that too was obvious, given the theft of *Long Shot*.

Louis's mind wandered away, fizzing with inspiration, seeking other puzzles.

Where was the Hindmost? Aboard *Hot Needle of Inquiry*. A ship built like a glass bottle could still be furnished with hidden control rooms. Where was *Hot Needle of Inquiry*? It didn't matter. Louis could reach the ship by stepping disk, and that was all that mattered, unless—was it flightworthy? He'd have to learn.

Why was Tunesmith's nose so large, when Proserpina's was almost flat?

Did Louis Wu have children or N-children among the ships of the Fringe War?

Where was *Long Shot*? Tunesmith might be studying the ship where he'd worked on *Needle* and the autodoc, in the Launch Room beneath the Map of Mons Olympus. The Launch Room was roomy enough. It was the first place Louis would look, if he ever got over this . . . torpor. It felt like he was thinking very fast, but his mind was like ten thousand butterflies in a field, lighting everywhere, going nowhere. His body . . . he couldn't tell.

He hid, and he ate.

Where had Roxanny taken Wembleth? She'd fled from Louis Wu and his protector allies. Of course she must have burned her bridges behind her: changed settings on the stepping disks, maybe burned out the last one before hiding herself. How would he ever find them?

One hundred and fifty-one days flickered past. Then it was as if he'd wakened from a doze.

He stayed where he was, half buried in dirt and plant stalks. His hands moved over his face and his body, finding a new shape. Swollen joints. Vanished testicles, penis shrunken to nothing. His skull had softened, expanded, hardened again, leaving a minor crest of bone. His face was a hard mask, lips fused to gums and ossified. His nose was enlarged. He'd look like a clown. And his sense of smell had become almost magical.

Hah! He'd solved it, the problem of the noses.

A human nose forms a kind of hood: it will hold a bubble of air for a swimmer. Apes don't have the hooded nostrils because they don't swim. Humans have evolved halfway in every direction, including the aquatic: most of their skin is bare, like the smooth skin of a dolphin.

Fate really did intend mankind to swim.

Breeders lose most of their sense of smell because it would drive them crazy. They would kill any stranger who came near their children, even doctors and teachers. They would protect their children from *everything*, driving *them* crazy.

Louis's nose told him that the Penultimate's arcology-sized refuge was empty of enemies. The only life here was burrowers and insect analogues, and an old scent that went straight to his hindbrain.

He looked at the watch tattooed on the back of his hand. Swollen knuckles and wrist bones distorted the digital display. It was telling Canyon time. He did the math and found that he'd been dawdling for two falans. Far too long. But it was right, he'd counted one hundred fifty-one thirty-hour days. An old ARM record said that Jack Brennan had changed to a protector much faster than that.

Something had slowed his metamorphosis.

He tried to stand up, already guessing the answer.

He couldn't stand straight. He'd been half-healed when he began to eat yellow root. The injuries were embedded in the regrowth pattern. He'd become a protector, but crippled. His knee, leg, hip, and ribs on the left side were twisted out of true. His body was nearly fat free, the fat burned out of him during too long an estivation.

He limped through the hanging garden, learning how to move all over again. A protector who couldn't fight. He reached for something badger-like and caught its leg only because it was so slow. He ate it in haste, and judged it was enough.

A few ramps below was the scorched and half-melted

service stack. He limped down and had a look. It had cooled, of course. He tried to pop the controls open, but melted metal had fused it shut.

He climbed painfully onto the stepping disk. Nothing happened.

His fist slapped the rim hard.

Mars! He twisted and reached up to slap both hands against the inverted stepping disk before he could fall away. A moment later he was in a handstand in a field of high grass. He rolled to his feet *quick* (where was Tunesmith?) and found himself under a blue hemisphere, in the tree-of-life garden where he'd killed Teela Brown.

Tunesmith?

Nowhere.

He popped the stepping-disk controls open and began to play. First things first.

There was a mile-long craft on the Great Ocean. *Hidden Patriarch* had brought Kzinti to conquer the Map of Earth, centuries ago, and on that ship was a stepping disk. Louis didn't remember its code, but he found it.

Hidden Patriarch. He flicked in wire-tense, ready to fight or die.

Nothing came at him. He could see a bronze fractal spider web looking at him from a rusted iron wall: one of the Hindmost's webeyes. Otherwise the location didn't seem to be guarded.

He'd left *Hidden Patriarch* almost beneath the Ringworld's starboard rim wall. Such a view could reduce a man to the size of a proton. Mountains as big as Everest lined its base, green with riotous life. Spill mountains were all seabottom muck, all fertilizer.

The librarians hadn't moved the ship. The Hindmost said they'd been returned home. *Hidden Patriarch* might well be empty.

Louis popped the controls, taking this disk out of the network. Now he was unreachable.

For a few moments now, Louis only thought. His memories were muzzy—a long lifetime of breeder memories. His memories of this last hour were diamond clear.

Long ago, it seemed, he'd studied a map of the Hindmost's stepping-disk system. Now he reached back into those memories to find settings and placements for various locations. They were mostly lost . . . but what he needed was a disk only recently put into service. Thought and memory gave him the code by which the Hindmost designated stepping disks. Wouldn't Tunesmith keep that system? It would give Louis a handful of settings to try.

He'd better have a pressure suit.

He popped aboard *Hot Needle of Inquiry* and yelled, "Hindmost's Voice! It's Louis!" Despite changes in his throat structure he made himself *sound* like Louis Wu.

"Don't move. You are not Louis Wu," said a flat voice like the Hindmost's.

Louis didn't move. He was in the crew cabin. For an instant he considered familiar food, a shower, and a change of clothes, but it just didn't matter. He said, "Tell the Hindmost Louis Wu has become a protector. I need to talk to him."

"Louis? I warned you!" said the same voice.

"I knew. Don't tell me where you are. I've come for a pressure suit. Have you been watching the Fringe War? Has anything happened?"

"An antimatter missile destroyed one of the ramjets on the rim wall," the puppeteer's voice said. "Twenty-eight Ringworld days ago. The explosion was tremendous, not just antimatter but kilotonnes of confined plasma under fusion. Spill mountains melted. I couldn't learn what faction did that. I thought chaos would follow. I made ready to depart, but nothing happened."

"Those attitude jets always were too vulnerable. Tunesmith must have set up something else by now." Louis's mind ranged ahead of his words. "The Ringworld builders never did want rim wall ramjets as anything more than a temporary fix and a safety feature. They built the super-conductor grid to move the system magnetically, push against the sun. Tunesmith controls that."

"You're guessing."

"I guess good. I'm a protector. Free me, Hindmost, and I'll get off your property."

"What's it like?" the Hindmost asked.

"I feel confined. I'm crippled," Louis said. "I can't fight and can't run. I can think faster than I ever did before. I see more answers. That's confining too, in a way. If I see the right answer every time, there're no choices.

"Tunesmith has a plan. I won't interfere unless he threatens my N-children, but I should talk to him. It's just that there are things I have to do first. What about you? Do you have a plan?"

"Run away when I see a chance."

"Good. Do you remember where Tunesmith worked on *Needle*? Do you have webeye cameras in there?"

"Beneath Mons Olympus."

"Is *Long Shot* there? Is it functional?"

"He took the ship apart and put it back together. He hasn't tested it since."

"What about Carlos Wu's autodoc?"

"It hasn't been touched."

"It's still spread out across the floor?"

"Yes."

"Watch for me to cause a distraction. Then get the autodoc aboard *Long Shot* in working condition. Can you do it?"

The scream of a demented orchestra. "Why would I even consider committing burglary on a protector's turf!"

"But you'll have a protector on your side. Hindmost, we are under a deadline. Tunesmith will not consider your convenience. He will act as soon as he can, because he can't predict when the Fringe War will go to hell. If we can't get off the Ringworld soon, you'll lose your home forever, and so will I, and worse."

Into the silence that followed, Louis said, "You're thinking you could hold me prisoner until you turn me over to Tunesmith. Buy something with that. Shall I tell you why you can't do that? Do you remember three chairs in the Meteor Defense Room, on booms?"

"I remember."

"Tunesmith only needs one."

The Hindmost understood. He was as quick as some protectors. "Triumvirate."

"He let me see that on purpose. It's a message, a promise. Tunesmith, Proserpina, and me. He extrapolated a surviving Pak protector, and he knew he could feed me tree-of-life. He didn't expect me to be running loose. He probably won't mind finding me crippled like an ancient Greek slave. He needs my input. He can't guess what the Fringe War will do as well as I can.

"See, you can sell me to Tunesmith, but you'll have to deal with me afterward."

"You're free to move about the ship," the Hindmost said.

Louis let himself slump into his more natural twisted pose. "Give me access to the stepping-disk master controls. I need to rewrite some instructions."

"To make yourself hard to find? I can help."

"Me and a couple of others. I don't need help."

After he had finished reprogramming the stepping-disk system, Louis flicked into *Needle*'s cargo bay. He extruded a pressure suit. It didn't fit him well in his twisted condition, but it would do. He took some gear: a rope, mag specs, a flashlight-laser.

He tapped at stepping-disk controls and flicked out.

He was in orbit. He'd thought that might happen. The settings he wanted were the most recently deployed, and some of those would match orbiting service stacks.

He spent a few moments looking down at the Ringworld's face. This was a region he'd never seen in detail, partway between the Great Oceans. There were ochre deserts, and tiny pockmarks of impact craters, and three little knots of cloud: eyestorms.

Tunesmith wasn't making repairs unless he had to. Given what he was doing, Tunesmith might be glad to find places where the landscape was ripped down to the scrith.

Aircraft and spacecraft he saw none. That was better than his predictions. By now the Fringe War might have worked its way down to the surface. Louis still had time.

But he would have made this side jaunt despite the Fringe War. A protector didn't often have choices. He tapped in another setting.

Still in orbit, but elsewhere. An ARM camera the size of a gnat was looking at him from two meters away.

That tore it! Now they had a verified protector sighting. Or would the pressure suit and his twisted shape hide his nature for long enough? He tapped and flicked out quick.

Night wasn't particularly dark on the Ringworld. Nothing was here but sand and scrub and Tunesmith's service stack, and the calm surface of a sea. Louis prowled about for a bit, but the sand wouldn't hold footprints.

But it held a trace of a scent.

They'd flicked in here, but they hadn't stayed long. They had a flycycle to play with. Louis walked around the island, using mag specs to study the distant shore. A flycycle ought to stand out.

Nothing. Try again.

Nowhere. He flicked in and was trapped in branches and thorns.

He looked about him, he felt about him, before he tried

to move. The thorns didn't do much harm to his leathery skin. Behind his hardshelled face his mind grinned.

Tunesmith had sent a service stack to rendezvous with Louis's flycycle.

Half a year ago. Roxanny, riding the flycycle, might have moved several times before she gave up. Tunesmith's programming would hold: the service stack would follow the flycycle. For all Roxanny knew, it might be covered in sensors and cameras! Finally she must have run it into a jungle and let thorn plants grow over the flycycle and service stack both.

Louis did some careful cutting with the flashlight-laser. The brush started to burn around him. Not a good thing. He crawled down through the thorns, around the edge of the stepping disk, picking up scratches, cutting more brush as he went. Popped the rim and turned off the stepping disk, and lofted the stack of float plates before the fire could roast him.

The forest ran a fair distance, following a river, and he'd been in the middle of it. Now he was above it, with a fine view. Where would a pair of strangers go after abandoning their transportation?

Not far. Wembleth would lead Roxanny to the nearest center of civilization: *he* knew strangers were welcome everywhere. Follow the river downstream and they'd find *something*.

What Louis found was a convergence of two rivers and a small village. He drifted toward the conical houses. Somewhere a voice shouted, "Vasneesit!" and Louis thought, "Stet."

A fire was growing in the forest. A pillar of smoke to gather attention, right where Roxanny and Wembleth had left their vehicles. Looking toward the fire, they'd see a stack of float plates limned against smoke. And what then? Would they hide, or flee?

Hide. They couldn't run faster than a service stack.

Louis sniffed. Population of a thousand to fifteen hundred, smelling like meat eaters, not many elders, lots of parasites but little disease. And—

There.

He set the stack down in the village square. Locals gathered. They were short, brawny, wolfish-looking men and women. Eyes faced front from deep sockets. Small sharp jaws protruded a little.

An elder tried to speak to him. Louis couldn't understand the language, but he tried to placate the man with body language. When that didn't work, he nipped the elder's nose, then knocked him down. A brief shoving match and the man was groveling.

Fair enough. Louis followed the scent. The source had changed houses, but it would have been stronger if they'd moved through open air. Were there tunnels under the village?

A young man popped out of a doorway with Roxanny's sonic in his hand.

The buzz just brushed him before Louis's laser beam touched the metal butt. *Carefully!* The man dropped the sonic and ran inside. He wasn't one of the Wolf People. He was only a few centimeters shorter than Louis, curly brown hair around the face and head, bare skin elsewhere. He was clearly human. Louis's nose knew him.

"Wembleth!" Louis limped after him. "I just want to talk." He moved inside, afraid they'd outrun him, but he was limping faster than they could move. His hand caught metal swinging toward his head, turned and had a wrist and metal bar. "Roxanny."

The fight went out of her. She stared at him in fathomless terror. "What are you?"

"Don't you believe in Vashneesht?" She didn't react. Not funny? "I'm Louis Wu," he said. "Your sonic left me twisted, but otherwise I'm a protector. You were lucky. You would have eaten tree-of-life if we'd gone where you pointed me."

"Louis."

He sniffed: she was carrying a child of his own blood.

She could kill him before he harmed her now. He said, "Do you know—?"

"I'm pregnant. It happens." Roxanny looked him in the eye. "You said you were fertile."

"It's Wembleth's child. I can smell."

"Stet. *Why* were you fertile? Most men use up their birthrights. Didn't Louis Wu?"

"Roxanny, *every* life is unlikely."

Her smile was a mere flicker. "And why am *I* fertile? You sure didn't arrange *that.*"

Louis said, "Someone jiggered your med specs. You all used the same 'doc aboard *Gray Nurse,* didn't you? Someone wanted to get you pregnant so he turned off your sterility patch." It was the most rational answer.

Roxanny said, "Coroner-First Zinna Hendersdatter. She thinks I took Oliver away from her." She had her aplomb back. "So protectors make mistakes?"

"There's never enough data. It's why protectors second-guess each other. Roxanny, I just want to talk and then I'll be gone. Wembleth?"

"Don't hurt her."

Wembleth's head and arms poked out of a hole in the earthen floor. He'd been there for some time. His beard was brown and somewhat curly, tipped with white. Boosterspice had made him young, and in that state he looked something like Teela Brown and quite a lot like a young Louis Wu. He had a crossbow.

"You don't have to come closer," Louis said. He let go of Roxanny, who backed away. He held still, wondering if Wembleth would fire, wondering if he could catch a crossbow bolt. "You've been practicing Interworld speech?"

"Yah, Roxanny wants to join the ARM fleet."

How? Louis wondered. If he'd seen a way, he'd have had to block it.

"Roxanny," he asked, "where did you leave *Snail Darter*'s library?"

"I took it aboard *Gray Nurse*," she said. "Why?"

"My children, their N-children, one or two might have joined the ARM fleet. I have to see the roster. There'd be a current copy in every ship in the fleet."

She laughed. "There are tens of thousands of men and women in the ARM ships! Are you going to scan them all?"

"Yah."

She shrugged. "Maybe Proserpina picked it up."

"You'll have to leave here," Louis said. "I brought the service stack. I'll reprogram it so it'll stop following the flycycle. It's very important that you can't be found. I got this close to you by just following the programming in the stepping disks. I followed your scent from the forest, Wembleth."

"With a nose like that, I'm not surprised," Wembleth said rudely.

Louis touched his enlarged nose. "Do you know that you're my son?"

Wembleth snorted in disbelief. "I would have thought you might be mine! But you're older than you looked."

"You're younger. I never saw a human being who hadn't used modern medical techniques. No depilators, no tannin pills, never a dental program. I thought you were another species. But Teela Brown was your mother," Louis said.

Roxanny shook her head. "She'd have had a five-year patch."

"She must have decided she wanted my child. She'd have to have had her sterility treatment reversed before we left Earth. It would have taken both of her birthrights. She never told *me*."

Wembleth said, "Wait. You mean it? *You're* my father?" He seemed horrified.

"Yah—"

"Why did you leave us?"

"Teela left *me*. I thought then that she left me for Seeker—"

"But what did you *do*?"

"I didn't protect her." How could he, against her own luck? "She went into an eyestorm and we lost her. When we found her again, she was with Seeker. She'd have been carrying you when I left them near the Great Ocean, and as for what she did after that, I'd be guessing."

"You are Vashneesht," Wembleth said. "You're good at guessing. I've never understood. Why did mother leave us?"

Louis knew he should be going. Every second might be precious. Once upon a time Proserpina's people had cleaned the Ringworld system of every menacing rock. Now it was infested with ships. . . .

But in the presence of his son and growing grandchild, Louis was inclined to stay; and Wembleth needed reassurance.

He said, "I left Teela near the Great Ocean. There weren't any stepping disks on the Ringworld then. Seeker—the man she left me for—he might have known how to use the transport that runs along the rim wall. It's a magnetic levitation system, Roxanny. They found something to get them there; there's enough Builder technology lying around. They took the maglev system all the way around to the Other Ocean.

"You'd call that crazy unless they were running from something fearsome. Not from me, I think, but maybe it was what she thought I'd bring. The Fringe War. Teela might have been afraid of puppeteers. Nessus meddled in her life, pretty well destroyed it, and she didn't want that to happen again. She knew any of us would look where we last saw her.

"So they found a place halfway around the arc, and she settled down and made a life with Seeker and you. I hope she was happy."

"Mother was happy," Wembleth said, "but restless too. She never had any more children—"

"Course not. Seeker wasn't her species."

"She and—Seeker—my father," with a bit of a glare, "took turns exploring. I never knew what they were looking for. One of them had to stay with me. They did more of that after I was older. I was near eighty falans when she disappeared."

"And never came back?"

"Never did," Wembleth said.

"She found tree-of-life." *Teela's luck*, Louis thought. *Poor Teela. If anything, it was her genes that were lucky.* He said, "I don't know just how it happened, but that tuber grows on every one of these maps of the Pak world, and most maps once held a protector prisoner. A few prisoners must have found some way to infect roots with tree-of-life virus, just as Proserpina did. I think Teela found the Penultimate's garden. It would have got Seeker too if she hadn't been exploring alone. She woke up as a protector. Wembleth, she wouldn't ever leave you unless it was to protect you from some greater danger."

Wembleth scowled.

"No, really. She saw what we all saw. She must have guessed what was under the Map of Mars. Roxanny, it's a huge volume, an area to match all the land masses of Earth, and forty miles high. You can't miss it. It's the Repair Center for the whole Ringworld. Teela could see that most of the rim-wall ramjets were missing. Somebody had to get into the Repair Center to try to stabilize the Ringworld before it brushed its sun."

She'd wanted power too, Louis thought. *Futz, she was a protector.* He said, "She rode the rim-wall maglev system, and then anything that could reach the Map of Mars on the Great Ocean," his mind running ahead of his mouth. "Maybe she went to the Map of Earth first, to see how the archaic Pak were faring, and picked up *Hidden Patriarch* there. That's how the ship got to Mars—"

Roxanny said, "Say what?"

"It doesn't matter. What happened next was that Teela tried to murder Bram."

Roxanny said, "Bram?" and Wembleth said, "Murder? My mother?"

Louis said, "There was a protector already inside the Repair Center. Teela didn't *know* about Bram, but she knew that *if* there was anyone on site, he wasn't doing his job. He was letting the rim-wall attitude jets be stolen. He'd have to be replaced.

"Wembleth, I talked to Bram. I got his version of what happened. Bram wasn't the brightest of protectors. He never figured out this next part.

"Teela was a protector. She did what she had to do. She took an older man off one of the other maps, probably, and disguised herself. She went with him into the Map of Mars as a pair of breeders. They went exploring through the Repair Center. By the time they found the tree-of-life garden, Teela must have seen enough, or smelled him. Somewhere there was a protector. She let the man eat tree-of-life, and she ate too.

"The man died. Teela pretended to go into a coma. She might have lain motionless for several turns. Bram was supposed to come and examine her to find out what she was, then kill her before she could wake up as a protector. She would have taken him by surprise and killed *him*.

"But Bram didn't come. He must have decided to let her wake. She had to go to Plan B. She left the Map of Mars without ever letting Bram know she knew about him. She set about repairing the rim-wall jets, and then . . . she contrived to get herself killed."

"How? Louis, how?" Wembleth demanded. He was still holding the crossbow.

She had attacked Louis and his companions, and contrived to lose the fight. Louis had killed her himself.

He said, "Bram had us at his mercy. We were hostages for as long as Teela was alive. She'd have been his servant, and he was incompetent. She had to die to save the Ringworld, and she did."

"But—"

Louis rode him down. "What matters now is that I would do anything for you. In practice, what I have to do is lose you again. It's indescribably important that the ruling protectors, Tunesmith and Proserpina, be unable to find you."

"What would they do, kill us? Question us?"

"They'd protect you."

Wembleth set the crossbow down. His hands were shaking. "Vashneesht! Stet. I like these people, but we can move again. Must you know where?"

"I must not," Louis said firmly.

He went outside. Wolf-people youths were clambering over the service stack. Louis shooed them away. He reprogrammed the stepping-disk controls and the float controls too.

Wembleth and Roxanny had followed him out. "I'm going to flick through," he told them. "After I'm gone, change this setting, then *tap the crosshatch button*, here, and flick through. Then go wherever you like."

"Can't we be traced?"

"I fixed that, Roxanny. You're ghosts as long as you tap the crosshatch before you flick out. Even so, Tunesmith will solve that pretty quick, so bounce around for no more than . . . half a day, give me that much . . . then stop flicking around and get away from the service stack." Louis flicked out.

20

TELLING A TALE

Launch Room. Louis only needed an instant here. He wanted to see the workspace, *Long Shot*, and the nano-tech autodoc.

Carlos Wu's rebuilt autodoc was spread around the stepping disk he'd flicked onto. Tools lay about. He could guess their intent, most of them. Cables and rainbow threads of laser light led to a score of instrument stacks. This maze would take minutes to disentangle . . . an hour or more for the Hindmost.

Long Shot loomed, a bubble a mile tall. At first sight it looked partly disassembled. A curved hatch as big as a fairgrounds gaped near the bottom. Equipment was piled about, and there was lightweight packing stuff everywhere.

Look again: that stuff wasn't intrinsic to any likely hyperdrive system. Here was a General Products #2 ship, a lifeboat. Those were tanks. Those, inflatable habitats for ground and orbit, and a deuterium refinery fitted to suck up seawater. Some of it was mere misdirection. Distorted hull fittings turned out to be a holoprojector left running.

Tunesmith had cleaned out cargo and packaging to get at the works, done his investigations, and rebuilt the ship. Close that hatch and—Louis couldn't instantly see how it would exit the cavern. Hmm?

The linear cannon roared like the end of a world. Lightning ran through the hole in the floor, up and out through Mons Olympus. In the silence that followed, Louis heard Proserpina's shout.

"They'll notice!" In Ghoulish.

They were over by the hole, looking down along the linear cannon: Proserpina, Tunesmith, and two little protectors either of whom might be Hanuman. Tunesmith bellowed, "They know I'm here. They'll guess I'm active. The ones with brains must have deduced what's under the Map of Mars by now. Some may even rest easier because I'm closing holes in the Ringworld floor."

". . . Risk?"

"The missiles most of these factions have been using, one antimatter explosion wouldn't tear up much of the Repair Center. An enemy couldn't *know* he'd hurt me, and he'd anger me, and I might find him. I admit there's risk. I'm stalling. I don't want the ARM and the rest of them wondering what the Mars protector is up to. So this is what I'm up to, closing holes. Keeps me out of mischief."

They wouldn't scent him: Louis was in a pressure suit. Louis couldn't smell anything either, so he kept looking around. He saw a few Hanging People protectors. They weren't near him. He saw a webeye camera sprayed on the 'doc's Intensive Care Cavity. He waved at it, *Hi, Hindmost!* and wondered if Tunesmith was linked into the same cameras.

". . . need the holes?"

"I'm through with them. We're almost . . ." Their voices dropped as their hearing came back. Louis wasn't going to learn more this way.

He saw them cover their ears, so Louis covered his. As lightning roared up the linear cannon, Louis picked up a grippy and flung it at Proserpina's head, sixty meters away.

Proserpina caught it and sent it whizzing back at him . . . almost: it would hit the service wall, shatter, and shower him with slivers. Louis danced around the service wall, caught the grippy as it struck, and flung it slantwise at the floor, to ricochet at Proserpina, who caught and returned it. Suddenly other objects were in motion, tools and a random chunk of concrete and a long dead animal as big as Louis. The animal disintegrated in his hand. Louis caught the rest and returned them. He turned a spigot on a tank and was behind the service wall again, popped *up* and returned the grippy and a block of lava tuff, then threw himself behind the puff of featherweight packing plastic that had emerged from the tank. He kicked it upward and was behind the tank while they looked for him there. The grippy burst through the foam plastic, shattering it—

But there were too many things moving now, and elements in his torso and hip were trying to tear themselves apart. He caught what missiles he could, juggled them, and presently set them down. He limped toward the protectors.

Proserpina said, "Funny man—"

"What makes you feel so safe?" Tunesmith demanded.

"You left me a chair. You fiddled with my metabolism."

Tunesmith said, "Louis, everything has happened out of sequence. You ate early and finished your change late. An ARM ship exploded early. We could have taken our sweet time extrapolating the behavior of all these factions in the Fringe War. Now—talk to me. What will they do?"

"A sanity check first?"

"Whose?"

"Have you solved how *Long Shot* works?"

"Yes."

"And embedded the principle in a quintillion nanotech devices? Made from a much-altered experimental autodoc?"

"The numbers—"

"And run nanodust into the superconducting network under the Ringworld, so that its structure can be altered?"

"Yes, with help from Proserpina and our associates."

"Proserpina, are you with this?"

"Yes, Louis. There weren't enough holes in the landscape, so we had to drill in spots—"

"Is it *working*?"

Tunesmith said, "I think so."

"Stet, I'm sane and so are you, or else we're all crazy. Is the system ready to go?"

"It may be, if my power storage holds. I can't include the shadow squares or the sun. At best I can only run for a little more than two days. But, Louis, I'm not sure the nanosystems have finished infecting the entire grid. I need to know how much time we've got. What will the Fringe War do?"

Louis's mind was dancing down a new path. "You can build a new day-and-night system. Tunesmith, why not build a real Dyson sphere? Ten million miles diameter with a sun at the center and the Ringworld around it. Make it thin like a solar sail so light pressure will inflate it. Give it windows to let daylight through to the Ringworld. The rest of the material is a photoelectric transformer. You'll be collecting most of the power of a sun."

Proserpina said, "You're fresh, Louis." In Ghoulish speech that implied meat not ready to eat: unacceptable immaturity. "Protectors can be scatterbrains. You must solve one problem at a time. We're still looking at the Fringe War fleet. When will they strike?"

"There's another matter—"

Tunesmith bellowed, "No! Already some faction has destroyed one of my attitude jets. Who? What motive? Was it a deliberate provocation?"

"Show me the event. Meteor Defense Room."

They flicked out.

He absolutely couldn't signal the Hindmost. The puppeteer would have to move *now*.

Meteor Defense. Proserpina and Tunesmith took their chairs in a jump. Twisted Louis had to climb to reach the third chair. He looked for where stepping disks ought to be. The one he'd come through was clearly marked. A Hanging People protector, Hanuman, flicked through an unmarked site and awaited orders. Others might be concealed *there* or *there*. Bet on three or four, no more. Why were the chairs on these booms so massive?

The wall displayed the Ringworld system as if viewed

from the sun. The Ringworld was a mere outline, white threads against starscape. "I need a pointer," Louis said, and found touchpoints on a knob. "Stet. These are Outsider ships, right? Two. Do you see more?"

"No."

"We're not really of interest to anything that different. These," he highlighted lenses and spheres, "are Kzinti, and these are ARM," long levers studded with lesser ships. "I don't see the Sheathclaws' ship."

"It went away."

"Probably ordered off, or they might have run from Kzinti. Kzinti use telepaths as slaves. What are you wondering about?"

"Interactions," Proserpina said.

He needed a way to use up some time, then send the protectors off on some sort of distraction. Louis drew a net of lines linking various ships, and added vector arrows. "See? Distance and velocity and gravity, you need to take it all into consideration, so it's complicated—"

Proserpina snapped, "It is not! It's only different. We did this all the way from the galactic core to the Ringworld site! They've arranged a standoff, but it's unstable *here*—"

"Yah. And this balance won't hold if—if some dissident faction, say the One Race contingent, is actually running *this* ship or—"

"I don't see how it held this long. I don't see how it could hold much longer," Tunesmith said. "But you know them all, Louis."

"It won't hold. You're missing the effect of the Outsiders. They're more powerful than the other factions and everybody knows it. Just being here, they've made it all more stable until now. Everybody's been wondering what the Outsiders will do. What the Outsiders will do is nothing, and the whole Fringe War is gradually coming to know that."

He was seeing it now, the disintegrating patterns,

strength built up here, bluff here. Two bar-shaped ARM ships poised to destroy one great Kzin lens. Thirty-one ships edged up around one Outsider ship in hope of protection that would vanish like dawn frost on the Moon. Futz, the balance just wasn't there.

"Tunesmith, this whole house of cards could come down at any second. Don't wait. How fast can you get us moving?"

"Half a day, with luck."

Louis turned, shocked. "Why so long?"

"I need to run all the power in the shadow square system into the superconductor grid. If I did that too early, it would leak—"

"Can't you get magnetohydrodynamic power from the rim ramjets?"

"What a good idea. It would have required a certain amount of redesigning, say twenty to thirty days and a thousand spill mountain protectors. I need half a day, then *go*, and no more Fringe War."

"Start now," Louis said.

Patiently Tunesmith said, "You've only just arrived. We don't even know, *you* don't even know who attacked us twenty-eight days ago. Where's the danger coming from? Can I just kill it? The superconductor net has been rewiring itself for only two falans, crystallizing into its new configuration. Even if the change is complete, I need to test it."

Sometimes you just have to gamble, Louis thought. But Tunesmith wouldn't act fast enough without more pressure. "Show me how it happened," he said.

The sky changed: ships moved, stars didn't. The Ringworld went solid. A frame zoomed on one of the attitude jets, a gauzy glittering net molded magnetically into a hyperboloid of rotation with a line of white fire running down the axis. Suddenly it was bright, bright, dimming—the motor was gone, and a piece was bitten out of the rim wall. Along its foot, spill mountains were burning.

"Is *this* all you've got?"

"Various frequencies."

Replay, hydrogen alpha light. Louis waved it off. "It's too overt for puppeteers, too restrained for Kzinti. Maybe a Kzinti dissident. There are ARM dissidents too; we could ask Roxanny. Or anyone who'd like to see both sides reduced a little. I've never been sure about Trinocs, or puppeteers."

"Not much help," Tunesmith agreed.

"Tell me what you know about Teela Brown."

Proserpina asked, "Who?"

."An insane puppeteer scheme," Tunesmith said. "She was a victim. General Products, the merchant arm of Pierson's puppeteers in human space, set up a birthright lottery on Earth. The attempt was to breed for lucky humans. In practice what they got was a few statistical flukes, like Teela Brown. She . . . Louis! *Did you have a child with Teela Brown?*"

Louis said nothing.

"Where is your child?"

Louis said nothing. Among protectors, a poker face is easy; body language is hard.

He waited until he saw motion. Proserpina left her chair in a long jump. Tunesmith jumped in a different direction. Hanuman looked uncertain; he remained at the visible stepping disk, the far one. As soon as the protectors were committed, Louis jumped toward Tunesmith's chair.

One of these chairs *had* to be a stepping disk. It was a natural hiding place. Two would be redundant, though all three had been made too thick and too wide—and Tunesmith would have claimed the right one. But other stepping disks in this room had to be guarded. If Louis was right—and he was, because Hanuman instantly launched himself toward the same chair.

Hanuman got there first. The chair started to swing aside, but Louis was there. Hanuman caught Louis with a powerful kick, but Louis had the mass. He slammed

Hanuman into the stepping disk and reached around the dazed hominid to pop the rim and turn the disk on. They both flicked out.

Heel of the hand, a blow to Hanuman's head. Hanuman went limp. Louis pushed, sent him flying. Grinding pain in his hip: Hanuman's kick had broken something.

They were underground, somewhere beneath Mars. He popped the disk's rim and tapped controls, *fast*.

Louis flicked in, popped the rim. If Tunesmith tracked him to this sandy, barren island—or Hanuman signaled him a minute or two from now—he'd find Louis's footprints, hours old. He might even find scent traces of Wembleth and Roxanny.

And if Teela's genes were lucky, Wembleth and Roxanny and their child would be well out of Tunesmith's reach by now. But *every* surviving gene pattern is *insanely* lucky, and Teela's luck didn't matter a tanj to Tunesmith. What mattered was this:

Louis Wu could never give a dispassionate, trustworthy answer to Tunesmith's questions while he could shade his answers to favor his bloodline.

One more move. Louis tapped controls, then hit #, and flicked out.

In the crew quarters aboard *Hot Needle of Inquiry*, Louis rapidly typed up a bleu cheese and mushroom omelet and a salad. He stripped off his pressure suit, then his clothes. He dialed up a falling jumper and put it on. He turned on the shower just long enough to wet the bag. He half-expected to hear the Puppeteer's Voice, but it didn't come.

He flicked into the cargo bay. A flycycle would have been too big, but he typed up a flying belt modified for magnetic lift. He ate most of his salad and omelet while he waited, a hairy four minutes, for the flying belt to be built. Put it on, flicked back to crew quarters.

Now, where would a puppeteer hide a stepping disk? An escape hatch had to be here: the Hindmost might find himself trapped in crew quarters by a man and a Kzin. The toilet seat? Too small. The shower?

The shower *ceiling*. It was the right size. The code would be puppeteer music: Louis could never sing it. Maybe he could hack it, but first—

He set his hands against the shower ceiling and said, "Hindmost's Voice, put me through."

He was in the control room. He used the stepping disk there.

Neither Hanuman nor Louis was where the first flick had taken them. The second flick put Tunesmith and Proserpina on a barren island. They found Hanuman groggy, trying to sit up. Proserpina examined him. He didn't seem badly hurt.

Tunesmith asked, "How are you?"

"Injured, not badly. He held my life and released it," Hanuman said.

"That shows good self-control. Proserpina, see if you can find traces of your escaped guests. Hanuman, rest." Tunesmith went to work on the stepping-disk controls.

"I find their scent," Proserpina called. "Falans old. In rut."

"This changes all," Hanuman said. "I must warn my people."

"Your people are tree dwellers! How can they hide from what must come?"

"Stet. I know what to do."

"Do it after we're gone," Tunesmith said. "Then rejoin us in Meteor Defense." He and Proserpina flicked out.

Launch Room. Little Hanging People protectors were all lying prone about the cavern below Mons Olympus. The Hindmost was working on a laser projector. "How are you doing?" Louis called.

"I'm still disconnecting instruments. It's hard to tell where it's safe."

Louis began disconnecting laser and cable attachments, pacifying Tunesmith's instruments where necessary. He wished he could move faster. Something with sharp edges was loose in his hip; the flesh was badly swollen. "You're not safe on the Ringworld," he said. "How are you going to move the 'doc components?"

"I hadn't decided."

"I was hoping you'd think of something. Stet. This next part is risky." Louis finished disconnecting sensors. The 'doc's components were still connected to each other. Louis left them that way. "I'll be gone at least an hour. Get this stuff ready to be lifted with magnetic fields. Leave the roof open."

"Wait. What are you about to do?"

"No time."

"Where are the protectors we're robbing? What can I accomplish when death may find me in a moment? Tell me what you've *done*!"

Better if he knew, and Louis had already cost himself an hour at least. Give the Hindmost a minute. He said, "I tried to tell Tunesmith that the Fringe War is about to blow up—"

"Eee!" A raucous chord of dismay.

"—Just as I'm telling you. If you tuck your heads under you, you will die in that position. Do you believe me?"

"Yah."

"I let Tunesmith guess I had a child—yes, a boy with Teela's genes. Congratulations, they survived. Your breeding program is still in force—"

"What of later inbreeding?"

"Oh, Hindmost, there must have been other ships crashed on the Ringworld. Wembleth's children will find mates."

"Stet."

"I flicked out to a few places, ended where Tunesmith

can find traces of Wembleth. Then I used my block on the stepping disk and went to *Needle*. It won't take Tunesmith long to get around the block. When he does, he'll find out I went to *Hot Needle of Inquiry*, took my sweet time there, and didn't leave.

"I must be still aboard. I went to get Wembleth, right? It follows that we're trying to leave the Ringworld. The Fringe War balance must be ready to fall apart *right now*. No protector would otherwise risk his child's life this way, in a ship that can be shot down by Fringe War ships or blocked as easily as Tunesmith can block *Needle*.

"If Tunesmith and Proserpina followed that line of logic, then they're getting ready to end the Fringe War, and they will not disturb us here, as long as you keep these protectors asleep and take care to shut down these cameras. Can do?"

"Trust me," the Hindmost said.

Louis took a moment to think that over. The Hindmost knew how to open the roof into Mons Olympus. *Long Shot* was too big to launch using the linear cannon, so the ship would rise slowly, on fusion jets, making too good a target. The Hindmost wouldn't have the nerve, and it was far too dangerous anyway.

So he wouldn't launch without Louis, Louis could trust him, and that settled *that*. Louis flicked out.

Meteor Defense. "We never did *locate* the ship," Tunesmith said. "Can you block his takeoff?"

"Yes. And I can search near space for any ARM ship coming for him. He can't possibly escape me. He must be mad. A failed transition to protector can warp a breeder's brain."

"Sudden understanding can do that too. Mad with fear?"

"But is he afraid of the Fringe War, or of what we'll do?"

Proserpina's eyes half-closed. She looked a little like

Hanuman in that pose. She said, "He didn't expect to delay us long. He'd have just enough time to get clear, if we begin now and ignore Louis Wu and his freemother child."

Tunesmith looked up at the crowded sky. "Begin," he commanded.

Hanuman flicked in on a ridge of bare scrith. He looked down across miles and miles of forest, reviewing his options.

Louis Wu was the protector who had no children on the Ringworld—*unless* he'd had a child by Teela Brown. Louis-protector could have no interest in Teela, who was dead, *unless* she'd left a child; and that child would be Louis Wu's. The chain of logic was so straightforward that even a Hanging People protector could follow it.

Tunesmith had seen it in a moment. And in that moment, Louis Wu had gone to rescue his child and get him to safety.

It followed that the Ringworld's death was likely and immediate. Tunesmith would act.

And what now? Hanuman's people were tree dwellers! They didn't have minds; they couldn't follow instructions even if he had any to give. How was he to hide them from the sky?

Wish for a rainstorm?

Find and fetch Teela Brown's lucky child, bring the creature here, *then* wish for a rainstorm?

Hanuman decided.

He detached a float plate from the depleted service stack. He stayed above the forest, enjoying the scents of thousands of his people below the canopy. Brothers, sisters, N-children. He did not dip down to see them. There wouldn't be time.

Tunesmith would move immediately. Where a treetop blocked the sun, already Hanuman could see a glitter to the shadow squares. Power was being beamed down.

He settled his disk on raddled earth. A few Burrowing People emerged. He spoke to them.

"You must stay underground for two days. For you this is easy. Do not watch the sky. Spread the word as far as you can, but be underground before shadow hides the sun.

"There will be lights beyond your experience. Do not look at the sky until the light fades. Afterward the sky will be very dark. Go spin-and-port to where you will find Hanging People. Help them. They are mine, and they will have gone mad."

21

IN FLIGHT

Penultimate's Palace. Louis flicked in and rolled off the burnt stack of float plates. Nothing fired on him.

The flying belt took him out and down. He skimmed above the yellow lawn, wondering at the black markings. One pattern must be the Penultimate's name or portrait . . . there, traces of a cartoon, very simplified, a style weirdly reminiscent of William Rotsler. The other would be speech.

He had guesswork for a Rosetta Stone. What would a protector say to an invader? That might be a pictograph pun: a word you could read as "Enter" or "Extinct"; "Greetings" or "Epitaph." Could you extrapolate a language from that?

Nah.

Louis flew low, enjoying the skill it took to weave between trees. Maybe they'd conceal him if Proserpina came looking for him on her own turf. (Nah. She had his scent.) Hard turns and high gees and a brief freedom from intellectual problems.

Proserpina's sunfish ship rested among the trees near

Proserpina's base. Lesser trees had grown up through the gridwork. Louis set the flying belt behind a thick trunk, stripped off his falling jumper, and left that too. He made his way forward on foot. *See the naked, limping breeder.*

Here was the ARM 'doc from *Gray Nurse*. Louis wondered what the diagnostic readings would say about him. Mutated? Not human? Dying? He walked past it without a pause. No time!

He stopped by *Snail Darter*'s library. *No time*, but protectors didn't always have a choice.

He'd watched Claus and Roxanny work this device. It wasn't hard to persuade it to summon up a roster for the Fringe War fleet. There were dozens of Wu, and six Harmony: his first daughter had married a Harmony. An ID number sequence would identify his line of descent—

A grandson and his daughter had joined the Navy decades ago. Wes Carlton Wu was Flight Captain aboard *Koala*, a lurker ship, with Tanya Haynes Wu as Purser. Another quick pass found no other blood relatives, and time was shrinking.

Louis approached the sunfish ship.

Think like a Pak. A protector might kill any breeder who smelled wrong, to leave more space for her own breeders. But you're Proserpina. Accommodation has been your survival for a million years. You don't want to hurt a breeder. It might be some powerful enemy's N-child!

There were no steps up to the cabin. Louis climbed up like a Hanging Person.

It was roomy inside. There were handgrips everywhere, and footgrips: just how prehensile were Proserpina's toes? And sensors and touchpads and toggles and levers, randomly placed. There was a horseshoe of couch, but only one control chair, and it would not fit Louis. He'd have to change it—but he'd better give some thought to convincing the ship he was Proserpina.

Louis was disappointed in the Hindmost. He had

steered the destiny of a species whose tools and learning beggared mankind's. Why couldn't he move a few kilotons of medical equipment? It would have saved Louis considerable trouble and two or three hours' time.

Maybe the Experimentalist faction on the Fleet of Worlds was more like New Orleans' traditional Fool King. Set them going, but watch them. Turn them off when they do something excessively expensive or dangerous. Sometimes they'll do something worthwhile—

He was getting distracted.

Thou shalt have no Proserpinas before me. She'd have set defenses to prevent a protector from manipulating the ship. Unless—would Proserpina really set a death trap for someone like Tunesmith, acknowledged as brighter and more dangerous than Proserpina herself? Retaliation could be terminal.

And what about protector slaves? This chair looked like it had been altered to fit a Hanging Person, then adjusted for Proserpina again. Hey, she must have let Hanuman fly it!

Futz! The ship wasn't defended. She *was* the defense. Who would dare steal Proserpina's ship?—and that was the point: *risk* for Louis Wu was *do nothing*. He adjusted the chair and sat down, strapped himself in, and lifted.

Trees had grown into the ship's metal lacework. They tore loose. Louis lofted the ship above the atmosphere, then turned toward the rim wall.

Was the sun starting to roil? He'd burn his eyes out if he looked hard. There must be a way to dim the glass, right? And Tunesmith would have the meteor defense going. Louis zigzagged his path a bit, and studied the controls. Here?

It didn't just darken the view; it was light-amplification too. He turned it very dark, and looked up.

A solar prominence was reaching out and out.

Louis jogged the ship at high gees. The ground flared below him. He could see the beam tracking and avoid it, even guide it a little to miss a populated spill mountain, and then he was off the Ringworld and dropping, easing back and under the Ringworld floor.

He had to follow the arc halfway around, three hundred million miles. Now the nontrivial danger was alien ships. Louis zigged along the magnet grid, accelerating hard, hearing a *toc, toc* of multimolecule-sized cameras hitting the skin of the ship. The Fringe War would be after him soon enough.

Something flashed on the Ringworld's underside. Louis zagged almost into another flash. Maybe he'd started a war himself.

Tunesmith's Meteor Reweaving System had closed Fist-of-God. Louis came up around the rim instead. He made for the Map of Mars, a little over half a million miles away. The sun was roiling again.

A spark struck upward: a launch from Mons Olympus. Louis slid the sunfish ship beneath the path of the meteor package, just for a moment. Tunesmith wouldn't have set the meteor defense to fire on those! He slowed, descended through the crater, and set the ship to hover.

He crawled halfway out of the cabin and shouted down. "Hindmost! Close it!"

The crater's lid began to close.

Louis began to play with the sunfish ship's controls. The 'doc's Intensive Care Cavity rose, twirled in the air, and settled a bit jerkily into the bay in *Long Shot*. Then the Service Wall, trailing loose cables. Then other, smaller components. Then the lifeboat.

Then a tank Louis had identified earlier.

The puppeteer was shouting something. "—tied down?"

Louis settled the tank in with the rest of the 'doc. He brought the sunfish ship down and got out.

The Hindmost came trotting up. He asked, "How will you tie these components against shock of takeoff?"

"Tunesmith was using a tank of foam plastic. Let's set it going and close the ship up, then board."

The tank was spraying foam plastic as Louis closed the lid on it. He'd taken the pilot's seat without comment. Hey, it was built for humans. The Hindmost asked, "Shouldn't we open the crater again?"

"Hindmost, let's try something else." He activated the hyperdrive. The cavern disappeared. The Q2 ship launched itself straight down into a boil of colors.

Map of Earth. Shortly after nightfall Acolyte begged audience with Chmeee.

One of the guards said, "Play elsewhere, child. Your father is busy." And grinned.

"I bear a message from Tunesmith."

"An odd name."

"Chmeee will know it. Tunesmith who lives under the Map of Mars."

The guard was bored, and he toyed with Acolyte a bit longer. Then he went into the tent. When he came out, he asked, "How did it come, this message?"

"There were flashes of light from the mountains to starboard."

Acolyte was allowed entrance. He groveled before his father, who asked, "Is this the Tunesmith who wants to give me the Map of Earth? I've heard nothing since you delivered his message."

"He says you may take the Map yourself, after the other prides have gone mad."

It had gone quiet: Chmeee's courtiers were paying attention.

Chmeee asked, "Mad?" and studied his son, whose subservience seemed laid over a whiplash eagerness. "Lecture me, then."

"Tunesmith instructs us to hide ourselves from the sky for two full days. We must be under a roof or tent, all of us, even females and kits. We should sleep if we can. We must all be under cover, or blindfolded, before shadow reveals the sun."

"So soon? How shall I manage that?"

Acolyte dared to grin. "What would Louis Wu say?"

" 'That's why I get the big money.' What is to happen to the sky?"

"That was not told. You have seen ships leaving tracks of light across the sky. You have heard talk of the Fringe War. I watched it in Tunesmith's Meteor Defense Room. It is told that Tunesmith will end the war."

Chmeee nodded. "Are you ready to run? It is well." His voice rose to a bellow. "All in my hearing, you are each an emissary to my far provinces! Divide the contents of my kitchen to feed yourselves. Go where I send you. Carry a blindfold ready to use. You will know when to use it. Fools will go blind or mad.

"You are each more valuable than those you will speak to, and you will be under cover before the shadow square passes. Two days hidden, or answer to me. The rest of us may conquer the Map of Earth if we so choose."

The boy Kazarp was gazing open-mouthed at the sky. Shadow had covered the sun, but the shadow squares were glittering in a way he'd never seen. Presently he raised his instrument and began to play.

Over the music he heard a stealthy shift in posture, too close for any stranger, and he said, "I knew you were there."

"Don't turn around. I am become Vashneesht."

His father had disappeared falans ago, and now this: a thing out of fantasy, awesome and terrible. Kazarp didn't turn. "Father? Does mother know?"

"You must tell her. Tell her gently. Then tell her she must hide from the sky for two days, and you too, for fear of going mad. Spread the word. A burrow would be better than a roof. Afterward there is a world of mad folk to care for, and far more feasting than our folk will ever want."

"Will you stay?"

"Not now. I will visit when I can."

Long Shot's cabin was at the bottom of the sphere, between four fusion-drive nostrils. In hyperdrive *Long Shot* flew ass-backward into the unknown. Louis launched straight down, into and through the Ringworld floor—feeling a touch of drag from the superdense scrith—and out into space.

He was moving away from the sun and straight into the thickest gathering of Fringe War ships. Not that that mattered. Those ships were all in Einstein space, this close to a large mass. Louis was flying blind, of course, through hyperspace. What he hoped was that this faster ship would outrun the eaters.

The puppeteer was wound into a tight knot. *He* wouldn't be of much help.

How fast would *Long Shot* move near this great a mass? He'd wondered if it would even exceed lightspeed. Tunesmith might have worked out the QII system's behavior, but Louis didn't have enough clues. He'd learn soon enough. When the crystal sphere that was the mass detector began working, he'd be outside the "singularity."

Eleven hours later, Louis knew that even protectors could grow tired. He could ignore that, and hunger and thirst, and pain in guts and joints, headache and sinus ache, that properly belong only to an aging savage. It didn't matter. He'd got clear of the Ringworld. Of thirty trillion Ringworld hominids, a fat percentage would survive. Wembleth and Roxanny and their child were lost in noise. If Tunesmith worked out what they truly were, he wouldn't even search. With luck, though, he'd think Louis had taken Wembleth to the stars.

Winning could compensate for a lot of pain.

The window was the floor, and it would darken, light-amplify, record and display recordings, or zoom. Louis watched flow patterns of colored light, and a dark comma zipping past.

He saw the view change. The window wasn't there: his eyes slid around it.

Louis looked at the mass detector. There should have been lines of light crawling toward him. Nothing showed. It was just doped crystal.

Louis hit the cutoff.

He saw showers of stars. The universe was wide and beautiful below his feet. He was in Einstein space.

It would have pleased him to sell *Long Shot* to some band of freebooters in human space. Or form his own! Now that looked unlikely. Louis set the window to zoom, then darkened it a little against the zodiacal glare. The Ringworld eclipsed the sun except for a tiny sliver of light.

Six light-hours from Ringworld system—he measured it—the sun wouldn't light up *Long Shot* very much, but putting the ship in the Ringworld's shadow would leave it black as space. He hadn't used fusion motors at all: nobody would find him via neutrino flux. The rest of the electromagnetic spectrum might reveal him to the Fringe War if they happened to look. Louis thought they'd be too busy for that. They'd hunt for Proserpina's sunfish ship until something more interesting happened . . . real soon now.

The rec room above was as tiny as the cabin below, but there was a game-room wall, a food dispenser, and a shower bag. He noticed also the hatch in the ceiling. That was new. It led into a maze of man-wide access tubes he could see through the wall. They were hard to follow, a neat puzzle, but one led to the storage room where he had stowed the lifeboat and autodoc. *Good.*

He took time for a shower. Hey, if he missed the event, *Long Shot* would catch the light wave further out.

Nothing had changed when he'd dried himself. He sank his fingers in the Hindmost's mane and dodged a hind leg kick—almost. "Wake," he said.

"Did I hurt you?"

"Doesn't matter."

"Why are we at rest?"

"I want to watch something. Also, I can't use the mass detector."

"Eee!" the Hindmost whistled.

"It's a psionics device. You'll have to fly the ship yourself. But we're loose, everyone I love is safe, the Fringe War won't be looking for us, and the way lies clear to Canyon."

"To Canyon?"

"Well, or the Fleet of Worlds, if you like. I just assumed you'd brought your mate and children with you when you left the Fleet."

"Of course."

"If we can work out details, there's something I need."

"You're bluffing, Louis, as you did once before. You're dying, aren't you?"

"Yah. I was too twisted up when tree-of-life started to change me. I'm dying, stet, but not bluffing. Everything's worked out fine. But I'd be pleased if we could get Carlos Wu's autodoc running again."

"That would take . . . mmm."

"Considerable trouble. Hard physical labor. What can I offer you?"

"*Long Shot* moves too fast. Collision with some star is nearly certain. I don't have the nerve to fly us to Home."

"Not Canyon?"

"Home," said the puppeteer. "I didn't think I could hide us on Canyon. Too small. Home is very like Earth, Louis, and has a wonderful history."

"Home it is," Louis said agreeably. "Hey." The magnified sun glared, etching the control room with sharp-edged shadows.

The puppeteer turned one head, then both. The pupils irised nearly shut. His voice was a monotone: the Hindmost was upset. "Where is the Ringworld?"

"Yah."

"Yah?"

"Yah. Tunesmith used nanotechnology to change the entire superconductor grid to the configuration he found in *Long Shot*. He's off like a bunny under Quantum II hyperdrive, and he took the Ringworld with him."

"How far?"

"What?" But this was the only ship that could catch it. A little more than two thirty-hour days at Quantum II hyperdrive . . . a light year in 5/4 minutes . . . "Three thousand light years before Tunesmith runs out of power. That's *way* out of human space. Telescopes won't see anything for a hundred generations. You might catch that much mass shifting around with a gravity-wave detector. What were you going to do, chase it down?"

"The wealth," mourned the Hindmost. "All gone. I lost my place as Hindmost chasing the Ringworld's wealth of knowledge. And those you spoke of, those you love, Louis, what of them?"

"I'll never find them. Hindmost, that's the point. Now let's fix that autodoc before something intimate tears loose inside me."

"I think we can ignore the tidal effect," Tunesmith said. "Don't you?"

Proserpina's fingers danced. The wall display—which showed nothing, a kind of curdled gray everywhere—went black. White hieroglyphs danced across it in a Pak mathematical system millions of falans old. "The sun's gravity pulled up and a bit inward along a very narrow angle, when the Ringworld had a sun. With the sun gone," she said, "all the seas will tend to flow toward the rim walls. We're in flight for two days? Stet, that's negligible. What I'm worried about," hieroglyphs danced again, "is the approach."

The sky had gone crazy. Roxanny and Wembleth wriggled out of the tent, Roxanny a little clumsy, and stared into a light-show that would have won awards. Wembleth asked, "What is happening?"

"I swear I have no idea. Some supersecret weapon. Futz, I hope it isn't Kzinti. I don't see any ships at all, unless—what was that?" A little black comma fell wiggling across the sky, starboard to port. It left a pockmark near the top of the rim wall, visible through mag specs.

"I don't know," Wembleth said.

"A ship bigger than *Long Shot*? No species *I* know makes one."

"It's changing again, Roxanny."

For an instant the colors faded, and then the whole *sky* was gone, and they were both blind.

It was hard to remember that there had once been sight. "It's the Blind Spot," she said. Roxanny had been trained: she looked at her feet. Yes, there they were. "Futz, I can't believe it. We're in futzy hyperdrive! Look down. Lower your—" Wembleth was wandering off, still blind. Roxanny followed him and, still without looking up, felt her way up his body and tilted his head down.

"Let's get into the tent," she said.

They lived in the pressure tent for two days. When they had a sky again, it was stars glaring on black. "This is going to drive a lot of your people crazy," Roxanny said. "The Ringworld was never this dark. The headlights on the flycycle are going to be priceless."

"I never saw stars so bright," Wembleth said. "It's a whole new age, Roxanny. You said there are Ball Worlds around most stars? They could be our children's inheritance."

One bright star was growing brighter above the portward rim wall.

The sky had returned to the Meteor Defense wall display.

Proserpina said, "We'll have to find us a sun, stet? And shift the whole Ringworld sideways to get to it. The mag fields are useless without something to push against, so we'll be using just the attitude jets. Line up with a sun, fall toward it, use the fields to stop ourselves. The seas will shift, Tunesmith."

"I know. I've found a yellow-white star with nearly our own velocity. There, the bright one, do you see it?"

"Yes. Zoom."

The star expanded, and darkened. "Increased X-ray output in this region," she said. "We'll need to boost the ozone layer until we can build a shadow square system."

"Yes."

"I'm more worried about tides."

"Yes, there will still be stress on the seas and oceans."

"I thought of letting them freeze, but we can't. We—"

"Of course not, but we can use magnetic effects on the sun itself. Look, I found a way to skew our path so the star comes straight down the axis. We'll ring the sun. We'll bob a few times stabilizing ourselves; that sends the seas back and forth, not just all in one direction, which would be disastrous."

White hieroglyphs danced across the starscape. "It would work," Proserpina said. "We'll lose much of our population, even some species."

"I know."

"I have a request. Tell me if it's feasible."

"See if you can describe it."

"Leave the sun bobbing back and forth along the Ringworld axis. We'll get tides. We'll get seasons, changing weather."

"What, like a Ball World?" Tunesmith laughed. "Like your world, the Pak world. What about breeders? Won't they go crazier yet?"

"Anyone who kept his mind through these last two days will get used to anything," Proserpina said.

22

BREEDER

Louis Wu woke aflame with new life. Cautious in free fall, he waited for the coffin lid to move aside. A hologram Hindmost was looking down at him.

Louis wriggled out. "Nothing hurts."

"Good."

"I was used to it. Oh, futz, I've lost my mind!"

"Louis, didn't you know the machine would rebuild you as a breeder?"

"Yah, but . . . my head feels futzy. Full of cotton. I never felt so much *myself* as when I could think like a protector."

"We could have rebuilt the 'doc—"

"No. *No*." Fist against coffin lid. "I remember that much. I have to be a breeder, or dead. If I'm a protector, I *will* track down Wembleth and Roxanny, and Tunesmith and Proserpina *will* follow me."

"But they would certainly protect your blood line."

"They would, yes. But if Wembleth is loose on the Ringworld, his luck . . . hey."

"You don't believe in Teela Brown's luck."

"I didn't. But when I was a protector . . . it's not good science, stet? Because it's not falsifiable. But look at the pattern. He stole my woman, stet? She fell into his lap. The only woman in reach who could make Wembleth young again, and bear his children too. He's the only survivor of a village that died of asphyxiation, and he'd be dead if rescue hadn't fallen on him from interstellar space!"

"Louis! Teela wasn't lucky!"

"Stet, and Wembleth lost all his friends, and ended up a hunted refugee. What if it's the genes that are lucky?

Teela's genes want to reproduce. You can always argue either way.

"It could still be all moonbeams. Anything that doesn't make predictions that can be disproved isn't science. Maybe Teela was only a statistical fluke until we found her. After that, whatever happens to her, you can always explain it as luckier than something else that might have happened. Read *Candide*."

"I'll look it up."

"Unfalsifiable. If it's wrong, you can't prove it. When I was a protector, I didn't *dis*believe. Maybe Teela's children are the Ringworld's luck. If their location is uncertain, they protect the whole Ringworld. Basic quantum mechanics. And it's going to need that! They've all gone out into the universe at a minute and a quarter per light year—"

"Louis."

"What?"

"We haven't moved since you went into the 'doc, two months ago Earthtime. We're a warm spot on the sky. Sooner or later the Fringe War will notice us. What else has that heterogeneous mob got for entertainment but to track us down and take our ship?"

"Right." Louis climbed back through the maze of access tubes, getting lost once, guided by the puppeteer behind him. He set himself in the pilot's chair and jumped to hyperdrive. Radial lines indicating stars edged out of the mass detector, and Louis turned *Long Shot* toward Home.

FLEET OF
WORLDS

DRAMATIS PERSONAE

HUMANS / CREW OF *LONG PASS*

Diego MacMillan   *Navigator*
Jaime MacMillan   *Doctor*
Sayeed Malloum   *Engineer*
Barbara Nguyen   *Captain*

SOL-SYSTEM HUMANS

Sigmund Ausfaller   *Amalgamated Regional Militia (ARM) investigator*
Sangeeta Kudrin   *Senior executive at the United Nations*
Julian Forward   *Physicist (native of Jinx, in the Sirius system)*
Miguel Sullivan   *Racketeer*
Ashley Klein   *Racketeer*

CONCORDANCE COLONISTS / CREW OF *EXPLORER*

Kirsten Quinn-Kovacs   *Navigator and a math whiz*
Omar Tanaka-Singh   *Captain*
Eric Huang-Mbeke   *Engineer*

CONCORDANCE COLONISTS / OFFICIALS OF THE ARCADIA SELF-GOVERNANCE COUNCIL

Sven Hebert-Draskovics   *Colonial archivist*
Sabrina Gomez-Vanderhoff   *Governor*

Aaron Tremonti-Lewis   *Minister, Public Safety*
Lacey Chung-Philips   *Minister, Economics*

CONCORDANCE CITIZENS

Nessus   *Political officer on* Explorer; *Experimentalist
          neophyte*
Nike   *Deputy Minister, Foreign Affairs; Experimental-
         ist radical*
Eos   *Leader of out-of-power Experimentalist Party*
Hindmost / Sisyphus   *Leader of the government and
          the Conservative Party*
Baedeker   *Engineer at General Products Corporation*
Vesta   *Nike's senior aide*

FLEET OF WORLDS TIMELINE
(All dates in Earth-standard)

2095	Ice World begins its interstellar journey.
2197	*Long Pass* signals to the Ice World, spotted one light-year away.
2198	*Long Pass* is boarded.
2645	A supernovae chain reaction is discovered at the galaxy's core.
	The Fleet of Worlds begins its flight to safety.
2650	First expedition of *Explorer* to the Gw'oth world.
	In Known Space, UN authorities renew their search for the recently vanished Puppeteers.
	Political crises brew on Earth and Hearth.
	Colonists seek the truth about their past.
	And so: Many events, on several worlds, ensue.
2652	New Terra charts its own course.

PROLOGUE

Earth date: 2197

Long Pass crossed the sky in a series of shallow curves, because Diego MacMillan willed it so.

Interstellar space is not uniform. The tenuous interstellar medium isn't just a few atoms of hydrogen per cubic inch, forever. There are pockets of greater density, some thick enough to form strings of stars, given time. Between the dense patches there is nothing. A Bussard ramjet like *Long Pass,* which eats interstellar hydrogen and accelerates by spitting out fused helium, must coast between the denser clouds.

This is worse than it sounds. At any reasonable fraction of light speed, interstellar muck comes on like cosmic rays. As much as propulsion, a Bussard ramjet's purpose is to guide that lethal muck away from the life support system.

Every simulation run in Sol system had reached the same inconclusive conclusion: Course tweaking to exploit density fluctuations in the interstellar medium was "likely to be" unproductive. Between Sol and the target star the muck was thick enough. Sure, a course tweak might funnel a bit more hydrogen into the ramscoop *here,* but was it enough to compensate later? A slight diversion at these velocities took a heavy toll in kinetic energy. And what would you find when you reached the end of a detour? Maybe that was where the law of averages caught up with you, and the near-vacuum of interstellar gas became vacuum indeed.

Of course, flatlanders had built the models. Diego MacMillan had nodded noncommittally at their advice. Technically he was also a flatlander—spacers pinned that label on every Earthborn—but he had traveled across the solar system. Once *Long Pass* launched, whether he undertook the experiment was beyond their control.

The question had never before come up on a manned mission. *Long Pass* was experimental, a crew-rated ramscoop. In the abstract, Diego respected the mission planners' conservatism. The ship's failure could discredit the new technology for a long time.

Flatlanders! He and his wife were aboard. That was more than enough to keep him from taking foolish chances.

So *Long Pass* had followed its wobbly curves for decades now. Maybe he'd saved a few months' travel. That was okay. Studying the variations, plotting alternate courses, assessing probabilities—they kept him busy. What had the experts imagined the ship's navigator would *do* for decades?

They could never have imagined what, in his obsessive peering ahead, he would find.

"And to what do we owe this honor?" Captain Nguyen asked.

Meaning that by the current schedule Diego would normally be asleep. It was all he could do not to blurt out the answer. *One step at a time,* he told himself. "All will be revealed," he intoned with his best mock pretension.

The ship's population numbered just above ten thousand. Most were embryos, sharing the freezers with forty-three hibernating adult passengers. The crew numbered only four, between them covering three daily shifts. Together, they filled the ship's tiny dayroom.

He had arrived early to configure the claustrophobia-denying decor. Undulating, verdant forest, the Andean foothills of his youth, receded into the digital wallpaper. Fluffy clouds scudded across the brilliant blue sky glowing overhead—he had no use for the cave-parks his Belter crewmates thought normal. Leaves rustled and insects droned softly in surround sound. Most of one wall presented a well-remembered mountain lake on which a sleek, two-toned power boat cruised. Its hundred-horsepower inboard motor was throttled down to a barely audible purr.

Nothing, alas, could mask the ubiquitous odor of endlessly recycled air, nor could the rough-hewn planks projected from the dayroom table disguise the plasteel slickness beneath his fingers. He twiddled the cabin controls, tuning chirps and twitters down a notch, while his curious shipmates took coffee and snacks from the synthesizer.

Barbara Nguyen sat first. She had the tall, gangly frame of a Belter, and her head was shaved except for a cockatoolike Belter crest of thick black hair. She was their captain and the most cautious among them; which was cause and which effect remained stubbornly unclear to Diego. Throughout their hitherto uneventful voyage, she had let decisions emerge by consensus. With luck, consensus-seeking had become a habit.

Sayeed Malloum, their engineer, was taller still but stocky for a Belter. Each of them handled the tedium in his own way. Sayeed's latest affectation, dating back several weeks, involved dyeing his crest and disposable jumpsuit in matching colors. Today's hue was chartreuse, shading to deep yellow.

Jaime MacMillan, ship's doctor and Diego's wife of fifty years, slid into the last chair. She was built to earthly scale, nearly matching his six feet, but otherwise illustrated the old adage about opposites attracting. She was lithe while he was pot-bellied, blond where he was dark, and as fair as he was swarthy. Those were shipboard skin tones, of course. Flatlander full-body dye jobs and elaborate skin patterns had been left on far-off Earth.

Jaime slipped a hand beneath the tabletop to give his knee a reassuring pat, although not even she knew what he was about to reveal. With a start, he noticed she had printed her jumpsuit in Clan MacMillan tartan: another silent vote of confidence. How anxious did he seem?

Barbara cleared her throat. "Spill it, Diego. Why did you call everyone together?"

Oh, how the details and analyses, all the terabytes of specifics in his personal journal, yearned to be free. This was not the time. "Have a look." Above the picnic-table illusion he projected a navigational holo. Amid the scattered pink, orange-white, and yellow-white specks of the nearest stars, a brilliant green asterisk blinked: You are here. As his friends nodded recognition, he superimposed, in tints of faint gray, a delicate 3-D structure. Would they see it? "Density variations in the interstellar gas and dust."

Sayeed frowned, likely anticipating another pitch for rerouting the ship on one more just-a-bit-off-our-planned-course wrinkle in the void.

"You've shared density plots before. It's never involved much fanfare." Barbara eyed him shrewdly. "And you've never before struggled so hard not to bounce in your chair."

Words alone would not suffice—not for this, not with Belters. That was not a criticism. Growing up inside little rocks, they lacked the background. Diego said, "Jeeves, give us Boat One."

"On full throttle, sir, as you had specified." The virtual speedboat slewed until its stern faced them and the shore. With a roar, the boat's bow rose. A great vee-shaped wake formed. Diego tracked the boat as it receded, the ripples of its wake dwindling as they spread.

Sayeed's gaze flicked between the simulated lake and the 3-D graphic that still hung above the table. "There's a shock wave in the interstellar gas. A . . . a *bow* wave."

Barbara narrowed her eyes in concentration. "I concede the resemblance, but we're comparing two simulations. Diego, are you certain about the underlying data?"

It would be *so* easy to dive into minutiae about years of observations patiently culled and collated, about converting those observations from the ship's accelerating frame of reference to a stationary frame, about estimating and correcting for the perturbations of stellar winds. He could have discussed at length vain efforts to match his readings to the sky survey with which they had departed Sol system. He yearned to explain the extrapolation of the full pattern from the mere fraction so far glimpsed, even after so many years and light-years of observations.

He must have had a fanatical glint in his eye, because Jaime shot him the warning look that reminded: There's a fine line between scary-smart and just scary. Diego kept his response to a confident nod.

Barbara said, "I'll want to go through it later, step by step. No offense, just captain's prerogative."

"What could have made this bow wave?" Sayeed asked.

That was the right question. Diego started another simulation. A more nearly uniform background wash, modeled from a century-old survey, replaced the translucent ripples in the stellar display. "This is what we expected to encounter. And . . . now."

A new speck, this one bright violet, materialized in the holo. Gathering speed, it recreated the 3-D shock wave.

Jaime stood, squeezing behind his chair to study the image from another perspective. She poked a finger into the image. "Then whatever caused the waves is here?"

"Obviously, the simulation runs faster than real-time. I've given you no way to gauge the compression factor. The object producing the wake is moving at one-tenth cee, and we're nearly a light-year apart. To look at it, we aim"—Diego tweaked a program parameter, and a backward-extrapolated trajectory materialized—"where it *was*."

He linked their main telescope to the display. A dark sphere shimmered, faintly aglow in a false-color substitution for IR. Mountain peaks and hints of continental outlines peered out from beneath an all-encompassing blanket of ices.

Sayeed leaned forward to read annotations floating above the globe. "An Earth-sized world. At one point, it *was* Earthlike, its oceans and atmosphere since frozen. It's a bit warmer than the interstellar background, which is why we can detect it, perhaps leakage from a radioactive core. And somehow, you say, it's racing by at one-tenth light speed. How can that be?"

Barbara shook her head, setting her crest to bobbing. "A fair question, but I have a more basic one. Diego, you might have *begun* by showing us what you'd found. Why didn't you?"

"Because this isn't about an out-of-place planet. I need you to accept the years of observation and the model that showed us where to look." Diego took a deep breath. Would they believe? "They prove that that world has been accelerating steadily at 0.001 gee.

"*Someone* is moving it—someone who controls technology we can't even imagine."

"Are you awake?"

Diego was reasonably certain he'd been prodded in the ribs to assure a positive response. "Uh-huh," he answered groggily. "What's on your mind?"

Propped up on an elbow, long hair looking stirred from tossing and turning, Jaime stared at him. "Are we doing the right thing?"

For days, the four of them had gone around and around on this. Even Nguyen had come over. The big day was *tomorrow*.

But decisions feel different in the dark. "Jeeves, lights to quarter bright," he told the onboard computer. It had the good judgment to comply without speaking. "Hon, we've all agreed. We can't let Earth decide! They're almost fifteen light-years away. Whether they signal the aliens directly—which they wouldn't, since there's no guarantee the planet won't change course in the meanwhile—or they tell us to proceed, that'd be nearly a thirty-year delay.

What does *that* do for us?" Despite himself, a yawn interrupted his response.

Then she surprised him. "That's not what I meant. Maybe we shouldn't contact them at all. What if they're . . . hostile?"

That brought him fully awake. Ascribing violent intent was a good way to get sent for medical help—but aboard this ship, *she* was the medical help. "Advanced civilizations are peaceful," he said cautiously.

"I know." She raked a hand, fingers splayed, through her mussed hair. "War was a societal psychosis. With the resources of a solar system at our disposal, and with Fertility Boards to keep population levels under control, there's been peace for more than a century. We left behind violence with the era of scarcity that the mentally ill used to excuse it." The words came out like the secular catechism that they were. "They"—no antecedent was needed—"move entire worlds. How could they possibly covet the resources humans administer?"

She was shivering! Sitting up, he put an arm around her. "Then why are you worried?"

She snuggled against him. "Because aliens must surely *be* alien. Can we presume to predict their social development?"

"Can we presume to decide for mankind *not* to try contacting them? We're almost a light-year apart. We're moving at thirty percent cee. The ice world is moving at ten percent cee, and accelerating. Contacting them by comm laser already requires extrapolation and faith. Deferring to Earth could mean losing the opportunity." He kissed the top of her head.

"We're not making this decision only for ourselves," she said softly.

He said, "There's a reason our computers, like every starship's computers, carry the UN's standard First Contact protocol. Sending us off with the protocol means the UN recognized we might have to—"

"I mean our children." She shifted into a sitting position, careful not to dislodge his arm. "Diego, they may be only frozen specks, two among thousands, but the decision we've made affects them."

The children they were permitted only by leaving Sol system behind. "I think companionship in the universe will be a wondrous gift for them."

For a long while, the omnipresent hum of fans was the only sound. Then she said, "I might be worried about nothing. There may be no answer to our signal. Some unknown natural phenomenon could explain that planet's movements." She squeezed his hand. "The first extraterrestrial intelligence or a brand-new cosmic force. Either way, you've made one heck of a discovery."

If its acceleration was constant, the ice world had taken about a century to reach its current velocity. In that time, it would have crossed a bit over five light-years. A red-dwarf star lay more-or-less in its backtracked direction, at about that distance. One of its worlds, a gas giant alongside which Jupiter would seem puny, had a separation in its satellite system, a gap at odds with the accepted theory of planetary formation. "It could be a natural phenomenon," Diego agreed.

But he didn't believe that.

The normal course of shipboard events was that there were none. One could get very bored, even at full cruising speed, between encounters with significantly sized dust motes. Every excuse for a celebration was quickly embraced.

Four birthdays and New Year's Day (despite Diego's railing at the pointlessness of commemorating a random spot on the orbit of an increasingly remote planet) left long stretches of mind-dulling routine.

The liquid in Diego's glass was undeniably of that morning's vintage. "Jeeves, did you *taste* this stuff?"

"Harmless," the Jeeves program said. "Mostly harmless."

"Good enough," and Diego raised his glass. Fine wine would significantly overtax the synthesizer's capabilities. Today the four of them celebrated something *real*. Ice World, months ago promoted to proper-noun status, should now have received the first-contact greeting lased more than a year earlier. Should . . . for such a simple word, it conveyed a satisfying and very newfound conclusiveness. They had signaled to where they projected the distant, speeding planet would be—if it continued without interruption on its steady course and acceleration.

It had.

A miniature Ice World, unanimous choice for the party's décor, glittered above the dayroom table. Months of continuous observation had yielded details far beyond the crude holo he had first shown his shipmates.

His shipmates. With a start, and to Jaime's knowing smile, he returned his attention to the party. "To new friends!" Glasses clinked, contents sloshing a little, and were enthusiastically emptied.

Sayeed shrugged. In the steadfastness of the Ice World's hurtling trajectory, which three of them saw as evidence of intelligent intervention, he saw a mindless, if unknown, natural force. On one point all agreed: At least one of them was spectacularly wrong. Long after the discovery of pulsars, astronomers still remembered the hasty misattribution of the celestial rhythms to aliens. None of *them* planned to be forever remembered for announcing imagined aliens—or for failing to recognize real ones.

"In another year-plus. Two if they ponder and muse for a while about how to respond." Barbara poured another round of the *vin* très *ordinaire*. "I wonder what, still assuming someone *is* there, they will have to say."

Any alcohol is potable by the third serving. The day was special; they imbibed enough of today's wine to render it superb. Eventually, they had Jeeves draw virtual straws. Jaime lost. She was taking a very strong stim when the rest of them headed to bed.

The voice of Jeeves brought Diego instantly awake. "All hands to the bridge!"

He burst through the cabin door shouting, "What happened?"

Barbara beat him onto the bridge, but only because her cabin was closer. He and Sayeed were left to loiter anxiously in the corridor. The bridge couldn't accommodate them all.

"Radar pulse hit us." Jaime's chair spun as she relinquished it to the captain. "There's nothing on our sensors."

"Jeeves, alarms off." The warbling screech mercifully faded. Barbara settled into her seat and triggered a ping. Above a monitoring console, a spherical volume grew and grew: the representation of the space probed by that pulse. "Nothing," she finally concluded. She downed the stim pills Jaime offered. "That's as it should be. We must have a flaky sensor."

Diego nodded jerkily. *They couldn't have reached us.*

A new alarm blared. Parallel rows of floor lights blinked, painfully bright, their sudden manic cycling drawing Diego's attention down the curved corridor. Emergency hatches slammed; the siren and the whooshing stopped. "Hull breach in storage bay D," Barbara said. "Check that out, Sayeed."

Diego's head pounded. He dry-swallowed the pills Jaime now offered him. The alarms resumed, joined by the windstorm of a second breach aft. Something was poking holes in their ship. What, if nothing were nearby, had breached the hull? They were moving at thirty percent of light speed. What could possibly overtake the ship from behind? *Light speed! They couldn't have reached us!*

"Jaime! Trade places."

They squeezed past each other and he dropped into the lone chair beside the captain. Radar, lidar, maser—the instruments reported nothing, regardless of the frequency they sent.

Oh.

"Barbara, let's just *look*. No active sensors, just Mark I eyeballs." She spared him a sideways glance—light-years from the nearest sun, what could he expect to see, and how? But she did as he proposed.

The exterior cameras spun with the hull. Computers compensated for the gravity-simulating rotation, projecting a stationary star field onto the bridge. The stars behind were reddened and dimmed; the stars ahead flared, visibly shifted toward blue. And to one side: a large, circular patch of pitch-blackness. Whatever blocked the starlight was huge, or close, or both. Its immobile appearance meant it was orbiting them, matching the ship's rotation.

"What the tanj *is* that?" Barbara focused their radar and lidar on the apparition. "Still no return signals. The echoes are being nulled somehow."

"They're—" Jaime bit it off, but Diego could finish it for her. *They're poking holes in our ship!* Enemy aliens. She thought they were under attack.

"Sayeed, report." Diego's words echoed from speakers across the ship. There was no answer.

Another alarm. More wind rushing from the bridge. More emergency bulkheads slammed shut. "I'm on it." Jaime's voice quavered as she dashed off.

There was precious little privacy in the *Long Pass;* by mutual agreement, the corridor cameras had been powered down early in the mission. Muttering under his breath, Diego hunted for the command sequences to awaken them. The first reactivations came a tantalizing few moments late. Was that shadow disappearing around a corner Sayeed's? Jaime's?

One more ear-piercing alarm and again sudden wind

tugged at his clothes. This alarm, too, faded as Barbara reset it. What was that scurrying sound?

"Pressure continues to drop throughout the ship. I'm closing all interior hatches," announced the main bridge computer.

"Thank you, Jeeves. Give us the corridor cameras."

At last they were all on. Diego cursed as one revealed Sayeed, crumpled and motionless, face down on the deck.

Black, many-limbed figures scuttled past the camera at a nearby corridor intersection, moving too fast for Diego to integrate what he was seeing into a meaningful picture. Aliens, or robots, or alien robots. . . .

Barbara had seen it, too. "We've been boarded."

The bridge hatch burst inward before he could respond. There was a brief glimpse of serpentine limbs, an impression of something pointing at him, and a nearly subsonic vibration.

Then there was only darkness.

EXILE

Earth date: 2650

1

Alone in his cabin, behind a triply locked hatch, within a vessel constructed from the most impenetrable material ever made, light-years removed from any conceivable hazard, Nessus cowered.

"Nessus" was a label of convenience. His actual name, Citizen speech requiring two throats for proper articulation, was unpronounceable by his crewmates on the opposite side of the sturdy hatch. He had once overheard an irreverent Colonist remark that his true name sounded like an industrial accident set to music.

Curled into a ball, heads tucked safely inside, Nessus saw and heard nothing. He unclenched only enough to breathe. The herd pheromones continuously circulating in the ship's air would eventually calm him. Meanwhile, surely, his anxiety was appropriate.

How could he *not* panic? He represented a trillion of his kind. Only the merest fraction of the Concordance could bear to take leave of the home world. Yet here, by his own initiative, he was—because the alternative, for all of the trillion, was even more unthinkable.

The panic attack ebbed, and a head emerged for a peek. Sensors hidden throughout the ship reported that conditions remained normal. His three Colonist crew were unaware of or properly respectful to his mood. Two were within their respective cabins, one softly snoring; the last stood watch on the bridge.

Had he truly thought: normal? Normality existed only on Hearth, in the time-tested rhythms of life, amid the teeming multitudes of his kind.

He rolled once more into a tight, quivering orb. Without

radical changes and much luck, everything *normal* was doomed.

You never saw hyperspace; quite the opposite. The brain refused to acknowledge that a dimension so strange could exist. Objects all around a cabin window somehow came together, the mind denying the nothingness between. You covered the window, but a coat of paint or a scrap of fabric only taunted you that oblivion lurked behind. You had to get used to hyperspace, and some never did. Hyperspace had driven many people mad.

Kirsten Quinn-Kovacs, alone on the bridge, studiously ignored the covered view port. There was much else to do, and much more to occupy her thoughts. Everything was new and wondrous. Merely to be aboard was a tremendous honor.

At every moment, the strangeness of it all threatened to overwhelm her.

The bridge of *Explorer* was a chimera, a superposition of improbable parts. Chimera: The word itself was a fanciful novelty, describing a fantasy creature. Nessus had taught it to her, claiming to have learned it on an alien world far, far away.

What could be more improbable than that *she* was on her way to study an unexplored alien planet? Though there was little chance she would set foot on that new world, this trip was an amazing opportunity. Except as a passenger or on training flights, always within sight of the Fleet of Worlds, no Colonist had been on a space ship— until now.

She stretched and her crash couch stretched with her. Whoever had built it truly understood Colonist physiology. The flight and navigation controls within her reach were likewise comfortable and intuitive. The General Products company knew their stuff. It amazed her that *Explorer* was only a prototype.

The other seat on the bridge, a padded bench, was as

clearly meant for Nessus. The console before Kirsten had its analog near that empty couch. She could, in a crisis, interpret those other instruments; she could barely operate those controls. Her hands did not begin to approach the dexterity or strength of a Citizen's lips and jaws.

Although half the bridge's seating accommodated Colonist physiology, the room itself was clearly designed to Citizen standards. There was not a sharp corner to be seen. Consoles, shelves, instrumentation, the latching mechanism on the hatch—everything looked melted and recongealed. Citizens perceived an unnecessary hazard in every crisp edge and pointed corner.

The nothingness that was hyperspace whispered to Kirsten, daring her to acknowledge its presence. She fixed her eyes instead on her console. The heart of the instrumentation was a large transparent sphere: the mass pointer. Each blue line radiating from its center represented a nearby star. The direction of the thread showed the direction to the star; the length of the thread represented the star's gravitational influence: mass over distance squared. The longest thread by far pointed straight at her: their destination.

Logic said that a glance every shift or two was more than sufficient—even at hyperdrive speed, they took three days to cross a light-year—but logic seemed a flimsy thing indeed while the nothingness stalked her mind. She shuddered. Ships in hyperspace that too closely approached the singularity around a stellar mass vanished. The mathematics was ambiguous. None knew where the disappeared had gone, or whether they even still existed.

Monitoring seemed like a process that could be easily automated—simply drop out of hyperspace when a line got too close—but it was not possible. The mass detector was inherently psionic; it required a conscious mind in the loop.

Even splitting the responsibility three ways, the stress was intense. They dropped into normal space every few days, if only for a moment to remind themselves that stars were more than hungry singularities reaching out to devour them.

"Does a thirty-day journey still seem like a simple thing?" The voice was a rich contralto that women envied and men found disturbingly alluring.

Kirsten looked up, the clatter of hooves on metal decking that should have alerted her to Nessus' approach only now making a conscious impression.

One head held high, the other low, he watched her from two directions at once. With the instinctive caution of Citizens, Nessus had paused half-inside, half-outside the hatchway, poised to dash in any direction.

Her whole life she had been beholden to Citizens. So it had been for generations. But while Kirsten knew about Citizens, and respected and revered them, she had *met* few of them. Her people, like sharp corners, were an avoidable risk.

Now, in the emptiness behind the void between the stars, Kirsten reawakened to how dissimilar Citizens and Colonists truly were.

Nessus stood on two forelegs set far apart and one complexly jointed hind leg. Two long and flexible necks emerged from between his muscular shoulders. Each flat, triangular head featured an ear, an eye, and a mouth whose tongue and knobbed lips also served as a hand. His leathery skin was a soft off-white, with few of the tan markings common among some Citizens. The unkempt brown mane between his necks covered and padded the bony hump that encased his brain.

He raised a neck. His heads swiveled toward each other, eye briefly peering into eye, in an ironic laugh. Her brave words at the start of the journey had not gone unnoticed. Despite her embarrassment, she was relieved that he had come out of his cabin. Relieved, but not surprised: The surprise would have been his continued absence as they neared their destination and its unknown perils.

Of course had Nessus not emerged in another shift or two to oversee the ship's arrival, she would have hit the panic button. The looped recording of a Citizen screaming in terror would bring him to the bridge, no matter what.

The room must have looked safe enough. Nessus entered and straddled his thickly padded bench, arching one neck forward to more closely examine the mass pointer. "We will arrive soon," he said. The simple statement ended with a hint of rising inflection that was surely no accident.

He had run the experimental training program for Colonist scouts. Surely questioning his protégés was by now second nature to him. But what was the question? Whether preparations had been completed while he hid in his room? No, that topic would be reserved for the captain.

Twenty of the best and brightest had been winnowed from the Colonists' millions. Whatever their avocations or interests, until this time of crisis *every* Colonist contributed directly or indirectly to food production. The trillion Citizens on Hearth consumed vast amounts of food, and left scant open space on which to raise it. How she, Omar, and Eric performed on this mission would be taken as proof whether *any* child of farmers and conservationists could rise to the occasion.

Before departing the Fleet, the biggest risk the three of them had imagined was a lack of challenge. The unsuspecting aliens whose faint radio emissions had drawn Hearth's attention might prove too primitive. They might offer the crew no opportunity to show their talents.

How naïve those fears now seemed!

Risks motivated Citizens, risks and finding ways to avoid them. If Nessus was questioning her, most likely the unstated subject was risk. He wanted to know: Did she understand the dangers?

The only tasks in hyperspace were routine maintenance and monitoring the mass pointer. The one was tedious, and the other nerve-racking. In such a small crew, everyone took turns. They were about to emerge from hyperspace, though, and this time not only for a reassuring peek. When they did, the star that had been their target would instantly become the brightest object in their sky. In that instant, the crew's roles would cease to be interchangeable.

She would be a navigator once more, once more with stars to steer by.

"We'll assume orbit well outside the singularity," she answered, guessing at his implied question. "I can't imagine how they could detect, let alone waylay us—but if they do, we'll reengage hyperdrive and be gone."

Two bobbing heads, alternating high and low, left Kirsten convinced she had guessed correctly. She smiled too, in her own Colonist way.

Explorer burst from hyperspace at furious speed.

The courage that enabled Nessus to be here meant that he was, by definition, insane. Kirsten had never met a sane Citizen, because they never left Hearth. Her hands never left the flight controls, but her eyes kept darting involuntarily to the right where Nessus rested upon his crash couch. He could take control of the ship from her at any time. The knowledge was simultaneously reassuring and demeaning.

The Fleet's velocity at *Explorer*'s departure was "only" 0.017 light speed. Setting out, that initial impetus had seemed a meaningless crawl in the context of the light-years they were about to cross. That same intrinsic velocity as they reentered normal space was an altogether different matter.

Under Nessus' watchful eyes, Kirsten shed excess speed using the ship's gravity drag. Three times she micro-jumped them back to hyperspace, looping them around their target for another braking pass. *Explorer*'s fusion drive would have accomplished the task much faster—but a miles-long column of fusing hydrogen, hotter than the surfaces of stars, would have shouted the news of their arrival to anyone watching.

"Well done," Nessus finally said.

"Thanks." Her mentor's words seemed both sincere and tentative. As Kirsten steered *Explorer* into orbit around the distant spark named G567-X2, she initiated a deep-radar scan. It was both doctrine and enigma. Neutrinos passed right through normal matter, so what were they looking for? "It is good practice," was the only explanation their trainer had offered. "Nessus will know what to do if there is a return signal."

As busy as she was, Kirsten could not help wondering what the aliens called this sun. Nessus would not care. Citizens exhibited curiosity only when their safety might be imperiled. At other times, they considered inquisitiveness to be at best a distraction.

Perhaps their curiosity made Colonists better explorers, and that was why they were here. Or perhaps Colonists were only expendable. Her parents and brothers thought the latter. *And if no one were willing to scout ahead of the Fleet?* Her family had no answer to that.

With a sigh of relief, Kirsten raised her hands from the controls. "We're in orbit," she announced over the ship's intercom. To Nessus, she added, "We're safely outside the singularity, as promised."

With one head high and the other low, he studied her. "Good. Our work here begins."

2

Of the solar system they had come so far to survey, only the star that they distantly circled was visible to the naked eye. Their instruments reported one gas giant and three rocky worlds, plus an unexceptional assortment of asteroids and remote snowballs.

Radio signals had brought *Explorer* here; radio signals emanated now from only one spot in the solar system: the third moon of the gas giant. On close examination—*close* denoting high magnification, not proximity—that moon was tidally locked to its primary, airless, and sheathed in ice. Great cracks crisscrossed the icy surface. Nessus remembered seeing another world quite like it once, a long time ago. It was called Europa.

"There is probably a world-spanning water ocean under the ice," Omar said. He was pacing the narrow aisle of the relax room, which, after the machinery-packed engine room, was the largest chamber aboard the ship. Eric and Kirsten were tucked into small spaces on either side of the treadmill.

Nessus watched from the doorway as Omar led a review of their early findings. Most of what they discussed was confirmation rather than discovery. The Fleet's instruments were *very* sensitive. The crew's findings would be matched to what the Fleet already knew. Nessus hoped the three of them had not figured that out.

". . . So by process of elimination, whoever is generating the radio signals is beneath the ice," Omar concluded. He glanced from time to time at Nessus for approval.

Captain Omar Tanaka-Singh was tall, wiry, and slope-shouldered. An unruly mop of brown hair—Nessus had wondered: Was that a conscious imitation of my mane?—emphasized the pinched features of his face. Omar organized and administered shipboard activities; he did not define them. Nessus, in role if not in title, was the mission's Hindmost: he who leads from behind. The captain coordinated such tasks as Nessus delegated.

Before his selection for training as a scout, Omar had been an agricultural logistician. In that role he balanced projected demand with long-term weather forecasts with transportation availability with plant-pest mutation probabilities with, doubtless, many more fuzzily defined factors. The work demanded multidisciplinary analytical

skills and a broad tolerance for ambiguity. And yet—
while deciding what to plant and when to harvest it was
important, things agricultural changed *slowly*. How would
thought processes attuned to the growing season adjust to
scouting of the unknown?

Some things were unknowable from a distance. Were
that not the case, Nessus mused, there would be no need
for scouts. "Omar, how do underwater beings make radio waves?"

"Eric, why don't you handle that?" Omar responded.

Eric Huang-Mbeke was their engineer. He was stocky
and short, with ocher skin, thick lips, small teeth, and
dark and intense eyes. His naturally black hair was dyed
in long, colorful strands elaborately braided in imitation
of Citizen style.

Explorer's ability to sense through the ice was limited,
but that constraint wasn't the chief difficulty. Why would
the aliens deploy radios at all? Sound was a more suitable
mechanism for underwater communication. Radio waves
attenuated quickly even in pure water. *Explorer* had observed enough water bursting through fresh surface cracks
to measure the covered ocean's salinity, and it was high.
Radio could not be a useful medium under the ice.

And even more puzzling: How could parts for a radio
or its antenna be fabricated under water? While Eric hy-
pothesized about forays above the ice, unknowingly echo-
ing speculations of the experts on Hearth, Nessus found
his attention wandering.

Did any Colonist truly understand how coiffures en-
coded social status among Citizens? Nessus doubted it. His
mane was unadorned because he considered the custom
an affectation.

Nessus could have worn an elaborate style if he so
chose. Powers high in the Concordance government,
within two levels of the Hindmost himself, had authorized
this mission. Those who had appointed Nessus to lead it
mostly disdained him for the very traits that made him

qualified. Nessus returned their not-quite-hidden sneers by wearing his mane not only plain, but occasionally disheveled. His parents were Conservatives; he had ample experience coping with disapproval.

He hoped his conduct toward the Colonists was less judgmental than what he had so often received. Eric in particular deserved better: His devotion to the Concordance was beyond question. With each new generation, more Colonists took their comfortable existence for granted. Eric would never be one of them.

The irony was not lost on Nessus. For all that *he* questioned authority, instinctive loyalty to the current, utterly conservative, political order was a primary selection criterion for this crew. He would have it no other way. His safety might someday depend on their reflexive deference.

"Nessus?" Eric prompted respectfully.

Nessus quickly ran through his mind the highlights of Eric's briefing and Kirsten's occasional insightful interjection. On the one head, they had raised no points new to the Fleet's analysts. On the other head, despite being pioneers on their first separation from their own kind, their findings so far seemed sound. He could not reasonably have expected anything more.

"You've made some interesting observations. How would you propose we proceed?"

"I would like to get closer," Eric said. "Perhaps we can locate their above-the-ocean bases."

"Absolutely not." Omar glanced at Nessus for support. "That's why we carry unmanned probes."

Explorer's distant orbit around G567-X2 was not, as Nessus was happy for his crew to believe, a precaution taken against the still-unseen aliens. Out here where hyperdrive could be used, the hyperwave radio hidden in his cabin could *also* be used.

If *Explorer* headed sunward, they would leave behind a hyperwave radio buoy, with which the ship could then link by conventional radio. The light-speed crawl to the relay, however, was the problem. It would delay his access to Hearth's experts. The illusion of infallibility would be lost without fast access to a world of experts.

As Omar turned anxiously to Nessus for support, Nessus wondered whether his staffing decisions might already have proven him fallible. Perhaps the captain was *too* much like a Citizen. In a crisis, would Omar become hysterical or withdraw? Of course, Omar's wariness was another tool Nessus could use to mold and guide the crew. Problem or not, Nessus took satisfaction from having had the insight. He was getting to truly understand them all: cautious Omar, loyal Eric, and quiet but clever Kirsten.

This must be what it's like to raise children. The comparison seemed appropriate: If Nessus expected ever to have his own children, he must demonstrate success with these Colonists. He had once overheard his parents discussing the need for extreme caution in having progeny: "The disadvantage of advanced medical technology—we have to live with our child for a *long* time." It did not matter that Nessus was eager to take that chance, for there was no prospective mate in his life.

Success could change that.

Flight from danger was instinctive for Citizens. He certainly had the same reflex; no doubt there would be times he would regret the decision he was about to announce. Fortunately for the trillion on Hearth, he, and a precious few like him, could overcome the impulse.

Perhaps it was the prospect of a mate when they succeeded. Whatever the cause, a manic mood seized him. It was familiar from his other travels and at the same time wondrously strange. They were inside a General Products hull, made from the most impenetrable material known to his or any other species. Without a black hole or large amounts of antimatter, there was nothing the ice-moon aliens could possibly do to harm them. He felt liberated, even giddy.

Nessus fixed Omar with a hard, two-headed stare.

"Actually, Omar, I think the level of hazard is acceptable. Everything we have discussed here suggests the aliens use only quite primitive technology. I believe we'll be quite safe.

"Let's go get a closer look."

Eric was leaving the tiny galley as Kirsten arrived. He loitered while she got a glass of juice from the synthesizer.

He had been wearing the bold colors of a man seeking a wife and children, ready to settle down. Fair enough. But aboard this ship were only Omar, who was already mated and had two daughters, and Eric, and Kirsten herself.

She had worn only gray—and a pale gray, at that, for added emphasis—to make plain that she was not presently open to any relationship. She had done so since the final crew selection, before *Explorer* ever departed their world of NP4. If asked, she would have told a partial truth: that her sole focus was on the success of the mission.

Eric's colors were bolder today than ever, his jumpsuit an eye-poppingly vibrant green. She had never encouraged him. That intense color, that overt proclamation of his interest, was the equivalent of a leer. He watched her drink. "You're looking very relaxed," he told her.

His clothes did not match his words, and Kirsten decided to address only the latter. "Relaxed" certainly overstated things. She could admit, however, to being relieved. "I'm just happy to be here," she said.

To be anywhere, in fact, besides hyperspace—merely thinking of the nothingness made her twitchy. After finding their way across ten light-years, wasn't she entitled to feel a bit of accomplishment and relief?

Eric said, " 'Here' is going to be a disappointment. You *getting* us here, and presumably home again, may be the highlight of the whole trip."

Was he mocking her? She had rejected his advances in training, politely, she thought. No word had been spoken; only clothing styles and body language expressed her disinterest. His attitude ever since, whenever they were alone, was inappropriate. It might be suggestive, or sarcastic, or belittling, or something else entirely.

Nessus had assembled a *very* bright crew—considering them individually. Perhaps it was too much to expect him to anticipate how three isolated Colonists would interact. Or maybe—Omar having a long-term relationship contract back on the continent of Arcadia on NP4—maybe Nessus considered himself a matchmaker between her and Eric. *That* idea made her fume.

She hiked enough to be fit, she supposed, although the treadmill in the relax room was a poor substitute for cross-country treks. Maybe she cleaned up all right. Neither was justification for Eric's unwelcome persistence. Regardless, the easiest way to deal with him was usually to ignore the subtext.

She said, "What we're here to do is *important*."

"In a way," he answered. "In the way that practice is always important."

She knew she was staring. Words refused to come.

"No, really. The mission can't be anything else." Eric perched on a corner of the room's small table. "We were sent to assess this specific solar system, of all those along the Fleet's path. *No* artifacts are visible, not from the Fleet, not even here on the borders of the solar system. There are only alien radio signals, too faint and intermittent to interpret over just a few light-years."

"Right," she agreed, wondering where he was going.

"Trust your friendly neighborhood engineer on this: The aliens' equipment could not be any more primitive." She must not have looked trusting, because he continued. "The signals we came ten light-years to investigate were scarcely more than big sparks. They evidently encode some kind of on/off system for sending information.

"These guys on their ice world are hardly a threat to anyone. We learn, or fail to learn, anything interesting about them, and get our final grade. If we're lucky, we show ourselves worthy of exploring someplace that really might be a potential threat. Regardless, the Fleet flies past in seventy years, by then accelerated up to three-tenths light-speed. If realistically there were any danger here, would Nessus be willing, even eager, to go for a closer look?"

Was Eric right? Might this be simply one more exercise? In her disappointment, Kirsten almost overlooked a subtlety. "Were, you said. Their signals *were* little more than big sparks. Are they something different now?"

"Well, yes," he admitted. "The signals are better controlled now. They've substituted an absurdly convoluted transmission scheme. The broadcasts remain staticky. They use spectrum with horrible inefficiency. Even their most sophisticated format has a slow, jerky frame rate, low resolution, and it's all in two dimensions. The content is mapped into an analog representation, of all unlikely choices. Despite the many oddities, I have most of the details worked out."

Big sparks was a much shorter description. Was he implying progress? "You're describing video," she finally said.

"True, in the sense a sled is like *Explorer.* They're both for transportation." Eric slid off the table. "Look, Kirsten, I didn't mean to upset you. Forget I said anything. Be as relaxed or tense as you wish, and I won't comment further." With a patronizing smirk, he was out the door and into the corridor.

Hyperdrive had brought *Explorer* across ten light-years, so Eric's big sparks were first broadcast just ten years ago. Was sparks-to-video in ten years fast development? The Concordance's vastly superior technology was *old,* mature long before the first Colonists arrived at the Fleet of Worlds. Maybe she could extract something germane about technical history from *Explorer*'s data archives.

Eric could be obnoxious and offensive, but he was also damned smart and he paid attention to politics. What if he was right? What if this whole trip was an elaborate exercise? She presumed that by getting them here she personally had passed. It did not seem like enough. Surely an equally important part of the test was threat assessment. The *mission* would flunk if they too quickly dismissed the aliens as a prospective danger.

Think like a Citizen, she told herself. Any avoidable risk should be avoided. Nessus had an expression about leaving no stone unturned. She got a sandwich and more juice, wondering all the while why that odd saying nagged at her.

Three-tenths light speed. Stone. She nearly dropped her plate as the realization dawned. In the presence of quite modest technology, the Fleet's very speed was its worst vulnerability. Strew some pebbles in its path, and the Fleet's velocity transformed them into fearsome kinetic-energy weapons.

Was such a scenario remotely likely? Sparks-to-video in ten years seemed rapid to her, but truthfully she could not say. She intended to find out. What about alien intentions? If the ice-world denizens could harm the Fleet, would they?

From the Concordance's perspective, the better question might be: Who could say they would not?

Space was a dangerous place, as her ancestors had found to their misfortune. A chill came over her—and a wave of gratitude for everything the Citizens had done for her people. Training exercise or not, *she* would take this threat assessment seriously.

Eric was quite mistaken. She was *hardly* relaxed.

3

Perhaps mathematics was not such an impractical career choice after all.

The Colonists' world was Nature Preserve Four, NP4 for short, and theirs solely through the great magnanimity of the Concordance. At that they held only the continent of Arcadia. With few exceptions, and Kirsten was not one of them, the Colonist population enthusiastically embraced their assigned role as ecological stewards. Much of their world was dedicated to biodiversity sanctuaries; the rest of NP4, including most of Arcadia, was intensively farmed. The Colonists produced huge quantities of food, for the vast population on Hearth and the few millions of themselves.

Not everyone is meant to be a farmer or preservationist, and that, too, was part of the Citizens' vision. People were needed to maintain the irrigation systems, manufacture the tractors and combines, process and transport the harvests, educate the children, run the power generators, maintain the records, house and clothe everyone . . . it took a great many skills to maximize production in a sustainable way. Sustainability was the key—Citizens planned for the long haul.

For all the breadth of Arcadian society, though, it took real creativity to justify a career in mathematics. Kirsten found enough unresolved problems in weather forecasting and seismic prediction to make it work. Interstellar navigation was not an application she would ever have imagined for herself, but she could not fault herself for overlooking it. Things change.

Until five years ago, none of a trillion Citizens anticipated that the galactic core had exploded.

With that revelation, nature preservation took on a much broader meaning. The radiation blast from that long-ago supernovae chain reaction would sterilize this part of the galaxy in another twenty thousand or so years. It was impossible to imagine the Citizen flight reflex operating on a larger scale: the migration of Hearth and its five nature-preserve companion worlds to safer surroundings. In so doing, the Concordance was once again rescuing her people.

Nessus did not admit to knowing the aliens who had reported the core explosion. Maybe there was even sense to his refusal to say much about his past travels. "All aliens are different," he liked to say. "The less I share, the less I'll warp your thinking about what we encounter on this flight."

Kirsten liked Nessus a lot, and not only for having selected her to train as a navigator. Few Citizens could do what he did. Yes, the Fleet of Worlds was running *from* danger, but without someone scouting ahead, who could know what dangers they might be speeding *into*?

Sighing, she switched off her sleeper field and settled lightly to her cabin's floor. The universe had a way of keeping her awake. She might as well get up and *do* something.

Nessus was probably unique. Padding down the corridor to the treadmill in the relax room, she surprised herself by thinking: There may not be another Colonist who can do what *I* can—

And I have the pictures to prove it.

With five equal-sized, tapered, tubular limbs spaced equidistantly around a flat core, the aliens seemed equally adapted to swimming the world-spanning sea and crawling along sea-bottom muck. Prehensile spines covered their leathery skins. Their five writhing extremities made them gross parodies of Citizen and Colonist alike. From time to time, some of them would entwine, or crawl over one another, or manipulate unrecognizable objects for unknowable purposes. Most of the activity took place inside ice or stone structures. Nothing in the images offered Nessus any sense of scale.

He was marking a flat projection when Kirsten entered the relax room, a towel over one shoulder. She was svelte and athletic, fair-skinned with high cheekbones and a delicate nose. Her auburn hair was pulled back in a short ponytail, with unruly bangs that somehow made her dark brown eyes that much more striking. From the way Omar and especially Eric looked at her, Nessus guessed she was a desirable mate by Colonist standards.

She hopped onto the treadmill. "Are you learning much from the recovered video?"

Nessus said, "Despite what I always say, a picture may not be worth a thousand words."

She laughed, and Nessus guessed her good humor had little to do with his turn of phrase. While Eric had been disparaging noisy, low-quality signals and a primitive broadcast format, she had mathematically deconstructed the modulation scheme. Crisp video had popped right up after she mathematically described how to filter out superimposed data flows. It appeared she had found an audio channel and annotations of some kind where their engineer had suspected only noise.

Presumably the experts on Hearth would come to the same conclusion, which was something he himself would never have accomplished. The only numbers Nessus found truly interesting were polls. Success in the Colonist scouting program could give him the start he had so long wanted in politics. A mental image of his disapproving parents, near-catatonic with fright these past five years since the first news of the core explosion, almost made *him* laugh.

None of these ruminations were suitable for the crew. "What do you think of our new acquaintances?"

"They're sure busy doing *something*, but I can't begin to guess what." Her arms pumped as the treadmill kicked up to a higher speed. "It should get easier when the translator software starts making sense of the audio channel."

Nessus put his heads to use tweaking the projector controls. He was stalling: His attention was not on the magnified area he slowly panned across, but on what not to say. Concordance technology must seem limitless to the Colonists. There was much to be said for keeping them in a state of awe.

This manic phase would not last forever. Soon enough, Nessus thought, I'll surrender to tucking my heads tightly between my forelegs. When that happens, I'll just a bit safer if these three understand what *Explorer* is, and is not, capable of.

"We can't translate the broadcasts. The way it usually works"—and the thought brought him *very* close to retreating into a tightly coiled ball—"is in a faces-to-face encounter. We say something, and it's unintelligible. They say back something unintelligible. There is much pointing and miming. The translator has to build the context. At first, only scattered words make sense. In time, there will be phrases, even sentences, but with maddening gaps for unrecognized concepts. Full translation takes a while."

"That's . . . logical," she huffed. Her ponytail flipped from side to side as she now ran full-out. "So we need to land and meet them."

A mosaic filled his mind's eye, populated by swarming hordes, grasping tentacles, and sharp-edged daggers of stone and ice. He had met aliens before but not like this: A first contact could go wrong in *so* many ways. Up here, in the ship, they were safe from anything such primitives could do. Faces to face was a very different situation. "It would be prudent to gather more information first."

Sweat dripped down her face and neck, to be wicked away and evaporated by the nanofibers in her tunic. She ran in silence for a long time. "Here's a thought. Most likely, some of the audio corresponds to the video information.

Suppose—" and she fell silent again. "Okay, try this. We use scene-analysis software to model what's going on, tagging with English text our hypotheses about each object and activity. Most images are ambiguous, so we start with probability-weighted decision trees. Then we correlate the tagged scenes with the concurrent audio information.

"Sure, some of the seeming audio may be an independent voice channel. It might be music, if they have such a concept. The thing is, over time, the only statistically significant audio data will be speech that's related to the concurrent video. Everything else will be washed out by the significance filters."

"You could do such an analysis?"

Retrieving her towel, Kirsten blotted her face and neck without breaking stride. "Sure. Not easily, exactly. It will take some programming, and probably some experimentation with the weightings of alternative interpretive models. . . ."

Her math ability constantly impressed Nessus, but her casually assumed prowess at programming made him tremble. No, be honest—this *kind* of programming scared him. It scared all Citizens. Nothing was more intrinsically related to intelligence than language. Programs that modeled intelligence could, it was feared, all too possibly become intelligent. Translators, in certain circumstances, were a necessary evil, but . . .

I'm more like most Citizens than I realize, Nessus thought. Still, he was one of the very few to have visited civilizations that dared to undertake AI research. None had run amok yet. And her approach, if it worked, might eliminate the need for a landing.

"That is an excellent idea," he began to say in support.

The rapt expression on Kirsten's face made it clear no encouragement was required.

"Cute little Fellas." The curl of Eric's upper lip revealed his words as sarcasm. "Still, it's interesting to watch what the starfish are up to." He had proposed the name, and was all the prouder of it because it amused Nessus.

At times, Kirsten found Eric's deference annoying. Have your *own* values, she wanted to shout. She kept her response to a noncommittal grunt and returned her attention to the video. Officially, her interest was in ways to improve the correlation and decoding models. Interpretation of the data was more Omar's department. In truth, she was hooked. The more she learned about the aliens, the more fascinated she became.

Holos surrounded the video, each offering another perspective of the main scene: partially translated conversations; interpretations of any alien artifacts in view; the location on the globe of the video source; a highly magnified view from synchronous orbit of the encampment and a few roving aliens, taken by one of *Explorer*'s recently deployed probes. Kirsten said, "They call themselves Gw'oth, Eric. It's Gw'o if you're talking about just one."

"Maybe that translates to *starfish*."

"Whatever it means, they're adventurers, space travelers in their own way." He was so enamored of Citizen culture—just look at the curls and intricacies of his hair!—that Kirsten doubted he would ever appreciate how incredible the Gw'oth were. She felt compelled to try. Maybe she could reach him on *his* terms.

"Someone I know once suspected this trip was a test. If so, part of our grade will certainly depend on how well we figure out these guys. Think about it, Eric. They evolved in the ocean. Living underwater means no fire and no use of metal. Their first venture above the ice, into the *vacuum* above the ice, was a heroic undertaking."

If their scene interpretations and partial translations were correct, those first forays had involved the most primitive of gear. The early protective suits looked like no more than translucent bags trailing tubes back to underwater pumps that were little more than flexible bags manipulated by Gw'oth remaining beneath the ice. Bags, suits, and hoses all seemed to be made from the tough skins of deep-sea animals. She pulled some old imagery from *Explorer*'s archive. "Just look at this."

Nessus joined them in the relax room. He had a way, Kirsten had noticed, of appearing whenever a conversation became interesting. "Don't mind me," he said. "I just came for a bite to eat."

"So the starfish," and Eric looked to Nessus for approval, "cut a hole in the ice with stone tools and climb up wearing leather bubbles—where someone is already on the ice to capture it all with a video camera? Was that chipped from stones, too? Kirsten, that makes no sense."

Citizens ate often, but they ate with one head and kept watch with the other. Nessus was observing them now while he ate. Trying not to think about him assessing them, Kirsten gestured at the video she had just pulled up. "I assume it's a reenactment. Maybe that's a Gw'o who likes the challenge. Maybe it's a history show, or education, or entertainment.

"You're right, Eric, about one thing. They could not have had video cameras, or any type of electronics, until after they went above the ice. Their only prior experience with gases would have been from undersea volcanic eruptions, or vacuum boiling of the water in a fresh ice fracture. Look at them now: We've got video of them wearing their pressure suits inside their above-ice buildings so that they can contain an atmosphere. Why? They need fire! Fire for what they still see as new industrial processes." She wished she could say more, but it was far beyond her knowledge to guess what alternate paths to technology had been involved.

Nessus set down his bowl, the gruel within it still untouched. "Eric, what do you think? Is such a scenario plausible?"

Eric struck an increasingly familiar pose that made Kirsten strangely uncomfortable: worshipful presentation to their mentor. "It's possible, Nessus. A big ceiling lens in an airtight room could focus enough sunlight to gradually photo-dissociate water. That would give a hydrogen and oxygen atmosphere. Such a lens could be carved from ice or a crystal like quartz. They'd need something they could add to the oxy-hydrogen mix to make it less explosive. Biological processes like digestion or respiration probably produce other gases, like carbon dioxide, in small amounts. They might have found catalysts to produce or separate gases. Yes, it seems possible. But how could they figure this all out?"

Nessus gave an involuntary shiver, the kind Kirsten associated with a mood swing to depression and withdrawal. "I certainly hope we convince ourselves they somehow did. The alternative is that an advanced, space-faring species has visited this solar system without our knowing anything about it."

He did not need to remind them that this solar system lay near the Fleet's planned path.

From fire to fission in two generations.

From the depths of his tightly coiled body, Nessus took solace that it could have been worse. At least the analysts on Hearth thought the Gw'oth had developed their technology on their own. And at least their report had reached him through the still-secret comm link in his cabin. The Colonists had not seen him in panic.

Those advising the expedition from the safety of Hearth had assigned a multitude of computer and math experts to enhance Kirsten's models. How many experts? His inquiries never got an answer. It probably did not matter, and it even amused him to picture their unease. None of the experts had had her insight to augment the standard translator.

Regardless, between *his* expert and the many at home, there was now an answer to Eric's question: How could they figure this all out?

With great force of will, Nessus unwrapped himself. Without a doubt, this mission had already established the value of Colonist scouts. It was hard to be happy about that when a threat to the Fleet was involved.

The disturbing analysis from Hearth lay unannounced in the ship's main receive buffer. With a coded message, he released it to the comm subsystem on the bridge. Omar, currently on the bridge, would "receive" it while Nessus innocently made his way to the galley.

"All hands to the relax room," Omar called out over the intercom. Omar read fast.

Kirsten stumbled down the corridor, groggy from being awakened suddenly. She found the rest of the crew in the relax room before her, discussion already begun. A laugh caught in her throat, because Eric's usual construction of elaborate braids was a straggle matted on the left. How much time, she wondered, did he normally spend to maintain that coiffure?

". . . Scientists back at Hearth have decoded a portion of a big Gw'oth data archive. What we've seen by tapping their broadcasts is a small part of what's available. The good news is, there's no evidence of spacefaring visitors helping the Gw'oth." Omar gestured to a complex holo graphic whose meaning was far from obvious.

Yawning, Kirsten almost dropped the bulb of stim juice Eric lobbed her way. She needed the caffeine badly; it took her a moment to synchronize her thoughts with the conversation.

It had turned out digital data streams were sometimes modulated over the analog transmissions between the bases above the ice. Reverse-engineering the protocol and cracking its associated simple authentication model had revealed to her a new surprise: a Gw'oth digital communications network and associated archives. Likely there was no way beneath the ice to develop electronics or other sophisticated technologies, but devices built above the ice could operate below. The wired network deployed below the ice seemed far larger than what they could directly see. Its addressing scheme implied planning for a very large network.

How much, she wondered, that was hidden from sight will now be revealed?

That, Kirsten realized, was what this no-notice gathering was about. The experts on Hearth had analyzed the archive. She felt a twinge of jealousy. She could apply only the computing power of this single ship. They had a world's computers to sift and organize the data.

"The timeline surprised the analysts," Omar said. "The Gw'oth calendar is based on the solar orbit of the gas giant they circle. We can translate their dates precisely. They first ventured above the ice fifty-two of our years ago. Roughly two Gw'oth generations."

Our year. It was an arbitrary unit of measure, maintained for consistency with old Citizen records. The Citizens had long ago moved Hearth far from its sun, as that star prepared to swell into a red giant. "Year" had been arbitrary long before the Fleet began its latest journey.

Looking around the room, Kirsten could see that everyone was struggling to absorb the news. Not that long ago, the only bit of technical history she wanted to better understand was the likely progression between broadcasting techniques. More sophisticated transmission was such a small part of what was implied by Omar's timeline.

Someone had to comment first, so she did. "Fifty-two years seems incredibly fast progress." It *had* been done, so she had to believe it. How could they learn so much so quickly? They had to build the tools to build the tools to build the tools, through untold iterations. They had to produce an atmosphere in which to first create fire to first smelt ores with which to craft their first metal tools. She could just barely believe the full sequence was achievable starting with a detailed knowledge of the underlying sciences. Experts on Hearth said there were no outside parties imparting the knowledge. So how?

The hideously complex graphic floating in the aisle suddenly made sense. It represented the many parallel and entwining technological projects the Gw'oth had undertaken. "They knew from the moment they cracked through the ice what they wanted to do and how to accomplish it."

"That is what's now believed," Eric said. "What I don't get is *how*. How could they create the plan before they had the environment in which to do the experiments to develop the science to envision the plan?"

Kirsten had no answer, but neither did anyone else. She pointed into the holo. "Is that a *nuclear plant* at the end of this sequence?" No one corrected her. "How could we fail to notice nuclear power plants?"

"They're beneath the ice, on the ocean floor," Nessus said. "We had noticed the heat sources, of course. We assumed they were seabed volcanoes. Checking those locations with full instrumentation, deep-penetrating radar, and radiation sensors leaves no doubt what they truly are. From fire to fission in two generations."

Nessus' body quivered, as though he resisted fleeing to his room or rolling himself up. "And there is one more detail we collectively overlooked. Radio signals don't propagate past the horizon, unless by bouncing off of an ionosphere. The ice moon has no atmosphere, but we never stopped to ask ourselves how the starfish communicate between their distant bases."

"Long wires run under the ice?" Omar guessed.

Nessus reached a head into the graphic. "No, low-orbiting communication satellites. So far they use only primitive chemical rockets, but it's a start toward space travel."

Comm sats. No one could claim *those* were out of sight beneath the ice. At least, Kirsten thought, Eric had the decency to look embarrassed.

4

The walls were rough-hewn stone, the lighting an eerie bioluminescent green, and the occupants five-pointed sea creatures. Purplish-green fronds grew from cracks in the floor and walls, swaying in unseen currents and eddies. For all the strangeness, the setting suggested an office.

"What are you working on?" Kirsten asked rhetorically. She was watching the Gw'oth through a camera conveniently placed by the aliens themselves. Were they recording an important meeting? Monitoring workers for purposes of security? She had no idea. The camera was video only. That was too bad, because their translator was getting better. It produced logical-seeming results from nearly half what it was given.

Beep. Her viewpoint switched to a storeroom somewhere beneath the ice. Their scanning program probed Gw'oth network addresses at random, but as far as she could ascertain, a network address conveyed nothing about a camera's physical location. Maybe it didn't matter. No one was in the room, and the translated labels on the boxes identified only various foods.

Beep. Beep. Beep. Two random attempts had gotten no response. Another room, this time with two writhing Gw'oth. Alien sex, she thought. She was still blushing when the vantage point shifted again.

A knock rattled her cabin door. "How is it going?" Omar asked.

"Fine." It was a rote answer. Eric was investigating the primitive Gw'oth satellites—in plain sight, now that he knew to look—and scanning the surface for launch sites. Omar was assisting Nessus with analysis of the archive translations streaming to them from Hearth. By process of elimination, that left her to sample the array of Gw'oth cameras. She only wished her assignment had produced something useful. "I've tagged several scenes for ongoing monitoring. How goes your analysis?"

"The little guys are making me feel really stupid. I'm just glad we have a big head start, and the Fleet will be past here soon."

The little guys: Omar's favorite nickname reflected a small bit of progress. A medical database had provided typical Gw'oth body dimensions in their own units of measure. A physics database had shown the correspondence between their traditional unit of length and hydrogen wavelengths. An average Gw'o was no longer than her arm; its torso at its thickest was the length of her hand. "Keep me posted, Omar. I'll let you know if anything interesting pops up here."

The next beep-beep drowned out Omar's parting words. Receding footsteps suggested he had not expected an answer.

Bigger surprises than the size of a Gw'o lay within the medical databases. Each of the five muscular tubes was nearly an independent creature in its own right. Gw'oth researchers believed a distant ancestor of theirs was some sort of primitive colony. Omar, the closest among the crew to a biologist, suspected they were correct. It would take genomic databases to prove or disprove the theory, and so far nothing of the sort had been found. Gw'oth science seemed not to have ventured far into genetics.

The next scene showed a single Gw'o operating an apparatus she did not recognize. Whatever it was, the creature used four extremities to control it. The lack of an annotation said the translator could not identify the equipment either. "Pause scan." She watched for a while without enlightenment. "Keep recording this channel. Queue a copy to Eric." After staring a little longer without result, she added, "Resume scan."

Beep. An empty corridor. Beep. A writhing mass of Gw'oth: an orgy. She averted her eyes until a tone signaled a scene change. Beep beep. A vast spread of sea-bottom plant life, perhaps a farm. Beep . . .

She stood and stretched. The little guys were keeping their secrets, she thought, followed by: Why do I care that they're smaller than me? Several more uninteresting scenes beeped by before she decided. It's a *defense mechanism*. Omar is not the only one they make feel slow-witted.

"Pause." Maybe her reaction did bear thinking about. It wasn't just that the outpouring of Gw'oth creativity shocked Eric and Omar—and her. In truth, Colonists had little experience developing technology from scratch. Her people's science and engineering was doled out by their patrons. Whatever she had learned before, she had always been aware it was merely a subset of Citizen knowledge. No, what was truly eye-opening was that the Gw'oth rate of learning astonished *Nessus*.

It was not her first such rude awakening. . . .

When Kirsten was twelve, her parents took her and her brothers hiking in a forested conservation zone. Dad practically had to drag her there, stepping disc by stepping disc. Voluntarily leaving the grid seemed ridiculous. To intentionally walk into the wilderness was the most peculiar thing she had ever contemplated.

Still whining petulantly, she popped into a small woodland clearing where Dad and Carl awaited her. She took a step forward, and her mother and her baby brother appeared on the disc she just vacated. Teleportation: *That* was how civilized beings traveled. A ten-digit code was emblazoned on a nearby sign; she committed the stepping-disc's address to memory. It seemed impossible that there would be *no* more stepping discs in their path. She had vague hopes of finding one, evading her parents, and teleporting back along a chain of stepping discs to home and friends and urban comforts.

Five globes—four blue and white, one bejeweled—hung overhead in a straight line: the rest of the Fleet. She had never set foot on any of them; she did not expect she ever would. Still, any of those worlds, even Hearth itself, was less alien than the myriads of trees all around her. Each of those worlds had stepping-disc grids, too.

She had known in the abstract that farms and ranches and seas lay outside the stepping-disc network. Never before had she *felt* it. Her parents worked in a tractor factory. The factory and their neighborhood were in the heart of the grid.

A hundred paces into the woods they lost sight of the forest-ranger station and its end-of-the-line stepping disc. Chirps and rustles in the undergrowth made her shrink close to Dad despite her displeasure at being here. She knew both he and Mom carried some sort of Citizen-sanctioned stunning device in case an animal got too close.

Dad led the way into the park, babbling about permutations and combinations of trees. She did not share his enthusiasm. She remembered a downhill section along a stream bed, and a packed-dirt path. Had it been trodden by animals? The thought made her cringe. Occasionally they climbed hills for their different-only-in-the-details views, between longer periods spent among the trees and undergrowth. Much of her time went to keeping track of little Philip.

Dad's commentary grew sparser and sparser. They came to a halt beside a pond she thought seemed familiar. He and Mom traded looks that said plainly: This is not what I expected. Mom checked her communicator, and shook her head. No reception.

"We're lost, aren't we?" Kirsten was scared and angry and ready to slug Philip, just because he was there. "Why would you bring us here? No stepping discs, no communications"—and a sudden thought hit her—"and no food."

"It was supposed to be a fun outing, Kirsten," Dad said. "I thought we were following a circuit that would lead us back to the entry disc, but obviously we missed a turn. This park *seemed* small enough that we couldn't go very far astray, and safe enough, because it's surrounded by farms.

"So yes, we're lost, but there's no need to worry. The park staff will surely find us. They know we're in here. Or our friends will call them when we're late coming home."

The sky darkened with clouds, and the rain began. They huddled together for warmth under a rocky outcropping that kept off little of the rain. Philip hid his face in Mom's side, and even Carl was quiet. As the last of the orbital suns set for the night, the temperature plummeted. Her teeth chattered.

Were they animals, to die alone in the forest? It seemed insane.

Three yellow blotches in the dense cloud marked the visible worlds of the Fleet, a bit of normality in an existence suddenly become surreal. Through the clouds, she could not tell one world from another.

It was a useless skill, but she had deduced how to tell the time of day from the position of the worlds in the sky. It amused her, and provided a smart-aleck answer to Dad's questioning the value of studying math.

Wait! The line of the worlds had seemed different at the start of their trek. "Dad, you said the park is surrounded by farms." Farms meant warmth and food, and workers who could show them the nearest stepping discs.

"Yes. We could hike out of here if we could walk in a straight line." His shrug was barely recognizable in profile in the nighttime gloom. "Following stepping discs isn't the same, is it? I mean, a stepping disc or a sign for one is always in sight."

"That's the thing." She pointed skyward, suddenly excited. "We *can* walk in a straight line. It's even easy." She turned to face squarely the three glows overhead. "Just walk towards the Fleet."

They made their way slowly with only flashlights to guide the selection of a safe path. With Dad at her side, Kirsten led the way. Another world had set, leaving but two to guide them, when the edge of a cultivated field appeared through the trees. It was her first feat of navigation.

That near-disastrous outing was at once the start of her love of nature and the loss of innocence. Thinking her parents wrong and stupid about everything somehow had not yet translated into a visceral realization that parents did not know everything. But no one can know everything, not even parents. It was all right if she knew something they did not.

That wilderness adventure, her first act of navigation, was also the first step on the path that had brought Kirsten to the stars.

So even *citizens* don't know everything, and Eric's question hung over the mission like a dark cloud. How *had* the Gw'oth planned their no-wasted-efforts, no-missteps, technological eruption before they mastered the environment in which to do the experiments to develop the science to envision the plan? If the four of them could not answer that, how could they begin to predict whether the Gw'oth represented a risk to the onrushing Fleet?

Running often helped Kirsten think, and the only place onboard to run was the treadmill. Her arms and legs pumped, and cityscape streamed past her in a wall projection, as she tried to reconcile the irreconcilable. She had a theory that only an applied mathematician could like. The Gw'oth could have *simulated* everything— science, engineering designs, and development projects— until they were ready to put their plans into effect. With sufficiently massive computing power, models and calculations could replace much messy experimentation. She had taken basic science classes on Arcadia. Simulation was a much more reliable guide to how the world worked than her typical lab technique.

But the Gw'oth wouldn't have computers until they developed above-the-ice industry. The riddle made her head hurt.

Dinner time came and went; she kept loping on the treadmill. She needed a clear head more than a synthed meal.

Not only would the Gw'oth need computers to do the simulations, but as far as their investigations had revealed, the aliens *still* did not have major computing capabilities. They had huge data archives, and specialized devices to facilitate sorting and searching and networking that data—but computers? The scouts had not found any computing centers to speak of.

Her arms and legs burned and trembled; she ached from overexertion. Knowing she had overdone it, she slowed the treadmill to a cool-down gait.

Even Citizens don't know everything. How much less do I know?

5

The four scouts watched a cluster of stone structures climb skyward from a mountain peak that poked through the ice. In the fast-forwarded playback, Gw'oth workers in pressure suits became nearly invisible blurs. Completed rooms and outbuildings were sprayed inside and out; whatever water did not immediately boil away froze into gas-tight seals. More and more test bores gaped nearby, giving the site the overall appearance of a mining camp. From the apex of the mountain rose a metal structure, too early in its construction to be conclusively identified. A steerable dish antenna on a tower pointed skyward; analysis showed it was tracking low-orbiting comm sats as they flew past.

This was a full hologram, the imagery taken by *Explorer*'s forward probes. *Explorer* itself shared an orbit with the ice moon. The gas giant they both circled blocked starship and moon from any direct view of each other. Chains of tiny stealthed buoys, each in a transparent and indestructible General Products #1 hull, relayed messages between *Explorer* and its observation satellites high above the ice moon. We're surely safe here, Kirsten thought. How much are we impeding our own investigation by hiding here?

They had gathered again in the relax room. Nessus gestured with one head at the holo. "Omar, what do we know about their building project?"

"Know? Not much," Omar said. "The project was well under way before we happened to notice it. It looks like the little guys are putting up a big antenna. I would guess they're going for a high-gain antenna to use with synchronously orbiting comm sats."

"We could land and *ask* them," Kirsten burst out. More and more, the Gw'oth impressed her. Observing them was fascinating, but she wanted to get to *know* them.

Nessus swiveled a head toward her. "Ask them what?"

Whatever, she wanted to shout. Her impatience and frustration surprised her. "What are they building? What is their approach to science? Can we trade information with them?"

The core question—will you become a threat?—could not be asked directly. Eric wanted to know how and from where they launched the satellites; she wanted to know why she had found data archives but still no major computing centers. Inquiries about either topic risked revealing their own spying to the Gw'oth. It's tricky, Kirsten thought. Our investigations might make *us* seem a threat to *them*.

"No landings yet," Nessus answered with a shudder.

"We don't announce our presence, either. The Gw'oth probably do not even know that other intelligent species exist. Why reveal that fact, and perhaps in the process make them more likely to notice the Fleet?"

Eric was frowning at the fast-changing holo. "They might know sooner than we'd like, that they're not alone, I mean. That could be a radio telescope they're building."

"I'll continue to watch it," Omar promised. "We might also try an experiment to elicit more information."

Something about *experiment* sounded provocative to Kirsten. "What do you mean?"

"Incapacitate one of their satellites to see how they respond. It was Eric's suggestion, and rather good."

Kirsten struggled to find a suitable verb, finally settling on a word that described the behavior of predatory animals. "Attack them?"

Eric nodded. "We would use a laser-equipped probe, waiting until its line of sight to the Gw'oth satellite misses all other satellites and the ice moon itself. They won't see anything. There is no evidence they have lasers, so they won't have a clue what happened. A lost satellite will put a hole in their communications network, so they are likely to replace it as soon as they can."

"So yes, an attack," she replied.

Nessus plucked nervously at his unkempt mane. "We know they have *some* sort of spaceflight capability. We need somehow to extrapolate whether that capability can grow into a threat to the Fleet. Given their rapid progress in other fields, that risk could be substantial."

"I still feel we should start out by *asking*." Only as she realized she was shaking did Kirsten grasp how strongly she felt. "If radio contact with them does not work, I volunteer to go down myself."

Omar switched off the projection. "Kirsten, we are *far* from home. Your primary job is to get us back. After Nessus, you're the last of us I would put at risk."

She found herself thinking again of that long-ago hike in the woods. No one knows everything.

She just wished she knew whose ignorance—that of Nessus, or herself, or the still-mysterious Gw'oth—was the issue here.

From deep within a comforting nest of pillows in the sanctuary of his cabin, Nessus considered Kirsten's unusual request for a private audience. He had already reached his decision about the aliens. His full focus could now be on assessing the Colonists. "Please come by my cabin," he decided.

The knock on his cabin door was timid, but Kirsten had wasted no time getting to him. "We're making things worse, Nessus."

"What do you mean?" he asked.

"I believe our actions are stimulating the Gw'oth to develop in ways contrary to the Fleet's interests."

That was also his suspicion. "I don't see how that could be," he lied.

"You know we're deep inside their communication networks and data archives. There is no sign they know *Explorer* is here, but their R&D is being influenced by how we study them. We map their cities with deep-penetrating radar, and they detect radio-frequency anomalies. Their radio and radar research expands. We destroy one of their satellites, and they quickly develop a rapid-launch capability. The pattern goes on." Kirsten looked around the cabin for someplace to sit; finding none, she leaned against a wall. "The longer we test the Gw'oth for capabilities we consider undesirable, the more likely we make it that they will develop just those capabilities. Our very presence may give them the theoretical potential to endanger the Fleet as it passes."

She was methodical and insightful. If that intellect could be combined with Eric's devotion to the Concordance, how useful their children would be.

Thoughts of Colonists mating made his stomach roil. "Kirsten, do you *admire* these primitive aliens?"

"I do," she said. "That's all the more reason not to groom them into a threat meriting any action on our part. Respectfully, Nessus, I recommend that we leave this solar system now."

Kirsten was raising valid points. The Gw'oth were erecting large observatories above the ice. How could they not notice the Fleet when it approached? They already had primitive chemical rockets and fission. Would interplanetary capabilities follow? In the seventy years until the Fleet passed by, it was surely imaginable—which crossed his risk threshold—that the Gw'oth would have spacecraft exploring the fringes of their solar system. Should such probes be stealthed and maneuvered to lie undetectable in the Fleet's path . . .

Why do *anything* that might advance progress among the starfish?

The correct course of action was obvious. Nessus had decided several shifts earlier on his recommendation to those who led from behind. The Fleet should adjust its course slightly. Over seventy years, even a minor course modification would steer the Fleet far from any possible Gw'oth danger. Slamming a comet into the ice moon was a last resort, and even if it came to extreme measures, he could imagine far more subtle actions.

"Nessus," she prompted him apprehensively.

Unfortunately for Kirsten and her crewmates, the investigation of G567-X2 was always his secondary objective. "I appreciate your input, but I believe we must continue assessing the Gw'oth."

She flinched at the gentle rebuke. "May I use your holo projector?"

"Of course." He wondered where this would lead.

Kirsten called up a file from the ship's archives. A bumpy sphere appeared: the hidden ocean floor of the ice moon. Scattered dots glowed, some blinking. "The red dots are major data archives. The blinking dots are archives associated with major Gw'oth development centers."

"They had to do their engineering somewhere. What is the significance of the locations?"

"Now look at this," she answered. Her face reddened as a second holo appeared.

It was a squirming mass of twisting, entangled aliens. His stomach churned as the view changed to another such scene, and another, and another. There were chains of convulsing aliens, pulsing arrays, and writhing piles. That the aliens performed these acts on camera revolted him.

Reproduction was a private matter. Among Citizens, sex meant reproduction. No Citizen was comfortable discussing sex with any other species. To sound sternly disapproving took no effort. "I have no interest in others' sex lives."

Her face reddened further, but she stood her ground. "I know what this looks like. When such scenes appeared on our random video surveys, I turned away. Then an amazing thing happened. The longer we have been here, the more frequently such scenes appear in our intercepts.

"The outpouring of technological change, the above-ice journeys of exploration, perhaps suspicions of unseen observers—it must be very stressful for the Gw'oth. At first I thought, and please excuse me for this indelicacy, that they respond to stress with increased sexual activity."

She could not meet his eyes, and he guessed he knew why. Humans must also react that way to stress. Reluctantly, he gestured for her to continue.

"Then I noticed a perplexing correlation. This . . . activity corresponds with the growth of data in the archives. The activity is most prevalent where the archives are fastest growing. What could that mean? In desperation, I made myself watch these scenes." She froze an image. "Look closely," and she swallowed audibly, "and you'll notice that each Gw'o has, umm, linked tubes with four other Gw'oth."

Nessus forced himself to confirm her observation. As best he could ascertain, there were sixteen Gw'oth in the image, all linked as she described. "Why is that significant?"

Kirsten searched the cabin once more for a chair. Finding none, she settled onto a pile of cushions. "What I've not yet mentioned is near which data archive this scene happened. It's an archive specializing in rocketry development. *This* group interaction has been ongoing for days, starting and stopping, aligned with the apparent work schedule of the surrounding Gw'oth city. As this activity continues, there has been extensive growth in datasets related to rocket-nozzle design."

Rocket nozzles? Nessus struggled to imagine the need to design such things. It seemed as archaic as inventing a pillow or table. Such things had been standardized on the homeworld for many millennia. Yet his people, like the Gw'oth, had had to originate the technology sometime. He supposed the design process had had to consider variations in heat and pressure throughout the nozzle volume. Ah. "Three spatial dimensions and time. You're likening four-way linkages"—and despite himself, he could not keep disgust from his voice—"to a four-dimensional matrix calculation."

She leaned forward on her cushions, eyes bright. "Exactly. I found similar correlated expansions in other archives, where the number of inter-Gw'o links matches the apparent mathematical model. Lines of linked Gw'oth and simple, one-dimensional gas-diffusion models. Three-way connections and 3-D models of molecular bonds. I found more examples."

He was beginning to believe. "How is such a thing possible?"

"We already suspected from their medical records that the species evolved from a colony organism. The individual tubes are like hollow worms, with at least a vestigial version of every organ required for independent existence.

Omar thinks the ancestral forms linked nervous systems and eventually evolved a large, shared central brain. It looks as though nervous systems can also connect at the *other* end, the freely moving end, of the tubes. If that's right, such connections would form multiperson minds."

Nessus' purpose was not served by admitting anything, but he was fascinated. "Biological computers. That would explain why you've found large archives, but no computing centers. It's an interesting hypothesis, although this may be only a coincidence." Could it be true? "But even if you are correct, why should I care?"

"Don't you *see*? We all wondered, and worried, about this sudden, unexplained outpouring of creativity. The Gw'oth must have been preparing for ages to break through the ice, waiting to act until they had a very detailed plan. Remember all the seabed ruins we've seen in deep-penetrating radar images and intercepted video— this is an old civilization. The eruption of capability only *seems* sudden."

He had never been more convinced of the value of the Colonist scouting program. Would Citizen scouts have ever reached such a bizarre—but quite possibly correct—conclusion about the Gw'oth? He doubted it, even ignoring the difficulties in assembling an entire Citizen crew.

"Kirsten, say you are correct. Throughout their history, the Gw'oth have been limited to the energy of muscle power and tides and perhaps volcanic heat. Their collective memory was limited to what could be recorded on some underwater analogue of paper. They remained stuck beneath the ice.

"Now those constraints are all lifted. They have nuclear energy. Above the ice, they've had the means to create vast data archives. And they're on the verge of space travel, with all these other moons at hand. Perhaps all that remains unchanged is the will that sustained them until they could entirely plan their renewal. Consider how dangerous that focus might be coupled with their vastly expanding resources."

Her mouth gaped in shock. "Nessus," she finally managed. "They don't know we exist. They don't know the Fleet exists. They have done nothing to threaten anyone. And we all agree they're smart—if they do spot the Fleet, an undeniably more advanced civilization, why would they provoke us?"

"What are you suggesting, Kirsten?"

"What I proposed earlier. We should just leave."

A succession of insights was not Kirsten's only surprise. Obviously, she had developed an emotional bond with those *Explorer* had come to study. He sensed there was yet more she was thinking but not admitting to him.

How would her feelings for the Gw'oth affect her behavior? Might she oppose the application of defensive measures, should the Fleet's safety require such? He needed to know. "Your findings have brought me to a different conclusion. We must strive harder to understand certain implications."

His Colonists had compellingly proven their abilities to be great scouts for the Fleet. Now, Nessus pondered a dilemma that had never before occurred to him.

It remained to be proven whether they would be loyal servants.

6

Starlight glistened off the icy, potato-shaped body on which Kirsten stood. With her visor photomultiplier turned up, it was as bright as a cloudy day on NP4. Boulders were scattered in the ice beneath her feet, and more rock protruded from the surface. Eric tramped nearby, crouching occasionally, inspecting the ancient and pock-marked surface of the proto-comet.

What made this region of the snowball safe for them to work on was what it lacked: gas pockets. Although they were much too distant from the sun for any significant heating, they had used deep-penetrating radar to find an intrinsically stable area for their landing.

This was her first time off *Explorer* since they had left the Fleet. *I'm on another world, if only a small one.* Not long ago, a mere chance of such an adventure would have elated her. Knowing the purpose of the excursion now sucked the joy from the experience.

Explorer floated at a safe distance. As Kirsten watched, a port opened, through which a small sphere emerged: a General Products #1 hull, not much larger than her helmet, hardware glittering within. Omar remote-piloted it toward them.

"Success," Eric called with satisfaction over the public channel. "Here's a suitable spot. I've got a clear view into the ice for as deep as my flashlight will shine."

She walked over carefully to see. The improvised crampons on her pressure-suit boots did more to hold her to the surface than the snowball's feeble gravity. She believed him, but wanted to speak alone. Private channel two, she gestured. "This is wrong," she began without preamble.

He dialed his flashlight-laser to its highest intensity setting and aimed it downward. Steam instantly boiled from the surface, luridly illuminated by the laser beam. "What do you mean? If we're careful, which I am being, this is perfectly safe."

"Not unsafe, wrong." How long did she have before Nessus became curious or suspicious? "We're endangering another intelligent species, Eric. We shouldn't be doing this."

He released the laser's ON button for a moment, allowing the steam to dissipate so he could have a look. "A nice shaft," he said to himself, before he resumed drilling. "No one is hurting them, Kirsten. We're testing them.

The question is: Will they see and respond to a comet-collision threat? It's our best bet at predicting how soon they'll be able to detect the approaching Fleet, and whether they can launch anything that might endanger it. After we watch for a while, see whether they react or not, we'll divert the comet."

"Will we really?"

The laser beam wobbled as he jerked in surprise.

"Careful with that! I'm serious, Eric. This test is happening because the Gw'oth *might* be a threat to the Fleet. We know nothing about what they're like or how they think. Admit it: We're endangering the Gw'oth. And why? It's purely because they've acquired some basic technology. Ask yourself what Nessus will do if our monitoring shows they have detected a collision risk and made plans to divert our comet."

He switched off the laser. When the steam dissipated, he grunted approval at the hole gaping near them. "Kirsten, I have to talk to Omar now. I'm going public." He tapped buttons on his sleeve. "Omar, give me control of the probe."

The sphere approached slowly. "Reactionless drive. *There* is a technology I bet our little buddies don't have," Eric said. The tiny ship settled into the hole he had excavated, smacking the bottom with a thump they could just sense through their boots. "Piloting something that is practically indestructible makes the job a lot easier."

With his flashlight-laser dialed to a broader beam, Eric began fanning the surface around the hole. Less steam erupted than before, and the tube collapsed inward on itself. He slowly fanned the area until all that remained of the shaft was a shallow depression. Kirsten waved her flashlight laser about, too, but her beam was set so wide it contributed only harmless light.

Eric gestured for a return to the private channel. "You know this test isn't a danger to the aliens. At worst, they'll think it is. The thruster we just planted will slowly change the proto-comet's orbit, to make it a near-miss threat. If the Gw'oth don't see it, or if they are unable to respond, the thruster will be used later to nudge it off an intersecting course."

She knew the plan, too. It would seem from a distance as though the typical random eruption of gases from the comet had changed its orbit to something safe. "Or our embedded probe could re-aim the comet for an impact on a later orbit. Or the probe could rip through the comet on full thrusters, and shatter it into several large pieces to make it all the harder to divert."

"I guess you two wanted to be alone," Omar kidded on the public channel. "Fine, take a little while. I assume you know Nessus thinks every unnecessary minute you spend out there is a sign of insanity."

"Kirsten, what is this really about?" Eric asked.

"We have just built the means by which the Gw'oth civilization could be destroyed. Maybe the entire species. A comet striking their world would kill millions. To create such a device just in case . . . are we any better than those who attacked our ancestors?" She stared down at her boots. "Is the Concordance?"

He grabbed an arm and jerked her around to face him. "How *dare* you make such accusations against Citizens! Someone, and we'll never know who, attacked the starship transporting our ancestors. It was a Citizen vessel that found the hulk, dying and adrift. You *know* how fearful Citizens are, and yet they boarded the derelict, they rescued the frozen embryo banks, and they salvaged whatever few artifacts they could carry in a vessel no larger than *Explorer*.

"Kirsten, they might have left the hulk lost in space, and our ancestors with it. Instead, they saved us. They created a whole language and culture for us. They gave us our whole world. So don't expect *me* to think ill of them or their motives."

Every word he spoke was true, and yet . . . together, under Nessus' tutelage, they had created this frightful device. How could any sense be made of that?

Eric was staring at her. She had to respond to his outburst *somehow*. "I don't know what to say. Maybe this is just too far from home for me."

"I'm going back on public in a moment," Eric said. "But yes, we are a long, *long* way from home."

Meaning he accepted her rationale? Meaning he took her almost-apology as a long-awaited acquiescence to his advances? In either case, she breathed a sigh of relief. It seemed that her unworthy misgivings would, at least for the moment, remain between them.

7

Kirsten did not know whether they had passed or failed.

All she knew—all Nessus had told the three of them—was that he had decided to return to the Fleet. Any danger from the Gw'oth was far into the future. The Concordance government could choose a course of action, which might be simply to change the Fleet's path slightly.

And the Gw'oth? Nessus assured them the comet experiment had been canceled. The altered snowball would stay far from G567-X2. She could neither confirm nor refute, much as she yearned to, that the danger to the ice moon had passed.

Nor could she cajole Nessus for reassurance. Once they had exited the singularity and reentered hyperspace for the flight home, he had locked himself in his cabin, and answered no inquiries. His manic phase had given way to its opposite.

On the other head, Nessus' withdrawal during the long journey home gave her unsupervised time to think.

* * *

Gw'oth ventures above the ice fascinated Kirsten. How brave they were to explore such a hostile domain with only the most primitive of technologies to sustain them! Their quest for knowledge, the expansion of their capabilities, and the vigor of their efforts were inspiring—

And they awakened in her a new attitude toward her own kind.

Colonists did not have pride. Why would they, without successes to call their own? NP4 had been tamed before they first set foot on it. Their technology had been handed to them, and even that technology, everyone knew, was far beneath what the Citizens controlled. Their benefactors considered them unworthy, or unprepared, or in some other as-yet undefined sense not ready, to share in all that the Concordance had researched and invented.

Knowing in the abstract of whole worlds with indigenous civilizations was one thing. Observing the strivings of the Gw'oth was so much more. The experience made the lost home of her kind *real* to her. Somewhere out there was a world, a place as real and unique as the ice moon of the Gw'oth.

In her mind was a pale blue spheroid that resembled NP4, but with all outlines blurred. Her ancestors must have tamed that world, and developed their own technology, and ventured unaided into interstellar space. If she could respect the Gw'oth for their accomplishments, how could she not admire her own ancestors?

What were they like? How did they organize themselves? To what goals did they strive? What language did they speak? Surely it was more logical and structured than this English the Citizens had invented for them.

Her newfound interest made all the more troubling how little could be found in *Explorer*'s library about the Colonists' long-ago rescue.

Three on the bridge was a tight fit. Omar and Eric sat side by side, hips touching, sharing Nessus' padded bench.

Omar had brought in a tray with three hot bulbs of stim juice. "Thanks for coming," Kirsten began.

"What's up?" Omar waved at the controls in front of him. She took the gesture to mean: Do we need Nessus here?

That Nessus continued to hide in his cabin served her purpose. Her ability to formulate such rebellious thoughts remained new enough to surprise her.

She had decreed a sanity break in normal space. Diamondlike points of light shone through the bridge's presently uncovered view ports. The distant Fleet remained invisible to the naked eye. "It's really *empty* out here, isn't it?"

"That's not exactly big news," Omar said.

"No, but it's hard to truly grasp *how* empty until you're living with it." She let them consider that for a moment. "Imagine how unlikely it was that a Citizen ship should encounter our ancestors adrift." How very unlikely, given that hyperdrive-equipped ships dropped back into normal space only occasionally. How especially unlikely, if adrift meant, as was always part of the story, that their saviors noticed a ship whose fusion drive was inoperative. *Explorer*'s sensors could not spot such a derelict unless it was nearly on top of them.

Eric glanced in the direction of Nessus' cabin. "We were lucky, I suppose. We should be thankful."

Had that passing look denoted fear? Skepticism? Warning? She would know soon enough. If she was correct, this would be the hardest on him. "You both know I've been researching primitive technology. I thought it could be instructive to contrast the Gw'oth experience with what Citizens have seen in their travels."

She called up a holo to summarize her findings—or rather her paucity of findings. She opened a second display. "Here's how I queried the library. Am I doing anything wrong?"

Omar studied the images. "Your queries look fine to me."

"Nessus *told* us he didn't want our investigations influenced by knowledge of other aliens," Eric said. "I'm not surprised he removed such material from our library. He was obviously right—*some* of us couldn't be trusted not to look."

Kirsten ignored the criticism. "Next, I wondered if the history of the Citizens themselves might have relevant material." Two more holos she opened implied another excision from the library.

"Kirsten, *why* are we here?" Omar asked. "It wasn't to sympathize with what Nessus chose to exclude from the library."

Her eyes twitched involuntarily toward Nessus' cabin. Had her precautions been successful? "Bear with me." She offered another query. It was the opposite of what she had queried for before: everything *un*related to prespaceflight technology history.

A warning message chastised her for her overbroad search. The only hint the library provided as a measure of the relevant results was two very large numbers. One number was merely the count of related files. The second number, an even more prodigious value, showed the extent of the data in those related files. "Consider this, gentlemen. I ran complementary queries. The first asked for everything related to early technology history. The second asked for everything *not*. The combined results should encompass the capacity of the library. They don't."

"Obviously," Eric sniffed, "Nessus anticipated your prying. The unaccounted-for storage must be files he reserved for himself."

"Obviously. As a confirmation, consider *these* queries." Her next requests sought what was, and what was not, in the library regarding hyperdrive technology. It was no secret Citizens reserved hyperdrive theory for themselves. To no one's surprise, Kirsten's paired searches revealed another large inaccessible region. "Are we agreed? This is a valid way to measure the extent of hidden data on a given topic?"

Saying nothing at all this time, Omar looked pointedly at Nessus' controls.

Perhaps there was more to their captain than Kirsten had suspected. She ignored the apparent warning. "It works with searches using date parameters, too. Would anyone be surprised to know there's an off-limits region that continues to grow even as we travel home?"

Omar stood, clumsily dismounting from the padded bench. A shoe-tip caught, and he fell across Nessus' control console. "Crap!" He got back to his feet, juice all over his shirt, his beverage bulb squashed flat. "That's hot." The liquid beaded quickly, unable to adhere to the nanocloth, and trickled to the deck.

More stim juice dripped down the controls. Omar removed his shirt and with it blotted ineffectively at the console. Reflexively, Kirsten looked away—it was unseemly for her to see Omar's bared chest. But she looked back at what his hands were doing.

That was no random spot on the console! Growth in the archives even while they remained in hyperspace suggested Nessus did not limit his eavesdropping to the Gw'oth. Kirsten had found a sensor hidden on the bridge—exactly where the spill had occurred and the location Omar's wadded shirt now covered and muffled. He, too, had located the concealed camera.

"We can get away with this only once." Omar was suddenly more direct than Kirsten had ever seen him. "Nessus may be suspicious regardless. Whatever you have to say better be important. And Eric—do *not* ask."

Eric looked ready to explode, but he stayed quiet.

"There was an unfortunate spill before I called you both here," Kirsten said. "Hopefully it worked." Nessus would never believe two innocent accidents could occur so close together. "I'll tell you what's so important.

"We've all been raised on the heroic tale of the rescue of our ancestors. How dangerous the tumbling derelict was, its hull agape, the victim of unknown and unknowable assailants. How back-projection along its apparent path suggested no plausible candidate sun for hundreds of light-years. Perhaps it had been adrift for a *long* time, or its crew had changed course in a desperate run from peril. Either way, there was no clue to its point of origin. After the embryo banks were rescued, the wreck was abandoned in deep space, its fate unknown. All in all, what we've been taught is how very little the Concordance knows of our past. Now watch."

Her final two queries revealed yet another inaccessible region within the library. Its topic was "pre-NP4 history of Colonists" and its extent was vast.

Nessus had begun to dare to hope that this mission would be deemed a success. The Colonists had functioned well as a team, operated the ship effectively, and learned a great deal about the Gw'oth.

As importantly, they had proven loyal. Kirsten's assertiveness, as respectfully expressed as it had been, had briefly worried him. He need not have been concerned. When the time came, she had helped implant the comet with a thruster-equipped probe. Obedience to Citizens was an ingrained part of Colonist society.

The Fleet would have more scouts and better preparation for its dash from the galaxy . . . and those happy, risk-reducing results were because of *him*. When he returned in triumph, in this, the Fleet's time of need, all things would be possible for him.

So many had doubted him. It had gladdened him to imagine what consternation his unorthodox success would evoke in his heads-under-their-bellies parents. He had daydreamed of recognitions and honor from his new friends, the Experimentalists. The achievements of this mission could result, quite possibly, in that most precious of rewards: a mate. And not just *any* mate—

When he returned in triumph, even subtle, graceful Nike would surely be approachable.

Yes, he had begun to dare to hope . . . until the private recall message had arrived. Its few brief words left him cowering in his cabin, all thoughts of personal advantage forgotten. Nothing seemed to matter. He ate from the small synthesizer in his room. He could not be bothered to replace the sensor that had shorted out on the bridge. The Colonists would get him back to Hearth whether he paid attention or not.

The unexpected message read in its entirety: "Return immediately to the Fleet. Wild humans are close to finding us."

"I can't explain what's going on," Kirsten said, "beyond that the Concordance knows far more about our past than they have shared. I intend to discover the truth. To begin with, I'm going to find our ancestors' ship."

"That's impossible." Eric sat slumped on Nessus' bench, his belief system shattered. He looked deflated. "It was abandoned hundreds of years ago. How can we possibly know where to begin?"

How can *we* possibly know? He believed her! Kirsten set aside all her doubts and uncertainties. "Whatever clues there are will be found where we are now going.

"Whatever secrets the Concordance has, they hold on the Fleet of Worlds."

QUEST

Earth date: 2650

8

Nike's office was a stepping disc away from his apartment. Barring emergency, he never commuted that way. Teleportation offered efficiency, but neither comfort nor information.

He teleported now to his arcology lobby, walking briskly off a stepping disc there and pressing through the gentle force field that divided the climate-controlled atrium from the exterior walkways. Buildings extended up and down the mall as far as the eye could see. The least of the arcologies towered to a thousand times his height.

Herd scent embraced him like a warm bath. With a sociable nudge, Nike plunged into the unending stream of pedestrians. Chance bumping and brushing of flanks was as reassuring as it was unavoidable.

Heads craning as he walked, Nike surveyed utility belts and decorative sashes, the ribbons and jewels adorning manes, and ornamental brooches. As always, he spotted the greens of those declaring their Conservative loyalties and the orange shades that identified Experimentalists.

Declarations of allegiance to hobbies, professional affiliations, and social clubs greatly outnumbered any factional color. The spectrum of adornment only highlighted a reality Nike had sadly accepted: Passions had cooled in the years since the discovery of the explosion in the galactic core.

And why not? The sky glow of continent-spanning cities masked the shifting of constellations. Only sophisticated instruments could discern the operation of the reactionless drive that continued to accelerate the Fleet of Worlds. Departure from the galaxy would change nothing for the vast majority of Citizens, or their children, or their children's children, for countless generations—for those who still measured the passage of time in generations. Births were as rare as deaths among the Citizens.

Thus the extraordinary had become mundane had become all but forgotten. Escape from the galaxy had been entrusted to Conservatives too unimaginative to have initiated it. This was how the Concordance dealt with every emergency. With a tremble of frustration, Nike straightened the large orange brooch pinned to his utility belt.

Conversations ebbed and flowed all around him. They dealt with family and friends, art and theatre, shopping and government. The little political discussion he heard involved nuances and trivia, nothing that might favor reconsideration of those most suited to lead from behind.

Of course, few shared his knowledge. With that recollection, Nike declared this unscientific poll sufficient for the day. Nearing a public stepping disc embedded in the walkway, he dipped a head into a pocket. With nimble lip nodes he retrieved an address from his personal transport controller; his tongueprint authorized access to a secured file. The disc flicked him instantly to a restricted location: the employee vestibule of the foreign affairs ministry.

"Sir," whistled the guards who encircled the entry area. Taking turns, they briefly lowered their heads in respect. The motion began with the guards standing nearest to Nike and traveled around the group, so that at all times most sentries remained attentive to the discs.

Pulling his head from his pocket, Nike assumed the wide-legged, no-need-to-run stance of confident leadership. "My greetings," he chanted formally. He gestured, and two guards sidled away to clear his path. He walked briskly to a second group of restricted discs, discs that provided access to workspaces within the ministry. Another tongue-locked address delivered him to the maximally secured complex of offices that was Clandestine Directorate.

Functionaries emerging from their warren of work

nooks repeated the gesticulations of esteem. "Deputy Minister. Sir. Your Excellency." Nike most savored grudging bows from the Conservatives in this herd. With the Conservatives in power, of course the Minister was a Conservative. *All* ministers in the present government were Conservatives.

Whatever the political balance, however, most positions of responsibility in *this* ministry remained with the Experimentalists. Despite generations of acculturation, few Conservatives could bear to deal directly with Colonists. There were never enough, and anyway, managing the Colonists was the simplest part of the ministry's mission. Only the truly exceptional could cope with wild aliens, and none but Experimentalists had the flexibility of mind to work with the exceptional. The Clandestine Directorate was and would remain an enclave of Experimentalists.

Too many in Nike's party bemoaned the short memories of the masses. He did not. To deny the wisdom of the majority was the very definition of insanity. Those who now led the Experimentalists from behind had resigned themselves to another epoch of powerless opposition.

Which was why, thought Nike, when we Experimentalists next return to power, the party will not be led by any of them.

Nike straightened again into the stance of supreme confidence. Heads held high, he strode toward his private office. Its personal door bespoke his high status. Just before shutting it, he announced to all, "I am not to be disturbed."

". . . Disappearance of General Products representatives continues to stoke interest in Puppeteer affairs. United Nations authorities continue their full search for your home system. They rationalize the hunt by claiming that in GP's absence some contractual commitments might go unfulfilled or warranty obligations become unenforceable.

I have yet to gain access to the investigators' files, but it is thought a wide-ranging analysis of astronomical anomalies might—"

Nike paused the hyperwave message. The human in the recording stood unmoving. A thousand details, from her bold skin-dye pattern to the cut of her clothing, made clear that she was not one of the Colonists.

Her use of the term "Puppeteer" told Nike the same. When representatives of the Concordance had eventually revealed themselves to the indigenous civilization within the tiny bubble of stars so presumptuously deemed Known Space, the human explorer Pierson had likened Citizen anatomy to a three-legged centaur with two sock-puppet heads. The name Puppeteer had stuck.

The wild human's mouth had been open at the moment the image was frozen. Just now, that gaping orifice made the torrent of bad news seem unending. At least having a personal office meant Nike might compose himself a bit in private.

Perhaps the wild humans would have the last laugh. Following the success of the Colonist experiment, many Experimentalists had taken human names as an affectation. The appellation he had chosen was suddenly like ashes in his mouths: Nike, the deity of victory.

The question was: victory for whom? How might wild humans react if they were to discover the Fleet—and with it, the Concordance's human servants?

At least the wild humans continued to look, mistakenly, for a home world still anchored to a solar system. Not even the most trusted human agent had been told that six worlds had flown free of their sun.

Nike found himself pacing around the soft, padded work surface that occupied a significant fraction of his office. He needed to calm himself. With one mouth holding a comb, the second a mirror, he meticulously smoothed and layered and arranged his braids. As always, the grooming routine soothed him.

His intercom lowed. "Your Excellency." His assistant's voice was softly respectful over the intercom.

"Yes," Nike replied.

"It is nearly time for the rally. You asked to be reminded."

With a few deep breaths Nike banished a slight trembling from his limbs. What his distant agent reported made it vital that the Experimentalists reclaim power.

That, in turn, made his rally all the more crucial.

Nessus trotted as quickly as the teeming throngs permitted, hooves clicking on the hard surface of the wide boulevard. His destination remained unseen no matter how much he craned a head, but it never occurred to him to use the public stepping discs that might have sped him the final small fraction of his journey. "What a beautiful day," he hummed softly to himself. Despite the din of the crowd, several heads twisted his way in inquiry. He could not resist responding with a one-eyed blink. Why *not* smile? He was delighted to be off *Explorer*. To be home. He was *so* happy that his mane, although not stylishly coiffed, was uncharacteristically neat, combed and pulled back by two orange ribbons.

The walkway broadened as he neared the park. Greeters spaced every few body lengths bobbed heads in welcome, bunches of bright ribbons for the party faithful clasped in their mouths. Nessus took two brilliant orange-and-gold streamers and merged into the waiting crowd. Many had draped their new ribbons about their necks. Nessus happily followed their example.

A Citizen to Nessus' left tapped his shoulder. "It's an excellent turnout."

"I completely agree." Nessus had spoken only English with the Colonists for *so* long. It still felt wonderful beyond words to warble and trill, to roll long arpeggios from his tongues, to harmoniously entwine elaborate speech with himself and others—to truly *talk*. The Gw'oth seemed only a distant memory. "It's for a great cause."

"Have you been to other Permanent Emergency rallies?" asked his new friend.

"Some." Not as many as I would like, Nessus thought. He made no mention of his long absence. Even the partial truth he was permitted to share, that he had been away on NP4, would cause most people to back away. Association with the insane was but another risk the majority shunned.

Before thoughts of separateness could ruin his high spirits, Nessus immersed himself in the moment. The contrapuntal themes of thousands of voices, the milling herd, and the scent-rich air enveloped him. And soon enough, *Nike* would orate.

Speaker after speaker crooned about risks and perils, about the many dangers from which Experimentalists had saved the Concordance in times past. It was familiar and exciting at the same time. Nessus' heads, like those around him, bobbed agreement: up/down, down/up, up/down, down/up.

"Our flight from the galaxy is likely the first," warbled the current speaker. "It will surely not be the last. Race after race must follow us, all the more desperate for their unwise delays. Imagine their panic as the wall of radiation from the core explosion draws near. All the laggard races desperately seek energy and supplies where wiser races have already refueled and resupplied. Now picture some of these needy, desperate refugees encountering the Fleet of Worlds. They detect our prudently collected resources. Will the Concordance be safe then?"

"No!" The tens of thousands packed haunch to haunch in the small park roared as one. Around Nessus, hooves pawed at the ground in anxious contemplation of distantly glimpsed perils.

"Is the danger passed?"

"No! No!"

"Is our course of action so clearly a matter of routine

that we should entrust the existence of the Concordance to Conservatives?"

"No! No!"

"When will it be safe?"

It began in a thousand jarring dissonances, and then converged into a chord of tremendous power. "After the emergency!"

After the *permanent* emergency, that was. It was a concept too new to judge, an upending of all norms, breathtaking in its audacity—and for that, frightening in its own way. Even most Experimentalists balked at the concept. For Nessus, scarcely split from his Conservative upbringing, it remained too great a leap. It did not matter. In his hearts, Nessus knew his interest in the Experimentalist Faction of the Permanent Emergency was not about policy.

A delicate figure materialized onto the park's central knoll, magnified many times in an overhead holo. His skin was a pale tan, without spots or other markings. Delicate filigree of orange and gold blended with the waves of his tawny mane, gleaming under the spotlights. Other than on the Hindmost himself, and perhaps on the would-be Hindmost who led the Experimentalists, Nessus had never seen such an elegant coiffure.

Nike stood, legs far apart, totally poised, in the stance of confident leadership.

Amid tens of thousands of ululating stalwarts, Nessus acknowledged a private truth. He would do *anything* to win the heads of, and the right to have children with, the beautiful and charismatic leader.

Every arcology offered many dining halls. The myriad conversations in each assembly freely started and ended, coalesced and diverged, waxed and waned to reflect the interests and experiences of thousands of diners. How could it be otherwise, with so many professions, hobbies, political opinions, and individual interests represented?

And yet, as Nessus exited a stepping disc into his usual dining hall, one topic clearly predominated: Nike's speech. The din was inordinate. How loud would it be, he wondered, without noise cancellation?

Row after row of triangular tables receded into the distance. Nessus paced deep into the vast room, searching for familiar faces. He nudged his way into the gap between two acquaintances, settling astraddle a long padded bench. Signaled by his weight on the bench, a shallow trough of mush, a loaf of bread, and a bowl of chilled water materialized on the tabletop in front of him. The shipboard freedom to select his own diet was already a fading memory.

To each side of him, a head bobbed in welcome. Nessus knew both Citizens from the dining hall, suggesting they lived somewhere in the arcology. An orange ribbon on one and orange utility-belt pockets on the other marked them as fellow Experimentalists, just as an absence of gold suggested they were not of Nike's faction.

A lack of contact with humans, wild or domesticated, was no obstacle among Experimentalists to the selection of a human-style nickname. In his dining companions' case, musical hobbies provided ample inspiration.

"Euterpe, Orpheus," Nessus acknowledged. He spoke with one-head informality, his other already busy with his food. He had skipped a meal in favor of an earlier start to the rally, and now he was famished. "How goes the latest composition?" Honestly, he did not care. It was a question likely to evoke two long answers during which he could eat.

His plan failed.

"Good, good," answered Euterpe. Setting down his half-eaten loaf, he double-warbled a short, mellifluous passage. Partway through, Orpheus joined in. "That can wait. We were talking"—Euterpe made a gesture with one sinuous neck that encompassed the whole dining hall—

"*everyone* is talking, about Nike's latest speech. Did you hear any of it?"

There was an undertune of skepticism to Euterpe's words. Nessus answered cautiously. "Some."

"It's amazing. No, worse—it's unprecedented," Orpheus said. His disdain did not hide in mere undertones.

Nessus tapped a keypad on the table to recycle the rest of his synthesized grain mush, his appetite lost. The half-filled trough vanished. He said, "The chain reaction of supernovae at the galaxy's core is unprecedented. The wave front of radiation that will sterilize everything in its path is unprecedented. Is it so surprising that our course of action must also be unprecedented?"

"Not the course of action." Orpheus paused during a long sip of water, his opinion evidently too important to convey with a single throat. "Most people, well, most Experimentalists, would agree with you. Whatever our response is or becomes must surely be without precedent. But once we have followed that course of action for a time—Nessus, does it not become precedent? *Has* it not become precedent?"

From beyond Orpheus, a homey smell made itself known: manure. The soft plop had barely penetrated Nessus' consciousness. The dropping was already whisked away.

Tables covered with stepping discs to deliver sustenance. Aisles paved with stepping discs, imprinted with filters that passed excrement, and excrement only, directly back into the synthesizers. Grazing and fertilizing—the herd had done both together since before it became aware of its own actions. Technology merely made the process more efficient.

No other known intelligent species was herbivorous and only herbivores eliminated where they ate. Part of Nessus' preparation for visits to other intelligent species had been bowel training. Once again, he felt out of place.

"Nessus," fluted Euterpe impatiently. "Do you not see Orpheus' point?"

Sadly, Nessus did, or rather the deeper reality that lurked beneath his herdmate's observation. Success created familiarity, and familiarity bred complacency—even among Experimentalists. His travels had revealed but the tiniest fraction of the galaxy, but that limited exposure often amazed him. The Gw'oth were merely the latest wonder. What other surprises, what unimaginable perils, yet lay in the path of the Fleet?

In the unprecedented flight from the core explosion, complacency could kill them all.

Once more, companionship shifted without warning into an unbearable reminder of how maladjusted, how unlike his own kind, he had become. Excusing himself, Nessus took the closest stepping disc that would return him to the doorless, windowless little cube that was his home.

Nike, he realized, was correct. Escape from the core explosion was a permanent emergency, or so close to permanent that the difference could not matter for many generations.

For all Nessus' dread on behalf of the Concordance, his heads now tucked snugly between his forelegs, he could not help but notice the irony. The very fear that threatened to immobilize him also provided his best hope of finally meeting the object of his affections.

9

Waves crashed against the rocky cliffs that rimmed the Great North Bay. Salt spray leapt high into the air. Between crests, phosphorescent foam undulated and sudsed amid the scree. Atop the craggy heights at the head of the bay, it was just possible to sense the wall of water onrushing from its mouth. A gorgeous blue-and-brown-and-white world, the source of the oncoming tidal surge, hung overhead, dominating a clear night sky aglitter with stars. NP3's single string of orbiting suns was doubly bright for their reflections from its equatorial ocean.

"Wow." Omar's mouth opened and closed experimentally a few times, but he failed to find any word more suitable. "Wow," he repeated.

Five companion worlds meant ten tides every day, and nowhere on NP4 did the tides surge as high as in this remote fjord. Kirsten had been awestruck on her first visit. She had not budged from the spot for days. Remembering, she grinned. "Then it's all right that I rousted you guys a little early from your sleeping bags?"

"It would have been wrong to come this far and *not* see this." Eric paused for effect. "Now about coming out here at all . . ."

"You have *got* to be kidding, Eric," Omar said. "We all grew up in cities. The woods we hiked in through and this rugged coast are as exotic as anything we found on the Ice Moon, but *this* we get to experience in person. How can you not appreciate such a spectacular view?"

Eric wiped salt spray from his forehead with the back of a hand. "You're right. I am kidding. Good idea, Kirsten, to drag us out here—even if it is the farthest corner of Arcadia."

The night was chilly. She raised the heater setting on her coveralls before answering. "We don't really see much of even our own world, do we?" She let them think about that as, with a roar, another great wave smashed into the cliffs. "Truthfully, only our own continent."

"Arcadia is more than ample. If this were our world entirely—" Eric began.

Omar cut him off. "We know, Eric. One isolated continent given over to the species preserved on our ancestors' ship. The remainder of NP4 dedicated to growing crops for the Citizens. Kirsten, I can't help but think there is more to this outing than the view. What, exactly, is out here?"

More to the point, she thought, was what was *not* out here: any Citizen presence. The closest stepping disc was half a day's hike distant through thick forest. Not even Nessus would care to approach this precipice and its spray-slick rocks. "Privacy is out here. Privacy to discuss my doubts."

Omar leaned against a nearby boulder. "Meaning the pre-Arcadia history files you found hidden aboard *Explorer?*"

"I was taken aback by that, too." NP3 light gave Eric's face a blue tinge. "I've had time since to think it through. Maybe I overreacted."

Implying that *she* had overreacted. "We've been lied to. I don't like that."

"I acknowledge information was withheld from us," Eric said. "At a minimum we were lied to about that information's existence. But have Citizens lied about anything substantive? We have no reason to believe so."

Kirsten felt her eyes widen in disbelief. "Why keep our history secret from us?"

"To protect us," Eric said. "Maybe our ancestors did something shameful, and they want to spare us the knowledge."

Something shameful? Her mind spun. "Or maybe the Citizens did something shameful to our ancestors, and want to keep *that* secret from us!"

Omar broke a lengthening, awkward silence. "Either way, the Concordance knows things about our past that we don't. It's a big file. They're hiding a lot." He stood and walked nearer to the precipice to stare at the surging tide. "We're not the first Colonists to see such discrepancies."

She remembered that Omar, too, had known about the sensor hidden on *Explorer*'s bridge. "Omar, who are you really?"

"You mean other than your captain: above all reproach,

beyond any question, and more than a little obsequious?"
Omar smiled, and Kirsten could not help but think how
different this self-confident, self-deprecating man was
from the Omar who always deferred to Nessus. "I'm
someone who was asked in confidence by someone in the
Arcadia Self-Governance Council to keep my eyes open.

"I'm glad that you arranged this secluded outing. It's
time we started working together."

There was a bit of conventional wisdom in which Kirsten
had never placed any stock, that any Colonist was only a
few degrees of separation removed from any other. As she
kept her eye on her cousin's next-door neighbor's visiting
friend's mate—who just happened to be the chief archivist for Arcadia—she thought she might have reason to
reassess.

The apparent chance meeting was Omar's doing, or at
least he had brought the opportunity to her attention. Her
questions about how he had identified the opportunity
elicited only a knowing smile. Leveraging her celebrity
status as an *Explorer* crew member to obtain an appointment with Sven would have been easy. The trick was to
talk with the archivist without leaving an audit trail. Were
Citizens monitoring the network activities of *Explorer*'s
crew, or of Sven Hebert-Draskovics, the archivist, or of
Omar's undisclosed contacts in the Self-Governance
Council? The microphone hidden on *Explorer*'s bridge
made such unannounced supervision all too plausible.

This community party provided a perfect venue for an
innocent encounter. People filled the streets, food and
drink in hand, chatting and milling about. Kirsten eventually wandered to where Sven stood in conversation with
someone she did not recognize. With casual nods and
comments on the day's fine weather, she worked her way
into the conversation. In time, Sven's friend went looking
for a fresh beverage.

"What do you do?" she asked after a while.

"Nothing interesting, I'm afraid," he answered. "I keep dusty old records."

"Dusty?"

Sven laughed. "Pardon my whimsy. Of course, most records are computerized. That was a metaphor, to denote age."

"You lost me," Kirsten said.

"That's one of my skills." He glanced about for someplace to exchange his empty beer bulb for a full one. "I deal with obscurity for a living. I'm the Colony archivist."

"I didn't know we had an archivist," she lied. "Dusty old records, you say. You must know all about the founding of the colony, with all that information at your disposal."

"I generally deal with more modern times. Production data, census compilations, weather statistics, that sort of thing. Still, I may know more than most about the early days." He looked a bit wistful. "That may be less than you would expect."

"Hold on." Kirsten grabbed the sleeve of the man walking by with a tray of sliced cheese. Feigning disinterest in what Sven had just said, she took her time pondering her selection. Did her lost ancestors have words for devious and unsanctioned data collection? Certainly the vocabulary developed for the Colonists did not. "Sorry. You were saying something about 'less than I'd think.' "

"Few records and artifacts survive from those early times."

Despite herself, Kirsten blinked in surprise. "I didn't think information was ever lost. Citizens have backups and backups of backups."

"Of course," Sven agreed. "That is, Citizen computers are massively redundant and frequently backed up. The Citizens who established Arcadia colony chose not to interface the recovered computers to their own networks. They were concerned a connection would be unsafe. Events proved them correct."

Youngsters dashed past, flapping their arms and whooping, their antics random as far as Kirsten could judge. She let the noisemakers recede before cautiously following up. "Recovered computers? Oh, you mean salvaged from our ancestors' drifting starship. Did they matter?"

"Nothing mattered more." Sven ran a hand, fingers splayed, through his thinning black hair. He wore a marriage ring and a progeny band with three small rubies. "Maintenance of the embryo banks, real-time control of the artificial placentas, nutritional requirements of the newborns—it *all* depended upon our ancestors' computers. And it's all lost."

"Lost? How?"

"A fire. It's believed a piece of the recovered equipment must have started it."

Of course Citizen equipment could never fail dangerously. But still . . . "Sven, I'm confused. That equipment maintained the embryo banks safely from the attack until a Citizen ship arrived. Then it withstood experimentation while Citizens learned how to operate it. It ran long enough thereafter to gestate at least one generation, or none of us would be here. And *then* one day it burst into flame?"

"Unfortunate, I know." He coughed. "There's no helping it, though."

Her ancestors' computers were insufficiently trusted to be connected to the Citizen network. The same computers were entrusted with the primary Citizen records of the founding of the colony! At least one of those statements *must* be incorrect. Perhaps both were.

What would the archivist have to say about the extensive, if inaccessible, pre-NP4 history files she had unveiled aboard *Explorer*? "So our past is lost. As you say, there's no helping it." Smiling to show she was joking, Kirsten added, "We won't know until we inspect the derelict. I don't suppose you have any records where it went."

"Now there's a crazy idea," Sven laughed. "Imagine, finding that ancient ship, lost in space, after all this time."

Doubtless, it was a crazy idea. Like Nessus, Kirsten was not about to let a little matter of insanity stand in her way.

10

The summons was both exhilarating and unnerving. Approaching the appointed time, Nessus tongued the message's stepping-disc coordinates.

His tiny sleeping quarters vanished; he reappeared inside an even smaller, clear-walled chamber that looked into an unoccupied waiting room. A blue beam scanned him, presumably checking for dangerous implements even as it took his retinal prints. His gentle rap on the foyer wall confirmed his suspicion: This was no ordinary entrance. He was enclosed in the near-impregnable material used in spaceship hulls. Ceiling-mounted high-intensity lights shone brightly on him. Their intensity could surely be raised to lethal levels—and visible light was one of the few things that could penetrate General Products hull material.

Nessus was suddenly outside the security chamber, delivered by the stepping disc on the isolation booth's floor. "Welcome to the Ministry of Foreign Affairs," a recording fluted and trilled. "Please wait here."

He settled onto a pile of plush cushions. Nessus took no offense at being made to wait; the security precautions had unnerved him. He appreciated having time to regain his composure. Of course, much more than security was on his mind.

Had he ever *not* been infatuated with Nike? For as long as Nessus could remember, the charismatic politician had been a darling of the media. Nike had such vibrancy and wit, such presence and poise—and such beauty—that he was constantly in the news. Nike's exotic political positions had only increased Nessus' fascination.

Parental disapproval had only encouraged Nessus' youthful obsession. He recorded Nike's every major public appearance, viewing them again and again. Many political events were open to the public; Nessus had attended at least sixty. Intellectually, he knew Nike's positions had changed repeatedly over the years. In his hearts, those shifts made no difference.

To his supporters, Nike was creative, flexible, and original. To his detractors, Nike was ambitious and bold. Ultimately, which description best fit did not matter. Nessus abandoned his family's generations-long tradition of Conservative allegiance. His family abandoned *him*.

While most of Nessus' peers wasted their time in idle socializing and frivolous hobbies, Nessus had volunteered for every experimental project that might attract Nike's attention. None did, so Nessus proposed his own, even more innovative programs. His Colonist explorer initiative had supposedly risen to Nike's personal attention.

Today, he would finally meet Nike!

"Follow me." A tall, green-eyed aide, a green brooch pinned to his utility belt, had appeared across the room. His posture hinted at disdain for this scruffy visitor. "The Deputy Minister will see you now." Then he was gone.

Nessus trotted, hearts pounding, to the temporarily active stepping disc. He emerged outside an open office door. Merely the wide padded work surface visible through the doorway was larger than his living unit. Lush meadowplant covered the floor. The green-eyed aide ushered Nessus inside, bobbing farewell as, from the outside, he closed the door.

"Your Excellency." Nessus lowered both heads submissively.

"Be comfortable." Nike extended a neck gracefully,

brushing heads with Nessus in greeting as though they were equals. "You may wonder why I asked you here."

Nessus settled awkwardly onto a guest bench. Artwork lined the large office. Much was holographic, of course, but crushed meadowplant showed that several of the large sculptures were carved from rock or cast in metal. Physical art, like the oversized office, bespoke vast power. It was surely meant to intimidate—and it succeeded.

He had imagined this day so many times, in so many ways, that he was at a loss now for what to say. It was all Nessus could do not to pick at his mane—or to cross his necks flirtatiously. "Yes, sir."

"Nike. And may I call you Nessus? Good. Those human-style designations are especially apt given our subject—

"—The recent *Explorer* mission."

Faces to faces, Nike's elegance and charisma were overwhelming. Nessus had missed something in his delighted shock. What about the mission? His report on the Gw'oth? The crew's capabilities? That was it. "Yes, Nike,"—how he reveled in speaking the name—"I consider the trip a success. A longer stay would have yielded more data, but not changed my positive assessment of the Colonists."

"Did you know I personally approved the experiment?" Nike watched Nessus closely. "I did. The Concordance is gifted with too few individuals able to search for danger in our path. Your imaginative solution to our problem is to be commended." Nike paused, for no apparent reason other than to let Nessus bask in the compliments. "I did not lightly call you back to the Fleet."

"I understand." The praise was exhilarating. "Then why, Nike?"

"We face more immediate dangers."

Nessus had not forgotten the hyperwave-radio recall message. "Have the wild humans discovered the Fleet?"

"Not yet. Our agents on Earth report that a serious search is under way."

"That has long been the case." Very few Citizens could confidently say that, but Nessus was one. In his early attempts to advance among the Experimentalists, he had served as a General Products Corporation representative in Human Space. Quite possibly, he had recruited the human agents of whom Nike spoke. "They have yet to succeed."

"They never before expended such resources in the effort," Nike persisted.

The earlier, unexpected flattery suddenly made sense. Nike's newfound interest in Nessus was not about the *Explorer* mission. This summons was about Nessus' earlier experiences. A hundred human-standard years earlier, a mere fifty human-standard years after Citizens had made themselves known to wild humans, Nessus had first entered Human Space.

Remembered fear and isolation flooded Nessus' mind. Only Nike's presence kept Nessus from rolling into a cowering, quivering ball. He told himself: Nike needs me.

Would returning really be *so* bad?

Every human world, even Earth itself, was an unpopulated wilderness. The poorest human tenements wasted volume profligately in hallways, stairwells and elevators, and individual food-preparation areas. And conditions in Human Space were primitive. When the Colonists' point of origin had finally been located, wild-human technology had advanced little beyond that of *Long Pass*. The Concordance, directly or otherwise, was the source of what few improvements had been made since. How much of that technology, Nessus wondered, would have been transferred to the humans absent experiments and experience with the unsuspecting, easily manipulated Colonists.

Primitive, but still dangerous.

Nessus had challenged *Explorer*'s crew with thoughts of pebbles turned into kinetic-energy weapons. Should humans find the Fleet, a stealthed ship jumped by hyperdrive into the Fleet's path could utterly destroy Hearth. And if the wild humans were to discover the Colonists and their history . . . would that not guarantee hostility?

Concentrate! After striving for so long to meet Nike, how could his thoughts have strayed?

He heard, ". . . Agent quite highly placed in the United Nations bureaucracy. This United Nations search for the Concordance is wider ranging than any before."

Knowledge would impress Nike. "Respectfully, that search cannot be sustained. The wild humans' primitive economy had become dependent on our General Products Corporation. Now that GPC has withdrawn, their economy has contracted. It will suffer for years."

The idea for GPC had originated in a historical entry in the *Long Pass* computers: the British East India Company. Concordance influence was more subtle, of course, than the crown-awarded monopoly over trade with the East Indies. GPC sold humans its indestructible hulls and accumulated vast sums of human money—funds whose main use was the purchase of behind-the-scenes influence. And much as India's sepoy armies battled Great Britain's enemies, the wild humans were readily manipulated into constraining other spacefaring species that might otherwise grow to trouble the Concordance.

Nessus had left behind highly placed agents, including a deputy undersecretary of the United Nations. Most had been recruited—compromised or bribed—very indirectly. They might still be reporting by hyperwave radio to the foreign-affairs ministry.

"Nike, wild humans sought the 'Puppeteer' home world the whole time I was in their region of space. The progress of some such efforts I tracked myself through the human news media. The UN also hunted us in secret. My agents reported on those efforts to me, often without knowing it. The longer those quests failed to find us, the deeper into space the humans looked." Each time Nessus appeared without protection under their yellow sun assured them that Puppeteers had evolved nearby a similar star. "While they keep looking at yellow suns, they'll never find us."

"And yet, despite their failures, they keep looking," Nike said. "Tell me about the ARM organization."

"The Amalgamated Regional Militia." It was an uncharacteristically modest name for an extremely powerful entity. "The ARM evolved as the law-enforcement branch of the United Nations. Its operatives are called ARMs, too."

"Are these ARMs capable?"

"Some." Once more, Nessus found himself struggling not to pick and tug at his mane. "ARMs are given psychoactive drugs to make them paranoid. When one such is smart, too—"

"I am told Sigmund Ausfaller is such a smart one," Nike said. "He is the organizer of the latest United Nations search for us. Our source says Ausfaller feels the haste in GPC's withdrawal from Known Space might have left traces, new clues. I fear his assessment could be correct."

Ausfaller! "He is among the humans' very brightest, a natural paranoid, and not easily distracted." Nor, despite several surreptitious attempts, had Nessus ever found a way to corrupt him. What might Ausfaller attempt if he were to find the NP4 colony? And yet . . .

Nessus had the start of an idea. It was not fully formed, nor necessarily practical. He would have to do a lot of thinking before he dared articulate it to Nike.

On the other head, it just might be brilliant.

With a fine-toothed comb in one mouth and tiny scissors in the other, the stylist made the final adjustments to Nike's mane. The dyes had already been touched up, the

hair carefully teased and layered, and the braids reknot-
ted and arranged. Hundreds of jewels had been woven
into place. Nike craned his necks, admiring the effect
from all angles. His elaborate coiffure required the twice
daily ministrations of a master hair artist—and that was
the point. Only one as successful and powerful as he could
afford the expense.

Nike chanted his approval. The hair artist dumped his
tools and unused ornaments into a sack and vanished from
Nike's residence via stepping disc. The many instruments
could be sorted and repacked elsewhere.

The figure in Nike's mirror was virile and command-
ing. Surely few in the audience of tonight's ballet would
be more dashing. Completing a pirouette of inspection,
he bobbed his heads high/low, low/high, in satisfaction
with both what he saw and his upcoming appointment.

Nessus, despite his excellent record, had been distracted,
sometimes all but tongue-tied, at their first meeting. Was
he sexually infatuated? Another hero-worshiper? Either
way, after the evening to which Nike had invited Nessus,
the smitten scout would do whatever Nike asked.

Knowing just how spectacular he would look by
farm-world light, Nike had directed Nessus to meet him
on a shore promenade. They would go to the ballet soon
enough.

Nike dipped a head into a pouch of his decorative
sash—no utilitarian pocketed belt tonight!—and with a
quick manipulation of his transport controller left the residence. He emerged to a place, rare in the world, devoid
of lamps, chandeliers, and glow panels. Artificial light
could only detract from the view.

Rising from the blackness of the sea was the planet
NP1. Beneath its ring of equatorial-orbiting suns, that
most ancient of Hearth's companions shone in full phase.
Its seas sparkled in brilliant blues and greens; its icecaps
were pure white. Countless reflections shimmered on the

swells that rolled slowly up the shore. A crescent NP5 was setting on his other side. Its suns were polar-orbiting, to provide a more constant climate from pole to pole. The visible arc of that world revealed vast cyclonic storms. His still-to-be-conceived children would be old before those storms subsided and this most recent world to join the Fleet became fully tamed and productive. As for NP2, NP3, and NP4, Hearth's rotation had temporarily hidden them from view.

"It's breathtaking," Nessus said. The tremor in his voice suggested he had wished to say *you* are breathtaking. He stood nearby, one head resting on the stout railing that separated the promenade from the gently sloping beach. His mane was as plain as could be: unimaginatively cut, earnestly combed flat, and bound into large clumps by a few simple ribbons. Still, by comparison with the holos in his file, Nessus was being uncharacteristically formal. Nike appreciated the attempt.

"It is beautiful," Nike agreed. There was no need to mention the exclusivity of this location, for the restricted stepping-disc address, and the one-time-use access code, said it all. They were sharing one of the few, small parts of Hearth not covered in arcologies.

Also unspoken was the prospect that Nessus, by remaining in Nike's favor, might join the community of privilege. Nike felt a moment of shame. No promise would be uttered, but a thousand generations of social convention spoke as loudly as words. Peril to the Concordance *must* be averted. He would do what he must to see that Nessus returned to Human Space.

"This is not natural." Nessus looked himself in the eyes briefly. As Nike suffered another twinge of guilt, Nessus continued. "As beautiful as is this unending night, other worlds have suns to warm them."

Suns, not the waste heat of a trillion occupants. Alone among the worlds of the Fleet, Hearth had no suns. Nike extended a neck. He pointed a head, lips pursed and tongue extended, at NP1. "We can enjoy that perspective from here."

Nessus swung a head from side to side disapprovingly. "I know it will never happen, but I wish I could show you the beauty of a true sunrise. The sky shading from darkest, star-spangled black to pale blue. Clouds aglow in yellows, pinks, and reds." For a long time, they stood side by side, watching long waves rush far up the shore. "I will enjoy the sunrises on Earth."

The words meant success—and renewed pangs of shame. "It's getting late," Nike said. "We should be on our way."

11

Kirsten led cautiously through thick underbrush, bending foliage from her path with a sturdy fallen branch she had retrieved from the forest floor. The dominant plants ranged from waist-tall to twice her height. Dense shrubs that she might almost call hedges predominated; they failed to qualify because of their plethora of colors. Fruits and flowers might fairly span the rainbow, she thought. Leaves should be green.

Like Omar and Kirsten, Eric wore muted colors today. It wasn't just for concealment. He had eased off on the styles and colors of a man seeking a mate. Perhaps his intentions had evolved during their time together aboard *Explorer*. Certainly his manners had.

"What's with that one?" Eric asked.

He was huffing from the unwonted exercise, and Kirsten suspected a stall. She hid a smile. "Which one?"

From the boulder where he had settled, Eric pointed. "That red thicket to my left, with dangling purple tendrils."

"I forget the name, but it's an insectivore. Citizens once planted them on the periphery of fields to protect crops." As though to demonstrate her point, several tendrils on the nearest red hedge lashed out, converging with a *snap*. A bit of diaphanous wing fluttered to the ground, the remains of a purple pollinator.

Omar grimaced at the display, and dropped his backpack. The groundcover into which it settled with a soft whoosh was dusty yellow, mosslike in texture, with scattered spiky flowers. "And this little training exercise you talked Nessus into authorizing—you say it's safe?"

"Relax, guys," she told them. "We don't smell a bit appetizing to anything here."

Could anything here even smell them? Kirsten found the odors a bit overpowering. An artificial herd pheromone had permeated the air aboard *Explorer,* but that was a single scent. Countless pungent, spicy aromas surrounded them here. The next time, she'd bring nose filters.

Having twice navigated interstellar space, she had expected the jaunt across the ocean to the continent of Elysium would seem inconsequential. In practice, leaving Arcadia was visiting a whole new world, and the suborbital hop was the least of the experience. Amid all this strangeness, she had no impenetrable hull, nor even a sturdy spacesuit, to protect her. It was too easy to forget, especially when not a farmer, that most of NP4 was a *Citizens'* nature preserve.

Of course Citizens work here, she reminded herself. How dangerous could it be?

Omar and Eric were exchanging a look. "Now that you've brought up smell, did you know how badly it was going to stink?" Eric asked. "Did that detail make it into your research?"

The brief stop was encouraging her muscles to assert themselves: They were tired. Tough. There was a long way to go before anyone rested. Bending forward slightly at the waist, she shrugged her backpack into a more comfortable position. "I'd like to find someplace more suitable for camping before dark." They all knew she had a very specific spot in mind.

Grumbling, Omar retrieved his own backpack. "Someone explain again why we didn't step there directly and set up camp? First flying here and then all this walking . . . it seems so primitive."

"There's a limit to how much kinetic energy a stepping disc can absorb or impart." Despite having agreed to this adventure Eric looked embarrassed, as though admitting to a limitation in Citizen technology were somehow disloyal. "Simple example: We're on the equator. Half the world away on the equator is where we want to be. Both locations, being at the same latitude, rotate at the same speed—but their instantaneous velocities are in opposite directions. Do the math: We're dealing with big numbers.

"Across much of Arcadia, and surely all over Hearth, the huge number of stepping discs avoids the problem. If the velocity difference between two locations is too large for a single-disc jump, the system moves you through intermediate discs. It happens so quickly you never experience the intermediate points. We flew here because the ocean is too wide for a disc-to-disc jump. We're hiking now because this wilderness Kirsten is so keen to get us eaten alive in is sparse on discs."

Omar peered dubiously into purple underbrush where a scurrying *something* had set ground-hugging fronds rustling. "What's the limit?"

"Two hundred feet per second," Kirsten answered him. No one understood why Citizens had come up with English units of measure to accompany the English language they had invented. Maybe they only used them with humans. She had had to master standard Concordance units to fly *Explorer*.

"Let's get going." She lobbed a pebble beyond the rustling. Something resembling a cross between a Citizen and a koala, but smaller than her hand, burst from the bushes to rush past them. "If that creature isn't too *scary* for you."

That brought the laughter she had hoped for. They resumed their hike through the transplanted Hearthian woods.

Their path was mostly west. Until the final circle of suns set, the north-south line was unmistakable. She pushed briskly forward, leading them to the true objective of this outing.

Kirsten felt herself beginning to tire; her crewmates, who lacked her considerable hiking experience, were staggering. Around them, branches creaked and leaves rustled. Unseen animals chattered and scuttled in the brush and high in the trees. NP4's suns had long ago set for the day. The only illumination to augment their flashlights was Fleet light dimly filtered through the many-hued forest canopy.

Their goal was a safety shelter deep in the woods. She had wondered how visible the structure would be amid such a variety of foliage colors. Now her concern seemed foolish. The blinking lights that outlined the building would have been unmistakable even without their rapid but random color-hopping. This was a Citizen refuge— she should have known better than to worry.

The shelter sat in the center of a clearing, bathed in the light of worlds. Three were presently visible: a crescent NP2, a full NP1, and Hearth.

Sunless Hearth was a world like no other. Between oceans as dark as pitch, continents sparkled like a million jewels. Each of those lights was a city larger than any on Arcadia. No matter how often Kirsten saw it, the sight was humbling.

"Whenever you're done gawking," Omar panted. A smile took the sting from his rebuke. "Even a Citizen's padded couch will feel good about now."

"Or a padded floor," Eric agreed.

A fifteen-mile hike through the wilds entitled them to

be weary. They had gone farther than was rational given their mid-afternoon arrival on Elysium. Had it been important to get specifically here, a stepping disc from the airport, or from a shelter closer to their departure, would have made much more sense—to a Citizen. Tomorrow, after a hike back out, none would ever suspect they had been here. Except—

"We'll be limping tomorrow," she said. "We'll take it easy. I know massage, I'll do you both." She waited for their nods.

Unlatching the door activated the inside lights. Kirsten led them inside. "All the comforts of home, my friends, and no records in the stepping-disc system." Were records kept of who went where when? She did not know, and asking might raise suspicions.

Wincing, Eric dropped his backpack. "I ache in places I didn't know had muscles. Maybe food will help."

"It never hurts," Omar said. He was sitting on the floor, boots off, massaging a foot. "Besides, whatever we eat will make someone's pack lighter."

"Good point." Eric started digging through his backpack. "Kirsten, any requests?"

"Whatever sounds good to you," she answered distractedly. Where was the comm terminal? No Citizen shelter could possibly be without one. "Remember to pack up the wrappers and any waste."

The terminal was behind her, immediately next to the door. With a second head, she would have found it sooner. "Here it is. I'm going to work."

The questions that obsessed her could be answered nowhere on Arcadia. She could not prove that assertion, but even if there *was* something there . . . how likely was she to uncover secrets that had eluded Sven, and all the archivists before him? No, it made more sense to search on the public Citizen data net.

That was her theory, anyway. This was her chance to test it.

With fingers interlaced, Kirsten cracked her knuckles. Eric's queasy expression made her chuckle. "I only have hands. This keyboard is meant for a Citizen's lip nodes."

"Then it *does* have keyboard input," Eric said.

"As backup to the voice-command mode, like aboard *Explorer*." A pleasant aroma began to make itself known. Beef stew, she thought, from a self-heating pouch.

"Eat, Kirsten." Omar held out an open pouch. "Can you operate the terminal?"

Suddenly she was ravenous. She devoured a third of the contents before responding. "It's like Nessus' console on *Explorer*. Yes, I can use it." Barely. An experimental button push brought up the greeting screen she had expected. "Welcome to . . . Herd Net," she translated. Nessus had decided it was easier to teach his crew to read Citizen than to translate the shipboard library into English. "We'll know soon if I read well enough to make sense of the public databases."

Her first accesses were for the benefit of any logging software at the unseen public data center. They retrieved information any Citizen on Elysium might request. She navigated slowly through holos describing NP4 geography and climate, the flora and fauna of Elysium, and a brief history of the reshaping of the planet to resemble an archaic Hearth. As she read, she finished her stew and burrowed into her own backpack for a juice pouch.

Omar stood behind her, looking over her shoulder. "It's kind of interesting. Maybe we should save some of it. Agreed?"

"Uh-huh." She snapped a memory cube into the download slot. "If nothing else, copying this might make it less obvious which subjects really interest us." She returned to a previously viewed summary of NP4 history. Now she drilled down to Arcadia, the human settlement, rather than Elysium.

"Look at that." Eric crouched for a closer look. "I count

far fewer links than before. Was Elysium settled before Arcadia?"

"Let's see." She tuned her requests to consider just the past two hundred years. "No, there's still more information about Elysium."

"Apparently Colonists aren't interesting." Omar sounded insulted. "Is anything new here about Arcadian history? It might be my language skills, or lack thereof, but I see nothing surprising."

Nothing caught Kirsten's eye either. "In the details, maybe. To be fair, there are words I don't know." She waited until Eric shrugged. "Regardless, I've downloaded all of it. Time for the big experiment."

She carefully entered a refined query: pre-Arcadian Colonist history.

After an agonizing few seconds, a list of topics materialized before them. Kirsten struggled with unfamiliar terms. Some struck her as English transliterated into Citizen characters. "Earth, humans, Long Pass, ramscoop, United Nations."

"Ramscoop sounds promising," Eric said. "Our ancestors' starship supposedly scooped interstellar hydrogen for its fuel. We're told they didn't have hyperdrive."

She selected *ramscoop.* Another multisecond delay got them only a "restricted" disclaimer. She tried Earth: restricted. Long Pass: restricted. Humans: restricted. She began timing the delays on her wrist clock implant. Her earlier, for-show searches had gotten near-instantaneous responses. "That's interesting. The time lag is consistent with a light-speed round trip to Hearth."

"Not an unexpected place for the Concordance to keep its secrets," Omar said. "Unfortunate, but not surprising. I guess it doesn't really matter, since the data are restricted."

Aboard *Explorer,* she had watched Nessus access restricted files. However clever they got, she saw no way to mimic a Citizen tongueprint. "No, I guess . . .

"Or maybe I *can* do something." The display was in its default mode, a format that efficiently allocated viewing volume to minimal file descriptors. With a few keystrokes, Kirsten changed visual layouts to a maintenance mode— and shivered. The inaccessible files were now time-stamped and sorted by their creation dates. "Whatever these are, they predate the founding of Arcadia colony."

12

Recent bravery was taking its toll.

Nessus cringed in his personal quarters, swinging between exhilaration and panic, too keyed up from his rendezvous with Nike to sleep. Their time together had been everything Nessus had dreamed. More. And yet . . . Nike was surely destined for great things. How dare a motley loner like him aspire to union with a likely future Hindmost?

Nessus plucked two-headedly at his mane, the few decorative touches he had so recently worn already picked apart. In all honesty, it had never been much of a decoration: a scattering of ribbons and a few lopsided braids. Nike's coiffure had been a work of art. What could Nike possibly think of him?

And so much for his principled rejection of mane adornment.

It had never before occurred to Nessus, but the quest to become Hindmost, to *seek* responsibility for the entire Concordance, demanded its own type of courage. The dangers to be faced were not physical, but the duty was surely unending. How could *he* possibly hope to conjoin with such a partner? And yet . . .

Their time together had been *fabulous*.

Fifty dancers, gliding and twirling in ever more intricate patterns, their hooves clicking ever faster in a frenetic crescendo. Afterward, a bejeweled gathering he could never have imagined, where he brushed flanks with some of the most powerful figures of the Concordance. Broad rows of grazing tables covered entirely with *grown* fare: grains and roots and freshly squeezed juices, without a speck of the synthesized food that sustained most Citizens.

All of it experienced with Nike.

Quivering muscles bespoke another swing back into depression—and Nessus rebelled against his instincts. He stepped to a place that always calmed him.

The visitor gallery was always crowded at Harem House.

In Nessus's stage of life, Harem House was something of an abstraction. He could be on any of a thousand floors, in any of a hundred physical locations. Until he entered a registered union, until that pairing was awarded a license to mate, the stepping-disc system would continue to deliver him to a random viewing area. However often he returned, he was unlikely to observe the same Companion herd twice. Social convention held this was for his own good, lest he form an unseemly attachment to a specific female.

Where a Citizen arcology would enclose living units and offices close-packed like blocks, Nessus now saw an open, naturelike expanse. Meadowplant spread before him, interrupted occasionally by shrubs and stands of trees, by ponds and bubbling streams. Digital wallpaper extended the rolling heath to the distant virtual horizon, beneath a hologram blue-and-scudding-cloud sky. The mating fields were, of course, elsewhere and not viewable.

Nessus pressed through the milling throng toward the soundproof, one-way viewing wall. He tried to ignore the pitying looks from doting couples. The singles in the room were in the clear minority, and most were younger than he. Someday, Nessus thought, it could be Nike and me here, awaiting the birth of our child. It *will* be Nike and me.

The judgmental whispering stung. On past visits Nessus had occasionally lied that his partner had been detained, speaking a bit overloud to some sympathetic-looking pair of observers. His mood now was too complex for such pointless subterfuge.

"There is our Bride."

A new couple had edged up to the window to Nessus' left. The lovers stood side by side, their adjacent necks entwined. The one who had spoken was tall, with bright blue eyes and a lush, simply groomed red mane. His partner was nearly as tall, with a handsome tan-on-cream patterning that reminded Nessus of a panda. Both wore brooches suggestive of an avocation in abstract art.

Using his free head and a straightened neck, one was pointing toward a cluster of three Companions. Their sides heaved slowly as they cropped the thick blue-green meadowplant.

"The middle one?" Nessus guessed. She was the thickest of the three, so most likely with child. There had been no introductions; Panda and Red were serviceable labels.

"That's her," Panda agreed. "She bears our child."

"Prosperity for you and your family," Nessus said. The traditional answer was the safest.

"She looks strong, don't you think?" Panda continued proudly.

"Very," Nessus said. In truth, Companions always seemed delicate to him. The tallest of them scarcely reached half the height of a Citizen. That was not the only difference, of course. The torsos of Companions, although brown-and-white patterned like those of Citizens, were entirely covered in fur.

Panda and Red prattled on about the intelligence of their Bride, oblivious to Nessus' torment. He wondered if he would lose all objectivity if—when—his own turn came. Size was only the most obvious difference between Citizens and Companions. Another differentiation was in the mane-covered cranial dome between the shoulders. In Companions, the hump was much flatter—because there was far less brain under the dome. Companions could not speak, nor were they capable of learning much, although the brightest among them, Nessus had heard, could understand a few words, and seemed to grow fond of their husbands.

That was far short of sentience.

There were times when Nessus thought the structured and unthinking life of the females was idyllic, and not only for the unimaginable luxuries of natural foods in this meadow-like setting. How liberating it must be *not* to strive, *not* to wonder for most of one's life whether he would ever be deemed worthy of siring children. But introspection was his doom; the diminutive and unthinking creatures before him faced their own. . . .

Panda and Red eventually departed. Nessus watched the Companions for a while longer, until being there without a mate became too awkward and painful.

All the while the possibility that had come to him in Nike's office continued to sharpen in Nessus' mind.

Nike roamed distractedly about his office. Scouts are a precious commodity, he assured himself. They are exceedingly rare, no more than a very few identified each generation. Why, but for such scarcity, would he, a deputy minister, have studied the personnel records of all of them? Why else would he have deigned to *meet* one? Each scout was aberrant in his way, needful of coddling, jollying, and other distasteful encouragement. Their missions inherently relied upon self-direction, exercised in isolation, far from the Fleet.

Only a motivated volunteer could perform such duty.

How could it be otherwise? Safety in numbers had been wired into Citizen genes long before the first glimmer of intelligence. Beyond the herd waited predators patiently stalking, ready to pounce on anyone too young or too old, too infirm or too inattentive, to keep pace with the herd. Yet what if none were to scout ahead for new pastures? The whole herd might starve.

Hearth had long been purged of its native predators, but more sinister dangers lurked. Spacefaring alien races surrounded them. Hearth's once-yellow sun had swollen into a red giant, generations ago, initiating the planet's first epic voyage. The galactic core itself had erupted into a storm front of lethal radiation thousands of light-years thick. If none ventured ahead, who would warn the Fleet of new perils? Without scouts, how would the Concordance know where to flee from danger?

It was all a rationalization, of course. A secluded walk on the shore, the ballet, the private party after . . . Nike knew he had crossed a line with Nessus. The wild-eyed, mangy-maned scout was all too obviously smitten with him. Without shame, Nike had exploited that infatuation.

There was ample shame now, however belatedly, and Nessus had requested urgently to see him again. Nike had agreed. Very soon he must ask Nessus to undertake another mission. For the safety of all, no other race must ever locate Hearth.

What Nessus must do in Human Space was horrible.

A buzzer interrupted Nike's dark thoughts. "Yes?"

"Deputy Minister, your visitor is here," an assistant said over the intercom.

"Show him in." Reflexively, Nike found some minor details of his coiffure to straighten. His assistant appeared at the door with the scout. "Please come in."

Nessus was bursting with scarcely restrained enthusiasm. Two uneven braids offered a token acknowledgment to social norms. Faint compression marks hinted where a few ribbons might once have been found. "I have an answer!"

That sounded unrelated to the feelings Nike feared he

had so inappropriately encouraged. "How I envy you. What was the question?" he temporized.

Nessus shifted his weight excitedly between front feet. "An answer for the problem with the wild humans. I can save them. That is, I know how to preoccupy them."

Preoccupation sounded so inadequate. "Can you keep the ARM from finding us?"

"Yes, yes!" Nessus bobbed his heads in vigorous alternation. "I was at Harem House and—"

Had his encouragement already led Nessus so far astray? Nike's embarrassment deepened. Worse, the scout was not the only one influenced by their late private encounter. Nike found himself distracted by strange sympathies.

We Citizens, he thought, even the most ardent Experimentalists, are a conformist lot. What must it have been like to grow up tempted by curiosity, lured by risk? Somehow, Nessus had learned to wonder what lay beyond the next hill, and—more wondrous still—to go, necessarily alone, to look. His personnel file said Nessus was long estranged from his parents.

"—discrediting Earth's Fertility Board is the key."

An advanced civilization of only a few billions defied Nike's imagination. Regardless, the humans' United Nations had already instituted mandatory population controls. "You propose a scandal to divert the hunt for the Concordance."

Nessus fixed him with a two-headed stare. "Imagine if it were suspected Citizens were secretly buying Brides and the right to reproduce. How would our kind react?" Nike's horror must have been apparent, because Nessus added, "Exactly."

It made a certain depraved sense. Only the conviction that reproductive constraints were equitable made those restrictions bearable. Loss of faith in that fairness would incite strife even here on Hearth. How would wild humans react? With massive unrest, Nike supposed. With violence. It might very well preempt their security forces from speculative Puppeteer hunts. "Is it doable?"

"I believe so, given access to sufficient resources," Nessus said. "I envision our agents bribing some members of the Fertility Board, and compromising others by creating bank accounts in their names. The economies of the human worlds have yet to recover from the shock of General Products' disappearance. The more wealth people have lost, the quicker they will be to suspect conspiracy. Many will believe the rich are buying birthrights. A bit of innuendo here, some surreptitious funding to political opportunists there . . ."

It did not help communications that Nessus lapsed repeatedly into some wild-human language—Interworld, was it called?—for terms lacking in their common vocabulary. After several such digressions, Nike had an epiphany. For much of his life, Nessus had had only humans with whom to converse. Even when Nessus had finally returned to the Fleet, it had been mainly to the company of other humans: the Colonists.

Slowly, after many questions and lengthy discussion of wild-human traits, the proposed plan took shape in Nike's mind—if only in broad outline. "The retained earnings from the General Products Corporation are adequate to the task?"

"If the approach is valid, money will not be the limiting factor."

If? Nessus, who had entered Nike's office almost bursting with exuberant certitude, was beginning to slump. Nike saw he had pushed too hard. "I am very encouraged, but of course a great deal of detail must remain to be determined. I would like you to make this your top priority. Please get back to me soon with an update."

Amid the earlier torrent of explanations, Nessus had used a curious figure of speech. A surgical strike: It evidently related concurrently to primitive medicine, and warfare, and the application of force to points of maximum leverage. Nike had only partially grasped the metaphor, but that was sufficient. Nessus' gambit, if it could be made to work, would eliminate the need to lob stealthed relativistic objects at the human worlds. Gigadeaths, even among aliens, even in defense of the Concordance, should be a last resort.

And wild humans had proved helpful when deployed, however unwittingly, against the Fleet's other prospective opponents. Recalling the Kzinti, a fiercely aggressive species of carnivores who had repeatedly attacked—and been defeated by—the wild humans, Nike suppressed a shudder. If the Fleet were ever revealed, relativistic bombs might be directed at the Citizens' own inhabited worlds.

Terrible outcomes were easy to imagine: ARM hostilities upon the discovery of the NP4 colony. ARM survivors of a preemptive strike, even more enraged. And what if the Fleet were to be found by Kzinti no longer restrained by humans? Kzinti made even *more* aggressive by the knowledge of the humans' fate. Any of those results was unthinkable.

Thinking the unthinkable was among Nike's chosen tasks. Nike steeled himself. Any hope for an acceptable outcome depended on the maverick who stood trembling before him.

The office door was still closed. With feelings of duty outweighing shame, Nike leaned forward to intimately stroke Nessus' scruffy mane. "Come back soon. I am depending on you."

Someone from Nike's staff led Nessus to an isolation booth. Nessus knew his way out from his previous visit, but he was too wrung out from this encounter to object. His mane still tingled from Nike's gentle touch. Certain words had yet to be spoken, but some actions spoke for themselves.

The taciturn aide had not introduced himself. That was no surprise: Given the long chains of emerald-green beads woven into his braids, Nessus' escort was clearly a high-ranking Conservative. The bureaucrat was doubtless a factional watcher as well as an aide.

Nessus had worked himself into a manic state. How else could he have found the self-confidence to advise someone as hindward as Nike? But it was impossible to remain indefinitely self-agitated. Depression and panicked withdrawal could not be delayed for long.

Nessus stepped from the isolation booth to a nearby public nexus, and thence, in another step, to a favorite glen in a small park. Feathery purple hedges encircled him. Bright-winged germinators fluttered overhead. A few Citizens retreated from his wild-eyed stare.

His trembling worsened. He had promised much and implied yet more. His words had brought him, at the least, Nike's respect. He must return soon to Nike with a solution for every imaginable contingency.

For Nike, he would instill in his Colonist scouts the confidence they would need to explore ahead of the Fleet without him. For Nike, he would volunteer to remain in Human Space for however long the disruption and subversion of the wild humans required.

The task before Nessus would test and stress him like nothing he had ever attempted. His limbs trembled more and more; soon the fear of failure would exceed his ability to control. A final step deposited him into the cozy sanctuary of his sleeping quarters. Surrendering to the terror, he curled into a ball so tight he could scarcely breathe.

And yet, there was no doubt in Nessus' mind that he would undertake this mission. The safety of the Fleet was at stake.

To disappoint Nike—and so, to lose him—was unthinkable.

13

Three arcs of little suns, one directly overhead, beat down on the vast expanse of concrete that was Arcadia Spaceport. Cargo floaters, huge when they silently emerged over or vanished from above the freight-sized discs, were dwarfed by the great spaceships that they serviced. The ceaseless procession of cargo floaters, impressive as it was, handled only the largest and most oddly shaped items. Teleportation discs built into the decks of cargo holds were used to onload and offload most interplanetary goods.

With a hand raised to shade her eyes, Kirsten stood watching a grain transporter settle to the pavement. Its cargo of biowaste tanks would be exchanged for grain containers. The spherical ship was easily a thousand feet in diameter. The nearby tapered cylinder that was *Explorer*, about three hundred feet in length, was a toy by comparison.

Kirsten stood to one side of a group of Colonists. Four were family come to see her off; others were Omar's or Eric's friends and relatives. By habit, Kirsten checked people off by clothing and jewelry: these mated, these mated and pregnant, there a young woman unmated and interested—

She felt a tug on her sleeve. It was her niece, Rebecca, wearing the muted hues of youth and unavailability. "What is it, Honey?"

"Will you be safe, Aunt Kirsten?"

Nessus had yet to appear. Had a Citizen traveling companion been present, not even a six-year-old would have asked. "I couldn't be safer." The serious face looking up at her remained skeptical. "Ask your father."

Carl (pastels of a mated adult; a four-stone progeny

ring) gave Kirsten a brotherly hug. "Your aunt is right, sweetie. She'll be back before you know it."

Carl had ad-libbed the last part. Kirsten wished he hadn't. She didn't know how long they might be gone. True, this trip was her idea, but the argument she had made for it seemed weak even to her.

She was desperate to get to Hearth—and, once there, to find or make an opportunity to surreptitiously access Herd Net. No one was more surprised than she when the mission planners actually agreed to meet with the crew to get some Colonist-specific perspective.

Nessus' ready agreement, given with no questions asked, still puzzled Kirsten. It wasn't the only matter troubling her. Where was Nessus now? Why he had chosen to escort them? He might easily have arranged a ride for them aboard one of the grain ships that ceaselessly shuttled between NP4 and Hearth. It was rare, but not unheard of, for Colonists to visit Hearth. Those who made the journey, mostly associated with Arcadia's Self-Governance Council, rode cargo ships.

Nessus popped into view at a nearby stepping disc. He cantered forward, scarcely trembling despite the Colonist crowd, bobbing a head in general greeting. To Kirsten's surprise he sidled up to the group. After meeting Omar's and Eric's guests, Nessus made his way to Kirsten. She did the introductions; he chatted with her parents and brother as though they were old friends.

Nessus was in a manic phase, Kirsten realized. Had he worked up his courage merely to meet the crew's family? That seemed *so* unlikely. As she mulled that over, Nessus arched a neck to stroke Rebecca's fine, blond hair. "What do you like, little one?" he asked.

Kirsten glimpsed an unexpected motion out of the corner of her eye. A loud "Baa" confirmed her suspicions: Rebecca's pet lamb was bounding toward them. Schultz trailed his leash, rushing to play with Rebecca and her new friend. Hooves clattered on the rough surface. His mouth hung open, tongue lolling to one side. How often did animals bite their tongues before learning not to run that way?

Nessus pivoted to flee, and Kirsten realized what *he* saw: a large animal rushing toward him. Hearth was too crowded to keep around even harmless animals. She stepped forward and scooped up the lamb. He was nearly two feet tall now, and mostly legs. "Good boy," she cooed. Schultz wriggled in her arms, his tail wagging furiously. He licked her face. "That's a good kid." She scratched him between the ears. "Yes, you are. Yes, you are!"

Omar's wife, Evelyn (her tunic a rainbow of warm pastels: pointedly mated), whispered a bit overloud, "We've got to find Kirsten a man." Kirsten pictured Eric grinning at that comment and blushed.

"My apologies, Nessus," Carl said. "I'll take this little guy away." There was a flurry of movement, part farewell hug and part the transfer of the still wriggling lamb into his arms. His parting words to Kirsten, called over his shoulder, were, "Stay out of trouble."

If you only knew, she thought.

Nessus had turned back to the Colonist gathering, but his shaking had worsened. "I'll go ahead now. Join me when you're ready." One head tracked the squirming lamb until Nessus disappeared by stepping disc, presumably directly boarding *Explorer*.

Kirsten finished her goodbyes and followed. She found Nessus on the bridge, still quaking. "I'm sorry about Schultz. He was only being friendly. He wouldn't have hurt you."

"Do you like animals?" Nessus' voice was a monotone. He was still upset.

"I do." Clearly *he* did not. A change of subject seemed wise. "Nessus, I was surprised that you met us at the spaceport. I'm surprised you're on NP4 at all."

His heads swiveled so that he briefly looked himself in

the eye. "I wanted Colonist company. I've been in Arcadia for several days."

Huh? Kirsten had not seen Nessus faces to face since the Ice Moon mission. No one had mentioned having seen him. Who had he been visiting on NP4? And why?

Omar and Eric appeared at the hatch to the bridge. "Is everything all right?" Omar asked.

"I am fine." Nessus' response sounded rote. "I was aboard earlier, before meeting your families. *Explorer* is ready for departure. Take your duty stations." One head watched the two men leave; the second accessed an exterior camera. "Good. Everyone is at a safe distance."

A flurry of radio communications cleared *Explorer* for departure. "I'm sorry," Nessus answered Kirsten's interrogatory look. "Your qualifications are not the issue. Only Citizens may guide large masses near the Fleet."

The apology sounded mechanical, like the answer to Omar. That was not like Nessus, she thought. First, he had been manic; now, he was operating on reflex. What made him so edgy? Perhaps their scheming had been detected. Perhaps *she* should be nervous. Kirsten shrugged inwardly. If that were the case, the Concordance authorities would do whatever they wanted to Eric, Omar, and her. Could their jeopardy explain Nessus' mood? Maybe the Colonists' snooping had gotten Nessus into trouble, too.

"Trust me," Nessus continued. "You will find this trip interesting regardless." NP4 receded beneath them. The cooling system briefly hissed at full power as *Explorer* sped between two of the orbiting suns.

"What will we be doing on Hearth?" she asked.

"Trust me," he repeated. A trace of his earlier manic mood had returned.

Above the atmosphere and beyond the suns, where the sky grew black and the stars came out in their myriads, the Fleet of Worlds shone in all its glory. Kirsten's breath caught in her throat. Neither abstract knowledge nor a few trips off-world prepared her for the sight.

She looked down on the plane of worlds, above which their flight plan had taken them.

Six like-sized planets defined the vertices of a hexagon. They orbited the empty point that was their common center of mass, at a radius approaching 900,000 miles. The five worlds lit by necklaces of artificial suns were pale blue-brown-and-white siblings: the nature preserves. The sixth orb, magnificently brilliant in its own light, was Hearth. Its continents glowed with the radiance of megalopolises. Its oceans were mostly black, scattered with gleaming island cities, the pale blue reflections of the companion worlds, and the greenish-blue sheen of plankton blooms.

A fiery red point caught Kirsten's eye. The star was only a fraction of a light-year distant. Once it had nurtured all life on Hearth. It had been a yellow dwarf then, of course. The Concordance had moved Hearth and its entourage—a mere two farm worlds, so long ago—before its sun bloated into its present, red-giant stage.

Hearth's shift into a distant orbit had alleviated another challenge: ever more heat. The planet held only half a trillion Citizens then, but their waste heat was destroying the environment. The world could support more Citizens without a nearby sun. In the panorama spread before her, that wisdom remained on display. One large artificial sun at the empty center of mass would have equally warmed Hearth and its farm worlds. The smaller suns that circled individual NP worlds imparted little energy to Hearth.

"It is an impressive sight," Nessus said.

Impressive was such understatement. Kirsten shivered and did not answer. Beings too risk-averse to leave their homeworld had instead cast off the final ties to their sun.

As NP4 shrank, a part of Kirsten yearned to abandon all scheming. The Concordance had incredible knowledge. They wielded scarcely conceivable power. Who was she to question their actions? What if secrets *did* lurk in her people's past? What could Colonists accomplish in the face of such might?

She thrust aside her doubts. The truth mattered. Colonists deserved to know their own past. Kirsten planned to uncover it.

Final approach required two mouths. That was a disappointment: Nessus would have liked to observe Kirsten's reaction. He would settle for watching the replay from the hidden bridge camera. That bit of repair had been within his capability.

"Crew, prepare for docking," Nessus called. He allowed himself a one-headed peek. Kirsten startled nicely.

"Dock where? There are no ships nearby. Once we're past the moon . . ." Her voice trailed off as she studied her instruments. "The surface is perfectly smooth. There's almost no gravitational reading. That's no natural moon."

"Correct." Nessus tweaked their course as a large hatch irised open. He activated the intercom. "We're about to board an orbital facility operated by General Products Corporation. They make spaceship hulls. They made this one."

He set down *Explorer* with a barely perceptible bump. "All hands, prepare to disembark."

He and Kirsten found Eric and Omar already in the relax room. Nessus pointed at the discs inset in the cabin's floor. His other head was already in a pocket, mouthing the transporter control. "Are we ready?"

Omar and Kirsten nodded. "Absolutely," Eric said.

With the flick of a tongue, Nessus rematerialized them inside a factory waiting room. Omar's eyes widened. Eric and Kirsten merely grinned knowingly. Eric grabbed at the first wall bracket he floated past. He said, "Orbital manufacturing said it all, Nessus. Microgravity. Why else make things out here?"

That was quick thinking. Nessus had an epiphany: He

genuinely liked these Colonists. He could not say the same for all Colonists, of course, although increasingly they had his respect. The recognition made him feel guilty. Guilt-ier. Arcadia colony reflected long-ago Concordance med-dling. The imminent Fertility Board manipulation would be his personal crime.

A second realization crowded upon the first. He had been wise to spend the past few days in cities across Ar-cadia. Colonists in their millions still made him want to run and hide. Living among them was the best available preparation for a return to Human Space. He did not in-tend to reveal himself to many, if any, wild humans, not even to his agents. Still, humans would be all around him.

The thought terrified him.

Eric found the display control that turned a wall trans-parent, revealing the vast enclosed central volume of the factory. Nessus saw six hulls in progress. Surely, this ar-tificial world looked wondrous to them. Like the scenic flight plan he had chosen, this stopover was meant to in-still awe. He needed their dutiful diligence when—soon—he could no longer accompany them.

The nearest construct was a #4 hull, what Colonists knew as a grain ship. Its position near the view port was no coincidence. That placement hid a production space that was almost empty. Nessus had seen the same volume almost filled with ships. The export market no longer ex-isted, of course: The Fleet would soon leave behind the many races too foolish to immediately flee the explosion at the galactic core.

"Can we get a tour?" Eric asked. His eyes never left the factory region.

"Of course," Nessus promised. On cue, a General Prod-ucts executive appeared. He wore his mane in tight, closely packed braids, the hair a striking yellow-brown that approached a Colonist's ash blond. His utility belt and few ornaments disclosed affiliation only to the company. "Here is your guide."

Nessus exchanged introductions and greetings with the newcomer, who did not speak English. "I brought a translator. I'll activate it now."

"Hello," the executive said. "My name is . . . and I will be showing you around the facility."

Citizen names seldom translated. How should the Colonists refer to their guide? A label popped into Nessus' mind, unsurprising given his recent re-immersion in wild-human cultures. The word amused him, and with so much at stake he needed amusement. "For today, we'll call you Baedeker."

"I shall be Baedeker then. I'll start with an overview of our operation. We're looking into the main production volume of . . ."

Kirsten gazed into the enclosure that Nessus had so casually called a factory and she had mistaken for a small moon. Omar was subdued; she guessed he was as awed as she. Eric, though, seemed ready to burst with questions. Unless he overcame the habits of a lifetime and interrupted a Citizen, those questions would go unasked. One-headed speech evidently sufficed for the translator, and Baedeker never paused for a breath.

". . . Familiar with the Number 2 model, of course. We built your ship around such a hull. *Explorer* is unusual, though, in that it has a fusion drive. As part of this refit we'll replace the fusion drive with more and larger thrusters."

"Thrusters are more compact," Nessus said.

Why had Nessus made that comment? They knew all about thrusters. Only thrusters made sense near populated worlds, which was why *Explorer* already had some thrusters.

He clearly knew about this refitting. Why hadn't he mentioned *that*? Swap-out of the ship's main normal-space drive struck Kirsten as a major change. Eric's furrowed brow showed he was equally surprised.

"Our most popular model is the Number 1 hull." Baedeker held his heads about a foot apart. "They're excellent for free-flying sensors, small satellites, and such."

The air was redolent with a spicy chemical smell, reminiscent of the pheromones with which Nessus flooded *Explorer* but somehow different. These scents were more varied, Kirsten decided, more like the forest smells she had encountered on Elysium. Perhaps this factory/moon recycled its atmosphere biologically. Certainly it was large enough.

"We have prototyped several of the changes you Colonists suggested." Baedeker suddenly vanished. He had not moved from the room's stepping disc since his first appearance, a position he had maintained despite the microgravity conditions by hooking hoof claws through some of the fabric loops that surrounded the disc. Doubtless he was prepared to flee the Colonists. Perhaps the three of them were Baedeker's first.

A nudge against the wall sent Kirsten floating over the disc. It remained active; she found herself drifting in a chamber twice as large as the room she had left. This space was crowded, mostly with new computer cabinets. She was happiest to see keyboards whose layouts looked better-suited to fingers than to lip nodes and tongues.

Omar appeared before she could identify the other equipment, and then Eric. Nessus arrived last.

"Also, notice the modified crash couch we have designed for the bridge," Baedeker said. His second head adjusted the seat as he spoke. "I understand that for your next mission you will all be flight-trained. This reconfigurable couch accommodates whoever is piloting." He circled around his visitors to occupy a place above the room's stepping disc. "Someone try it."

"I will." On his first try Omar bounced from the chair. "This would be much easier with gravity. Can we get some in this room?"

"No," Baedeker said. "Is that comfortable?"

"Why not," Eric burst out. He seemed surprised at his own interruption.

Baedeker looked unhappily at Nessus. "Our manufacturing processes are quite sensitive to gravity. How is the couch?"

"It's a good fit for me." A nudge against an arm rest sent Omar floating free. "Someone else try it. Eric?"

"I'm an engineer," Eric said. Kirsten understood that to mean it took more than an adjustable seat to impress him. "Room-scaled artificial gravity produces minimal fringing fields. Pardon my curiosity, Baedeker. What is so sensitive?"

Shut up, Eric! This trip might be their only chance to uncover their long-hidden history. Excessive curiosity now could lose them that opportunity. Kirsten had to change the subject. Using a bolted-down table for leverage, she pulled herself to the prototype couch. "My turn."

Eric frowned, but he took her hint. He managed to keep quiet through a presentation about new sensors. Then he asked, "When will we see hulls being made?"

"You have seen that," Nessus said.

"I mean in person, Nessus. Up close."

"It is not allowed." Baedeker answered. "That region is a controlled vacuum."

"I'll wear my pressure suit. It's aboard . . ."

Baedeker's heads wobbled from side to side on the hinges of their necks. Kirsten had seldom seen the gesture, but knew it denoted strong disagreement. Eric needed to drop this! "It is *not* allowed," Baedeker insisted. "The traces of gas and dust that cling to the outside of your suit would contaminate the process."

"I don't understand," Omar said. "Nessus, you told us only large quantities of antimatter could harm *Explorer*'s hull. How can a bit of dust harm anything?"

"What I told you is correct," Nessus said. "I was speaking of completed hulls. During construction, hulls are fragile."

Eric would not let it go. "Extreme sensitivity to gravitational variations. Extreme sensitivity to trace contaminants. It sounds like a very-large-scale nanotech process."

Baedeker made a noise like a slow-motion boiler explosion. His howl did not translate. Nessus responded in kind, but louder and longer, until Baedeker lowered his heads submissively.

"General Products Corporation does not often disclose this information," Nessus said. "Given what you now know, it is best that you hear the rest. It would be unfortunate if you lost trust in your ship.

"*Explorer*'s hull is impervious to damage. If not, would I have ventured out in it? Still, there is a fact I had not shared. The hull takes its strength from its unique form: It is a single supermolecule grown atom by atom by nanotechnology. During construction, the incomplete hull *is* unstable. The slightest chemical contamination or unbalanced force can tear it to pieces. That's why there is no artificial gravity here, and why communication here uses optical fibers."

Kirsten gulped. As dependable as the rising of the suns, hundreds of grain ships visited NP4 daily. Each was like a soap bubble a thousand feet in diameter, grown atom by atom. How could such a thing be done? "Baedeker, are there only the four hull styles, each always the same size, because those are the superstrong molecular configurations?" In the back of her mind was the geometric oddity that there could be only five regular polyhedrons.

Eric disregarded both pairs of vigorously bobbing heads. "I don't think so, Kirsten. Hull shapes are standardized, but the details differ. Think about the number and placement of airlocks, the number and placement of openings for cable bundles, that sort of thing. And when I requested additional external hull sensors for *Explorer,* there were no restrictions on where to attach them or to route through the cable bundles. Since hull penetrations are that *un*constrained, I can't imagine how the molecular strength could stem from specific sizes or shapes."

Baedeker screamed again, louder and more discordantly than before. It only ended when he activated the stepping disc and vanished. Maybe he fled, Kirsten thought. Or maybe he was seeking higher authority.

"Too much logic?" Eric asked. The hurt look on his face added, "From a Colonist?"

"As I stated, this construction process is not widely shared," Nessus said. "You lack only one final detail. The supermolecule's imperviousness derives from interatomic bonds artificially strengthened using an embedded power plant. The stiffened bonds can absorb virtually any impact, and temperatures up to hundreds of thousands of degrees.

"Reinforcement of the bonds only becomes possible once the hull is effectively full-grown. Until then, as Baedeker explained, the construct is extremely fragile.

"Are you satisfied?"

Eric averted his eyes. Perhaps he had finally realized the extent of his assertiveness. "Yes, Nessus. I hope you will apologize for me to Baedeker. My professional interest does not excuse poor manners."

"Good," Nessus said. "Overhaul of *Explorer* will continue, but we have likely rendered ourselves unwelcome as guests. We will take the next available shuttle."

It wasn't until the shuttle was halfway to the surface, hull vibrating from the forces of reentry, that Kirsten took notice of a critical detail. Nessus and Baedeker alike had nodded at her analogy, moments later proven untenable, of four stable hull types. Up/down; down/up; up/down; down/up . . . like a Colonist's vigorous head nodding, it denoted firm agreement. Yet Nessus knew reinforced chemical bonds actually explained GP hull strength.

Nessus *lied* to us, Kirsten thought. What else has he lied to us about?

14

Explorer's crew exited the shuttle onto a vast expanse of concrete. Intellectually, Kirsten had known what to expect. Arcadia spaceport was merely one of several spaceports on one of five farm worlds. *This* was the main spaceport of Hearth itself.

Viscerally, she could not have been less prepared.

The unimaginable scale froze her in place. They had disembarked deep within an array of grain ships that extended in all directions. Cargo carriers, thousands of them, teemed everywhere. Strips of white lights embedded in the pavement provided ground-level illumination, while the clouds throbbed with the reflected blue running lights of arriving and departing vessels. In the distance, speckled blocks, prisms, and cylinders rose above the ships. To tower over the grain ships like that . . . those *were* towers. The smallest building must stand at least a mile tall. The tiny speckles were windows.

"I don't believe it," Omar said wonderingly. "I see it. I've read and been told about it. I still can't believe it."

"Believe it." Eric turned slowly, savoring every detail. "A trillion Citizens. One planet. Do the math."

Nessus watched them taking it all in. "Are you ready to proceed?"

They had exited the shuttle by stepping disc. They could have gone directly to wherever Nessus wanted them. Was his purpose a tourist excursion or understated intimidation? "Where to, Nessus?" she asked.

He pointed, neck and tongue extended, at the tallest tower in sight. "Soon enough, there. I arranged a meeting with a Concordance official to discuss scouting missions. Although almost anyplace is convenient to the spaceport by stepping disc, the deputy minister chose to place his department in sight of the spaceport."

"How long until then?" How long did she have to somehow gain access to Herd Net?

"I intended you to have an NP4 day here for sightseeing." Nessus picked at his mane. "That has changed. There were complaints about our visit to the General Products orbital facility. The deputy minister is rearranging his schedule to see us earlier. We have until we're summoned, no longer."

Was there an undercurrent to Nessus' reference to the deputy minister? A slight pause before the title? An especially careful pronunciation? Were Nessus a man, Kirsten would have had no doubt.

A nearby grain ship lifted off. Eric craned his head to watch it recede, running lights pulsing, into the perpetual night of Hearth's sky.

"Come." Nessus vanished.

Swallowing hard, Kirsten stepped onto the disc he had just vacated—and into complete sensory overload.

Unimaginably large buildings loomed over her, their tops hidden in low cloud. She stood in a plaza, amid tens of thousands of Citizens jostling together like . . . what? They clumped like sheep, flank by flank without visible space, but entering and exiting the flock, veering and converging, with intent purpose. Herd pheromones saturated the air, so pungent that her eyes watered. And the din! It sounded like a thousand orchestras tuning up at once, while tens of thousands of hooves beat a counterpoint on the pavement.

Blunt teeth grasped Kirsten's arm and tugged. "You must vacate the disc." Nessus spoke from one mouth, for his other one still grasped her elbow. She stepped back and Eric appeared. His jaw dropped; she felt better seeing his reaction.

By the time Nessus jostled Eric aside and Omar appeared, another impression struck her. "Nessus, everyone is staring at us."

"Colonists on Hearth remain a rarity." Nessus began

walking across the plaza. "Stay with me. You will not be bothered."

"We're in your mouths," Omar said shakily. "What can we see?"

The clear area around them moved with them, a bubble adrift in the sea of Citizens. Rare meant unknown meant, to Citizens, prospectively dangerous. What threat might the three of them possibly pose? she wondered.

"We are in a communal courtyard," Nessus answered Omar. "It is typical, although smaller than average. I did not want to overwhelm you."

"What are the surrounding buildings?" Eric asked.

"Three edges of the square are arcologies, modest by Hearth standards but you would consider each a large city." Nessus pointed at the fourth and nearest side, toward which they continued to walk. "This is a local entertainment and shopping complex."

Kirsten was about to ask a question when a distinctive warble intruded. "Excuse me," Nessus said. His head poked into a pocket of his utility belt. There were muffled orchestral sounds, and then his head reappeared. "That was the deputy minister's office. He will see us in a little less than an hour."

Kirsten's mind raced. A trip to Hearth had seemed their best hope to ferret out the facts about the Colonists' past. Among so many Citizens, with so little time, what chance was there to gain access to Herd Net? Would they have a moment without Nessus' supervision? It *had* to be now. After a high official had rearranged his schedule to get the three of them off-world sooner, she could not count on a repeat visit.

"Many artists exhibit in the main promenade." Nessus continued his recitation. "Classical holostatues remain the most common, but dynamic holoforms are increasingly popular. My favorite is—" He trilled something in both throats. "Sorry, his name has no meaningful translation."

He's manic again, Kirsten realized. The meeting is almost upon us, and Nessus is working himself up.

". . . A secondary entrance. The interior lobby has stepping discs, of course, for access to the stores and artistic venues. We can spare the time for a quick look."

As they reached an overhang, Kirsten encountered a slight pressure. A weak force field to keep out weather, she decided, pressing through into the lobby. Translucent holograms floated overhead, both abstract art and scrolling directories. Stylized fonts, rapid scrolling, and unfamiliar vocabulary rendered most labels unrecognizable. A few made sense: hair salons; stores selling jewelry, belts, music, and books; art galleries; concert stadiums. Aha! "Nessus."

He stopped. "What, Kirsten?"

"I'd like to get some souvenirs." She ignored Omar's baffled expression. "Maybe some picture books."

Nessus swiveled a head to scan the nearest directory. "Follow me." He vanished. This time Omar and Eric beat her to the disc Nessus had activated.

She emerged into a small, congested shop. Media players lined several shelves at the front of the store. Captions and illustrations floated over bins brimming with packaged media.

"Omar, would you mind picking out a reader for me?" She squeezed through the narrow aisles, Citizen customers staring at her, until she found a range of bins labeled "History." She plucked up a handful of coin-sized data disks under an assortment of titles. Most dealt with Hearth, but she included several about the NP worlds and Colonists. She added geography and art books from other racks.

Nessus was deep in conversation with another Citizen, a cascade of wild music, when Kirsten returned to the front of the store. She set her selections on the counter beside the media reader Omar had picked. As the clerk waved a scanner over everything, it occurred to her to wonder how to complete the purchase. Did stores on Hearth accept Colonist credits? "Nessus, may I pay you back?"

"Of course." He completed the transaction with a tongueprint on the scanner. "We must be going."

Nike's capacious office had acquired a human-compatible sofa since Nessus' last visit. Tuxedo-style, Nessus thought. Its purpose might be simple hospitality. More likely, Nike hoped to render the Colonist visitors careless with a gesture.

Astraddle a proper seat, Nessus listened as Nike chatted with Eric, Omar, and Kirsten. Nike's mane was resplendent, richly woven with orange garnets. Nessus had to concentrate not to stare. When they had last met, the cascading of Nike's braids had merely indicated unmated status, without interest in being approached. The current interweaving declared prospective openness to a relationship. This message is for *me,* Nessus dared to hope.

Despite the casual conversation, Nike remained behind a massive, new desk. Nessus guessed that a stepping disc hid beneath Nike's own padded bench for an emergency exit. "Tell me about the aliens you studied," Nike said via translator.

"They call themselves Gw'oth. Physically, a Gw'o is small." Omar held his hands about an arm's length apart. "It's five-limbed, in a star shape. The sense organs and the brain are in the central area. The Gw'o appears well adapted to life under water."

"And under the ice." With typical delicacy, Nike showed he had seen their report.

"You'll be more interested in their capabilities and potential," Omar said, taking the hint. "Eric will cover that."

Eric straightened. "They are newly industrialized. They had to master life in a vacuum to gain access to . . ."

While Eric described Gw'oth technology and Nike

probed Eric's depth of understanding, Nessus thought about the future. The crew *he* had selected and trained would warn the Fleet of any threats ahead. *He* would side-track the wild humans searching for the Concordance. *His* feats would earn Nike's undying respect and gratitude—and hopefully much more.

"My specialists say Gw'oth progress is exceptionally rapid," Nike said.

"I wondered about that," Kirsten replied. "We had no frame of reference."

Nessus' stomach spasmed at the implied criticism. His grand plans could unravel *so* easily. The complaints about the General Products visit already reflected badly on them. What if Nike insisted that he supervise the Colonists on their next flight? What if Nike canceled the Colonist scouting experiment altogether? Even the minor precaution of placing a substitute political officer aboard *Explorer* would be problematical. To prepare another Citizen to take his place on *Explorer* meant shared credit if all went well—and full blame if it did not.

"What impressed me most," Eric said, "is the Gw'oth rocketry program. We monitored several satellite launches. Every attempt succeeded. Each mission exceeded the last in sophistication and payload."

"The quality control, precision, and rate of learning impressed me," Omar added.

Good! The men appropriately respected the potential threat. This hastily rescheduled meeting would surely end soon. They would be safely out the door, his plans intact.

"On the other head, Nike, Gw'oth technology remains primitive," Kirsten interjected. "Their world is resource-limited. They are very unlikely to achieve deep-space capability before the Fleet passes them by forever."

It was all Nessus could do not to pluck and fuss at his mane. Generations of acculturation had yet to expunge from Colonists the casual human attitude toward risk. *Anything* dangerous was to be avoided. Likelihood did not matter. Humans curiously chose to ignore the unlikely. The marvel was that such self-destructive behavior had so far failed to cause their downfall.

"That is not a scout's decis—" Nike said.

"Excuse me, Nike." Kirsten leaned forward. "I believe you misunderstand my point."

On Elysium and again with a visit to the General Products manufacturing facility, Nessus had been sensitive to Kirsten's unfulfilled need to explore. Rather than satisfy her, he had emboldened her. Trembling with dismay and rage, he awaited disaster. No mere Colonist could interrupt a deputy minister.

"Explain." Nike's translated command was ominously curt and flat.

"I hadn't finished," Kirsten said. "Certainly we must avoid any danger to the Fleet. All we face now, however, is the potential for a threat. Should that threat materialize, Gw'oth technological limitations mean we can disable the aliens nondestructively."

Nike's necks tipped forward with interest. "How would that work?"

"Gw'oth networking is understandably primitive. It was neither necessary nor possible until they ventured above the ice, where they could no longer plug in as living computers. I can easily introduce a self-propagating, self-replicating program, let's call it a virus, to subvert their networks. The Gw'oth have no defenses against software attack. The virus would incapacitate everything their networks operate—including their launch- and spacecraft-control systems."

"Interesting." Nike ignored a discreet buzz that probably signaled another appointment. "But why respond that way?"

Nessus knew why. Kirsten disbelieved his assurances that he had deactivated the comet probe. She was correct, of course. Why not retain the option? Had he deactivated it, it was easy enough to build more.

"I'm considering the contingency in which we must preempt the Gw'oth from acting against the Fleet," Kirsten said. "If that happens, disabling their computers will limit Gw'oth casualties. The intervention would imperil anyone riding a computer-controlled conveyance at the wrong time, but most Gw'oth would survive."

"A surgical strike," Nike said.

The phrase obviously puzzled Kirsten; it spoke directly to Nessus. *He* had proposed a nonviolent stratagem against the humans. Now Kirsten proposed a ploy against the Gw'oth.

Nike's buzzer sounded again. "I have another meeting. Omar, Eric, and Kirsten, I found this discussion very helpful. Nessus informs me *Explorer* will soon depart on its next trip. I wish you an interesting mission."

Turning off the translator, Nike fluted four wonderfully complex double chords to just Nessus. "The human affinity to computing continues to appall me. Still, the opportunity to protect the Fleet without slaughter appeals to me, and these three seem capable and loyal. I accept your recommendation, Nessus. Next mission, they will fly alone."

15

Nessus pored over the shuttle's maintenance log, seeking composure in the routine. The ground crew had made a few annotations, none involving more than a small tweak to the calibration of one or another component within a massively redundant subsystem. A hundred such minor glitches could go unaddressed without endangering the shuttle.

He was shaking! By force of will, Nessus calmed his trembling limbs. A quick scan revealed his crew talking among themselves; he doubted they had noticed his lapse. Only now, the meeting safely behind them, did Nessus admit to himself the gamble he had taken. Had the session produced a different outcome, he might easily have lost any chance with Nike.

Omar stowed his duffel bag. "Nessus, thank you for arranging this trip. We all appreciate it."

"You're welcome." Nessus whistled a few parameters to the main bridge computer. It would record the data and uplink it to traffic control. "You three have done well."

"Thanks again," Omar said.

"Hearth is amazing." Eric checked instruments as he spoke. "Too bad *Explorer* can't accommodate four on the bridge like this shuttle."

Soon enough, *Explorer* would carry only three, although the refitting now nearing completion would retain a Citizen-friendly crash couch. Nessus decided the news could wait a little longer—until he achieved calm. "What struck you most about Hearth?"

"The crowds, even in what you called a small courtyard." Eric scratched his chin. "One thing puzzles me, though. Amid those throngs, I don't know if I saw any female Citizens."

Nessus froze. "You did not."

"Do they have their own communities?" Kirsten asked.

"Discussions of gender make Citizens uncomfortable," Nessus said.

"Everything seems fine." Eric looked up again from his own preflight checkout. "Nike is smaller than you and so elaborately coifed. I had wondered if Nike were female."

"Nike is also male."

"You would know, of course." Eric made a strangled sound, part laugh, part cough. "He kept looking at you."

Nessus had noticed that, too. Together with the mane signal . . .

"The few Citizens I've met are male," Kirsten said, "I would like to meet some Citizen females."

A lamb bleating and leaping playfully: Nessus remembered Kirsten hugging it and cooing at it. What would she think if she knew? What would any of them think? Their likely reaction was yet another worry pushing him toward withdrawal.

A traffic-control update let Nessus change the subject. "We're the third ship cleared for departure. Prepare for launch."

They took off soon after into the perpetually crowded skies above Hearth. He kept the bridge conversation focused on air traffic control, then space traffic control. His inner doubts, however, refused to be channeled.

What would any Colonist think who knew about the Companions?

The small world that was the General Products orbital facility receded in Kirsten's instruments. They had reclaimed *Explorer* quickly. Baedeker made no effort to hide his feelings. He was eager to be rid of them.

"I missed this ship," Kirsten said. "It's good to have her back."

"It's good that you like this ship," Nessus answered. He had slumped on his bench. "You'll be spending a lot of time on it."

He had been tense throughout this trip. Kirsten still had no idea why. "Shall I take over the controls? You seem . . . preoccupied."

"I appreciate the offer, but it remains impossible. Don't worry. I'll get you back to Arcadia." Nessus trembled, despite his assurances.

In hindsight, all her scheming for a visit to Hearth had been unnecessary. The trip's true purpose—for Nessus— was bringing them to meet Nike. Kirsten had yet to deduce his motives.

She probed. "Is Nike planning another scouting expedition?"

"Correct." Nessus straightened on his bench. It was a

struggle. "We're on autopilot. Now that we're clear of the GP facility, I have news to share." He activated the intercom. "Omar, Eric, meet us in the relax room."

For a short while, at least, they *could* use the autopilot. Even without a natural sun, the worlds of the Fleet warped nearby space-time too much to use hyperdrive. Kirsten felt more and more worried about Nessus piloting in his present condition. She had to do something: Citizens distrusted computers too much to permit automated landings.

They reached the relax room before Omar and Eric. Nessus tugged at his mane, undoing its final remnants of order as he waited. At their entry, Nessus looked himself in the eyes while whistling an impressive fanfare. "The meeting with Nike went well. Lest you become anxious, I kept to myself what might result from that meeting.

"Nike had final authority to approve a recommendation of mine. You three will take *Explorer* on its next scouting mission. I must attend to other matters."

Eric blinked. "Just us three. There will be no Citizen aboard?"

"Correct," Nessus said.

"But *why*?" Eric squeaked.

Was she proud or worried? Maybe both. The bigger question for Kirsten was: How would this affect the quest for their past?

"It is inappropriate for me to discuss my own mission," Nessus answered Eric.

"When will we go? How soon will you go?" Eric asked.

"I expect to go in a few days." Nessus' tremors grew. "Scientists in Nike's ministry must select destinations before you leave. Perhaps ten more days."

How much longer could Nessus last before hiding in his cabin? "Nessus, respectfully, you are distraught. *Please* let me do the piloting."

"I will be fine," Nessus said. "I'm returning to the bridge."

"I'll join you in a minute." After Nessus left the relax room, Kirsten took a pen and notebook from a storage locker. Had General Products hidden new cameras? There was no time to look—and no guarantee they would find them. She had to risk getting caught.

Kirsten hunched over the notebook, the better to block the view of any new sensors. The posture did nothing for the legibility of her writing. She passed the notebook, closed, to Omar.

Omar opened the notebook a crack, read her note, and nodded. He passed the notebook to Eric, who also nodded.

"Now I'll join Nessus," Kirsten said. He seemed too close to a nervous breakdown to bother watching them remotely. But what if she were wrong? Her presence on the bridge could dissuade him from accessing any secret sensors.

She found him quivering in a corner of the bridge. Tufts of his mane protruded in every direction, all trace of order vanished. "Are you all right?"

He looked at her dully. "I will be. I'm resting before we land."

She waited as long as she dared before calling Eric. "We're landing soon. Is everything in order?" It was not a routine inquiry about shipboard systems. Per her scribbled note, the question meant, "Do the Citizen histories have any new information about our people?"

"Everything is normal," Eric answered. "Nothing new at all."

She had bought the histories on impulse. "Nothing new" meant the Concordance told Citizens the same fables as it told the Colonists. The past she sought was a Concordance secret.

Her last hope for recovering that lost past would be in *Explorer*'s own archives—if those records had not already been purged. But perhaps Nessus would not delete his private records until he was done with the ship.

She saw only one chance.

"You're in no shape to pilot. Respectfully, you know it." Nessus said nothing. "Nessus, to land the ship yourself is dangerous. You could kill us and countless people on the ground."

"I know." A neck, as though with a mind of its own, curved slowly toward the safe place between his front legs. "Kirsten, a Colonist pilot within the Fleet is forbidden."

"You'll have to change that rule before *Explorer*'s next mission. Why not bend it now?"

Silence. "Traffic control cannot know," Nessus finally responded.

"No one need know, Nessus, but you must decide now. We reenter soon. There are only two *safe* options. One, I land the ship. Two, you give traffic control a reason for aborting into orbit around NP4."

He trembled in silence. Not even imminent danger was getting through to him. Could *anything* make him decide? Remembering the curious tone of voice whenever Nessus mentioned Nike, she took a chance. "Suppose we abort to orbit. *Explorer* is in perfect shape, just refitted. Will Nike still trust you for your own upcoming mission?"

The head about to hide between his forelegs whipped up to stare at Kirsten. "Would you keep this secret?"

"I promise," she said. "I assume I can communicate with traffic control solely by text messages and data transfers."

"Yes." He fell silent again until a fit passed. "I'll show you the message protocols."

She settled into her crash couch. "I'll need to be logged in as you."

"Right." He crept nearer. His voice trembling, occasionally verging on incoherence, he made his explanations.

When, the lesson completed, Nessus ran down the corridor to cower in his cabin, she fought to control two strong emotions. The first was pity for her stricken shipmate. Whatever his faults, Nessus had given the three of them unprecedented opportunities. The second was—

The urge to shout for joy.

Explorer sank through NP4's outer atmosphere, hull thrumming. They would be on the ground soon, and Nessus would likely emerge from his cabin.

Kirsten stared at a secondary bridge display. The pre-NP4 Colonist history files were gone. She pictured Baedeker gloating as he purged information meant only for Nessus' eyes.

Neither anger nor despair was the answer. What should she try before Nessus reappeared and revoked her temporary privileges?

Backup files: nothing. Temp files: nothing. Associative search: something! A few records remained in the library that pointed to the now-vanished information she sought. As she paged through those records, her hopes sank again. Hints and allusions, nothing more.

She continued scanning, and a familiar word caught her eye: ramscoop. It was one of the restricted terms they had encountered in Elysium.

The ground rushed toward them. Reluctantly, Kirsten abandoned the search to concentrate on their final approach. She exchanged messages with traffic control, carefully following the protocols Nessus had taught her. Too soon, they set down at Arcadia Spaceport.

She skipped the customary announcement over the intercom, hoping Nessus might not immediately notice they had landed. Instead, she shot Omar a message. "Wait outside Nessus' cabin door. Stall him if he comes out."

A query on "ramscoop" found only the one cryptic reference she had found earlier. What were the other terms from Elysium? United Nations: nothing. Long Pass: nothing. Humans: several hits! Humans might be a plural; she queried again with "human" and got more hits.

A corridor camera showed Omar on station outside

Nessus' cabin door. Kirsten skimmed the records that
mentioned human or humans. Nothing she saw meant anything to her, and she dared not pause to analyze what she
was reading. She copied her search results into new files
with innocent-sounding names, and then globally replaced
every occurrence of "human" in her copies with "squirrel."

The camera showed a cabin door opening. Nessus appeared, looking once more in control of himself. After a
short conversation, he pressed past Omar. Omar followed,
still talking.

Where but the bridge could Nessus be coming?

Logged in as Nessus, Kirsten had total access to the
ship's computers. Using that authority, she created a
pseudonymous account and delegated full privileges to it.
As Nessus' unmistakable contralto echoed in the corridor, she purged all traces of her searching from the audit
and security files.

Nessus entered the bridge. "Thank you for your help,
Kirsten."

"I was happy to do it," she said.

Nessus settled onto his bench. "I'm taking back control." Kirsten's display flashed, and all Nessus' privileged-
mode information vanished from it. "Thanks again."

The last file she had scanned mentioned a Human Studies Institute run by the foreign affairs ministry. Nike's
ministry on Hearth.

"I was happy to do it," Kirsten repeated.

16

Whom the gods would destroy, they first make mad.

Summoned by and left to wait for the Hindmost, Nike
wondered how many Citizens, even among those who
borrowed names from human mythology, had encountered Euripides. Probably none. The present crisis had

renewed Nike's fascination with humans, enough that he again rued the hubris of his assumed name. He did not feel victorious these days.

Had meeting Nessus's crew been a mistake? They seemed so *normal*. The harsh choices to be made about humans felt that much harsher after speaking with the Colonists. Perhaps it was madness to make such decisions. Perhaps it was madness not to.

Dark thoughts only amplified Nike's isolation in the posh, eerily spacious antechamber. He needed distraction. What, he wondered, was a suitable human name for the most powerful of all Citizens? One by one, Nike considered and discarded every option among the main members of the pantheon.

Perhaps a legendary mortal: Sisyphus. The Hindmost was crafty, and yet spent much of his time on pointless and endless endeavors. Fiddling while Hearth burned, as it were.

The Hindmost, of course, disdained such whimsy as a human pseudonym.

In a flurry of activity, the Hindmost and a small retinue materialized around Nike. All were resplendent in shades of green, none more so than the Hindmost. Nike's host wore his mane intricately coifed with emeralds and jade. Despite his advanced years, the Hindmost's roan coat gleamed with good health. "Thank you for coming," the Hindmost said.

Nike dipped his heads minimally, balancing respect with more assurance than he felt. The Hindmost's aides looked on disapprovingly. "I am honored to be asked into your home."

The Hindmost brushed heads briefly with Nike, as though greeting an equal. "We live in interesting times."

"That is true," Nike answered cautiously.

With a graceful twist of a neck, the Hindmost dismissed his staff. They vanished quickly. "Come. Let us enjoy the fresh air."

Nike followed the Hindmost through a virtual wall and weather-resistant force field onto a long, marble-tiled balcony. The house hugged the side of a mountain. The view, of wooded slope and crashing surf and undulating sea, was spectacular. A diffuse glow along the horizon hinted at a distant coastline.

The Hindmost paused while brilliantly colored flutter-wings zigzagged past in formation. "I received your recommendation for a course change."

Nike took a deep breath. "The ministry proposes an alteration in the Fleet's path. It is a matter of prudence, given that the wild humans seek us. In less than a year, the proposed small course change will interpose a dust cloud between the Fleet and the humans' home solar system."

"The recommendation said as much. That maneuver seems to be of marginal utility. The Fleet will remain observable—if they deduce where to look—from other human-settled worlds. And they can seek us from any vantage by using hyperdrive ships."

It was all Nike could do not to blink in surprise. When was risk *reduction* not a sufficient argument? "Hindmost, it is the home-system humans, their United Nations, who are most curious, most insistent—"

"The recommendation will have my authorization," the Hindmost interrupted. "I bring up its limitations to show that the ministry's advice receives my personal attention." The interruption wasn't jarring. It harmonized perfectly with Nike's woodwind/violin voice.

Long, slow combers washed up the broad pebbled beach, the foaming crests glistening by planet- and star-light. Offshore phosphorescence marked a sea-polyp colony. Clouds far out to sea sparkled with lightning. Despite the churning of Nike's thoughts—what was this meeting *truly* about?—he could not help but admire the view.

"This is a restful spot," the Hindmost said. "A stepping

disc away from anywhere and yet private and serene. Few places on Hearth can match it."

The sea breeze ruffled Nike's mane and raised a sigh in the woods that surrounded the mansion. He considered: Acceptance of the ministry's—Nike's own—recommendation. The gentle reminder who was in charge. The hint of potential rewards.

He was being tempted, as he had so recently tempted Nessus. The lure was of wealth and power, not mating, but this was seduction nonetheless. Work with me, the Hindmost implied, and the rewards will be great.

Nike had rationalized his manipulation of Nessus as vital to the safety of the Concordance. He would not sacrifice the Concordance for personal gain now. "Might we speak, Hindmost, about the coming consensualization?" The reassessment of the public mind and mood for which the Experimentalists were agitating.

The Hindmost swiveled his heads toward Nike. "Surely disturbing the public about a settled issue is unproductive."

"Respectfully, Hindmost, a revised policy is in everyone's interest."

"A policy of permanent emergency? I think not. And what else does your party have to offer? We are already embarked on the escape from the galaxy favored by Experimentalists."

"Some Experimentalists." Nike paused as far-off lightning bolts lit the sea. "The reality of the matter is: We flee because flight is in our nature. The explosion of the galactic core is frightening, and so we sought to leave it behind. Yet in my opinion, flight from the galaxy is our worst possible course of action."

"You would have us *stay*?"

"We run from a long-ago chain reaction of supernovae explosions—from radiation. To escape that peril, we will move fast and far, so that the wave front, already thousands of light-years deep, will dissipate before it can overtake us.

"Because all sane beings shun the perils of hyperspace, we must accelerate to relativistic speeds in normal space. Therein, Hindmost, is the paradox: As the Fleet flees the radiation from the core explosion, it produces radiation just as deadly—and will encounter it far sooner—with our own ever-growing speed. Interstellar dust and gas will impact our worlds as cosmic rays."

"Our planetary force fields protect us from the radiation in our path," rebutted the Hindmost.

"Those same force fields would protect us from the core explosion's radiation, were we to stay and await it."

"Indeed." The Hindmost blinked amusement. "Public beliefs notwithstanding, we can agree radiation is not a threat."

Had the Hindmost come to his point? "Meaning the threat is something else. The counterproductive results to our past approach toward our neighbors?"

"Guiding alien affairs to our own advantage seemed wisest at the time," the Hindmost confirmed. "Of course, every intervention introduced its own complication. Too bad. Colonists tending our nature preserves seemed such a good idea."

An aide approached, clearing his throats. "Your pardon, Hindmost. You asked to be reminded of your next appointment."

"Thank you." The Hindmost gestured dismissively.

Intervention was such a colorless word, Nike thought, and exploitation of the Colonists was but one instance. Now discovery of the NP4 colony by wild humans appeared to be the most imminent danger to the Concordance. "I see at last why Conservatives so quickly embraced flight from the core explosion. You seek to distance us from our neighbors, not the radiation."

"You are too judgmental." The Hindmost craned a neck downhill, sniffing the rich mélange of forest and sea scents. "Surely we agree that the safety of Citizens is ever paramount. That being so, wasn't a bit of social engineering preferable to genocide?"

Was concealed intercession in the wars between human and Kzinti mere social engineering? Was enslavement of the Colonists? How, Nike wondered, would Nessus react to the Hindmost's words? For all Nessus' quirks and idiosyncrasies, the scout was insightful—and increasingly an advocate for the Colonists. And yet . . .

How Nessus proposed to deflect the humans was more social engineering. What Kirsten proposed, if necessary, to hobble the Gw'oth was yet more social engineering.

In an epiphany, Nike grasped the Conservative vision. Where he would invoke permanent emergency to empower Experimentalists . . . the Hindmost sought permanent equilibrium in the emptiness between the galaxies. Hearth had already cast off its anchor to a sun; now, in the guise of institutionalizing Experimentalist policy, the Hindmost would have the Fleet cast off its anchor to even a galaxy.

There would be no more stars to misbehave. No more star clusters to erupt into a chain reaction of supernovae. No more alien races like those that had proven so difficult to control.

"Hindmost, let us not revisit past policy. For our own reasons, each party agreed that we must take flight. But to embrace the unknowable dangers between the galaxies—isn't this a risk?" Whom the gods would destroy . . .

"We can neither stay nor go," the Hindmost said. "Perhaps I have missed something."

The Hindmost had—but the course of action Nike might someday espouse remained unformed even in his own mind.

A proper discussion could not be managed before the Hindmost's imminent appointment. Nike settled upon a polite formality. "Surely the Hindmost would not miss anything."

The Hindmost motioned expansively at the private estate before them. "Consider what we have discussed." The advice served simultaneously as enticement, warning, and dismissal.

Whom the gods would destroy, they first make mad.

Alone in his apartment, Nike resisted the urge to wrap his heads in a tightly rolled shelter of his own flesh. What madness it was to meddle in the destiny of other races!

Yet meddling was what the Concordance did. How misguided that policy must be, when to escape its consequences even the *Conservative* Hindmost embraced a headlong plunge into the intergalactic unknown.

The choices before Clandestine Directorate were limited and stark. Preemptive genocide. Or do nothing, and risk the discovery of the Fleet, of humans trapped on NP4, and with it the unknowable—and surely justified—reaction of Human Space. That way lay mutual assured genocide. Or interfere yet again, undertaking more *social engineering*.

Whom the gods would destroy, they first make mad.

Feeling an unaccustomed empathy with the scout he saw no choice but to dispatch, Nike recorded a brief message.

"Nessus: Proceed immediately with your proposed intervention against the ARM."

17

Kirsten leaned forward in her chair, listening attentively to final guidance for *Explorer*'s upcoming mission. At least she felt her bearing was attentive. A discreet nudge against her left shoe suggested Omar read her posture differently.

Her hands hurt. Glancing down, Kirsten saw they were tightly clenched. Nessus might have understood white knuckles, but he was gone, destination undisclosed, purpose undisclosed. That had left Nike to oversee scouting missions, and the deputy minister lacked Nessus' in-person experience with Colonists. Best to play safe, though. She willed her hands to relax.

". . . The great responsibility entrusted to you," Nike concluded. "Do you have any final questions?"

"We appreciate the honor, Nike. We aspire to merit your trust," Omar said. Eric nodded agreement. "We thank you and Nessus for the confidence you have placed in us."

Through her left shoe, Kirsten felt renewed pressure against her foot. "I have no questions, Nike," she managed, envying Omar's poise.

She held her tension in check long enough to escape Nike's office and the foreign-affairs ministry. Stepping discs delivered them to the spaceport at which their ship waited. Their home, NP4, was visible only as a narrow crescent. Whether its appearance in new phase was auspicious, she could not decide.

Either way, it was time.

In the shadows beneath the curved hull of *Explorer,* Omar took her hand. "You're sure about this?" he asked.

"I am." She was sure she wanted to attempt it—while she dared. "We can't know if we'll get another opportunity. With Nessus away, Nike apparently felt he needed to brief us. Once Nike feels more comfortable dealing with us, or after Nessus returns, or when Nike assigns another Citizen to oversee us, there may be no more invitations back to Hearth." No other chance to uncover the facts of our past.

"Then I'm going, too," Eric blurted.

"Two of us going increases our risk of getting caught." She looked to Omar for support.

"Sorry, Kirsten. I agree with Eric," Omar said. "You can't know what you'll find."

Could they afford the time spent debating? "Fine, Eric, on one condition. You agree I'm in charge."

Eric nodded.

"Omar . . . if anyone gets suspicious, you don't know where we went. I just wanted to play tourist for a little longer while you finished shipboard preparations." Before he could comment, she stepped onto the nearest public disc and disappeared.

Kirsten emerged into a safety shelter indistinguishable from the one in Elysium. How long ago that seemed! She set the nano-cloth of her jumpsuit into a random conglomeration of red, purple, and yellow splotches. In theory, it would blend with Hearthian foliage.

Eric materialized behind her. His eyes widened at the unexpected change to her clothing, before, with a nod of understanding, he altered his own shirt and slacks to correspond.

"So far, so good," she said. "We have the place to ourselves."

He shrugged. "For the few moments we'll be here."

The exterior cameras showed nothing but empty woods, lit by the "daylight" glowing from the mile-high wall of a nearby arcology. She unlatched the door. "This is a *Citizen* park. There is nothing dangerous out there. You didn't need to come."

He edged past her through the doorway and into a small clearing. Bushes and trees, or at least their Hearth equivalents, soughed in the light breeze. "Maybe a third of the plants look familiar from our last hike. I don't suppose that matters."

"Probably not." Kirsten's attention was on the sky. By a succession of public stepping discs, and so, in theory, untraceable, they had jumped far around the globe. A full NP1 overhead instantly oriented her. "This way."

A few paces into the woods plunged them into shadowy gloom. Only Eric's fast grab saved her from a nasty fall as she caught a toe in an unseen root. He took a small flashlight from his pocket.

"Not even the Concordance can banish uneven ground," he said. "You could fall down a hill or into a gully—and then it's over."

He was right. "Thanks," she said, and meant it. They had miles to go, and they had to cross them quickly.

What would they find when they arrived? Perhaps the Human Studies Institute cited in files she had stolen from Nessus. Perhaps a home for wealthy Citizens. Perhaps nothing. The institute was "located" in the file only by its fifteen-digit stepping-disc address, highlighted in the manner that denoted an access-controlled location. Even if she had known Nessus' authentication code, the institute's entry was surely continuously monitored. The stepping discs into Nike's ministry were certainly well-secured from the uninvited.

It might never occur to a Citizen that someone would *walk* there.

Of course, walking there required knowledge of the institute's physical location. That critical detail appeared nowhere in Nessus' files. The institute went altogether unmentioned in Kirsten's souvenir books. That left only wishful thinking—and a hologram of the institute in Nessus' archive. The image showed an isolated hexagonal structure topped by a dome.

The murk grew ever deeper. Dim beams from their flashlights provided the only meaningful ground-level illumination. The overhead pattering that had begun early into their hike grew louder. Raindrops begin penetrating the canopy of leaves. Dense underbrush made the walking slow, and the uneven ground made it all too easy to veer off course.

Compass notwithstanding, were they even walking in the correct direction?

This expedition had seemed so much easier in the bright and warm comfort of her apartment. In the holo image, four NP worlds in various phases hung over the institute. The date stamp implicit in the image's file name indicated when the hologram was made. However computationally messy, it had been conceptually simple to derive the institute's physical location on Hearth. Those coordinates put it on the shore of a lake, deep inside one of Hearth's few large parks.

They talked of home and hobbies, of friends and family. Eric coughed. "How far do you think we've come?"

"Two miles, maybe a bit more."

"Less than half way. Kirsten, we're taking too long."

"I know." There was nothing they could do about it. At this point, they were committed. "I couldn't know how rough the terrain would be under the foliage, and I didn't think to plan for rain. The wet footing is slowing us down."

"I wasn't criticizing." His flashlight beam wobbled as, in a flurry of wet leaves, he slid down a slight incline. "What do you think we'll find?"

"I don't know." She batted aside a low-hanging branch. "I'm almost afraid to know."

"Humans," Eric answered. "Is that what we are?"

They crested a hill. Shadows hid the way down. "Maybe. Or maybe humans are another race the Citizens have encountered, who may know something about us. Or they're the species who attacked our ancestors' starship. I don't understand why they wouldn't just tell—"

Eric caught her arm as her feet slipped out from under her. A bit of wet clay? "Be careful," he wheezed.

Kirsten looked all around in growing panic. "I dropped my compass."

Crouching, Eric poked with his flashlight at the low groundcover amid which they stood. Fleshy, fan-shaped sheets filtered its light into dim pastels. "I don't see it." He chain-coughed as he stood.

"Are you all right?"

"Funny thing," he said. "Maybe not."

She stared at him. "What do you mean?"

"I had a condition when I was a kid. Asthma. Apparently, I still do." He sat on a boulder, breathing shallowly, as though he were sucking air through a sponge. "Humidity and chemical fumes can trigger it." A chuckle morphed into a hacking cough. "Stress aggravates it."

They were miles from anywhere, and the nearest structure was someplace they weren't supposed to know about. She patted a pocket, and was relieved to feel her communicator. "We can call for help."

"And wait for Citizens to extract us from the woods during a storm?" Another half-cough, half-laugh. He stood. "We might as well walk. At least that will avoid their questions."

Walk where? She had lost her compass. Thick cloud so suffused the NP glows that she could scarcely navigate by their light—and then, only in the occasional clearing from which the clouds were visible. The clouds hung only a few hundred feet over her, scarcely above the tree tops, blocking most of the now-distant arcology-wall light.

It suddenly struck Kirsten what an alien world Hearth truly was. It had no little satellite suns and no great fireball star. There would be no daylight to save them.

"I have an idea," Eric said. "The institute is on the lake, right?"

"Right."

"Maybe we can follow that creek"—he pointed toward a faint gurgle—"downstream to the lake, and then follow the shore."

"We don't know how much the creek wanders. The shore *does* wander. We'll have a much longer walk."

"You identified our destination mathematically." He coughed unproductively. "It's all right if we get there another way."

"Lead on." At the base of the hill she added, "I'm glad you came."

"I'm not." He coughed. "Well, that's not true. I had, however, envisioned our first date somewhat differently." Cough. "That's a joke."

"Why didn't I know about this asthma condition?"

Kirsten asked. Suddenly her face grew hot. She was thankful for the dark that hid her blush. She had been thinking like a crewmate; Eric would almost certainly fail to take her question that way. You *never* talked about hereditary medical conditions, unless with a doctor, or family, or a prospective mate.

Eric asked, "Can you keep a secret?"

"If not, we're in a lot of trouble."

The shallowness of Eric's breathing rendered his laugh horrifying. "Respiratory problems aren't that uncommon where I come from."

"We come from the same place." And she had never heard of asthma.

Cough. Wheeze. "Here's the secret, Kirsten. I grew up on NP3, a world away from you. There's a small Colonist settlement there. Apparently growing Colonists from the embryo banks was trickier than the Concordance wants people to know, and problems can—do—recur generations later. Some problems take a *lot* of medical care." Wheeze. "I was a success story. I owe them."

"I had no idea." The depth of his loyalty to the Concordance, his deference to Nessus, his sometimes questionable social skills, began to make sense.

"How could you know?" Cough. He crouched to peer below some branches.

No wonder he felt so indebted to the Citizens. She was afraid to ask why he had not informed on Omar and her. Why he was here?

Her doubts must have been written on her face. "Because it's important to you." As though afraid of her reaction he continued without pause, "I think I see the lake."

Moments later, she glimpsed the lake, too. A few more steps brought them out of the woods, to a narrow fringe of rocky shoreline. Around a curve of the lake, through the rain, she could just make out a hint of a domed structure.

The Human Studies Institute.

* * *

The "trees" by the lake loosely resembled red saguaro cacti sprouting fleshy round leaves instead of spines. Despite the increasingly heavy rain, the NP light that diffused through the cloud cover and reflected off the water allowed Kirsten and Eric to move quickly through the woods near the shoreline. The institute itself provided no light.

They were nearly to the isolated structure when Kirsten's communicator trilled discreetly. "You need to get back," Omar said. "Spaceport authorities are getting impatient. I blamed our delayed departure on a small technical glitch. If I don't 'resolve' the problem soon, they'll send tech support to help me fix it."

They were *so* close. "I told you to blame the delay on me: gone shopping. Now you'll have to find a way to stall. We're almost at the institute."

"If this doesn't work, I'm not leaving you and Eric to take the blame," Omar answered. "I'll do what I can, Kirsten, but *hurry*."

The building they had come so far to explore was scarcely taller than the surrounding trees. From where they stood, no doors or windows suggested themselves. She edged deeper into the woods to circle the building. "Follow me."

They stayed among the trees, straining to make out details of the building. "It's too dark," Eric said. "If there is a door, we might not see it." He crept up to the wall, hand over his mouth to muffle a cough. "Come on."

They reached the shore again, having closely examined four sides of the hexagon. The final sides, those nearest the lake, were sufficiently illuminated by sky glow not to need up-close scrutiny. They were unbroken.

"I can't believe it." Kirsten sat heavily on the ground, her back against a tree. "To have come so far . . ." She meant not only this hike, but everything they had been through. It had been a long and arduous trail here from the ice moon.

"Hmm." Eric studied the inaccessible wall, head tipped thoughtfully. "Remember Nessus bringing us to a shopping complex?"

"I do. Why?"

"It used force fields for outside access, not doors." He walked along the building, trailing a hand against the wall. "Just a hunch." As he approached a corner, his hand sank into the wall. "Aha." He stuck his head through briefly, then gestured her over.

"What did you see?" she whispered.

"A viewing gallery, I think, overlooking a roomful of Citizens and terminals. The gallery itself is empty."

Muddy splotches marked their approach. The rocky ground didn't take full bootprints. She pointed at her boots, covered in muck. "We can hope the rain will wash away our tracks, but that won't help us indoors. Our boots have to stay outside."

With a shrug, Eric sat down through the false wall. His head, shoulders, arms, and feet remained outside. He slipped off his boots, setting them just outside the holo wall, and then leaned backward to roll the rest of the way inside. His disembodied voice called, "Come on."

Faster than she could mimic Eric's entry procedure, he was flat on the floor, peering through the railing at the activity below. His clothes had become a pale blue that closely matched the corridor wall. She reprogrammed her own clothes and joined him. Below them, ten Citizens were seated near terminals, three walked about, and seven more stood watch over an array of stepping discs.

Holograms floated among and over the institute staff. Even the nearest projections were maddeningly indistinct at this distance. Images of Colonists—or was humans the correct term?—their activities unrecognizable. Impressions of text, none readable. The holo of a Nature Preserve world, clouds masking its surface. Holos of General Products hulls. It was all tantalizing.

It told her nothing.

Kirsten crawled around the balcony area, hugging the exterior wall. She was sopping wet from the rain and left a damp trail. She hoped strong winds sometimes blew in rain, or that the water would evaporate before a Citizen appeared up here.

The unattended terminal she sought was at the railing, a third of the way around the gallery. For all Kirsten knew, it offered only administrative functions unrelated to the purposeful activity below. She scooted backward with its wireless keyboard in hand until the wall touched her back. If she managed to activate the terminal and set its display into flat mode, whatever she did should be invisible from the floor below.

Murmurs and music whispered, snatches of speech from terminals and conversations below. Acoustical vagaries, echoes from the dome overhead, and her limited fluency reduced it all nearly to babble. Nearly, but not quite: Scattered words and phrases were intelligible. "Human" and "wild humans" were distinct enough, and several mentions of known space, and something she must have misunderstood, about a suspicious arm.

She could not get past the welcome display. Administrative or not, the terminal expected biometric authentication. Beyond turning the terminal on, all Kirsten had managed to do was to dim the display, still in floating holographic mode, to pale translucence. Faint characters continued to invite an authorizing tongueprint.

She caught Eric's eye. He shrugged, as unsuccessful as she at spotting anything useful. His face was mottled, pinkish-purple and pale. His chest moved shallowly but rapidly. She thought she heard wheezing. Whatever asthma was, she had to get him to an autodoc.

The hike from the safety shelter and its stepping disc had taken hours. Could Eric make it back? He needed medical attention *now*. Without a stepping disc, that meant making their presence known. Surrendering.

The still-scrolling characters of the welcome prompt

taunted her. She restored the terminal, as best she could remember it, to the brightness level where she had found it, and powered it down. It had all been for nothing.

As she slithered on her belly back toward Eric, her communicator trilled. Omar. "Not now," she whispered.

"Spaceport control has lost patience. In fifteen minutes, if *Explorer* is not ready to launch, they will send help. I'll have to tell spaceport control I've been covering for your absence."

On the level below, Citizen voices rose and fell, at once lyrical and discordant. Holograms floated about, appearing and vanishing to the unknowable purposes of the staff. Sentries still ringed the stepping discs. Even if they could be activated, they would only access another restricted area.

The only access she and Eric had found to the gallery was from outdoors. How did Citizens get to and from this level? They clearly never arrived at the institute by land, or there would have been guards outside. She began crawling the long way round to Eric. Halfway there she found a stepping disc in the floor. She waved for his attention. "Get our boots," she mouthed. "Wrap them in your shirt."

Most likely, the disc would only move them to the busy main area below the gallery. Maybe they could alter it . . .

Carefully, they pried up the disc. Eric, now shirtless, eyed the controls set in the edge. "It looks standard—with the minor problem that the customary maintenance keypad has been removed. Anything could be in the memory chip." His lips were blue and his breathing labored. "Maybe, if we remove the programming chip, it will reset to default settings." Cough. "Not that we know where its default setting would send us."

"There's no way to give it an address?"

"Only by communicator, and only then with an authentication code we can't give it."

They were out of options. "Eric, we have to turn ourselves in. You need medical help, and soon."

Cough. "I didn't know you cared."

"You came along to help me. That makes you my responsibility." And, if not in the way Eric would wish it, she found she *did* care. "Unless you have a better idea."

"You walk out. I tell them I came alone."

The offer made Kirsten feel even worse. "We're in this together."

The murmuring below continued to taunt her. Through the railing, holograms came and went: Colonists/humans. A grain ship. The nature-preserve world, now revealing enough continental outline through its clouds to suggest NP5. Still-indistinguishable hints of text.

Why a grain ship and NP5? The newest world in the Fleet was still being eco-formed. It had no grain to export. "Eric, that's NP5, isn't it?"

"I don't know." Cough. "Maybe. Judging by the amount of cloud cover. Geography isn't my strong point."

The Human Studies Institute had interest in NP5. That sufficed to pique *her* interest. Kirsten pointed at the disc. "Let's remove the memory chip. There's only one way to find out the disc's default address. Worst case, we'll surrender there."

"All right."

She pried out the part.

"Wait. Not like that." Cough. "Say we get away. The next time someone here uses this disc, they'll also be sent to the default location. Someone will check out the disc, and see that the chip is gone." Cough. "They'll see that someone has tampered with the disc." Wheezing, he took the chip from her, bent a pin and put the chip back into place. "Let them think the chip had a bent pin all along, and the bent pin just now came completely unplugged. Random floor vibrations, not intruders." Together they set the disc back into the floor.

He picked up an awkward parcel, their boots knotted inside his shirt, and stepped. He did not reappear on the level below. She stepped after—

To join him among a crowd of gaping Citizens. A holo-sign labeled the nearest structure as *Department of Public Safety.* The default disc address, of course.

"Let's go," she said. She took his arm and pulled/lifted him toward an array of public stepping discs.

After several random hops through public spaces, they popped aboard *Explorer.* Omar's eyes widened, and she could only imagine how bedraggled they must look.

"Two minutes to spare," Kirsten said. "I'll get Eric into the autodoc. *You* get us on our way."

18

Nessus bowed to no sane sentient when it came to caution. Of course, he was *in*sane and sadly aware of it. He could not otherwise be so distant from Hearth and herd. He could not otherwise be hurtling through the nothingness of hyperspace. Alone with his insanity, grazing absent-mindedly from a trencher of freshly synthesized mixed grains, he contemplated another's insanity—and wondered if he had finally met his match.

For Sigmund Ausfaller was paranoid, and his delusions of persecution made him a formidable adversary. Nessus understood paranoia, although among Colonists it was treated. Among the wild humans, within the ARM, paranoia was nurtured—even induced.

To be paranoid was to inflate one's importance, to see oneself as worthy of persecution. Paranoids found things to worry about that no sane person could. Such a fear might sometimes prove not so irrational after all. Where Puppeteers were concerned, Ausfaller's suspicions had become a self-fulfilling prophecy.

The meal was disagreeably dry. Nessus synthesized a flagon of carrot juice to accompany it. The beverage was totally without nutritional value for him but he liked it nonetheless. It was one of the few pleasures available to him aboard *Aegis*.

Another was the larger-than-life holo with which Nessus shared the bridge. He had taken the image at one of the earliest Experimentalist rallies he had ever attended. Perhaps Nike had meant the adoring expression for the entire crowd; Nessus chose to imagine it otherwise.

But first he had a mission to complete.

In his paranoia, Ausfaller hunted for Puppeteers years after all had departed. Nike had learned that fact from their most highly placed spy. Where, then, did the ARM seek? For what?

Reason as distrustfully as Ausfaller, Nessus told himself. Put yourself into his place.

General Products made its technology crucial to the economies of humans and their neighbors—and then disappeared, plunging those economies into chaos.

Perhaps it had been a mistake to humor the term "Puppeteer." To humans a Citizen's heads might look like a pair of sock puppets, but—imagine how a paranoid would interpret aliens embracing *that* label.

Put yourself in Ausfaller's place.

A world is too big to hide, hence it should long ago have been found. That worlds could be moved surely remained beyond the imagination of the wild humans, so failure to find the Puppeteers must only reinforce Ausfaller's theories of conspiracy.

A syllogism: All the UN's resources would have found the homeworld. The homeworld has not been found. Ergo: Some resources have been diverted, or some discoveries hidden.

Ausfaller deduced a Puppeteer secret agent in the ARM. QED.

Nessus shivered. The ARM had likely leaked news of his latest search, hoping to lure Puppeteers and their agents into exposing themselves. Any of Nessus' usual sources within the UN might now work with Ausfaller, or, unknowingly, be under his observation.

Nessus contemplated his dilemma, food and drink abandoned, picking anxiously at his mane. He needed a whole new approach to gleaning Ausfaller's strategy. He needed to recruit anonymously a whole new network. Could he act quickly enough to protect the Fleet?

All hope of return to Hearth and Nike receded into the very indefinite future.

Sol system was home to scant billions, but those few knew no fear. They filled its skies with interplanetary yachts and liners, tugs and freighters, Belter patrol ships and UN frigates. To those argosies were added yet more, the many starships that plied the void to far-flung human colonies and the worlds of Kzinti and Kdatlyno.

Nessus intended that his presence go unnoticed by all those teeming craft. He approached Sol system tangentially, rather than head-on, and at a steep angle to the plane of the ecliptic. He dropped *Aegis* from hyperspace into the anonymous outer reaches of the Oort Cloud—

And, from habit, he reached toward his console to run a deep-radar scan.

He jerked the head back. *Aegis* had just exited hyperspace far from the singularity, the better to let dissipate unremarked the unavoidable ripples of his emergence. Why emit a discretionary neutrino pulse?

Did he think to find a stasis box *here*?

He looked himself in the eyes, appalled and amused at the near-lapse. It could be worse, he supposed. He could be mystified, too, as Kirsten had wondered at being trained to emit a deep-radar ping on approach to a new star system.

Nessus burst into song as, with full thrusters, he slowed the ship's headlong plunge. *Ride of the Valkyries* in full orchestration. The music seemed somehow apt. Doubly apt, really, in that his erstwhile crew had once thoroughly enjoyed a performance.

Trust Kirsten to notice phonetic similarities between English and German. Coincidence, he had told her. What was one more deception?

Had she dutifully deep-scanned *Explorer*'s most recent destination, wondering what there was to be learned that way?

If she only knew.

Eons ago there had been a war of galactic extermination, of which naught remained but scattered artifacts preserved for eternity within stasis fields. Most objects recovered from stasis storage defied understanding. All embodied technologies of terrifying potency. The prevailing opinion was that these were weapons caches.

The one course of action more frightening than to locate and open a stasis box was to leave it for another race to find.

The stasis field was opaque to neutrino pulses. Only degenerate matter, like the collapsed central mass of a star, shared that property. A stasis field could not be missed—so it was foolish to look for a stasis box in such a heavily traveled region as Sol system.

As his singing swelled to a crescendo, enjoying his manic glee while it lasted, Nessus could not help wondering how Omar, Eric, and Kirsten were coming on *their* mission.

A water world sparkled through *Explorer*'s view ports. Other than the peaks of a few volcanic cones, only an immense, equatorial landmass interrupted the otherwise planet-spanning ocean. The continent's coastal regions were bright with greenery, its high central plains brown and sere. Nike, in his only active participation, had responded to an early report by naming the planet Oceanus.

Life teemed in the seas and jungles below. If she let herself, Kirsten could stare for hours every shift. Despite countless differences, Oceanus reminded her of NP4. She missed home.

"It does look nice down there." Eric sat on the relax-room deck amid a scattering of parts, things to be configured into yet another remote-sensing satellite. He had regained his normal color since the nearly disastrous expedition to the Human Studies Institute, but not yet his stamina. "In a bugs-at-the-top-of-the-food-chain sort of way."

"Nothing here to match the Gw'oth," she said.

"Not even close." As a tiny component went flying from his grasp, he muttered about fingers being too stubby and inflexible.

Rather than her smaller fingers, all she offered him was a question. "Why bother with more sensors? Nothing below can possibly be a threat to the Fleet."

"You really *are* down," Eric said.

He'd been like that with her, solicitous, since the autodoc let him out. His taste in colors had become subdued, too. She said, "It was a fool's errand. I was the fool. The best that can be said for our outing is I didn't get you killed—not quite—and we weren't caught." She trembled. She had no idea what punishment might have been meted out. Somehow, the uncertainty only made it worse.

"Kirsten, I insisted on going. I kept my medical condition secret. It's not your fault." A cough ruined his protest.

"I don't understand why the autodoc can't *fix* that." At least, if he healed completely, she would have only the failure of their quest to depress her.

"The 'doc can only treat my symptoms. It can't keep my body from producing the proteins that predispose me to asthma attacks. Only time stops that process." He sipped something from a drink bulb. "And no, the 'doc can't switch off some magic gene. There's some complex dependency involved: environmental, or multigene, or environmental *and* multigene." Cough. "That's me. I'm special."

Eric went back to his tinkering and she to planetgazing. She had a great deal of thinking to do. Either activity served to spend the time until his health would accommodate a return to the Fleet without raising unwelcome questions.

Unsavory.

It was the adjective Nessus associated with underworld figures. It could hardly be otherwise. To be unsavory, or worse, was surely a precondition for acting against the common good of one's species. Unsavory, fairly or not, was how he labeled the man and woman in the holo before him.

No matter that they had come at his summons: his minions.

The wild humans spoke from a light-second away. If they were surprised to encounter a hyperwave radio relay rather than a ship at the designated coordinates, they did not comment. General Products produced a near-impregnable hull, but a sufficiently serious impact would still turn *him* to jelly. A sufficiently powerful laser would vaporize the hull coating and then destroy anything within, the hull itself being transparent to visible light. There could be antimatter. . . .

This line of thought would soon have him cowering against his own belly, which he could have done without traveling so many light-years. It did nothing to protect the Fleet or to impress Nike. Better to concentrate on his goals than on improbable hazards. "What results?"

"Fertility Board records are not easy to come by," Miguel Sullivan began. He was swarthy and round-faced, with close-set eyes, a smooth scalp, and a scruffy mustache. An Earther scrubbed of body paint for space. "That was no small matter with which you tasked us."

It was no small retainer that had already been electron-ically transferred, from funds hopefully untraceable to General Products, with the promise of another payment upon success. "Your report," Nessus prompted again.

"Can I send you a file?" Ashley Klein's most prominent feature was a Belter Mohawk dyed shocking neon blue. Her pale blue eyes seemed almost colorless by compari-son. She towered over her colleague. The question was evidently rhetorical, because data appeared in an input buffer before Nessus answered. She said, "There have been billions of births on Earth in the past century. The overwhelming majority are what you would expect: one or two children approved for obviously healthy parents, and all Fertility Board rules clearly followed."

Nessus surveyed the file as she spoke. Those billions of births had been plotted against several different param-eters. Every chart showed a nice bell curve—which meant every graph had outliers. "Clearly some couples had a third, or even a fourth child. A few applications were ap-proved far quicker than the typical review period. There have been pregnancy complications, and a scattering of congenital disorders, despite all the screening."

"It's what I'd expect," Ashley said. "There's no more variability here than you'd predict with so many cases to be evaluated. Less, to be honest."

Nessus placed little weight in the self-professed hon-esty of criminals. Even his own. Even when, with only the evidence of their eyes and his virtualized transmission to guide them, he must appear a human she. "And you cross-matched those exceptions with family income?"

"Of course, since you asked." Ashley shrugged and re-ferred him to another graphic in the file. "It's the same lack of pattern."

A pattern would have been nice; a few data points would suffice. Nessus sorted a list of the outliers against family income. While proving nothing, it yielded more than a million cases of *plausible* connivance. He transmitted back his version of the data. "Here. Now look for associations with anyone working for the Fertility Board, or to their relatives and friends."

Miguel smiled humorlessly. "Then we put the squeeze on them?"

Unsavory and picaresque. The turn of phrase was new to Nessus, but its meaning was obvious. "No. For now, let the data trickle out. Reporters. Rumors. 'Net gossip. Be creative."

Ashley rubbed her chin. "Where's the profit in that? It'll only cause chaos."

"For you it will cause money." They had the good sense to be silent when Nessus paused for any further objection. "Good. Here is another credit authorization code."

"We'll head back into the solar system then," Miguel said.

Was there a nuance of complaint at Nessus' insistence on a remote rendezvous? He did not care. Closer to the sun would make detection that much more likely. Closer to the sun, he would be within the singularity, unable to flick away from danger by hyperdrive.

Thought of departure, however premature, reminded Nessus of another transaction. "There is something I would like you to acquire for me. A collection, actually." He transmitted the details.

The humans twitched in surprise. "You're serious?" Miguel asked. "That will cost you *serious* money. A few million, I'll say five, just to determine feasibility. Much more if it can be done."

"Approved." Fifty million would hardly touch the General Products accounts here in Sol system, and Nessus could hardly come all this way without bringing Nike home a souvenir.

Omar loped on the treadmill, sweat plastering his hair to his forehead. Only the wet hair suggested that he had been exercising for long. Sweat evaporating almost instantly through his nano-cloth jumpsuit kept the rest of him cool. He said, "I would defy even Nessus to find a threat down there."

Down there: the watery planet they had now orbited for twenty-two shifts. Close observation of Oceanus by remote-controlled sensors had revealed hive creatures, like especially retarded bees, and forests of sedentary sea-bottom creatures sieving the currents for the local algae-equivalent. Geometric structures in the ocean had provided the only suggestion of artificiality, an intimation that proved to be false. Except in progress reports to Hearth, the three of them never doubted these assemblages were naturally occurring reefs. Still, experience with the Gw'oth justified checking out the undersea features with methodical indirection. To stall while Eric mended.

Which, to Kirsten's relief, he had. She pinned Eric's feet as he did sit-ups. "Do you think we'll ever know where Nessus was sent?"

"Doubt it," Eric grunted. "Forty-nine. Fifty." He flopped back onto his mat, breathing heavily but with none of the wheezing that had been so scary. "I'm ready to go back."

"To Arcadia?" Omar stepped off the treadmill. Sensing the disappearance of its load, the machine came to a stop.

"To the institute."

"What?" Kirsten asked. She had championed that first excursion, arrogantly certain they would root out long-hidden secrets. That *she* would find a way into the computers, because that was what *she* did. "Why?"

Eric wiggled his feet. "Let me up." She did, and he stood. "There had to be meaning there. I keep looking."

"You keep looking," Omar said. "Present tense. How, exactly?"

"Where did I put it?" Eric looked around until he spotted his communicator, tossed into a corner when he began exercising. He tapped at its touch screen. "Here."

A holo swallowed his hand. "Enlarge."

Kirsten stepped back to take it in. "That's . . . the institute's main floor." She peered between the virtual railings at the remembered area below. In miniature, Citizens walked about, mimed conversation, guarded stepping discs, and labored at their workstations. Shadowy images floated above, phantoms of holograms past. The sequence ran less than a minute before looping back to the beginning.

"I took this video while you crept across the gallery floor to that terminal," Eric said.

"And you never said anything," she said.

"It shows us nothing." Eric shrugged. "The problem is, I can't help but believe that it should, or that it would have, if I had taken more."

"Can we enhance this?" Omar asked.

"I wish we could," Eric answered. "Now if we had a bigger computer we could safely put this on—but that's not going to happen until we're home."

"A bigger computer? We have all we could need." Kirsten leaned over, squinting. The indistinct images tantalized her. "With the superuser privileges I cloned from Nessus, I can delete all traces afterward."

Omar broke a long silence. "Let's do it."

A thousand-plus envelopes materialized at the appointed time inside as many unlisted transfer booths. The originating coordinates recorded by the receiving booths were nulled and untraceable. The compulsory authentication checks had been similarly bypassed. The identifications implicit in supposedly mandatory real-time payments were blanked out, should any of the recipients dare to inquire of the network provider. Lest the manner of message delivery be insufficiently instructive, each envelope bore in animation the snarling, ever watchful, three-headed guardian of Hades: Cerberus.

It was enough, Nessus thought, to instill dread in the recipients even before they saw what waited within.

Subverting the humans' primitive teleportation system was easy, since the underlying technology had been licensed from General Products in the first place. The device Nessus had provided his minions for the task would have self-destructed after use. The time might arise when he wanted to trust the transfer-booth system's integrity—in the sense of knowing that its vulnerability remained intact and unsuspected.

The envelope contents were as carefully selected as the recipients. Off-world bank statements with embarrassingly large balances. Dates and places of trysts. Intimations of various cooked books, stock manipulations, tax evasions, rigged bids, undisclosed product defects, and sordid collusions. Enumerations of criminal investigations stymied or inexplicably gone dormant, of pardons granted and sentences commuted. Gambling debts, drug habits, spousal abuses, embezzlements, youthful indiscretions . . .

It required an appreciation of human society far deeper than Nessus' to grasp exactly why most of the hinted-at disclosures were problematical. That lack of understanding scarcely mattered, because his minions understood. All Nessus had required of Miguel and Ashley was invisible influence.

He sought comfort from the beginnings of progress. Riots against Fertility Board corruption had begun. Those who would provide him with influence had been put on notice. Soon enough, the recipients of those Cerberus-emblazoned envelopes would be told the price of keeping their secrets. For most, the price of forbearance would be advocacy for Fertility Board "reform." For a few, the price would be much higher. Nessus would see into the ARM itself.

For all this preliminary success, Nessus trembled.

The pungency of synthetic herd pheromone could not disguise the knowledge that he was alone, the only one of his kind for light-years. It could not hasten the manipulation of the wild humans. It could not purge his fear of failure. It could not heal his aberrance, or make him more attractive to the one he loved.

Not directly, anyway.

The deliberate unfolding of the plan had one advantage. The gift Nessus wished to obtain for Nike *was* obtainable.

Its acquisition would also take time.

The video was low resolution, blurry, and shot from an oblique angle. Kirsten could do nothing about the angle, but everything else was amenable to computed corrections. She enhanced edges, interpolated new scan rows to sharpen the overall picture, compensated for the worst reflections, and adjusted for Eric's tremulous camera hand.

That was better.

Scattered letters that remained ambiguous to Kirsten were nonetheless identifiable by character-recognition software. Whatever had blurred and smeared the letters had likewise distorted the rest of the image. She dug into the character-recognition algorithms, and pulled apart the pattern-analysis and pattern-matching logic. One routine at a time, she experimented.

Eric, whom she had doubted, had persevered. She had despaired, and it shamed her. Not even the deflection of the Fleet's course away from the Gw'oth had cheered her.

Never again.

Step by step the image improved.

Omar ambled onto the bridge. "Welcome back."

She realized she had worked through the sleep shift. Her hands never left the keyboard. "What do you mean?"

"I mean, Kirsten, that you were whistling."

That made her stop, if only for a moment. "I guess I

was. I could kill that Eric, if he hadn't almost done it to himself already. This is *good data*."

"Only in your hands. And only when you were ready."

Omar was right, of course.

Her fingers kept working. There was always one more tweak to try. "Wish me luck." The still image hanging before her shimmered, then settled into crisper focus: the globe of NP5. This latest addition to the Fleet was always wreathed in cloud, still early in its transformation into a haven for Hearthian life. Beside the cloudy sphere hung an icon and a string of numerals.

"Luck." Omar settled on the arm of the crash couch beside her. "That looks clearer. See anything useful?"

Finally, Kirsten lifted her hands from the keyboard. She turned to look Omar squarely in the eye. "My guess is 'useful' seriously understates it.

"There's a General Products #4 hull circling NP5. For some reason we can't yet imagine, that ship matters to the Human Studies Institute. And *this*," and she poked her hand into the cleaned-up holo, to the string of numerals, "is the key to the stepping disc network aboard that ship."

19

With sinuous perfection, a thousand lithe figures twirled and leapt. Hooves kicked: unerringly straight and high, impossibly precise, preternaturally synchronized in each stroke against the rock-hard stage. Voices rang out, ineffably poignant in cadence and counterpoint, melody and mode. Lines formed, split, and re-formed. Formations melded and reemerged.

A thousand exemplars of perfection became one. A distraction, from questing humans and political ambition alike, that Nike sorely needed. As he watched, a much-

needed calm washed over him. His heads swayed sensu-
ally, drawn to the rhythms of the dance.

"Excellency," someone whispered.

Nike's heads whipped around. Who would *dare* at such
a time? The troupe had dedicated this performance to *his*
honor.

"Excellency," repeated the aide. His heads drooped
with chagrin and embarrassment. "There is an utmost-
urgency call for you."

Whispering apologies to friends and colleagues *he* had
invited to the performance, Nike pressed through the
throng filling the private viewing room into a corridor
empty but for some of his security detachment. The closed
door muted the singing, but had no effect on the pounding of three thousand hooves. The vibration of the building continued unabated as the performance continued
despite his absence.

He accepted a communicator from the cringing aide.
"That's all right. It was your responsibility to tell me."

"Hello?" squawked the communicator.

"With whom am I speaking?"

The name at first meant nothing to Nike. Then the
cocky attitude registered, and Nike remembered. This
was the General Products employee Nessus had dubbed
Baedeker.

"Deputy Minister, your staff resisted putting through
my call. I insisted." Baedeker's throats rasped with emotion. "The situation is unacceptable."

Why would this engineer think to contact him? "Start
at the beginning."

"It's the three Colonists, aboard *Explorer,*" Baedeker
said. "I can't hear them."

A ship lost? The staccato rhythms of three thousand
hooves waxed and waned, making the hoarse voice on
the communicator even more difficult to understand. "I
don't understand. How can a ship be lost? One of *your*
hulls!"

"No, sir. The ship is fine. I can't hear the crew. I can't *over*hear the crew."

For this he had been called from the grand ballet? "Continue."

"We equipped *Explorer* with listening devices with which to monitor the unsupervised Colonists. Their conversation is multiplexed into the outgoing telemetry stream."

Unsupervised Colonists. Nike chose to ignore the undertone of disapproval about the mission *he* had authorized. "What could interrupt the telemetry?"

"Nothing has. All data streams continue unabated. The Colonist recordings are fiction. Fiction!" Baedeker lapsed briefly into an unhappy hum. "They evidently altered the sensor feed into the telemetry subsystem."

Nike waited out a torrent of words about sampling techniques and autocorrelation. The details hardly mattered. *Explorer*'s crew had substituted random repeats of recorded conversations and ambient noises—and Baedeker had noticed only now. First the altercation aboard the General Products factory, and now this. Twice the Colonists had bested the engineer. Nike kept his amusement to himself, giving the Colonists credit for maintaining their privacy.

Citizens rarely wanted privacy. Colonists often did. Nike wished he could see *Explorer*'s crew, observe their clothing and jewelry. That would tell him much about their mindsets, almost what he could glean by observing a Citizen's mane. Of course a Colonist was a laborer. Laborers had little time for proper grooming of their manes. They took much less time over programmable clothing and nano-spun jewelry.

Thunderous ululations from the packed theater announced the end of the second dance movement. Nike asked, "What about the reports from *Explorer*?"

"They seem credible," Baedeker said.

That was rather grudging. "Do you see any inconsistencies in the data? Odd results? Any reason at all to question their findings?"

"No. If anything they are ploddingly thorough in their studies."

"Then let us accept their desire for privacy, and let them do their work for us." Setting aside thoughts of humans and Colonists alike, Nike reimmersed himself in the beauty of the dance.

Omar and Eric were rehearsing dialogue for a fresh voice recording, another faked bridge conversation. They were ad-libbing a little, trying to crack each other up, defying with their laughter the nothingness of hyperspace.

Kirsten stood unseen outside the relax-room door, listening, and asking herself one last time: Do I want to do this?

And realized that she very much did.

It scared Kirsten to remember how often she had spurned Eric's advances. Would he now spurn her?

He had matured into someone confident, supportive, and self-deprecating—into someone she very much admired. Perhaps that growth meant he would no longer have interest in her. She had to make a grand gesture.

She had to risk rejection as publicly as she had rejected him.

Kirsten stepped into view. "Eric," she called out. "May I have a word with you?"

Both men turned, and stared.

Eric followed her in silence into her cabin. The room was cramped, not much more than sleeper-field plates equipped with crash webbing. Eric managed to close the door without brushing against her. For a long time, he was at a loss for words. "About your outfit," he finally managed.

Her jumpsuit shone a fiery red, trimmed with warm

yellow accents, the colors more vibrant than any she had ever seen him wear. "I hope you like it."

He looked like he wanted to ask: why? Instead he said, "You already know my medical problems. They're genetic."

Kirsten took his hands. "I have wisdom teeth." When he looked puzzled, she explained. "Extra teeth. Too many for my jaw. If I hadn't had surgery, they could have grown horizontally or pushed out other teeth. In many people, the crowding causes jaw pain and headaches." The problem was easily corrected, and in fact the extracted teeth could be saved for transplants, but she wanted to make a point. No one was perfect.

His eyes narrowed appraisingly. She imagined he was weighing the risks to their hypothetical children, as society expected. All he said was, "That's not so bad."

"Anyway, now you know. And my grandfather ruptured an artery in his brain. He was hiking alone. Help didn't come in time. He was only seventy-one. I thought I should tell you."

Eric gave her hands a squeeze. "You're beautiful and fun and *brilliant*. How could teeth possibly matter? Kirsten, could you consider me a proper mate?"

"Yes. Yes. You believed in me. You brought me back when I had given up." Releasing his hands, Kirsten put her arms around his neck. He had been sweating.

He enfolded her waist. It felt right.

Like Citizens, Colonists seldom spoke about mating practices, but they did touch, and frequently. She could not help wondering: How much of this behavior is *human*? How much has been imprinted—inflicted—on us in hopes of more and fitter laborers?

She shook off the sudden cynicism. Now was not the time.

"Not being a total idiot," Eric said, "I want to join our lives. Shall we?"

"I bind myself. We'll still need genetic counseling,"

which was mandatory before a union could be made official, "but—" Kirsten trailed off, at a loss for words.

"And I bind myself." Eric broke into a grin as goofy as the one she knew she was wearing. "I have *got* to change the color of my clothes." To the pastels of a mated man, he probably meant.

"No," Kirsten answered. "You need to take them off."

20

"You're sure about this?" Omar called from the bridge.

"Yes!" Eric and Kirsten answered in unison. "For the last time," Kirsten continued, as she sifted backpack contents. "Are *you* ready?"

"We're holding position. Thrusters are working hard to do it."

Kirsten peered out the relax-room's view port. Even at full magnification, the institute's mysterious GP #4 hull was invisible. NP5, around which it orbited, loomed largest of the six worlds of the Fleet.

Explorer, under power, raced along a distant arc concentric with that orbit. Only a chance visual sighting could reveal their presence. *Explorer*'s space-traffic-control transponder was silenced, and its stealthing mode was active.

In theory, everyone in the Fleet thought *Explorer* far away, still studying Oceanus. In practice, Omar relayed reports and fictitious telemetry through the hyperwave buoy they had left behind. The doubled distance made no difference to instantaneous communications, and Hearth received the incoming signal from the expected bearing.

Are we really clever, Kirsten wondered, or delusional?

"We *are* better prepared," Eric said.

Could he read her mind? The unstated comparison was to the expedition she had planned, to the Human Studies

Institute. Or, more accurately, had scarcely planned. She answered, "If the stepping-disc network is configured as we expect."

"Even if Citizens weren't systematic by nature, why *wouldn't* there be a standard addressing scheme used aboard ships? Why waste the energy to invent one each time?"

If Eric was correct, the addressing scheme on that GP4 ship matched the stepping-disc network on *Explorer*. They would reappear unattended in a storeroom aboard the mystery ship. And if he was wrong? They could pop up anywhere. In a mess hall. Onto the bridge. She had never seen a Citizen's toilet—

"Guys," Omar prompted.

"We're ready," Eric said. Communicator in hand, he tried the first address in the presumed subnet range for storerooms. "Still here. Do you suppose there'll be gravity?" He tried another. A third.

And vanished.

Kirsten gave him ten seconds to pop back, if he had found himself somewhere unfortunate, or with a witness, or otherwise to simply vacate the destination disc. "Omar, wish us luck." She took her backpack and stepped—

Into a cavernous storeroom, dancing briskly toward a wall.

Eric caught her, sparing her from a fall. "It happened to me, too," he said. "Not the best velocities match."

What was the magic number? Two hundred feet per second was what she recalled. They must have been just on the cusp. A bit more velocity difference and the paired discs would not have allowed the transfer. A bit less and the momentum compensation would have been perfect.

If Citizens never envisioned an intruder crossing a few miles of predator-free forest, they *surely* never imagined a hundred-thousand mile jump between ships matching courses and speeds. "Under the circumstances, the match seems plenty precise to me."

They walked quickly through aisles until they found a terminal. Eric knelt to unload his backpack. He was still wearing pastels and a topaz ring that matched her own. "Look around while I do this. Keep an ear open. If we get caught, we're courting and a little goofy."

As though that would excuse a stolen starship and sneaking aboard one of the best-kept secrets in the Concordance. Kirsten smiled but said nothing.

The plan was simple. Crew communicators were portable; hence ships had wireless networks. So: In some deep recess of the storeroom, hide a network sniffer. It would catch and store the radio packets flying by. Also hide a vidphone with good lines of sight and hearing on the terminal.

On some future visit, they would retrieve the stored data. Keyed or verbal commands the gear captured during inventory draw-downs would provide an unencoded data sample with which to crack encryption on the shipboard network. Crew login sequences, if they could catch one, would be a bonus, although tongueprint biometrics was more likely.

Kirsten explored as Eric worked, snaking through aisle after aisle of tanks and bins. Finally past the raw-material repositories, she made her way between shelves piled high with everything from complex photonic components to large structural assemblies. Those must be either too complex or too large to synthesize quickly.

"Eric," she whispered. Almost certainly their communicators would go unnoticed here, but why take even that small chance? In her mind's eye, Nessus bobbed his heads, up/down, down/up, approving her caution. "Eric. How's it going?"

"Sniffer is hidden," he whispered back. "I'm working on a power hookup. It would be a shame if we couldn't get back aboard before the batteries drained. How are we doing for time?"

Her wrist implant was in stopwatch mode. "Eight minutes left." Eight minutes until Omar attempted another precise velocity match to enable their return. Thereafter, Omar would match courses again every five minutes, pacing the unseen ship.

She walked on. More bins and parts, components and supplies. Spare synthesizers. Emergency rations (grass and grains) in case the synthesizers all failed at once. Nothing instructive. The next glance at her wrist showed six minutes. "Eric?"

"I found accessible power lines for the sniffer and vidphone. I can use inductive taps. I'm snaking our power lines behind stacks of stuff."

Clever. Kirsten wouldn't have thought of that. An inductive coupler clipped over a power line, drawing off energy without ever interrupting the electrical flow. Very stealthy.

She reached a dead end. "Four minutes. I'm coming back."

The anticlimactic smoothness made her want to scream. We haven't *learned* anything, Kirsten thought, except that we can get aboard. In minutes they would return to *Explorer*.

"Done," Eric called. "Come on back."

There *must* be something here, some further clue in the long series of signs. To wait until they next managed to return, hoping to find decipherable data—it was intolerable.

Three minutes. Kirsten reversed course past emergency rations, chemicals, parts. . . .

She sped right past Eric, rushing through the aisles she had not yet explored, looking for something very specific and low-tech.

The storeroom held emergency rations and large structural elements. Survival gear would not be accessible only by stepping disc. Big stuff would not fit through the only stepping disc they had seen, in the storeroom's center. Logically, the storeroom had to have a physical door— and she still wasn't *sure* until she saw it.

A big square door with an inset window.

"Eric," she called. "Come here."

"Time's almost up," he answered from aisles distant.

"Now, Eric." She stared out the window, across a broad corridor, through a clear wall. A vast space, the central volume of the giant GP4 hull, gaped before her.

Suspended in its center was, undeniably, an alien spaceship. A ramscoop.

Faded English letters on its scarred and ancient hull declared it the *Long Pass*.

REBIRTH

Earth date: 2650

21

Side by side, Kirsten and Eric stared at *Long Pass*. Their wrist implants beeped almost simultaneously. Eric panned a quick view of the ramscoop with his communicator. "Omar will be matching course in a minute."

"Go ahead." Beyond the door and to Kirsten's left, a light flickered randomly. "I'll be right behind you."

Eric strode back into the maze of shelves. She took the cessation of footsteps to mean he had teleported back successfully. "In a few minutes, that is," she clarified now that he couldn't argue. *One* of them had to take back word of their find before anyone—she—took yet more risk.

She had seen old dates embedded within the serial numbers of some stockpiled parts. Dust covered the shelves themselves and most items on them. The flickering light outside the storeroom removed all doubt from her mind: This region of the ship had gone unvisited for a *long* time. Citizens would not leave a failing LED along the route to emergency supplies.

With a faint squeak, the door opened to Kirsten's touch.

She peered into the hall and saw no one. Feeling like a very small fish in a very large fishbowl, Kirsten ran, clutching her communicator, along the curved corridor to the spidery catwalk which led to *Long Pass*. With luck, software would compensate for the shaking and bouncing to render a good picture. She crawled onto the catwalk . . . but yes, there was gravity. She could safely run across.

Heart pounding, Kirsten dashed through the derelict's airlock, its hatches both open. Her wrist implant showed nearly four minutes until her next opportunity to return to *Explorer*. Thinking any ship must have something like a bridge, and that bridges belonged in the bow, she headed forward.

Crisp-edged corners, without trace of the melted look favored by Citizens. Beds and chairs glimpsed through open doors: Colonist normal. The latches on those hatches: equally ordinary, mounted at a height natural for Colonists. The ceiling glow that brightened when she stuck her head into a cabin was pleasant to her eyes. The holo cube she found lodged behind a small fold-down shelf showed men, women, and children.

In countless small ways, the vessel was undeniably Colonist. Or was the correct term *human*?

Kirsten kept shooting video as she sped through the ship, still seeking the bridge. Scarcely a minute until the next pick-up opportunity. She *should* return to the storeroom and its stepping disc.

She plunged ahead.

Another cabin, as familiar as anything on NP4. A larger room of uncertain purpose, on whose wall hung a mundane to-do list on curled, brittle paper—the tasks handwritten in English. Holos everywhere. An apparent cargo hold, its deck half empty, its shelves picked nearly clean. Tiedowns and braces on all the shelves. Gravity or free fall, the ship would accommodate both.

Beep. "I'll be back in five more minutes." Kirsten was not sure to whom she made the promise.

At last: the bridge. Crash couches. Controls meant for hands like hers. More holos.

Kirsten froze. That empty cargo hold! Without a doubt, its contents had been removed to Hearth for study. Its cargo probably resided deep in the bowels of the Human Studies Institute.

Maybe this GP4 ship had landed on Hearth, and the cargo had been extracted there. Maybe the cargo had been moved to a docking bay for offloading into a smaller Citizen ship for a flight to Hearth. It didn't matter which. The insight was that the cargo had been removed—and surely not over that narrow catwalk.

Kirsten raced back to the empty cargo hold. She found a stepping disc on the deck between two mostly empty shelves. Although she had expected to find it, the disc looked out of place. Grafted on. Her wrist showed a bit more than two minutes until Omar next matched course and speed. That gave her more than ample time in which to collect a souvenir.

She had noticed a decoration in one of the cabins, a handicraft of some unfamiliar kind. It hung on the same bulkhead as the hatch. No one could see the artwork's presence—or absence—without entering the cabin.

The artwork crudely rendered an image of flowers and shells in thousands of tiny knots and stitches. The background was tightly woven material. Texture could be a hologram, so she brushed it with her fingertips. Knots and background alike felt like natural filaments of some kind. The colors were muted—faded?—and the wooden frame battered. She took the decoration and frame, unsure why they seemed important. One corner of the wooden frame bore matching holes on its front and back edges. She guessed at a small animal's tooth marks.

Less than two minutes.

She dashed to *Long Pass*'s cargo bay. Her wrist beeped softly and she took one last video image. Then she activated her transport controller—

And stepped into *Explorer*'s relax room.

"Kirsten's back!" Eric said, presumably for Omar. "What happened?"

"I took a quick look around." She handed him the primitive picture in its wooden frame. "Impulse buy."

Omar appeared at the doorway. "Kirsten, what were you *thinking*?"

She projected the newest image in her communicator. The holo showed a small portion of the cargo hold, a stepping disc, and a nearby fifteen-digit label. "I was thinking that with this address and *Explorer* for course matching, we can board our ancestors' starship at will."

22

Thousands of humans swarmed the wide boulevard, waving placards and chanting slogans. Tens of thousands more shouted from behind barricades. Golden spheres the size of a grapefruit floated overhead: copseyes. The remotes carried sonic stunners; the beams they emitted were invisible, but not their effects.

The crowd grew frantic as more and more people fell. Then black-armored ARMs surged into the holo, shoulder to shoulder, rank after rank. The crowd stampeded, trampling anyone unfortunate enough to lose his footing. Soon the avenue was empty but for a few broken bodies and abandoned signs. A hand-lettered banner fluttered by, folds and tangles obstructing much of its message. "Bir . . . otteries Justic . . . eople." Sirens wailed, Doppler effects differentiating police vehicles in pursuit of the protestors from ambulances on approach.

"Where is this?" Nessus finally asked.

"Kansas City, Missouri." His holographic avatar must have conveyed incomprehension, because Ashley added, "That's a middling city in North America." She had come alone this trip, perhaps reassured by the knowledge that Nessus would only meet her over hyperwave relay.

"How many dead?" Nessus told himself these few had been sacrificed to spare countless more. Before spending months with only Colonists for company, that rationalization might have quelled his guilt.

"Twelve in this incident." Ashley squinted at him—at his avatar, anyway. "Why exactly is birthright policy so important to you?"

"How many worldwide?"

"Hundreds." She tossed her head, and her Mohawk quivered. Today it was bright orange. "Nessus, why are we *doing* this?"

"Conscience seems inconvenient in your line of work." Or his own. Nessus blanked the holo of riot coverage. "Never mind. The important question is: Has the ARM been diverted?"

"Some. Look, Nessus, Miguel and I had no idea you meant to stir up so much trouble."

Bribery, intimidation, and rumormongering raised no objections. It was comforting somehow to see his minions exhibit traces of conscience. "The right to have children should not depend on your political connections." Stealing a glance at a holo of Nike, Nessus wondered whose political system he questioned.

"Why don't we just focus on our business," Ashley said at last. A brittle tone conveyed her disapproval.

That was fine with Nessus. He had questions about several of Miguel's recent reports. How credible was the coerced information? Had new prey been made aware of incriminating deposits made in their names? Had spying devices been planted as Nessus had requested?

It all *seemed* to be unfolding according to plan. Sipping carrot juice, Nessus asked, "What news about that item I want to purchase?"

"It took most of your five million to be sure, but we feel we can acquire it." Ashley straightened in her seat. "Forty million more. Half up front, half on delivery."

"How soon?" he asked.

"Give us a month."

"Agreed." Nessus transmitted bank codes. "You and your colleague do excellent work."

"I guess we're done. Same time, next month?"

"Yes." Even a smuggler's ship, capable of doing thirty gees, needed time to reach the fringes of the solar system. He could not expect his Earth minions to come so far any more frequently. As Ashley reached out, likely to sever their hyperwave radio link, a new thought occurred to Nessus. "Wait."

Her hand paused in mid-air. "All right."

There were more ways to stir the pot. "The problem we have highlighted is that a few of the politically connected have bought birthrights. Perhaps we should separate the political and financial aspects. Surely the ability to make money is a proven survival characteristic. Why *not* sell birthrights legally?"

"You're kidding, right?" she said. "If that notion gets out, we'll have class riots, too."

"If you don't care for my money . . ."

Ashley swallowed but said nothing.

"See to it." Nessus had still another idea: gladiator fights. Winner gets a birthright; loser dies. Everything balances.

It turned his stomach, too. Maybe he would wait to bring that up. "I'll see you in a month."

But for his piercing, dark-brown eyes, the figure in the holo was unimposing: short and thickset, middle-aged, and moonfaced. His dark hair was thick and wavy, and a thin mustache was just growing in. The man paced in a small and cluttered office. He wore a jet-black business suit, doubly stark for being worn on Earth by a native, a flatlander.

His name was Sigmund Ausfaller, and he was the enemy.

Miguel's report, no matter how often Nessus reviewed it, never got better.

UN officials were no less corruptible than anyone else. If it were worth doing the calculation, Nessus thought he might find they were more corruptible. That this holo video had found its way to him proved that venality reached deep within the world government.

One problem with paranoids, of course, was that they assumed any temptation was a trap. Ausfaller had shunned all attempts to compromise him. At least, Nessus thought, the incorruptible ARM was on occasion within view of officials with fewer scruples.

Nessus returned his attention to the surreptitiously made recording. The holo had been taken by someone standing in Ausfaller's office doorway. The video caught an oblique view of the Bureau of Alien Affairs logo that shimmered on the surface of the open door.

"Sigmund is being secretive about his work, even by his standards." The comment was presumably dubbed after the video. "Maybe his computer display will tell you something."

Nessus zoomed in on the 3-D scatter plot that hung above Ausfaller's desk. Once he had reoriented himself to the human convention of showing galactic north on top, the holo looked like a star chart of Human Space and its immediate neighborhood, centered on Sol system. Almost certainly it was an information-free privacy image, popped up when Ausfaller heard footsteps approaching.

He fidgeted with his mane. Almost was not certain. "Match image with onboard navigational data," Nessus directed.

"All star positions match," the bridge computer answered.

A useless report—or was it? "Star *positions* match. Do the indicated stellar attributes differ from your records in any way?"

"Colors differ for some stars," the computer replied.

"Exaggerate color differences." Nessus craned his necks, eyeing the holo from all sides. The revised image muted most stars to a common dimness while brightening a few scattered suns. It still told Nessus nothing. "Which are the populated solar systems?"

Several stars grew pale haloes, both among the faint majority and the highlighted few that might be of interest to Ausfaller. Nessus still did not understand why. Perhaps Ausfaller's present obsession had nothing to do with the Concordance. The brighter dots clustered near the center and at the top of the map.

If the stars told Nessus nothing, perhaps starships would. The reports that had brought Nessus here said Ausfaller was investigating missing starships. "Computer, correlate this graphic with public records of interstellar travel." Such data was a very small part of what his minions had provided.

It was an expansive request. Nessus stared at the frozen image of Ausfaller as he waited for a response. "What are you looking for?" he warbled softly. The holo was as unforthcoming as the man.

"Computer, are all color discrepancies the same?"

"Yes."

This was getting him nowhere. Perhaps the star chart *was* merely a paranoid's meaningless decoy for the benefit of passersby. Am I not insane enough, Nessus thought, without inventing new reasons?

"I have a match," the computer interrupted Nessus' musing. "The falsely colored stars correlate with selective reports of human hyperdrive-ship disappearances. The selection criterion appears to be disappearances unassociated with incidents of warfare."

Nessus twitched. So much for his hope the display could be dismissed. "How many such ship disappearances have there been?"

"Twelve."

Humans had had hyperdrive for about four hundred years. Twelve ships gone astray in that time . . . excluding known Kzinti "incidents" . . . weren't many. Why was Ausfaller looking at this?

The cluster near Sol system made sense: human traffic concentrated here. Whether by equipment failure or pilot error, logically most accidents would happen nearby.

Why was there a second cluster?

"How recent are the three events near the top of the display?" Nessus asked.

"This one"—a dot momentarily flared—"two Earth years ago. The others, this year."

Suddenly Nessus realized why those dots bothered him. These recent ship losses appeared to involve exploration to the galactic north just beyond Human Space—

In the general direction of the Fleet of Worlds.

Nike refused to identify the scout responsible. Abstractly Nessus respected that. Who hardly mattered. What did matter was the bad judgment involved.

Not very long ago Nessus had by reflex almost triggered a deep-radar scan of Sol system. Such was not only *his* engrained habit. Most pilots—of all species—did it, certainly whenever they entered a new solar system.

The intelligent species of Known Space prized similar worlds, orbiting similar suns. The biological requirements were like enough and colonizable planets rare enough to have engendered wars, most recently between humans and Kzinti. Knowing which solar systems would most quickly draw explorers, Nike's unnamed scout had set traps in the wake of the Fleet.

The bait was elegantly simple: large masses of neutronium orbiting the most appealing planet of the most suitable solar systems. Neutronium occurred naturally only in the core of a neutron star—the collapsed remains of a supernova. Neutronium was incredibly dense. At one-hundred billion metric tons per cubic centimeter, a neutronium sphere a mere few meters in diameter was an enormous mass.

Arriving pilots, conditioned to scanning each new solar system with deep radar, would see what appeared to be a stasis container abandoned since that ancient war of extermination. Pilots could hardly be expected to wonder whether a compact opacity seen in their deep radar scans might be neutronium.

The lure would be overwhelming.

When an unsuspecting ship too closely approached the tiny moon, the gravitational attraction would be likewise irresistible. No ship. No report. No likelihood of exploration yet further into the unknown, and with it the possible chance discovery of the Fleet.

They had failed to consider what a few such disappearances could reveal to a paranoid like Ausfaller.

Nessus pawed restlessly at the cabin deck with a forehoof—but where could he run? Ausfaller could not be bought. He could not be coerced. And not even Earth's worst civic unrest in centuries had distracted the man.

Perhaps it was time to eliminate Ausfaller. For enough more money, Nessus' minions might well undertake that. Succeed or fail, how could that not raise suspicions? What sort of in-the-event-of-my-death message would someone as paranoid as Ausfaller have arranged?

Nessus pawed again, and with feeling, at the deck. He knew just where he had to run: toward danger.

The situation was not irremediable, not quite. He thought he saw one way out. It required that he have help—very specialized help—and not the sort of service Miguel and Ashley were qualified to provide at *any* price.

He would have to go deep into the solar system and enlist just the right physicist.

23

Burning profligately through their energy reserves, Kirsten eased *Explorer* through the atmosphere of NP4. The ship's thrusters whined in protest and strain.

Explorer was matte black and radar stealthed, the better to scout in secrecy. Its traffic-control transponder, silenced since their unauthorized return to the Fleet, remained off. Their deliberate, energy-gulping descent eliminated the fiery heat and ionization trail of a normal reentry. The only way their return might be detected was visually. Over the remote expanse of ocean she had selected, and at night, that risk was vanishingly small.

The ship settled into the water with a splash. Protective force fields activated by the impact squeezed Kirsten momentarily. "Is everyone all right?" she asked.

"In a mildly bruised way," Omar answered. He occupied the other crash couch on the bridge. "You, Eric?"

"I'm fine." Eric's answer came by intercom from the engine room.

Explorer wallowed in the swells, the undulating ocean surface sparkling by NP light. Clouds rose and fell in the view ports. Kirsten tuned out her queasiness to focus on status readouts. "The main thrusters are a bit warm, but that's the only off-nominal condition I see. Is everyone ready to submerge?"

"And get off these waves?" Omar looked pale. "I'm definitely ready."

"I will be once you release the refueling probes," Eric said. The probes were emergency equipment, little more than self-propelled stepping discs fitted with filters. They would transmit deuterium and tritium from seawater directly into *Explorer*'s tanks.

Kirsten ejected the probes, and imagined she could hear the splashes. Their hydro-jets started on command. "Probes away and reporting normally." There was no alternative to a low-power radio link for monitoring and directing the probes. "Down we go."

She pressed the bow into the water with maneuvering thrusters, and then engaged more thrusters to drive *Explorer* slowly beneath the surface. Air-filled, the ship was very buoyant; it slewed disquietingly until it slipped completely underwater. She increased thrust, driving them toward their target depth of three hundred feet. They hoped to be invisible there, even under daylight conditions.

I'm in an indestructible hull, she kept reminding herself.

"This is really eerie," Eric said from the corridor just outside the bridge. He stood in a slight crouch, the better to peer through the bridge view ports.

Kirsten looked up from her instruments. Through the deepening gloom she caught glimpses of ocean life, more often due to its bioluminescence than because it approached the hull.

Hearthian ocean life, she thought, surprised at a sudden rush of bitterness. What animals teemed in the seas of her ancestral world? If *Long Pass* had carried any specimens, she knew of none that had been introduced into the oceans of this world.

A bevy of creatures fluttered past, their maneuvering more reminiscent of Hearthian birds than the— humanistic?—freshwater fish Kirsten knew from Arcadia. She squinted, grasping for detail before they swam out of sight. She had to settle for impressions rather than a clear image. Webbed tentacles, undulating. Bioluminescent patches, in purple and gold. Ropy integument. With no way to measure the distance and nothing to use for scale, the swimmers' size was unknowable.

"Approaching three hundred feet," Omar said, watching the radar readings. "The sea bottom is down another four hundred feet."

"Thanks." Kirsten adjusted thrusters to just offset their buoyancy, and then cautiously engaged the autopilot. This was their first opportunity to test the software she had retrofitted to manage underwater hovering. *Explorer* wobbled and weaved as she lifted her hands slowly from the controls. Tilting and surging unpredictably, the ship jittered about the position where she meant it to stay. Kirsten tweaked program parameters until their orientation stabilized—which was, unfortunately, long after Omar had vomited explosively.

"I'll clean this up," Eric told Omar. "Change your

clothes. Wash up. Do whatever you need to do." Omar smiled wanly, and left to comply.

After scrubbing and wiping down the area, Eric settled into the empty crash couch. He pulled up status holos. "The probes are working properly, and we're getting fuel. In a few days, we'll be adequately fueled for flying around the Fleet." His expression seemed to ask where she thought they might go next.

Omar's return spared her from speculating. He had replaced his soiled ship's suit with formal attire. "I look forward to getting onto dry land." He swallowed hard as the ship trembled in its hover. "*Solid* land."

Kirsten adjusted her own garb until she judged it suitably casual for her next stop. "Eric, will you be all right here by yourself?"

He nodded.

She checked the content of her backpack one last time. "Then Omar and I will be on our way. Take care." She hugged Eric hard.

She walked with Omar to the relax room. He paused beside a stepping disc. "Join me when you can, Kirsten. I'll message you with the coordinates. Encrypted, of course."

Then Omar was gone.

Her communicator was preset with another address. Kirsten activated it and stepped—

To the public square nearest the Colonial Archives. She was thousands of miles from *Explorer,* and a string of suns hung near the horizon. Barring emergency, it was past working hours here.

Her "chance" meeting with Sven Hebert-Draskovics, seemingly so long ago, had not resulted in an exchange of communication codes. The publicly available code for the archivist connected her only to his voice mail. Rather than leave a message, she went inside the archive building and accessed the lobby directory.

Using a public communicator and a name randomly

chosen from Custodial Services staff, Kirsten called Sven's home. The little boy who answered listened uncritically to her story of a plumbing leak in the archive building and sent a location code for his father.

Kirsten stepped from the bustling square to a grassy expanse. Shouting children of all ages greatly outnumbered the watching adults. Some children flew kites, some climbed the monkey bars, and many ran about without apparent purpose. Most engaged in team sports. Shading her eyes with a hand—the suns here were directly overhead—Kirsten scanned the park.

That was Sven, along the sidelines of a football field. Young girls ran from one end of the field to the other, pursuing the black-and-white ball with far more enthusiasm than skill, kicking shin guards far more often than the ball.

Watching the girls play made Kirsten smile. She had been terrible at football. Citizens discouraged the game, calling it antisocially competitive. Football's ubiquity across Arcadia was a rare display of independence. Perhaps meeting Sven at a football game was a favorable omen.

"Which is your daughter?" she asked Sven. The grass had made her approach silent, and he startled.

He pointed. "Vicky. The tall girl with the curly black hair." After a long silence, he added, "I don't recall that you have children." The unstated question was, "Why are you here?"

"Then you remember me," Kirsten said. "Do you recall the rest of our conversation?"

"We discussed early NP4 history. You said something rather droll about finding the abandoned ship from which the Concordance rescued our ancestors." Cheers rang out: a goal. Sven clapped enthusiastically. He turned, finally, to face Kirsten. "This meeting is no coincidence, is it?"

"May we speak in private?" She began walking toward a nearby stand of trees without waiting for an answer. He followed. They stopped beside the copse, Sven waving vigorously as Vicky looked around for her father. "Sven, I have a brief recording for you to review."

The video, its projection kept small lest the game-watching parents take notice, came from Kirsten's dash to and through *Long Pass*. Sven watched without comment. The recording ended in the cargo bay, in a close-up of the grafted-on stepping disc. He studied the close-up from all angles. When Kirsten was about to burst from frustration, he finally looked at her. "That is quite interesting."

The disc? Not the ship? Her mind roiled.

"Once more please." Sven waved again at his daughter. "Slower, if you don't mind."

At one-fourth real time, Kirsten relived her too-brief exploration. The cavernous central volume of the GP4 ship. The exposed dash over the walkway to the scarred hull of *Long Pass*. Corridors and cabins aboard the ship itself, simultaneously ordinary and exotic. The cleared-out storeroom. The few neatly patched bulkheads evoked the same doubt and anger as always. A derelict abandoned in space?

What a lie!

"Interesting," Sven said. Head canted, he again studied the stepping disc through which she had returned to *Explorer*. He finally acknowledged her confusion. "Video is data. Data can be faked. This disc, though . . . zoom in, please?"

They *needed* Sven to believe. "What is so special about this disc? What about the *ship*?"

"Zoom in, please," he repeated. "Closer still. See the controls inset along the edge? Citizens are cautious. They upgrade their technology slowly. The stepping disc in this image is a model hundreds of years out of date. I've seen few like it. It lends a scrap of credibility to this recording. May I have a copy?"

"In confidence, of course."

"Of course." Squeals of glee rose from the field. Sven waved again at the players. "I don't suppose you will tell me how you came into possession of this recording."

"I shot it. I was aboard." As Sven's eyes grew round, she slipped off her backpack and removed a parcel wrapped loosely in cloth: the threadwork she had taken from a cabin aboard *Long Pass*. "Sven, how would you like to analyze a really dusty old record?"

Amid the hushed clutter of Sven's laboratory, Kirsten waited anxiously for Omar's message. The quiet would last only until the next workday and the return of staff. Before then she had to be gone, if not to the meeting Omar sought to arrange, then back aboard *Explorer.*

Sven flitted from workstation to workstation, all chewing on scene analyses of the video, and among the lab instruments with which he examined the artifact. About an hour ago, he had begun humming tunelessly. Kirsten allowed herself to hope that the droning denoted good spirits, and his good spirits the onset of belief in her report.

She had teleported ahead to the lab while Sven took his daughter home. Idly, Kirsten wondered what excuse he had given his family for returning to work. An archival emergency seemed *so* unlikely.

Then again, so did archival laboratories.

Sven shushed her when she asked about his progress, and tsked whenever she lost focus while answering one of his many questions. How long had it been since she last slept?

And *still* no word from Omar. He must be encountering the same skepticism as she.

Kirsten paced, eyeing lab equipment. Some she recognized: microscopes, both optical and electronic; spectrometers; chromatographs; crystallographic imagers. Some were mysteries.

A discreet buzz interrupted her survey. Her communicator, finally. It was Omar, and he looked exhausted. The backdrop of the holo told her nothing. "Kirsten, how is it going?"

From the minimal privacy behind a tall and unrecognized bench instrument, she brought Omar up to date.

"Is Sven convinced?"

"I think he's getting there. At least he seems excited about that framed art I brought from *Long Pass*. He refuses to say why. How are you doing?"

"I contacted some people I know in the Self-Governance Council," Omar said. "That led to a very exclusive meeting. I've been answering questions nonstop for hours."

"And now?" Kirsten asked.

"Now it's your turn." He transmitted a stepping-disc address. "Finish what you're doing and come here."

She could have asked if Sven was welcome—and didn't. Why ask, when she might not like the answer? "Sven." He looked up from a holo display in which cryptic codes slowly scrolled. *Genomic data*? "Sven, I need to go." She related what little she knew about the government meeting. "I would like you to join me."

Sven shook his head. "Not until I know more."

She could hardly drag him to the summit. He might even be correct in his priorities. "Here is the address, if you change your mind."

Kirsten stepped through into a dimly lit shed. Well-used farm equipment surrounded her, vaguely familiar from childhood tours of the factory where her parents worked. She had not known what to expect. Not this, certainly. An overhead door rattled open.

She blinked in the suddenly bright light. Omar signaled her to be silent. She followed him into a field that stretched to the horizon in every direction, the crop obviously Hearthian but otherwise unknown to her. Fibrous orange seed clusters pinched the dangling, red-and-yellow mottled tendrils that served as leaves. Combines floated in the distance, spraying orange streams into tiny floating trailers, from which the grain must teleport directly into weatherproof storage. Parallel rows of mulched stems and leaves showed the progress of the combines.

They topped a low rise. Kirsten blinked again, this time in surprise, at the people who stood below.

A slender woman with lustrous black hair and striking violet eyes stepped forward. She exhibited the indeterminate age modern medicine eventually bestowed on all Colonists, but she moved with a grace and economy of motion that hinted at advanced years. Her pink-and-red blouse was boldly checked with a matte finish. Her suede slacks had a luxurious nap. Texture and pattern alike bespoke great stature.

The hand extended to Kirsten bore a massive progeny ring, with four small rubies and at least ten emeralds: tokens of children and grandchildren. "I am Sabrina Gomez-Vanderhoff." The introduction was entirely unnecessary. Gomez was the governor of Arcadia's Self-Governance Council, and the colony's senior elected official. "My colleague is Aaron Tremonti-Lewis." He was the minister for public safety.

Public safety involved putting out fires and dispensing aid after storms and other natural disasters. It had never occurred to Kirsten that the function might extend to protecting Colonial society from its supposed patrons. She pondered where to begin.

"May I call you Kirsten?" The governor did not wait for an answer. "Kirsten, excuse me for being brusque. We are here," and her expansive gesture encompassed the broad fields to all sides, "lest we be overheard. Needless to say, we two disappearing for any length of time would raise unfortunate questions."

Citizen questions, that was. "I'll get right to it then," Kirsten said. "It all began . . ."

Gomez cut her off. "Omar explained. As interested as we are, for now we must limit the discussion to the review of a few points."

The questions came fast and furious, with follow-ups

and artfully leading paraphrases repeatedly interrupting Kirsten's answers. She was being tested. So many overlapping questions and comments kept her too busy to gauge the politicians' belief or disbelief. Was she telling the story the same way, citing the same facts, as Omar? Was she credible? This cross-examination was meant to shake her, to bare any weaknesses or inconsistencies in their story.

The governor had had her own dealings with Nike, especially since the last change in government—the Conservative Hindmost refused faces-to-face contact with Colonists. Sabrina's firsthand knowledge made her questions all the more incisive.

No wonder Omar looked drained.

Doggedly persisting through the interruptions, Kirsten conveyed the essential facts. Concern for the Gw'oth evolving into skepticism about Concordance policy to other species—including their own. The quest for hard data in computers aboard *Explorer,* then on the continent of Elysium, and even later on Hearth. The hunt for the Institute for Human Studies. The lightning visit to *Long Pass*, hidden in plain sight in orbit around NP5.

"Thank you for your patience," Gomez finally said. "Excuse us for a moment."

The hint was obvious. From a stream bed at least one hundred feet removed, Kirsten and Omar tried to read meaning into indistinct whispers and veiled expressions. Purple pollinators, Hearthian bees, chirped nearby. "How do you think it's going?" she finally asked.

"I honestly don't know." Eyes closed, Omar rubbed his temples. "I feel like I've been through a meat grinder."

Gomez shook her head insistently. Tremonti's face flushed. They disagreed about something. What? Kirsten resisted the urge to sidle closer. They would learn soon enough what the leaders concluded. "Omar, do they even believe us?"

Omar looked away, doubt plain on his face.

The debate ended abruptly. Gomez gestured to them to return. "We find ourselves unconvinced by your report, which has more inferences than facts. Assuming that everything you have reported is correct, it would still remain unclear how best to use the information."

"Assuming? Respectfully, Governor, these *are* facts." Kirsten shrugged off the hand Omar had laid on her forearm. Obsequiousness and restraint would accomplish nothing. "The Concordance has lied to us about our past. They have kept us from the ship in which we might find answers. For all we know, they obliterated our ancestors' home world.

"Don't you want to *know*?"

"Young woman, that's enough," Gomez snapped back. "Do you imagine you are the first to worry about the inconsistencies in our history? The first to encounter an anomaly? Don't flatter yourself. There is a *reason* your captain has our ear.

"Speculation and skepticism come easily. Before anyone accuses the Concordance of lying, let alone of whatever heinous scenarios you have imagined, there must be *proof*.

"You may be ready to put at risk the unprecedented opportunity of the Colonist scouting program. I am not. What if you found a replica, a re-creation, of some sort? What if your loyalty—and by extension, the colony's loyalty—was being tested? Perhaps you were *allowed* to find—"

"Hello?" The greeting floated over the hill, tentative and worried. "Kirsten?"

Kirsten needed a moment to remember having given Sven this address. Proof? Perhaps *he* had it. "Over here!"

Sven crested the hill, clutching the odd artwork from *Long Pass*. He stumbled as he recognized the high-ranking officials. "Am I interrupting?"

"I know you. You're the archivist," Gomez said. "What brings you here?"

"I invited him," Kirsten answered. "He may have the proof you're looking for."

Sven squirmed. "Kirsten asked me to assess her recordings . . . and *this*." He waggled the artwork. "It's very interesting, actually."

Tremonti coughed. "First, the data. Does that hold together?"

"It does, at least through a few hours of inspection." Handing the framed picture to Kirsten, Sven took a communicator from his pocket. "I've downloaded my main tests and correlations. We can access the raw data, if you like. But Governor . . . this artifact is the compelling evidence."

"Compelling?" Gomez frowned at the stitched flowers and shells.

"Let me explain." Sven straightened. "It's the materials that matter: the cloth backing, the fibers used in the design, and the wooden frame. Since they're organic, I carbon-dated them. These materials are thousands of years old."

"Thousands?" Omar repeated. "How can that be?"

"Exactly," Sven beamed. "Thousands of years seriously predates the official history of the rescue. It would make this artifact much older than all our records."

"How do you explain it?" Gomez asked.

Sven bounced on his toes in scarcely constrained excitement. "By recalling an underlying assumption of the method. Carbon dating is planet-specific. Carbon 14 can be more or less prevalent on other worlds. If this artwork is not an NP4 artifact, it might be any age."

Gomez considered. "Any age. Perhaps quite new, fabricated with materials found on a scouting mission."

Kirsten winced. Did her souvenir actually *hurt* their credibility?

"That would only deepen the mystery," Sven said. "I ran other tests. The materials are clearly related to materials we use."

"Clearly related." Kirsten was as lost as the rest. "Meaning?"

Sven tapped the wooden frame. "This is clearly oak—only it is of no species known to the archive. If it doesn't grow on Arcadia, where did it come from?"

Kirsten remembered Eric's disclosure about a human presence on NP3. Did the council know about that? "Could the artifact have come from another world in the Fleet?"

Sven gestured dismissively. "Calculations using the published atmospheric data for the other worlds gave me different results, but none any more credible. The organics would appear older still if they came from NP1, NP5, or Hearth. And there's too much C-14 for any of this to have originated on NP2 or NP3.

"Now consider the cloth fabric. Without a doubt it is linen, meaning its threads are made from the fibers of the flax plant. That's not merely a comment about superficial appearance, but consistent with what I saw under the microscope. Only . . ."

"Only *what*?" Gomez demanded.

Sven struck a pedantic pose. "You are aware that only a small part of a genome, any genome, serves a purpose? That most DNA consists of inactive segments, partial repetitions, and the like."

Tremonti nodded. "Junk genes."

"Exactly." Sven stroked the linen. "Most genes are junk genes, so most mutations have no meaningful effect. Not biologically meaningful, that is. Most mutations occur in the unused segments. The genetic drift rate then makes a fair molecular clock."

"A clock timing what, exactly?" Gomez asked.

"The interval since the harvesting of the flax in this linen." Sven paused dramatically. "Roughly five hundred years. I also tested several strands of the cotton floss. All imply the same approximate age."

Kirsten's thoughts raced. Five hundred years: scarcely longer than the supposed age of Arcadia colony. Those were Fleet-standard years, of course, the rotations of the NP worlds having been synched to the preferences of Hearthian biota.

A great bird soared lazily overhead, clearly Arcadian, undeterred by the extent of the alien fields. An eagle, Kirsten thought. It was majestic.

She hoped it was an omen.

Arcadian wood, either not of this planet, or thousands of years old. Flax and cotton as old as the colony. Surely now the politicians would have to accept—

"Excellent," Gomez said. "Perhaps there *is* something to this tale." She locked eyes with Sven. "You will accompany these two and their other crewman and find out for certain."

24

The summons was not unexpected. The venue was.

Nike materialized in a vast semicircular room whose great arc of transparent wall overlooked a wooded park. Far below his hooves, the undulating, multicolored leaf canopy glowed by the light of arcology-wall sun panels.

Abandoning the spectacular view, Nike scanned the room itself. Its floor was lush with meadowplant. Overstuffed pillows and dramatic holo-sculptures had been tastefully scattered all around. The ceiling, extravagantly tall and wasteful for an arcology, soared far above his heads.

A sinuous masonry partition subtended the clear arc. Water burbled down the rough-hewn rock face into a low, stone-rimmed pool. An unseen force field bent the water around the wall's central opening, which provided access to a long corridor in which many more doorways could be seen.

"Welcome." Eos, the long-time leader of the Experimentalists, capered through the vaulted archway. He was tall for a Citizen, with striking white patches around his eyes. He wore his mane informally today, in elegant waves confined by a few orange ribbons. He brushed heads with Nike in greeting. "Welcome to my new home."

New home? When had Eos come to possess such wealth? Nike managed not to react. "Your invitation referred to the upcoming consensualization."

"We will speak inside." There were ample benches and cushions—and privacy—in *this* room. Proposing somewhere else to talk failed to disguise an unasked-for tour of the residence.

They arrived finally in a den merely twice as large as Nike's office at the Ministry of Foreign Affairs. The few wall holos somehow emphasized the burnished wood paneling. Eos indicated a tall pile of cushions. "Sit, please. Now as to invoking the voice of the people—it is a critical matter, Nike, and one to which I have given much thought. I have concluded this is an inauspicious time for political uncertainty."

"I do not understand," Nike said. The party leadership had focused on awakening proper concern within the Concordance since the first news of renewed attention by the ARM. "The Fleet flees toward the unknown, while wild humans hunt us from behind. Circumstances could not better suit the Experimentalist cause." The mission of safeguarding the herd from its own complacency . . .

"Our travels into the unknown will last a very long time. How is *this* moment different?" Eos stared two-headedly, daring Nike to argue. "Some may think the Fleet is on a journey, a transient stage fraught with danger. I have come to embrace a different view. The Fleet has transitioned to our new way of life." The subtext went unarticulated:

With the transition complete, governance was appropriately entrusted to the Conservatives.

A decadently opulent new home. The abrupt renunciation of party belief. Eos' timing could not be more—

"I should share another matter with you." As he spoke, Eos traced vertical circles with his heads: a gesture of confidence and trust. "We live in challenging and perplexing times, Nike. The people call out to us, their leaders, for unity. I hear those voices, and so I am joining the present government."

The irony was unbearable; it demanded all Nike's self-discipline not to look himself in the eyes. He had dispatched Nessus to corrupt the wild humans with their own funds, money recycled through General Products Corporation. The Hindmost had co-opted and corrupted Eos with only a government penthouse.

However ironic, the situation was unambiguous. The near future would bring no appeals to or reassessment of the communal wisdom. This unnatural alliance between the leaders of the two parties doomed any possibility that a new vision might be forged.

Nike could scarcely bear to look at Eos. Looking around the room, feigning interest in this obscene ostentation was safer. This lavish home might even have been *his*. The offer had been clear enough. Now that Eos had been bought, temptation was being dangled once more.

The leaders of both factions were consumed with political and personal advantage, even as peril surrounded the Fleet on all sides. Whom the gods would destroy . . .

"Thank you for your hospitality." Unfolding his legs, Nike emerged from his nest of pillows. "If you will excuse me, however, pressing matters at Clandestine Directorate demand my attention." Surrendering to his roiling emotions, Nike left without awaiting a response from Eos, intent on locating the nearest stepping disc.

For affairs at his office *were* pressing. Having spurned

the enticements of the Hindmost and Eos, Nike wondered for how much longer Clandestine Directorate would be his concern.

Nike charged from stepping disc to stepping disc—across vast plains, around continental coasts, from remote island to teeming megalopolitan plaza to towering mountain crest—as fast as the ever-crowded walkways allowed. In impressions almost stroboscopically fleeting, he drank it all in: the sounds and smells of the crowds, the casual intimacy of brushing flanks with countless strangers, the randomly chosen waypoints.

Whenever Nike was troubled, a frenetic gallop across Hearth like this never failed to soothe him.

Until now.

The corruption of the elite threatened to overwhelm him. How tempting it was to find a quiet nook somewhere and then curl himself away from the world.

Tempting, but ultimately futile. Withdrawal would fail to console him just as this mad dash around the globe now failed to distract him. The problem was larger than him, larger than the world. Something, whether maturity or insanity Nike could not judge, demanded that he take a larger view. To hide beneath one's belly or on a single planet—the difference was only of degree, not of kind.

Sides heaving from exertion, Nike made his way home. This evil alliance between the Hindmost and Eos put the burden of safeguarding Hearth on *him*. If he were to be removed from Clandestine Directorate, who would address the *true* risks that confronted the world?

He had to retain his post, doing whatever that took—whatever the cost to his self-respect.

The sonic shower dissolved a patina of sweat but left Nike's thoughts as dark as ever. So many had joined him at the grand ballet, those he considered his friends and colleagues—and yet there were none with whom to share these doubts and misgivings. With a start, Nike realized the only one he knew to whom this star-spanning anxiety might make sense: Nessus.

What little order remained to Nike's coiffure after his mad dash had slumped in the shower. He sat before a mirror, a comb in one mouth and a brush in the other, trying to—

Bzzt.

An alert buzzer, insistent with harsh undertones. Only his most senior staff could get past his voice mail. An iconic image floated above the buzzing communicator. The still holo showed Vesta, his most trusted aide. "Nike."

Nike waited.

"I am sorry to disturb you." Vesta's voices trembled, and his necks slumped with worry. Tufts and gaps in his coiffure bespoke recent plucking. "An urgent matter has come up."

"There is no need to apologize," Nike answered. He had just flattered himself that he was irreplaceable. How fitting that there should be an immediate crisis. "What is the news?"

"We received a report from NP4. If only we had processed it sooner." Vesta lowered his heads submissively. "An unsolicited account by an informant."

"And?" Nike prompted.

A holo inset popped up, of a dour Colonist whom Nike did not recognize. "Her name is Alice Jones-Randall. She works in an office complex used by the Self-Governance Council on Arcadia."

Evidently she also informed on her coworkers to the directorate. Vesta's hesitance began to worry Nike. "What does she have to say?"

"She claims she saw Kirsten Quinn-Kovacs yesterday."

Kirsten was light-years away, aboard *Explorer*—but Vesta knew that. "Come as quickly as you can."

His aide teleported in moments later. "Thank you, sir. If I may? This video comes from a security camera." A new holo appeared, this one an urban setting. A timestamp counted up in a corner. Offices. Arcadian vegetation. Colonists everywhere.

Vesta extended a neck into the image. "Watch here."

Here was one end of a pedestrian mall, its surface tiled with stepping discs. Nike watched streams of Colonists walking around, appearing and disappearing. Vesta froze the image as yet another Colonist materialized.

"It could be her." Even side by side with an image taken during a visit *Explorer*'s crew had made to his office, Nike was uncertain. "Or not. See the pastel clothing. Kirsten is not mated."

"Facial recognition software says it is her," Vesta said. "We used a recent holo from her personnel file in the scout program."

"Run it again, with this image from my office."

Vesta reran the comparison. Another match.

Point by point, Vesta laid out the evidence. The suspected Kirsten walking across the mall into a government building. A second video watched her enter the lobby and scan an office directory. A match between her on-file DNA and dust from the lobby. Apparently humans regularly shed hair fragments and skin cells.

"How sensitive *is* that test?" Nike asked.

Vesta checked his files. "In such a well-traveled space, cleaned daily, all detectable traces would be gone in three to five days."

The proof seemed incontrovertible. Nike reluctantly accepted the identification. "Why was Kirsten there? Whom did she see?"

"We don't know." Vesta picked fearfully at his mane before unfreezing the latest video. In it Kirsten left the lobby without speaking to anyone. Returning to the pedestrian mall, she disappeared by another stepping disc. "This is our only sighting despite extensive searching of surveillance data. We might not find her again if she avoids security cameras."

And of course the stepping-disc system kept no records of transfers between public areas.

Only by good fortune did he know of Kirsten's unexpected return to the Fleet. How long might it be before anyone spotted her again, or found her crewmates?

Or, far more critically, their ship.

Eyes fluttering with surprise, Baedeker took Nike's unexpected call. "Your Excellency."

"We have a problem." Nike summarized the proof of Kirsten's surprise presence on NP4. "How can that be?"

Baedeker dipped a head in wary thoughtfulness. "She must have teleported off *Explorer* before it left on its mission. That's why the Colonists falsified the onboard audio recordings: so we would not detect her absence."

"Must have," Vesta echoed skeptically.

"Of course. Traffic control tracked *Explorer*'s departure. They still send their reports from . . ." Baedeker trailed off as a possibility occurred to him. "Perhaps *Explorer* returned secretly to drop her off."

"Perhaps? You don't track the location of their ship?" Harsh dissonances underscored Nike's displeasure. Had the Colonists deceived this arrogant engineer *again*?

"We know it by inference, Excellency. We continue to receive reports about Oceanus, and answers to our occasional inquiries, by hyperwave radio, always from the correct direction. It just occurred to me"—Baedeker lowered his heads submissively—"that a hyperwave relay could be involved. Hyperwave radio being instantaneous—"

"The ship could be anywhere," Nike said, completing the thought. "An indestructible ship designed for stealth, controlled by a deceitful crew."

No one spoke for what seemed a very long time. No one needed to. This was a nightmare scenario—and it was of their making. Sufficiently accelerated and aimed at Hearth, *Explorer* would be an apocalyptic device.

The corrupt pact between Eos and the Hindmost that had threatened to consume Nike receded into a distant, minor hazard. "Before *Explorer*'s departure, I assume General Products outfitted it with a failsafe."

High/low, low/high, high/low: Baedeker's heads bobbed

enthusiastic agreement. Did he see this as redemption for his many failures? "Of course, your Excellency. I did not use any ordinary paint—"

"I don't need to know details." It had been a mistake to meet the crew, Nike realized. He did not *want* to know details. That he had come to see Kirsten, Omar, and Eric as *people* made what must now be done that much more difficult. Possibly none of them remained aboard the doomed ship. He hoped that was the case. "Just do it."

25

"Welcome to Earth," Traffic Control said.

"It's good to be back," Nessus lied. He hoped his avatar had an honest face. As far as anyone in this solar system knew, this was a human ship.

The Mojave Spaceport sprawled in all directions. Rugged mountains loomed in the distance. Maintenance had evidently suffered since Nessus' last visit—greenery poked upward through cracks in the tarmac, a few grown tall enough to be recognizable to the ship's computer as young yucca and Joshua trees.

Aegis would look no different from many of the vessels around it. Despite the deep recession caused by the abrupt disappearance of General Products Corporation—or perhaps because of it—the company's indestructible hulls remained prized here. A used GP hull cost more now than it once had new.

Nessus trembled with excitement on his command bench. A manic phase was upon him, and it would be foolish not to act now. "Computer, proceed as planned." Then, since the plan relied upon the unwitting cooperation of a human victim, he went to the relax room to wait.

For a while he sampled the human media. Innuendo

about Fertility Board corruption. Unruly protests. Opportunistic politicians endorsing Birthright Lotteries. Vigilante attacks on "bought babies."

Necessity seemed such a facile excuse. Repelled by what he had caused, Nessus stopped watching. The reports would be in the archives when he could bear it again.

He was concentrating on one of the human histories that Nike so prized, by a flatlander named Plutarch, when an alert tone chimed. A caption appeared over the biography Nessus was reading: Sangeeta Kudrin, UN deputy undersecretary for administrative affairs.

He looked up. Behind a one-way mirror, a woman had materialized inside a booth made of hull material. She was petite with almond-shaped eyes and many facial piercings. She wore a conservative brown-and-orange suit; what little Nessus could see of her skin-dye job favored spirals in an assortment of blue tones.

She looked panicked.

Nessus set down his reader as his guest began pounding on the booth walls. "You will not be harmed."

"Where am I?" she demanded. "And who are you?"

Not: *How did I get here?* Nessus was impressed. She had already ascribed her abduction to subversion of the transfer-booth system. "You may call me Nessus."

"Where am I, Nessus?"

"That is unimportant." He let her ponder that for a while. "You have ceased to report as ordered." Ceased to leave information in designated transfer booths at designated times, so that his minions could retrieve it.

Sangeeta swallowed. "I have provided a great deal of information."

"Nevertheless." Her body heat would quickly warm the enclosed space. The filter-equipped disc in the booth's ceiling exchanged oxygen for carbon dioxide, but she could not know that. He waited.

"What do you want?" she finally asked.

"Information about Sigmund Ausfaller."

She flinched. "That is not feasible." Nessus waited until she added, "What about Ausfaller?"

"I want regular reports on his work."

"You want me to spy on *Ausfaller*? The man is a raving paranoid. Maybe you don't understand what that means. It means he suspects *everyone*."

Nessus waited in silence as beads of sweat appeared on Sangeeta's forehead and trickled down her face. Her eyes darted around, seeking an exit that did not exist. He said, "The ARM is part of the United Nations. There must be reports."

"I can tell you one thing." Furtive glances. "Ausfaller *knows*."

Nessus pressed on. "What does he know?"

"About the extortions! I'm trapped in here, but he's trapping *you*!"

"Explain," Nessus said softly.

"I'm guessing that you chose your victims, at least some of them, by clever data mining. I don't see how else you could have found *me*. My . . . creative use of UN funds." She slumped against a wall of the booth. "It appears Ausfaller had worried about just such an attack on the UN. He created a persona in the personnel files, gave it a suspect-looking past, just to entrap anyone doing exactly what you're doing."

Nessus quivered, his mania spent. "How do you know?"

"For the reason you wanted me here. I have limited access to his reports. At least I *had* access. He severely restricted everything soon after you tried to coerce his decoy." She laughed bitterly. "I wouldn't be here if I'd followed his example. He stopped using transfer booths right after the fake persona got an envelope with your Cerberus sigil on it."

What if Miguel and Ashley had, unknowingly, tried to blackmail the ARM? They would get disinformation from Ausfaller, surely. And Ausfaller would think to seek out other coerced parties, *real* UN personnel whom the hidden blackmailers might have threatened. If Nessus and his minions could find ways to intimidate them, Ausfaller could do the same.

Nessus quivered, wondering how much false data he might already have swallowed.

He resisted the urge to paw at the deck as the implications became clear. Assume Ausfaller knew the transfer-booth system had been compromised. Puppeteers were the obvious suspects. And the ARM already sought in the direction of the Fleet . . .

"Nessus!" His prisoner peered at the mirror, panting, hysteria in her voice. "Are you still there?"

He got his fear under control. "I have many sources at the UN. Ausfaller cannot know them all. I advise you to say nothing about our relationship or this conversation. If you inform him, I *will* find out."

Sangeeta shivered. From relief at the implication she would be released? In terror, that Ausfaller would learn of her thefts? Maybe both. "I'll say *nothing* to him."

Conscience aside, Nessus had no choice but to release her. The disappearance of a high-ranking official would only stoke Ausfaller's suspicions. If she *did* speak with Ausfaller, all she could reveal was the fact of her abduction and questioning. It would not endanger Nessus.

And Ausfaller himself? He remained untouchable. Nessus had to assume the paranoid had arranged an in-case-of-my-disability-or-disappearance message for authorities.

Nessus tongued the command that teleported Sangeeta from her cell to the transfer booth anteroom of her home. If she meant to keep her word to Nessus, she would need a moment of privacy in which to regain her composure.

As Nessus needed to regain his own composure. Without it, he could hardly expect to enlist a first-rate astrophysicist.

26

Darkness and an eerie silence greeted Kirsten's return to *Explorer.*

An unfamiliar acrid reek filled the air. She felt her way through the relax room to a light-activating touchpad. Dimmed LEDs she could have understood, but off? Her left shin smacked something massive as she shuffled toward the control.

Blazing lights revealed unfathomable disarray. Supply cabinets gaped open, their contents spilled to the deck. The treadmill lay on its side. Wall panels hung awry, baring the painted interior surface of the hull. "Eric?" she called.

No one answered.

As Kirsten forced open the suddenly stiff hatch, a flicker of motion registered in her peripheral vision. Sven. She said, "Clear the disc for Omar, but stay here."

The corridor, too, was dark. She tapped a lighting control to reveal chaos. Torn and shattered objects lay everywhere, the scraps scarcely recognizable. Scorching covered the bowed-in walls of the corridor.

What had happened here?

"Eric," she called. Silence. "Eric," she tried again, a little louder. She crept through the clutter to the bridge, where the situational holo cast enough light to hint at more madness.

Omar joined Kirsten as she studied the status display. Despite the all-encompassing disorder, despite consoles slid away from the walls to the limit allowed by their cabling, everything registered as nominal. "What *happened* here? Where is Eric?"

"I don't know." Her answer covered both questions. Kirsten swept a pile of clothing off her crash couch and sat to scan the instruments. "*Explorer* is where we left it, deep in the ocean. The refueling probes are working. Readings for temperature, oxygen, everything we routinely monitor, they're all fine."

Omar activated the intercom. "Eric." Silence. "Kirsten and I are on the bridge. Report."

Sven appeared in the doorway, looking anxious. "Is everything all right?"

She threw up her hands. "Honestly, we don't know. The readouts are fine, but *something* happened here. And Eric . . ."

"I'll search the bow," Omar said. "Kirsten, take the stern. Sven, stay here. We'll keep in touch by intercom."

Kirsten struggled aft through cluttered corridors. These halls had been empty, their walls straight and clean, just a day earlier. She activated lights as she went, checking inside each cabin, hold, and closet, finding only disarray until—

Eric sat on the engine-room deck, arms wrapped tightly around his knees, rocking, amid a jumble of tools and spare parts. Main thrusters and the hyperdrive were unbolted from their deck mounts and rudely shoved aside. A flicker of recognition appeared on Eric's face but he said nothing.

"Eric is in the engine room," Kirsten called into the intercom before settling beside him. "Eric. Eric!" No response. She shook his arm. "Eric, what's the matter?"

"I've been a fool," Eric said softly. "A fool," he repeated as Omar ran in.

"Are you all right?" Omar asked.

"Yes." With a shiver, Eric came out of his funk. He looked around as though noticing the disarray for the first time. "Welcome back."

"What happened?" Omar asked. "Why is everything torn apart?"

Leaning against an overturned cabinet, Eric got to his feet. He handed each of them a slender copper tube from a heap on a workbench. Wires protruded from one end.

"While you two were away, I decided to look for any more hidden sensors."

"For *that* you tore apart the ship?" Omar snapped. "With the telemetry bypassed, the sensors were harmless. We never revealed that we knew about hidden sensors. How do you propose to disguise this destruction when *Explorer* gets its next overhaul?"

Eric's eyes demanded Kirsten's attention. He seemed so *sad*. There was more to this mess than sensors. "Eric, these aren't listening devices, are they?"

"They're electric detonators." Eric laughed humorlessly at their evident shock. "After I found one, I got a little crazy. I found them all through the ship."

"Detonators," Kirsten repeated. "To detonate . . . what?"

"A good question." Reaching behind an upended supply cabinet, Eric scraped off a fleck of the paint-and-insulation layer that lined the hull. He sealed the paint chip, a detonator, and a sledgehammer inside a little GP #1 hull, one of many *Explorer* carried for use as free-flying probes. He strapped everything down on a workbench. "And presto."

Kirsten barely heard a loud *crack* before the engine room's noise cancellers kicked in. Vibrating madly, the GP #1 hull seemed unharmed—only its transparent shell had suddenly turned black. When Eric opened the probe's hatch, heat puffed out, and a stench of metal. She realized what now coated the orb's inner surface: the vaporized metallic head of the sledgehammer.

"The Citizens never trusted us. We were expendable." Eric's voice trembled with grief. "They were prepared to blow us up."

"They wouldn't . . . they planned for some remote contingency. . . . I don't see how . . ." Kirsten grasped for an explanation for the inexplicable.

"You think? Come with me." Eric led them toward the

bow. "This could almost be funny. A lifetime's deference to the Citizens almost killed me."

As they approached the burst hatch of Nessus' former cabin, Kirsten's jaw dropped. An explosion had destroyed everything inside.

Drifting off to sleep after hours of backbreaking labor restoring order to the ship, Kirsten realized why Eric looked so different. It was more than the pain in his eyes.

The elaborate braids and colorful dyes—every trace of the Citizen-mimicking coiffure Eric had so long affected—had vanished.

From adulation to doubt to anger and shock. Kirsten could not imagine how upset Eric must be.

Nor could she help thinking the Citizens would some-day come to rue it.

27

Julian Forward was a fireplug of a human, short and squat. He had arms as massive as most men's legs, and legs like columns. Forward was a Jinxian, and Jinxians bred for strength. That made sense on a world with nearly twice the gravity of Earth.

Nessus was happy to be thousands of miles distant.

Forward peered curiously and unknowingly into the hidden camera. His eyes, as though with minds of their own, kept sliding off axis. "Interesting," he finally said. He left briefly. Reappearing with a broom, he poked it into the transfer booth. Then, with a wry smile, Forward dropped the broom. He stepped inside the booth and picked up the package Nessus had sent.

This one was smart, Nessus thought, as quick as Kirsten. Forward's mind had leapt from the extra-dimensionality of the package to distrust of transfer booths to the realization that, had abduction by teleportation been intended, it would have happened without warning.

Optics far beyond human capabilities reconstituted the scene from rays scattered by their contorted path into the package's interior. Nessus watched Forward carry the object to another room. The nearest window offered a spectacular view of the Coliseum. Other windows gave equally striking views of the Grand Canyon, the Great Wall, and the pyramids at Giza. Boxes were piled all around, some still open, spoiling the simulated views.

All did not run smoothly in the life of Julian Forward.

"Whenever you're ready." Forward sat on his sofa, legs apart, facing Nessus' parcel. His eyes continued to slide off. "You have my attention."

"You are very perceptive, Dr. Forward," Nessus began.

Forward smiled. "You have a beautiful voice. Transfer in and give me a look at you."

"You are very calm for a man in your circumstances."

Forward brought his hands together, making a tent of his fingers. "A tesseract is a singular gift with which to get my attention."

"Your fame in astrophysical circles brought you to mine. But tesseract? I am unfamiliar with the term," Nessus dissembled. It was a small test.

"A four-dimensional 'cube.' Modern cosmological theories invoke additional dimensions beyond those we experience." Forward patted the tesseract; his fingertips bent oddly as they entered the volume of manipulated space. "To manifest one of those dimensions at macro scale—that *is* exceptional. And of course transfer booths somehow access those hidden dimensions to accomplish teleportation."

He was right, of course, on all counts—including, from the human perspective, that "somehow." General Products did not share the underlying science when it licensed transfer-booth technology. "Do you like Earth, Doctor?"

"Call me Julian. And you are?"

"Very cautious," Nessus answered. Over Forward's hearty laugh, Nessus added, "I wonder if you might consider a new professional opportunity."

"As to Earth—no, I don't much care for it. It's much too crowded for my taste."

"And yet here you are, Julian," Nessus said. "You have spent years on Earth. Attempting to prove a theory about the Tunguska Event, I believe."

"You have the advantage of me again . . . whoever you are. Yes, something fascinating happened in Siberia in 1908, something still unexplained. For all the devastation, that 'something' left no crater. And yet, trees remained standing near the epicenter. The accepted explanation, that a meteorite struck, simply fails to fit the facts." Forward frowned. "You need not have gone to such extremes merely to discuss my investigation."

Nessus knew all about Forward's research. After a hasty study, Nessus knew about most leading cosmologists in Sol system. Unfortunately, excitement and enthusiasm drove genius. It could not be coerced.

Few at the apex of human physics had seemed approachable. If the Jinxian would not serve Nessus' purpose, no one would.

And then Ausfaller would continue to stalk the Fleet.

"You are only the most recent to advocate that a quantum black hole, not a meteorite, struck Siberia that night. What you cannot answer, Julian, is when and where your hypothetical black hole, having passed through the Earth, then exited. If you determined *that*, perhaps you could deduce the black hole's orbit. And the historical records, such as they are, are all on Earth."

Forward stiffened. "This grows tiresome. Get to your point."

"The Institute of Knowledge funds your research, does it not?"

"It did." A scowl. "Apparently I failed to show sufficient progress."

And so we arrive at the hearts of the matter. Of course Nessus had the advantage. He knew why the Institute had *truly* canceled Forward's funding: they were bribed. Hence Forward was busy packing. "Then perhaps you would consider an alternative employment."

"Your convoluted methods do not evince confidence," Forward answered.

But they would evince curiosity. "All I ask for now is your confidentiality and consideration," Nessus said. "You will receive a handsome remuneration for this consultation." With the flick of a tongue, he severed the connection.

"Hello, Julian," Nessus began.

Forward had taken the call in his living room. Towers of boxes climbed higher than ever; today, only one box remained open. A sealed box hid the tesseract and blinded its camera. He removed a large box from the sofa and sat. "An unforgettable voice. And now an unforgettable face to put to it. When do I get a name?"

Forward had lifted the box effortlessly. The stack he had brushed past had tottered. These boxes were empty: props. The scientist was tempted—by the large honorarium, if nothing else.

Aboard *Aegis,* Nessus winked; his image in the call smiled. The avatar wore Kirsten's face. "You may call me Nessus."

"An unusual name for an unusual circumstance. What can I do for you, Nessus?"

"As I suggested in our last conversation, I have a complicated task that you might help me with."

Julian leaned forward. "Related to black holes?"

"Something less weighty." Nessus had his avatar smile again. "But only a little."

"And the work would be performed on Earth?"

"That is one of the complications," Nessus replied. "It's best to perform this project at a distance. You see, we're going to produce neutronium."

"At a distance." Forward's eyes narrowed. "Yes, some separation *would* be desirable, given that it takes a supernova to make neutronium."

"Is that a given, Julian?"

"Perhaps not." Forward stood. "Perhaps not for your kind."

Nessus somehow resisted the urge to snatch at his mane. He had no idea how the avatar program would represent that mannerism. "My kind?"

"Puppeteers." The silence stretched uncomfortably. "Now I have *your* attention."

"Do I *look* like a Puppeteer?"

"You look like an angel, which is hardly conclusive since this is a vid call. You *sound* like a Puppeteer. General Products pulled up stakes just five years ago. It takes much longer than that to forget just how sexy a Puppeteer sounds.

"More to the point, Nessus, is the tesseract you sent to get my attention. It embodies technology for which humans have no scientific foundation—much like making neutronium.

"While you consider that, Nessus, allow me to share an observation. In past dealings with humanity, General Products considered blackmail a perfectly acceptable business practice. The tesseract, and everything about it— and about you—that I know and could surmise, have been entrusted to a friend."

Nessus relaxed. *Blackmail* was a human term. Among Citizens, this was merely a stage of negotiation.

He had his native expert.

Crash!

Furniture suffered when Forward grew frustrated. His

newest table toppled, its top dented and a leg shattered by this latest blow. Tables, fortunately, were simple to synthesize.

"What now, Julian?" Only the relative safety of *Aegis* enabled Nessus' philosophical detachment. His native expert fulminated from inside the research center to which *Aegis* had berthed, the mined-out and repurposed Oort Cloud object immodestly renamed Forward Station. The Institute of Knowledge nominally owned the base; Nessus had anonymously arranged its lease.

"This derivation makes no sense. The third postulate here, to start . . ."

Forward ranted, not expecting a reply. The process had become all too routine. Experts in the Fleet would send isolated bits of theory, entirely out of context lest too much be disclosed. Then their responses to Forward's inevitable questions would be as unforthcoming as the incomplete information that had raised questions in the first place. As often as not they failed to grasp the limitations of human technology, blithely assuming Forward had access to instruments and means of fabrication available only in the Fleet.

An intellect any less brilliant than Julian's would have made no progress at all.

Despite the considerable pay Forward was accruing, he took no step until he entirely understood every nuance and implication. But for the passage of time the Fleet could ill afford, Nessus would have approved. The vast energies that they employed deserved the utmost caution.

So time passed—too much time—as Forward made the tools to make the tools to make the tools. It brought to mind Kirsten's musings, so seemingly long ago, about Gw'oth progress. How were his Colonist scouts faring? Nessus wondered. Nike declined to "distract" him with their progress reports.

How much quicker things would proceed if Nessus could only return to the Fleet for a neutronium generator! Alas, hyperdrive notwithstanding, he could not make the trip. Too much here in Sol system relied upon his constant attentions: Guiding his minions. Fomenting the Birth Lottery unrest. Anxious and indirect monitoring of Ausfaller.

And no one, regardless of Nessus' importuning, was available to deliver a neutronium generator to Sol system.

It all too often seemed that the fate of the Fleet rested on far too few freaks like himself. The pressure made Nessus yearn all the more for oblivion in a tightly rolled ball. For Nike, he reminded himself, countless times each day . . .

"I said I'm going to drop offline for a bit."

Nessus had once again let his attention wander. "Sorry. Doing what, Julian?"

"Uploading new calibrations for the implosion effect to the stasis-field generators. Baedeker sent new specs." Forward nodded at the holo of a nearby icy mass, its surface dotted with test gear. "While I do, perhaps you can re-check the instrument constellation." He referred to the halo of microsats, each a GP1 hull, which would monitor the coming experiment.

"Of course. And this"—the nearby mass of ice and rock, miles across—"will make how much?"

Forward grimaced. "About a cubic centimeter, Nessus. I hope this process scales up well."

To reproduce a neutronium trap here, to mimic what the ARM might find at any time in the Fleet's wake, Nessus needed a twelve-foot sphere.

They had their work cut out for them.

28

The acrid stench of explosives tainted everything. By the time *Explorer*'s scrubbers eliminated the last of the fumes, all traces of herd pheromone were also gone.

Somehow, Kirsten thought, that seemed fitting.

Sven was dazed, indifferent to symbolism, overwhelmed by his plunge without warning into intrigue and peril. The Concordance had tried to kill Eric, Omar, and Kirsten; *he* was endangered by staying anywhere near them. But if the authorities already suspected his involvement with the three, going home could be just as dangerous.

Perhaps, for as long as the Concordance believed *Explorer* destroyed, the safest spot for them all was onboard.

Kirsten shrugged. They would accomplish nothing by playing safe.

She found Sven in his cabin. The room had been hers until she had doubled up with Eric. Despite the bulging satchel at Sven's feet, he seemed reticent to leave. She said, "We're about to learn secrets every archivist before you would have given his right arm to know."

Sven smiled wanly. "I find I'm very like a Citizen. This seems foolhardy."

"Course match in ten minutes," Omar announced over the intercom. "Eric is waiting in the relax room."

She touched Sven's arm. "No one can make you come—but if you miss this opportunity, you'll regret it for the rest of your life."

Nodding, Sven picked up his bag. "You're right. Let's go."

Kirsten materialized in the ancient storeroom, its crisp right angles and emptied shelves just as she remembered. Sven stood nearby, his fears forgotten, enthralled by the handwritten list on a yellowed scrap of paper pinned by magnet to a bulkhead. Eric, who had previously only glimpsed the ship's exterior, looked about in awe.

At Kirsten's approach, Eric shook off his distraction. He burrowed into his backpack for a motion detector. It was just one of the devices he had prepared for this expedition. "Nothing detectable," he whispered.

For all Kirsten's certainty that this ship was abandoned, its contents long offloaded to Hearth for study, she sighed in relief. "Then why whisper? Let's look around."

"First things first." Tellingly, Eric did not attribute the expression to Nessus. "We've got sensors to distribute." One by one he dispatched tiny flying sensors to stepping discs throughout the huge GP4 hull. The robots, if anyone was aboard to notice them, resembled flutterwings midway through their nymph stage. For secrecy and power conservation, the robots would report only sporadically, in highly compressed low-power bursts. "All right. *Now,* let's look around."

Kirsten led them through the ship. Sven alternately muttered and rubbed his hands, declining attempts to draw him out. Eric clutched the motion detector, checking it ever more frequently as they neared the airlock. "Still nothing," he said. "Of course, *Long Pass* could be filled with or surrounded by sensors like those we distributed. A motion detector wouldn't see mobile devices that small."

Kirsten thrust her hands into her trouser pockets. "Clearly nothing was watching me during my last visit. If I had been spotted then, someone would have changed the storeroom's stepping-disc address. We wouldn't have gotten aboard at all, or we would have materialized inside a locked room with a receive-only disc, or been greeted by guards, or . . ." Her voice faltered. This expedition could have gone badly in so many ways.

And still might.

Eric laid the motion detector on the deck, facing the

open airlock and catwalk. "If anyone approaches, we'll know. If the remote sensors spot anyone aboard the main ship, we'll know. After I reprogram the storeroom stepping disc to require authentication, we'll be safe from surprise callers."

They followed that quick walkthrough with a systematic survey along each corridor and stairwell, and into every room. *Long Pass* was mostly machinery; there wasn't that much in habitable volume. Kirsten videotaped everything, narrating as she went. Data crunching would turn those recordings into a detailed 3-D map, complete down to the last closet, cabinet, drawer and cubbyhole. It would be too easy to overlook something vital without such an aid.

All the while, their teleported sensors found nothing to report. The big ship that enclosed *Long Pass* was unoccupied. They decided it was safe to explore separately. Eric began in the engine room. Sven began a more detailed examination of cabins and the mostly empty holds. Kirsten headed forward.

A savory aroma followed her onto the bridge. She tried to ignore the smell. Sven had mentioned planning to reconstitute one of the ancient packaged meals found in what she considered the relax room, but whose door was labeled "Dayroom." She would bring the sample to *Explorer* for testing when she traded places with Omar. However inviting the food here smelled, it might have turned poisonous. And its edibility would further prove whose ship this surely had once been.

Stomach growling, Kirsten inspected the instruments and controls. Their operation should be obvious, she thought. The keyboards had the familiar, inexplicable QWERTY layout. Cryptic icons shimmered in the holo display once she flipped a console's plainly labeled POWER toggle.

That was as far as she had gotten.

One does not randomly push buttons on a starship bridge. The almost familiarity of the controls stymied and frustrated her. Somewhere here were controls for navigation, shipboard status, external sensors—functions *Explorer* provided, functions any starship must implement. Functions she *should* recognize.

Drawers beneath the console ledges offered only dried-out pens, brittle papers covered in doodles and handwritten poetry, and the powdery remains of (she guessed) ancient snacks. What if the whole ship were like this? What if everything useful had been removed for study elsewhere?

"Eric," she called. The intercom controls, at least, like those of the synthesizer, were obvious and intuitive. "Have you figured anything out?"

"Mostly that this won't be easy," Eric answered. "We're hundreds of years distant from the people who built this ship. We're generations removed, Kirsten."

"Have you found any manuals?" she persisted.

"Sorry. No."

"Thanks anyway." She released the intercom button. "I need help," she admitted to herself.

One of the many enigmatic icons, a cartoon-ish head with somber expression and handlebar mustache, flashed twice. In a comically unctuous voice, the animation said, "You may call me Jeeves. How may I be of service?"

Sven and Eric had come running. When they talked over each other, Jeeves got confused or didn't respond. They learned patience. They laughed a lot. Hours passed while they played with the Jeeves program. At some point Eric stepped aside to cook several meals from their packs. They took turns napping, and had to be briefed when they woke.

After so long a search, so much had finally been revealed—everything, it seemed, except the one important thing: the location of Earth. Numbly, Kirsten tried to absorb it all.

From the captain's log: *Long Pass*'s discovery of and message to the Ice World, proven unambiguously by its ice-covered continental outlines to be NP5 en route to the Fleet.

From the video archives of shipboard safety systems: the takeover of *Long Pass* by robots clearly of Citizen design. Robots like those in the hold of the very ship that currently enclosed *Long Pass*. They had all seen such robots before, toiling alongside Colonists in fields and forests.

From an entertainment collection, musical recordings both familiar and wondrously fresh. How it must have amused Nessus to claim credit for *Ride of the Valkyries*!

From the ship's manifest: a listing of what, and who, had once been aboard, most notably the embryo banks and hibernation tanks that had given rise to a colony of laborers.

And the crew whose misfortune it had been to signal icebound NP5? Of their fate, Jeeves could offer no clue.

Gradually their questions ran slower. When Kirsten checked her watch, twenty-seven standard hours had passed. That long? *Only* that long?

Kirsten chewed without tasting something Sven had put in her hand. Part of her was overwhelmed. Part of her marveled at having come so far. Nodding belated thanks for the sandwich, she found herself remembering the football match from which she had so abruptly taken Sven. Girls running and screaming, embracing a game universally discouraged by Citizens.

Even Citizens didn't always get their way.

Kirsten went aft to the engine room, where Eric knelt staring in concentration into an open wiring closet. His new look, a long ponytail with no trace of Citizen-style coiffure, still made her pause, but she liked it. She gave him a long, hard kiss.

"I'm not complaining," Eric said, "but what was *that* about?"

She smiled. "It's about taking joy in making progress."

Omar sniffed appreciatively as the dayroom synthesizer filled a foamed plastic bulb for him. Coffee. She doubted he had tasted a normal beverage since the synthed food here on *Long Pass* checked out.

Normal? That was, despite her efforts to retrain herself, backward thinking. What this ship dispensed *defined* the standard. Black bitter stimulant. Bulbs for use in free fall, with a flat bottom because sometimes you had gravity.

"I've asked Eric this already." Omar paused to squeeze a sip from his coffee bulb. The nonchalance seemed feigned. "When do you feel we'll be ready to report back to Sabrina?" It went unstated that reporting back meant traveling back.

Omar had not mentioned Sven. There was no need. A few shifts earlier, every garment, doodle, or dust bunny aboard had fascinated the archivist. Now, with Jeeves' assistance, Sven had several hundred terabytes of databases to explore. He could not wait to analyze it on familiar computers running familiar applications.

First the casual pose. Then the ever so carefully worded neutrality of the question. *Omar* wanted to return.

Regardless, Omar raised a fair question. What *did* she think? Were they ready? "We don't know yet where we, where *humans* come from. We only have names: Earth, Sol system, human space."

"We may never know," Omar said. "If the coordinates aren't lost, I would think Sven and the archivist's lab present our best chance at recovery. He's copied everything accessible.

"Soon enough, *Explorer* will be declared missing—maybe by whoever tried to destroy it, maybe because we're no longer communicating—but by someone." Sad eyes added, "My wife and children will think me dead."

He shrugged off the hand she had sympathetically laid over his. "I know. I can't contact my loved ones even after we're back in Arcadia. But the sooner we report in . . ."

And her family, and Eric's.

It would be *so* easy to answer: I can mine the data anywhere. Easy, but was it true? Her gut spasmed. "I don't think we're ready, Omar. I'm working as fast as I can."

Her own hot bulb of coffee in hand, Kirsten headed for the bridge and more conversation with Jeeves.

"That data has been corrupted," Jeeves said. He always sounded apologetic, although he had spoken the same sentence scores of times. Any of a Citizen's devices, or any Colonist, would have become exasperated.

Kirsten rubbed her eyes. She was exhausted. How else could she approach this problem? She had asked in countless paraphrases about the location of Earth, Earth's sun, human settlements, human-settled solar systems, and any near-neighbors of Earth's sun. "I'd like to see this ship's course data."

"That data has been corrupted."

"Show me the stars used for navigational reference."

"That data has been corrupted."

Sven occupied the other crash couch on the bridge. An intricate, many-colored graphic, relating various recovered data files, she thought, floated over his console. He glowered—at her, Kirsten suspected—but said nothing.

"Show me the external sensor data for the five years before robots boarded this ship."

"That data has—"

"Kirsten!" Sven snapped. "All location data is gone. You have to accept it."

"Why is this one category of data gone?" she asked. "Did Citizens destroy it?"

"That data has been corrupted," Jeeves intoned.

"I don't begin to have your skills with computers," Sven said. "Maybe, given enough time, you can recover something. But think: Citizens have held this ship for generations. If the data were here, wouldn't they have gotten it somehow?" His expression softened. "Don't you *hope* the data is inaccessible?"

She shivered. If primitive chemical rockets made the Gw'oth a potential threat, how would the Concordance have reacted to her starfaring ancestors? How react, that was, beyond their unprovoked seizure of *Long Pass*? All too easily she imagined the preemptive destruction of human civilization. Trillions of people, in Kirsten's imagination, on human worlds spread across the sky, until the Citizens came. And after?

More than ever, she wanted to find Earth. She wanted to *know* the fate of her people.

"Jeeves," she tried again. "I would like to see data about astronomical observations made during the flight."

"That data has been corrupted."

Sven stood, shaking his head. "I'm getting coffee. What can I get you?"

"Coffee," she repeated mechanically. As Sven was leaving, she managed not to ask Jeeves about astronomical objects not examined during the flight. How tired *was* she? Even if that data weren't corrupted, the set of unexamined objects must encompass most of the universe.

And yet . . .

There was something else to try. She was sure of it. Something she *knew*. Something she had done before. Something about comparing two mutually exclusive sets.

By the time Sven returned with her coffee, Kirsten was pondering the fact that Jeeves deemed several terabytes of memory neither inaccessible nor accessible.

29

The nondescript stony lump that Julian had dubbed Forward Station waxed slowly in the radar display. In the forward view port, with photomultipliers set to maximum, evidence of habitation emerged: airlock hatches, strings of emergency lights, antenna dishes, the faint impressions of past ship landings. Nessus cautiously lowered *Aegis*, pressing another dent into the primordial surface.

Julian Forward netted in from an underground laboratory. "Welcome back, Nessus."

"Thank you, Julian. Are we alone?"

Forward's nostrils flared. "Nessus, I *told* you we would be alone, just as I've promised not to tell anyone about you."

Dismounting his padded bench, Nessus stretched necks and legs. "This must be a short visit, Julian. I would like to get directly to your progress report."

"Come in, and we'll get started," Forward said.

"This will go faster if I stay aboard." Had Nessus not worked closely with Colonists, he might not have recognized that rigid pose. Forward was offended—and strong enough to snap Nessus like a twig. Nessus hoped the Jinxian never learned how his research grant got canceled.

Colonists. Nessus did not want to think of them now. "Julian, your status?"

Forward never needed much encouragement to discuss his work. As always, the nuances surpassed Nessus' understanding, so he made noncommittal answers whenever a response seemed expected. He recorded everything for the experts on Hearth.

Still, the broad outlines were plain enough. More experiments: some successful, as many not. Imploding a stasis field was hard. So was maintaining symmetry as the field collapsed. Even harder was ascertaining what occurred, or failed to occur, within. Time stood still inside, within nanoseconds of the stasis field's activation. There-after, nothing but the mass within could be measured from outside.

"I'd make faster progress with proper equipment." Forward crossed his arms across his chest.

Ah. Nessus finally understood Julian's attitude. Freighters seldom called at Forward Station, deep within the Oort Cloud. A supply ship had recently come and gone—without the bulky, custom-built gravity meters Julian had ordered. They, together with more mundane cargo items, had been displaced, at Nessus' intervention, to make room for the merchandise from Miguel. "I apologize, Julian, but I need those packages. Are they ready for loading?"

Station cameras followed Forward down a dimly lit corridor into a cavernous storage space. He gestured at stacks of crates. Shimmering holograms showed the seals remained intact. "What's in these? Rocks?"

"They don't concern the project, Julian."

"They do when they delay critical instrumentation that I—"

"Julian, please." Unseen behind his avatar, Nessus plucked at his mane, resisting the urge to remind Julian who worked for whom. He dare not demotivate his native expert, especially just as it became necessary to leave the human unsupervised. "A time-sensitive matter has arisen. I leave immediately, and those crates must go with me."

Julian leaned against a crate, eyes narrowed in calculation. "When will you be back?"

A few months, at least, considering merely the round-trip transit time—assuming he came back. Nessus was not about to provide even that slight hint to the location of the Fleet. "To be determined, but we can keep in touch by hyperwave radio." And via repeater buoys ejected along the way to disguise *Aegis*'s path.

Nessus also answered as best he could the unasked

question: Would the project continue? "Funds already provided should last for a while. Your priority remains the
prototyping of a neutronium generator."

"And do you expect to return before the money runs
out?"

"To be determined," Nessus repeated. "I'll release other
funds, if necessary. Can we load while we talk?"

"Do you expect to return?" As he spoke, Forward casually set the first crate into a transfer booth. Nessus got
the impression Julian would be happiest if the funds and
knowledge transfer continued without the oversight.

The box was practically weightless here, but microgravity had no effect on inertial mass. What Forward
shifted effortlessly, Nessus struggled to lift off a stepping
disc. Box by box, deflecting queries as he labored, Nessus moved the cargo by floater into *Aegis*' main hold. The
overflow filled the relax room and several corridors.

Would he return? Nessus honestly did not know. If he
did, he would bring a proper neutronium generator. There
would be no further need for Forward's services.

Clandestine Directorate's latest message raised more
questions than it answered. *Explorer* was missing, its crew
unaccounted for. Nessus was recalled immediately, by implication to scout ahead of the Fleet.

Nessus launched as soon as he had secured the ship-
ment. The sooner *Aegis* reached the Fleet, the sooner Nike
would tell him the nature of the emergency.

And the sooner he might know what had happened to
three friends.

30

Explorer's relax room, its exercise equipment and furniture temporarily crammed into cabins, barely and uncomfortably accommodated the gathering. Considerations more basic than comfort had determined the meeting location. They dared not be overheard. If heard, they must be behind an impregnable hull.

Sweat trickled down Kirsten's forehead as the ventilators ran full out trying to cool the overcrowded room. Elsewhere heaters ran, as the frigid ocean depths sucked the warmth from a starship submerged beneath NP4's cold sea.

Sabrina Gomez-Vanderhoff stood in the doorway. "Let's begin," the governor said. "I don't see it getting any comfier in here."

No one had met everyone, so they circled the room doing quick introductions. Sabrina. The three crew. Sven. Aaron Tremonti-Lewis: minister of public safety. Lacey Chung-Philips, short and brunette, in the drab garb of widowhood: the economics minister. Lacey peered about the relax room, craning to see into the corridor, as though aboard a spaceship for the first time.

With a nod, Sabrina signaled Sven to begin. He projected a hologram. A spherical spaceship, backed by a storm-wracked rim of NP5, now glowed in the center of the room. "Eric, Kirsten, Omar, and I recently spent several days aboard this vessel. You probably associate ships like this with grain transport. Not in this instance." The picture changed into a panoramic view of *Long Pass*. "This is inside."

"Our ancestors' supposed starship," Aaron said. Lacey just stared.

"That's what we're here to discuss," Sabrina said. "That and what it would mean. Please let the man continue."

Sven laid out his findings, voice firming as he proceeded. Hull repairs consistent with the attack that began the colony's official history. The many artifacts aboard for people shaped like themselves. A primitive synthesizer that offered safe and nutritious food. Needlework art whose floss and linen predated the founding of Arcadia colony. The almost-as-old stepping disc retrofit to the ship.

"Suppose you *are* right." Lacey's tone dripped skepticism. "Why would the Concordance withhold this information? Why not admit that they had located our ancestors' ship?"

Kirsten took the projector controls. "*Here's* why."

Lacey gasped as Citizen robots overran *Long Pass*. She finally asked, "Can you authenticate this?"

Sven squared his shoulders. "It appears real, with no evidence of tampering."

"Sven is our expert," Sabrina said. "So: Presume *Long Pass* is our ancestors' ship. How do we handle the situation?"

"Situation?" Lacey asked. "While this information remains secret, there is no situation. Not until we confront the Concordance—if that's what you decide to do."

"Suppress what we have uncovered? Ignore it?" Kirsten quivered with anger. "You can't mean that."

"I may not *like* it," Lacey said, "but I mean it. Silence is our wisest course. Picture thousands of Colonists becoming as enraged as you. Imagine the chaos."

"Colonists reacting with hostility, you mean. Rebelling." Kirsten struggled to express herself with terms that described teenaged misbehavior. How did one articulate anger and purposeful enmity between neighboring cultures? There ought to be a word.

Jeeves spoke English. Clearly, so had the crew of *Long Pass*. Did English—true English—have vocabulary appropriate to their circumstances? What else had Citizens expunged, besides all clues to the location of their ancestral home, of Earth?

Maybe it didn't matter. Maybe hostility and rebellion would suffice. Perhaps the time had come for Colonists to grow up and take charge of their fate.

"Yes, rebellion," Lacey said. "That's exactly the problem. Suppose that we lash out like an immature teen. We could damage some Hearthian crops, certainly, or disrupt food shipments. We might even imprison or threaten the few Citizens on NP4. How do you suppose the Concordance would react? Before you answer, remember that they grew food on the nature preserves long before they found *Long Pass*.

"The truth is, the Concordance does not need us."

"Kinetic weapons," Eric said to himself. "Like the rigged comet in the Gw'oth system."

"What?" Sabrina asked.

Eric grimaced, struggling for a brief explanation. "The details don't matter. Smack a planet with something moving fast enough, and it wipes out everyone and everything."

"That's why we were attacked! *Explorer*, I mean." Kirsten was sure of it. "Someone realized we weren't following orders, and worried that we might use the ship to strike Hearth. But they already had the exploding paint in place! They were *prepared* to betray us."

Pensively, Aaron rubbed his chin. "So possession of a starship gives us leverage. What if we also seized the ships at Arcadia spaceport?"

"Stop it!" Sabrina shouted. She glared about her. "How quickly your minds turn to mass murder. We don't even know that the Concordance ordered the attack on *Long Pass*. Yes, an attack followed a message to the world which would become NP5. I assume a Citizen vessel was there to coordinate the planet's migration, probably the same ship that now encloses our old ship.

"Everyone here knows Citizens personally. Is it so difficult to believe that the crew on that ship panicked, that they lashed out on their own? Perhaps the Concordance has since done its best to make amends."

Lacey nodded. "Whatever happened happened long ago. Long-dead Citizens attacked our long-dead ancestors. If rebellion ever made sense, that time has passed."

Kirsten stared, her fists clenched. "I don't believe this. At the least, the Concordance hid that past—*our* past—from us. The lies continue to this day. How can we keep serving them? How can we live with them?"

She shrugged Eric's hand off her arm. She didn't want to be calmed. "Sabrina, there are things I must know. That every Colonist deserves to know. Where do we come from? Did the Concordance treat that civilization any more gently than it did *Long Pass*? Is there some way our people can go home?"

"*Yes,* Kirsten. We really *must* decide what we want. Not just information, not just apologies, but a way to confirm these things. And is it only information we want? And what do we have to . . . negotiate . . . persuade them with?" Sabrina too was having trouble with an English stripped of too many concepts. "One tiny spacecraft. I suppose exploding paint cannot be exploded twice, and we have you for a pilot and codes to fly it. But compare *Explorer* to—" She waved at the nearly featureless hologramic sphere: a General Products #4 hull. "They have thousands of those."

Eric said, "As for what we want . . . ? I suppose we want to leave."

Lacey: "Leave our *homes*? For what? This lost Earth?"

Aaron: "Maybe. If we knew enough."

The debate raged, every option unpalatable. Exile for a few, fleeing—to where, no one could say—aboard stolen starships. Futile acts of revenge. Provoking their own destruction. Shame and dishonor if they did nothing.

Kirsten finally stopped listening. Symbolic resistance or horrific destruction. Surely there was another way! Stomach churning, she mentally retraced the circuitous path that had brought them so close to the truth about their past.

The Ice Moon of the Gw'oth. The woods of Elysium.
The General Products factory. The arcologies of Hearth.
The Human Studies Inst—

The General Products factory and *Explorer*'s very thorough overhaul. Kirsten mused aloud. "While Nessus
still commanded, this ship carried a fusion drive." The
others stopped talking. They were actually listening to
her. "General Products replaced the fusion drive with
thrusters before we three were given control. Nessus had
a fusion drive aboard for a purpose. Just as surely, the
fusion drive was removed on purpose. I think I just realized that reason.

"A fusion drive directed toward a planet's surface would
also be a weapon—precise, controllable, and horrible. Easier to point—more effective, maybe more credible—than
a kinetic weapon."

Pointing at the hologram of an old ramscoop that
still floated in the center of the room, Eric articulated
the thought Kirsten guessed had leapt into everyone's
mind. "*Long Pass* carries a fusion drive, if only we can
use it."

Aaron shook his head. Lacey snapped, "Use it? It's—"

"It's locked in a box," Sabrina said. "An impenetrable
shell. Whatever horror you're thinking of perpetrating,
that old ship is of no use to us."

"Actually," said Eric, "It just might be the easiest part."

31

Their edges sharp, their corners treacherously pointed,
Nike thought the crates stacked before him looked out of
place even here in the bowels of the alien-artifact-filled
depot of the Foreign Affairs Ministry. They'd bite you as
you passed. Warning signs encircled the boxes, and a wide
aisle encircled the signs. Cargo floaters, material-handling

robots, and burly workers streamed all around, giving a wide berth to the mysterious delivery.

A worker shuffled forward, heads bowed. "I apologize, Your Excellency. Containers kept appearing, offloaded from the spaceport, marked to your attention."

The ministry depot, like almost anyplace on Hearth, was a mere step from his office. "You were right to contact me," Nike said. Besides his name, every container bore a prominent label: *Aegis*. Nessus' ship. Nike could imagine no peril here. He thought: I'm the *last* person Nessus would endanger.

He also thought, with less surprise each time it occurred to him, how much he had missed the scruffy scout. He would debrief Nessus soon enough, once Nessus rested from the tiring, long-distance, solo journey.

"What can you tell me about the contents?" Nike asked.

The worker straightened. He was short and broad, with dark brown eyes. Only the cloth gloves which covered his heads were transparent—and, of course, gas-permeable. The rest of the protective garment that covered his legs, torso, and necks had been turned blue to show his foreman status. Clothing on a Citizen, however appropriate the context, was jarring. The covered mane, scarcely discernable through the sturdy fabric, seemed especially disfiguring.

"Excellency, whatever you've been sent is very heavy. Scanners show only slabs of rock in foam padding. Nothing obviously dangerous."

Why would Nessus send a shipload of rocks? "Show me one." As the foreman stepped toward a wheeled scanner, Nike clarified, "Open one."

"Your Excellency?"

"It will be fine," Nike said. He sufficiently understood Colonists to recognize curiosity when, unaccountably, he experienced it himself. Or was this Nessus' influence again?

With impatience surely akin to the unaccustomed curiosity, Nike watched from behind a safety barrier as a robot carefully lowered the top crate from a stack. It pried off the top and sides of the container. Workers in protective garb converged to peel back the packing material. Finished, they stepped back in confusion, revealing figures carved with wondrous detail from the marble slab.

Nike wriggled his lips in unrestrained delight.

Nike rose as an aide ushered Nessus into his office. Nike was, as always, poised and immaculately coiffed. His mane gleamed today with gold and orange gems. "Thank you, Vesta," Nike said.

Vesta backed out, closing the door behind him.

"I see my gift arrived," Nessus said, admiring the marble sculptures that hung from one long arced wall. Heroic figures, on whom the draped cloth was elegant. Wondrous beasts. Flawless craftsmanship. Despite the spaciousness of the office, only a small portion of the art could be displayed. "They are finer than I dared to imagine."

"They are magnificent, Nessus. Are they what I think? The Frieze of the Parthenon?"

"Most of it," Nessus replied. "Acquired from the British Museum." Acquired was a neutral-enough term, and the humans themselves had quarreled for centuries as to the rightful owner. "Given your interest in human mythology, I hoped you would like them."

"Very much so." After a glance at the closed door, Nike crossed his necks flirtatiously.

How long I have waited for this moment? Nessus thought. And how circumstances have changed. He walked around Nike's desk, the better to study two groups of seated figures facing each other. "Even human scholars cannot agree on its meaning."

Nike moved closer.

"The frieze is said to celebrate the creation of the human kind," Nessus continued. "Some say these scenes represent a Council of the Gods, debating the wisdom of that creation. We see that the two groups, representing both points of view, are closely matched."

And humanity's fate again rests in the balance.

"It's time, Nike, to tell me exactly what happened with *Explorer.*"

Kirsten found light-years distant from where she belonged. The entire crew conspiring. *Explorer*, intrinsically a deadly weapon, missing under the control of the duplicitous Colonists. The destruction of the ship made perfect sense.

Logic did not lessen the pain.

Nessus slumped on a bench in Nike's office, the triumph of his gift washed away by grief. Months without sightings of or communications from the three. They were surely dead.

He wondered who would tell little Rebecca.

For all his anger at the Colonists' deceit, Nessus accepted his responsibility in the tragedy. He had selected them. Taught them. Championed them.

Evidently, he had failed them.

Nike stood before Nessus, stroking his mane, massaging his tense shoulders, intoning a wordless dirge. "It had to be done, Nessus," Nike said. "Truly, I'm sorry."

"I know." Nessus shivered. "I'll heal."

"I liked them, too," Nike said. "But they chose their path."

Nessus could not bear to dwell on his loss. "I assume this ends the Colonist scouting program. Once *Aegis* completes overhaul, I'll go out again."

"In time." Nike began combing Nessus' mane. "For now, I'm glad you are here."

Nike and Nessus circulated slowly through the crowd. Nessus sneaked another peek at their complementary braids. The hair artist so hastily summoned to prepare them could have been no more surprised than he.

The harmonized manes; the side-by-side walk, with flanks pressed together; their necks entwined in public, the introduction to each other's friends—all were affirmations. All were traditions that invited the scrutiny and approval of the community.

They were hardly mated, but a process had begun.

"Clio." Nessus repeated the name in greeting. "I am honored to meet you." His trilling sounded flat and discordant, but no one commented. How could he remember so many names? This social meadow in Nike's arcology teemed with Nike's friends, neighbors, and acquaintances. On the periphery, blending seamlessly, a virtual herd spread far into the distance.

They wandered among holo sculptures, dance performances, scent fountains, and mellifluous choruses, admiring the many forms of art with which most people filled their time. Sneaking another look at their coordinated manes, Nessus truly appreciated how much Nike and he had in common. They both worked.

Somewhere in their meandering, he and Nike joined a group of dancers. Legs flashing, hooves kicking high, voices raised in joyful accompaniment, Nessus realized: I'm *happy*.

This was not the mating dance, of course. Mating, should it happen, was far into the future. Still, amid the rich stew of crowd pheromones, sides heaving in exertion, throats thrumming accompaniment of a familiar ballet, Nessus allowed himself to envision the day he and Nike would walk together into the lush pastures of the Harem House.

In his imagination, Nessus saw a cluster of Companions. They grazed on a nearby hill, each lovely, each shy.

A Companion of surpassing delicacy and beauty glanced up from her nibbling. Twirling and leaping, he and Nike lured the fragile Bride with the perfection of their movements. She slipped between them and joined the dance, more graceful than anything he had ever seen. Their motions grew ever more intricate and sensual.

She broke free, and Nessus held his breath. This was the moment of decision.

The little one gazed up the hill to her friends. She could rejoin them, and resume the idyllic life that was all she had ever known. Or—

She looked back at her suitors. Slowly, she walked into the nearby circle of scarlet hedge. She settled onto a bed of lush meadowplant—

Their Bride.

A roaring crescendo celebrated the end of the dance. Nessus awoke from his reverie, sweat trickling down his flanks. Nike stood nearby, breathing deeply. Friends watched them both, blinking approval.

Never had the Bride-to-be been more real in his mind's eye.

Nessus permitted himself a moment of sadness for the Bride he had yet to meet. For after that glorious dance, after the tender moment of conception, after a year of doting by himself and Nike, would come childbirth.

And in giving birth to a Citizen, the Companion invariably died.

Exhilarated and exhausted, Nessus settled onto a pile of cushions. He owned only one small room deep inside an arcology, but Nike had a suite with an exterior wall. Craning his neck slightly, Nessus glimpsed woods below. The wall lighting panels were in their night setting, but the forest canopy shimmered in the light of the worlds.

Nike synthed a glass of carrot juice and another beverage for himself, then settled onto more heaped pillows. He seemed oddly withdrawn.

"What's wrong?" Nessus asked.

Silence greeted the question. Finally, Nike stood. He stared out the window, appearing not to focus on anything. "I would value your opinion on something."

"Anything," Nessus said.

"Do you know where we're going?" Nike began. As

though with a will of its own, a forehoof scraped at the floor.

"We?"

"The Fleet, Nessus."

Had he ever seen Nike not in total control of himself? Nessus' mind whirled. "To the galactic north, I think. That is our shortest path from the galaxy, to open spaces where we can set a straight course without stars to be dodged. Then outward, far from the core explosion."

"And then?" Nike prompted.

What odd manner of conversation was this? "To another galaxy, of course."

Nike exhaled a minor chord of great sadness before raising his heads high with resolve. In dire and portentous chords, he spoke—

Of the races the Concordance had wronged. Of Sisyphus seeking endless, eventless stability in the darkness between galaxies. Of Eos' corrupt bargain. Of Nike's own worst fear: That the Concordance, devoid of stimuli, was doomed by its timidity to self-absorption, decadence, and eventual decay.

Nessus' mind had never ranged through fields this wide. Nike's ambitions were frightening. He would shape the race itself.

"What would you have us do?" Nessus asked.

"We should go inward, *closer* to the galactic core. To a place rich with stars and resources, yet past the risk of a supernova chain reaction. To a place vacated by potential competitors, where, in temporary isolation, we can consider how better to coexist with other races. En route we will find species who could not flee, who will welcome our help."

Compared to the fate of the Concordance, Nessus thought, how trivial his worries seemed, even the deaths of three Colonist friends. As he searched for words of solace and hope, an alert buzzed stridently. An icon materialized, and Nessus recognized one of Nike's aides.

"Connect," Nike said. "What is it, Vesta?"

"Excellency, my apologies. You will want to see this immediately." Vesta looked surprised to find Nessus in Nike's home, but also relieved. "You, too, Scout."

"Speak."

"This must speak for itself," Vesta said. His off-screen head tripped something, and a hologram replaced him: humans, life-sized, too many.

32

As the old Colonist woman walked into the close foreground, Nessus screamed in chorus. He settled into the meadowplant rug, heads snaking under his belly . . . then pulled one out, and the other. Weirdly, terribly, he saw Nike doing the same.

The woman glared. "I am Sabrina Gomez-Vanderhoff, Governor of the Arcadia Self-Governance Council. I speak for the humans who have been repressed and exploited on Arcadia for half a thousand local years—"

Humans! How did she know that *word*?

But it wasn't just her. It was everything. Nessus forced himself to watch, made himself believe. *Preserver,* the ancient grain ship converted for exploration, and *Long Pass,* the old human-built interstellar ramscoop, and tiny *Explorer,* somehow unharmed. The three ships were in computer composite, surely not part of a physical scene, but their mere juxtaposition spoke of terrible secrets now revealed. In the foreground stood a crowd of Colonists as close-packed as Citizens. Despite his shock Nessus was relieved to see his three friends, still alive, among them.

Sabrina talked. Nike and Nessus listened.

"We have had enough of secrets and lies," Sabrina finished. "You will accept our demands, or pay a very high price. To begin, we are prepared to broadcast your secrets across the Fleet unless you contact us very quickly."

Turf flew as Nike pawed the floor in anger and fear.

Long Pass, long hidden, now revealed. Colonists further provoked by Baedeker's botched attack on *Explorer.* The Colonial government threatening to reveal everything. Predictions—thinly veiled threats—of civil unrest and food-export disruptions. Insistence upon free access to everything pertaining to their past, on every world of the Fleet.

And they demanded what no Citizen would dare admit to knowing: the location of Earth.

He and Nessus had stepped through to his office at the ministry, where the marble tableau now mocked him. The Council of the Gods, debating the wisdom of creating humans, arrived just as the wisdom of creating the colony arose anew.

Nessus sidled up, pulling at a mane again unkempt. "They know too many Fleet secrets to ever have contact with wild humans. But to tolerate a hostile world within the Fleet—or to undertake to destroy a world here within the Fleet—both choices are mad."

Nike quivered agreement. He had seen simulations. A kinetic-weapon strike that eradicated the Colonists would blast loose mountains of debris. Most would fall back.

Some wouldn't.

How much of the ejecta would fly free? How much be captured by the complex gravitational dance of six co-orbiting worlds? How much would bombard Hearth itself? These were questions beyond the capacity of any computer to determine. Flaming mountains falling among the arcologies—

And no what-if scenario had ever considered that a Colonist-controlled, stealthed starship might retaliate in kind against Hearth.

And yet . . .

Nike willed his posture to straighten, his hooves to cease their restless pawing. Slowly he paced, pausing only once to seek inspiration in the eyes of Zeus.

"Nike," Nessus said. "Are you recovered?"

The demands of the Colonists. The needs of the Concordance. The futility—for all sides—of open hostilities. Secrets now beyond keeping and secrets yet secure. Possibilities and perils coursed through Nike's thoughts. "I'm fine, Nessus. Give me a moment."

Flight from the galaxy had somehow become familiar to the masses. But aggrieved neighbors living on a world so near as to raise tides on Hearth? *That* danger had no precedent, and Experimentalists always took their opportunities when the danger was most extreme.

It seemed the Colonists meant to restore *Long Pass*. They might intend only an act of respect for or identification with their ancestors. They might have come to the wily realization that a fusion drive loose in the Fleet would affect the strategic balance. It mattered not. Locked safely inside a General Products hull, even a restored ramscoop represented no threat—except to the complacency of the Conservatives.

A well-managed crisis here within the Fleet would bring Experimentalists—dare he hope? Would bring *him*—to power.

Only more deception would do, perpetrated by one with great skill at controlling humans. "Nessus, do you love our people? Do you love *me*?"

"Yes and yes!" Nessus sang. "What do you need?"

As Nike summarized the plan—as much, anyway, as anyone but himself needed to know—he felt the eyes of gods boring into him.

He tried not to worry about the warning from Euripides.

33

Omar loped on the dayroom treadmill, confident and secure, and not at all the obsequious shipmate Nessus had once known.

"Tell me about Oceanus," Nessus said. He had seen enough reports to know that nothing there represented a danger to the Fleet. The distant ocean world was merely a neutral topic of conversation.

"Wet. Primitive. Probably a good . . . refueling station." Omar blotted his forehead with a towel as he ran.

"Refueling?" That was perceptive. The Fleet would not pass Oceanus for years, during which time much deuterium and tritium could be extracted from its seas. Hearth's own fusion resources needed periodic replenishment, while the less depleted oceans of the Nature Preserves served as emergency reserves. "Good idea."

The treadmill slowed. Omar adjusted his pace. "How much about this did you know?"

"This?" Nessus asked.

"*Long Pass,*" Kirsten said. Nessus' right head whipped around. He had not seen her enter the dayroom. "NP5. The way to Earth. Who did this to us."

"Hello. I wish I could answer your questions"—which was true, however misleading—"but you ask about things no one can know. Still, I know more than some."

He knew more than the technicians did. These were a dozen Citizens whom Nike had provided to work with the Colonists on *Long Pass.* They served as proof of Nike's good intentions. They brought technical skills or an interface to factories that could fabricate unique parts. They did not carry dangerous historical knowledge. And they were instructed not to share what little they might know about the Colonists' past.

"Separately, I want to congratulate you on your new relationship with Eric."

"Which you have, several times now. You can't change the subject forever, Nessus."

"My apologies. I mean no offense."

Coffee smell permeated the dayroom as she synthed a serving. "So how much about this did you know?"

"Which *I* have explained repeatedly." Nessus chose his words carefully. Since leading the small Citizen team to *Long Pass,* he doled out a bit more information with each repetition.

"Most Citizens don't know these things. You can believe that much! I could not have known you would buy histories while on Hearth. We're dealing with information held by a few officials. These are long-suppressed secrets the current government would still resist revealing."

Secrets that made it plausible this alliance of convenience must remain clandestine and restricted. Nike had convinced the Colonist leaders, at least for now, that this coerced cooperation must remain confined aboard this ship. That Experimentalist agents and Colonist rebels alike must avoid the suspicions and scrutiny of Concordance security authorities. Doubtless Sabrina and Nike both thought to exploit what they learned, to improve their negotiating positions later on.

Just as the technicians aboard conveniently knew only approved history, Nessus guessed he knew only a fraction of Nike's plans. That was for the best. Nessus could not let slip in error what he did not know.

He would rather that Nike trust him completely.

Omar and Kirsten exchanged skeptical looks. Nessus took it as a sign he was being too coy. "I've told you what I know about *Preserver.*" The ship that encased the little ramscoop. "*Preserver*'s crew deployed the planetary drive on the Ice World. As they escorted that world toward the Fleet, a comm laser contacted them. They panicked.

"Extrapolating the migratory planet's course, your ancestors would have been looking at the comet band around Red Star. They'd have seen five worlds in clearly artificial orbits. A gravitational rosette is stable, but it doesn't happen naturally.

"Then as now, the Concordance considered the secrecy of Hearth's position essential to our safety. *Long Pass* was attacked lest it signal the Fleet's position. By hyperdrive, the trip was a matter of days."

The treadmill stopped. Omar hopped off. "Nessus, that doesn't make sense. We're discussing two ships nearly a light-year separated, communicating by laser. *Preserver* responded to a year-old message. *Long Pass* had that same year to signal home."

"*Preserver*'s crew lost all reason to their fear. In a way, it appears they guessed right. Your ancestors evidently had not yet signaled home." Nessus could hardly admit *knowing* that human records made no mention of a wandering Ice World. *Long Pass* itself appeared in UN records, the official cause of its disappearance "unknown."

Unofficially, everyone blamed technical failure.

A ramscoop swept up interstellar hydrogen for fuel, using intense magnetic fields hundreds of miles wide. Fields that intense were deadly to advanced life, so ramscoop technology was reserved for robotic craft. Crewed vessels, carrying their own fusion fuel, followed robotic scouts to the stars at much slower speeds: slowboats.

Long Pass's designers had built a bubble in the magnetic field, a safe zone to contain the life-support compartments. The briefest interruption would have killed everyone onboard. Ramscoops were proven technology. At the time, safety bubbles were not. Everyone assumed bubble failure had doomed *Long Pass*. What else could happen in the emptiness between stars?

More than two centuries had passed before humans crew-rated another ramscoop.

Eric said, "Guessed right. They *guessed*?"

"Please understand, I do not condone the attack."

Nessus didn't back away from Eric's rage, but it was hard. "I meant only, strictly for keeping secret the Fleet's location, that they met their goal."

"You so carefully always say *they*," Kirsten observed. "Were you involved?"

The long-awaited question. "Absolutely not. This all happened before I was born."

Being entirely honest about something felt good. The opportunity so seldom presented itself.

Preserver, more than a thousand feet in diameter, enclosed twelve cargo holds, three parks, hundreds of cabins, a network of interlocking hyperdrive motors, miles of corridors—and, in the central cavity which once transported a reactionless drive of planetary scale, *Long Pass.*

A visitor setting hoof anywhere in *Preserver* inevitably spiked the temperature reading of some room sensor, the effect slightly more pronounced for Colonists than Citizens. By calibrating reporting thresholds with room sizes, Nessus turned the environmental-control subsystem into a serviceable tracking system.

Within the privacy of his cabin, Nessus watched the Colonists wander about *Preserver.* Some things about humans never changed, with curiosity high on the list. Eric soon limited his forays to the engine room and its technical files. Kirsten mostly visited the bridge. Omar and Sven entirely lost interest in the great ship. Despite crowding, they spent most of their waking hours aboard the ramscoop.

Then came the flash of empathy. *Long Pass* was built wholly by and for humans. It incorporated no Concordance technology. It made no compromise for the caution or convenience of visiting Citizens. In every detail, from ambient lighting to color combinations to door-latch and table heights to the taste of the air, the ramscoop proclaimed its independent origins.

No Colonist had experienced such an environment.

That the long-emptied ramscoop ship called to the Colonists made it simpler to keep them from coming upon anything unfortunate on *Preserver.* For that, at least, Nessus was grateful.

He burrowed deeper into a mound of cushions. Much had changed between him and his erstwhile crew, some subtly, more often not. Eric's close-cropped scalp was only the most glaring instance. Kirsten and Omar remained, warily, his friends. The newcomer, Sven, might become one.

Gone was the deference inculcated by generations of indoctrination. It was as though Nessus shared *Preserver*— and its many secrets—with wild humans.

Disaster loomed, and Nessus trembled.

A dot blinked red on the wire-frame holo of *Preserver,* which floated before Nessus. A warm body had appeared on the bridge. With a two-throated lament, Nessus stood. *Preserver*'s bridge was but a step by disc from his cabin. He guessed he would find Kirsten there.

It would not do for the Colonists to know he tracked them. Rather than onto *Preserver*'s bridge, Nessus stepped to the disc closest to the gangway onto *Long Pass.*

He found Sven in the dayroom, deep in conversation with Jeeves. Eric and Omar stood in the ramscoop's engine room, discussing technical esoterica with a General Products specialist.

Something suggested Colonist progress, something that Nessus could not at first put a tongue on. Then he had it: the absence of the fat power cable that had snaked from an auxiliary fusion generator in *Preserver,* through the open airlock, along corridors and down stairways, to the main power-distribution panel in this room.

Long Pass was now sufficiently repaired or refueled to generate its own power.

Nike needed time for a purpose not yet shared with Nessus. Let the Colonists waste that time restoring this ship—it would never fly again. Nanotech had sealed the great doors that once opened to swallow *Long Pass*. Like entropy itself, the extension of the super-molecule was irreversible. *Preserver*'s hull, except for small hatches, was now seamless.

It must be Kirsten's body heat that had set off the temperature sensors. She was unattended on *Preserver*'s bridge, where, doubtless, she poked about in the main computer. Data archeology was an activity for which, Nessus had belatedly recognized, she had few equals. "Where's Kirsten?" Nessus asked to cover for what he already knew. "I wanted to talk with her."

"The big ship's bridge," Eric interjected into the ongoing technical conversation. The rudeness miffed Nessus, although it spared him having to elaborate his story.

A stepping disc later, Nessus found Kirsten leaning against a padded bench on the bridge of *Preserver,* head tipped backward, eyes closed in thought. Holos surrounded her: navigational, graphical, and textual. "Hello, Kirsten."

She started. "You surprised me."

"I wondered how you were doing," Nessus said. "Eric said I'd find you here."

"You wondered *what* I was doing."

"There's no need to think that, Kirsten."

"Yes, there is. Too many secrets have been kept from us Colonists. We've been told too many lies. *I've* been told lies."

She didn't say by whom. She didn't need to. "Yet here you are, aboard this ship. Tell me truthfully, Kirsten. Did your path to *Long Pass* ever stray from total candor?"

She reddened. "We were inventive, of necessity."

Nessus said, "Then perhaps you can understand I also operated under constraints."

"You can see I'm fine." She turned away from him.

One of the floating holos caught Nessus' eyes: more material Kirsten might find troubling. "The planet en route, I see."

She enlarged that video.

At many times real time, the world that would become NP5 spun, swirled in clouds. The star that was no longer its sun shrank to a spark. Something in the display logic—Kirsten's contribution?—maintained apparent brightness as the star receded.

Storms raged as land and oceans surrendered their heat. The cyclones grew and merged, and the ocean spawned yet more storms, until thick cloud completely hid the surface.

"A world in its death throes," Kirsten said, her tone flat with disapproval. She set the playback rate yet faster. Cloud churned and whirled, its texture subtly changing. The clouds thinned. "Lakes and streams have frozen. Finally ice coats the oceans themselves, starving the storms." She fixed him now with a hard stare. "Now the atmosphere itself freezes, one gas at a time, covering land and ocean ice alike with new layers.

"Fast-forward, to arrival at the Fleet." Necklaces of little fusion suns streamed across space to ring the ice-sheathed planet. Storms formed anew as the atmosphere started to thaw. "An almost instant, oxygen-rich atmosphere, ready for eco-forming. Nothing above single-celled life could have survived the deep freeze to compete with Hearthian life forms."

Nessus straddled one of the bridge benches. "It was a primitive world. It would not otherwise have been taken."

"Primitive. Like Earth?"

Nessus jerked, realizing: She thinks us monsters. "Not even like Oceanus."

She did not respond. The silence grew oppressive. "You *know* the Concordance eco-forms worlds," Nessus said. "First, NP1 and NP2. They were arid worlds relocated within our original solar system, but further out. Before moving them, we bombarded them with comets. The collisions melted the ice. We massively seeded the new oceans with tailored single-celled organisms.

Transformation of the primordial atmosphere took thousands of years."

Nessus pointed at her holo. "A world with ocean and oxygen-rich atmosphere is quickly productive, ready for soil treatment as soon as the thawing storms dissipate."

"Like NP3 and NP4, I suppose," Kirsten said. "And NP5, soon enough."

He had to appear to cooperate with the rebellious Colonists. That precluded blocking her access to *Preserver*'s computers. What he couldn't block, though, he might monitor—and so he had hurried here. Better still would be to divert her interest.

Computers aboard the old ramscoop had been exhaustively studied. Earth's location was *gone*. Nessus was supremely confident that not even Kirsten could recover the coordinates of any human world from those computers. He was far less confident that no proscribed data lurked in *Preserver*'s systems, if not residual from the ill-fated mission, then carelessly uploaded after its return to the Fleet.

He needed to distract her.

"The strange thing, Kirsten, is that the Fleet flees an abundance of worlds just like that." He extended a neck at NP5, huge beneath the bridge view port. "Every once-habitable world in the galactic core has been wiped clean. More and more will be sterilized as the radiation front passes. Millions of worlds, Kirsten, ripe for eco-forming."

Swiveling his heads, Nessus looked himself in the eyes. "If only those worlds were safe to approach before all that wonderful but reactive oxygen recombines."

With a shiver for effect, he dropped the ironic pose. "Enough gloom. Let us return to *Long Pass* for coffee and carrot juice."

As she vanished, stepping ahead of him, he permitted himself a much needed stirring of his mane before following.

* * *

Nibbling delicately, Nike sampled the grass-and-fruit medley offered to him. The simplicity of the snack emphasized the naturalness and freshness—the expense—of its ingredients: another transparent offer. "Excellent," Nike said. With delicacy was exactly how he had to manage this meeting. "Thank you for agreeing to see me, Eos."

Eos gestured expansively. At the luxurious dwelling his venality had gotten him? At politics and life? At the presumed deal about to be made? "Of course. Always glad to see you. Have you considered what we discussed on your previous visit?"

"I have." Nike bowed a neck with feigned unease. "Will the Hindmost definitely propose a unity government?"

"Very soon," Eos said. "The time is right. The migration proceeds smoothly."

Smoothly? Wild humans still sought them. By disregarding that truth, Eos had betrayed his position. Had forfeited the right to continue as leader of the Experimentalists.

Nike decided: My conscience is clean. "A point worth making when you and the Hindmost announce your association."

"Indeed." Eos paused from refilling his trencher with more grain-and-fruit medley. "Is that important to you, Nike?"

"As leader of Clandestine Directorate, I am expected to watch objectively for problems. . . ." Another contrived bending of the neck.

"I see," Eos said. In the head not encumbered with a snack, lips wriggled with amusement. "It is more appropriate for you to agree that our circumstances are safe, especially to a suggestion *I* offer, than to volunteer that same assessment."

Nike lowered his heads submissively.

"I see your point." Setting down his trencher, Eos whistled a wry, double-throated arpeggio. "Then we have an understanding."

"We do." Nike straightened. He felt no shame for his lie.

Once Eos made his ill-advised declaration, and the Colonist crisis followed almost immediately, the whole Concordance would reach an understanding:

The current leader of the Experimentalists was unfit.

34

Snoring softly, Eric turned lazily on his long axis, releasing Kirsten. Finally. She collapsed the sleeper field, easing them to the deck. She stood aside and reactivated the field before he stirred. He snorted in his sleep and she smiled.

Resenting her insomnia—or his easy sleep—accomplished nothing. Kirsten headed to the relax room for a sleeping pill from the autodoc. En route, she changed her mind. She stepped directly from *Explorer* to *Long Pass,* the former docked alongside *Preserver*'s outer hull, the latter locked within.

After a detour for coffee, Kirsten went to the ramscoop's bridge. She found Sven already there.

"Oh, hello," he said. He continued shuffling papers.

"I'm sorry to see you can't sleep either."

"Coffee. We're all addicted."

She took the other seat on the bridge. "I hoped to chat for a bit with Jeeves. Will that bother you?"

"Nah." Sven spread the papers across a console ledge. "If it does, I'll move. I'm only here for a change of scenery. I can as usefully be stumped in my cabin or the dayroom."

"Thanks. I'll talk quietly." She swiveled toward the console, giving Sven the semblance of privacy. "Jeeves, this is Kirsten."

A cartoon of a round head with a moustache smiled

widely. "Good morning." It was, just barely, by ship's time.

"What can you tell me about Earth?" she asked.

"Very little. It's where humans come from. *Long Pass* was built in and launched from high Earth orbit."

"And you don't know where Earth is." Kirsten sighed. She already knew his answer.

"That data has been corrupted," Jeeves said regretfully.

She slouched in her chair, still not tired, but weary. Discovery of the ancestral ship was supposed to provide answers. Kept busy restoring the ship, Eric and Omar did not share her frustration. She did not share their intuition that mastering their forebears' technology would prove useful. Somehow.

Concentrate, she chided herself. "Could we, Colonists, live on Earth?" She had transferred basic knowledge to him, files about Hearth and the Fleet, about NP4 and Arcadia, hoping something would correlate with an otherwise useless scrap of his memory.

"Presumably," the AI said. "You can live in this ship."

"We may never know," Sven said, rearranging and crinkling papers. "The Concordance wants no one to know its location. Earth's authorities might have felt the same. Perhaps the data was only in the navigator's head. Perhaps they had a plan to erase it if they encountered others."

However logical the speculation, Kirsten could not bear to accept it. So *much* had gone into getting here. In the end, would they be left with only Citizen fables of their past? The possibility broke her heart.

She leaned back and stretched, stiff joints cracking. Sven had again rearranged his stack of papers. Task lists. Sketches. Snippets of inventory, some items checked or lined through. "Jeeves has terabytes of data. Why spend so much time dealing with these few bits?"

Sven shrugged. "The crew also had those terabytes. They found this worth recording by hand. It's worth a fraction of my time to wonder why."

"But doodles? At that, mostly doodles of flowers."
Kirsten was reminded vaguely of the needlework she had
taken her first time aboard. "Sure, we found them all over.
After years in this cramped, sterile environment, I'd yearn
for a bit of nature too."

"Even the flower drawings are interesting," Sven said.
"You recognize them, of course."

Kirsten sipped the dregs of her coffee, now scarcely
tepid. "A few. Buttercups and daisies. Irises, I think. That
means the ship carried the seeds."

"Tyra, my wife, is quite the gardener. I recognize all
these flowers, except maybe one." Sven tapped several
sheets. "It looks like a fuchsia, except that every fuchsia
I've ever seen has four petals. These all have five petals."

"Odd," she mused. "Maybe they brought seeds for
those, too, but the breed didn't take."

Sven stifled a yawn. "Jeeves?"

"My inventory never included such a seed." The AI
paused. "At least I do not think so."

In the corner of Kirsten's eye, Sven yawned again. She
said, "Don't let me keep you up."

"Fair enough." He gathered up his papers. "So you see
why I look to these few papers. The fuchsia discrepancy
may mean nothing. Or it may show us that not only navigational data has problems." Big yawn. "But more likely
nothing." He shambled off the bridge, presumably bound
for his cabin.

Not even Sven's yawning had any effect on her. "Jeeves,
remember the block of corrupted memory we last talked
about?" The region somehow neither accessible nor inaccessible, of whose content and purpose Jeeves denied all
knowledge. "Show details."

A graphic materialized: a fast-scrolling hexadecimal
dump. The data sped past, telling her nothing. At so low
a level of detail, how could it? "Pause. Is this program
code or data?"

"A little of each," Jeeves said. "It's mostly meaning-less."

Neither program nor data? "Is this unassigned storage? Something released by a program and not put back into use?"

"Unlikely," Jeeves said. "It's not queued for reassign-ment. Nor has it been initialized for reallocation."

Kirsten drained the last of her coffee. She had stud-ied Citizen computers, not human computers, but surely they shared some common underlying principles. No one worked with such minutiae as memory allocation—such bit shuffling had long ago been optimized and standardized—but obviously data structures underpinned everything. "Jeeves, does this mysterious block belong to *any* data structure?"

"Yes," he answered. "Not a useful one. It's tagged not to be reused, as though it had a physical fault. If so, the fault is transient, because it passes all my diagnostics."

Back and forth the conversation went, without progress. Her mood darkened under the futility of it all. Jeeves did not know what he did not know.

What *she* did not know was simple: how to give up. "You said there is some data in this region. Does it use any data structure with which you are familiar?"

Jeeves shook its animated head: no.

Hmm. "You also said there is program code. That *must* correspond to a meaningful structure, or else you could not distinguish it from data. Correct?"

It nodded, the tips of its mustache bobbing slightly.

Kirsten jumped as the ventilation fan kicked on. She had ground to a halt. Maybe she might yet get some sleep this shift.

But first—"Jeeves, I'm thinking we should try to ex-ecute the suspected code segments. Can you recognize and intercept anything unsafe they might do, before they do it?"

"Clarify unsafe."

She thought. "Changes to program or data. Operation of shipboard systems." Attempting to fire the fusion drive while inside the enclosed space of *Preserver* would kill them quick.

"Then, yes, I can."

Kirsten rubbed her eyes. After disallowing all that, how would she know if those mysterious programs did anything at all? "Corrections. One, permit memory modification within only the anomalous region we're discussing. Two, on this console," and she pointed, "allow display and speech."

"Done," Jeeves said. "Shall I begin running the suspected code segments?"

"Go ahead."

The corrupted memory region held eight possibly executable code segments. Four, given the opportunity to run, did nothing. Three tried to transmit garbled commands over the main shipboard network; Jeeves blocked their attempts and terminated them.

The final segment opened up a primitive hologram at Kirsten's console: a narrow rectangle with a blinking square at one end. It might be nothing.

Or, she thought, it might be a login dialogue.

Not long ago, to bond with Nike had seemed the unlikeliest of occurrences. Somehow, though, that had happened. So perhaps the news broadcast from Hearth should not have surprised Nessus.

Instead, Nessus found himself struck tuneless.

The Hindmost himself had invited Eos to join the government. Eos himself had agreed, citing the new era of security well established by years of uneventful Fleet voyaging. The sanguine announcement mentioned neither questing ARMs nor rebellious Colonists.

Nike refused Nessus' calls, pleading pressing duties.

Behind his locked cabin door, heads below the delusional safety of his belly, Nessus marveled. There were forms of insanity far worse than scouting interstellar space.

Preserver stored huge volumes of deuterium and tritium. Like *Explorer,* but on a much grander scale, its tanks were refilled through stepping discs and molecular filters. Operated in transmit mode, those same discs refilled the fuel tanks of fusion reactors across the ship. Thus were all of *Preserver*'s auxiliary vessels refueled, and its robots, and even its trash disposals.

Once Eric completed retrofitting a few stepping discs, *Preserver* would also replenish *Long Pass*'s tanks.

While Eric attended to refueling, Omar and Sven consulted with Jeeves about old inventory records, Nessus sulked in his cabin, and the Citizen technicians ignored them all to debate the latest political news from Hearth . . . Kirsten fretted.

After finding that single semi-functional code fragment, she had been too excited to sleep. No, be honest: too depressed. Say that she had found a hidden application. How could she possibly log in? Her exhaustion went beyond coffee's powers; she switched to stim pills.

Arms folded on the dayroom table, head down on her arms, Kirsten visualized the display invoked by that mysterious code. The blinking square was likely a cursor. Presumably the long rectangle was a data-entry field. If so, the field accommodated six characters. Random typing had proven the field did not expand to permit more.

So, twenty-six letters and ten digits. She would be an optimist, and assume the password contained no punctuation marks. Six character positions. That made thirty-six to the sixth possibilities. Two billion, more or less.

Guessing would not solve this problem and whoever

had set *this* puzzle was doubtless wily enough to have defended against a brute-force attack.

Guessing would not solve this problem.

When the stim pills finally kicked in, Kirsten noticed she was hungry. She tried another experiment from *Long Pass*'s synthesizer: pepperoni pizza.

Sven had covered one dayroom wall with old flower doodles. She couldn't tell most flowers apart, except for their differing numbers of petals. Why had someone spent so much time drawing these things?

The synthesizer disgorged her pizza. It smelled wonderful. The first bite seared the roof of her mouth.

Flowers everywhere. Flowers on that handicraft from her first time aboard. If those flowers meant something, why were the fuchsias drawn wrong?

More cautiously, she took a second bite. Pizza tasted wonderful. An Earth recipe, she decided.

And Earth flowers? Was a message hidden in the flowers?

Kirsten stared at the wall of drawings, desperate to see a pattern. Messy sketches. Many varieties. Petals and leaves. Something about the petals. The number of petals?

On one sheet, flowers with three, five, and twenty-one leaves. On another sheet: three, eight, and five. The next: eight, three, and five. Something teased her memory.

Across all the drawings, the flowers exhibited only a few distinct numbers of petals. She sorted the list: three, five, eight, thirteen, and twenty-one.

She saw a pattern, but no meaning. Three and five are eight. Five and eight are thirteen. Eight and thirteen are twenty one.

She finished the pizza and went to the bridge. A Jeeves animation was deep in discussion with Sven and Omar. There was no room for her inside. "Jeeves," she called from the corridor. The AI could multitask. "Three, five, eight, thirteen . . . what comes next?"

"Twenty-one, thirty-four, fifty-five. They're all in the Fibonacci series, Kirsten. Starting with zero-one-one-two, every number in the series is the sum of the two that precede it."

Omar looked up, impatient at the interruption. "Kirsten, can you play number games later?"

So the series had a name. Did it have a purpose? "Jeeves, what is the meaning of that series?"

"The Fibonacci series occurs frequently in nature. In botany, for example, Fibonacci patterns appear in the spiraling of petals, leaves, and pine cones, the clustering of seeds, and the growth points at which plants branch and rebranch. In zoology, the Fibonacci numbers appear in the dimensions of successive compartments in the shell of the nautilus. The so-called golden rectangle . . ."

"Kirsten," Sven grumbled. "I've found my way to a listing of species once carried on this ship, including marine species new to me. Can your fun with numbers wait?"

She ignored Sven, too. "Jeeves, you said the pattern occurs in nature. Did you mean all nature, or earthly nature?"

"Earthly nature," Jeeves said.

So: She had found a code fragment, with what might be a dialogue box. A secret program hidden in the earthly computer, possibly accessed by a secret password. A secret *earthly* password?

Might the flowers everywhere carry a message? Something that only humans might notice? Fibonacci numbers. Flowers with three, five, eight, thirteen, and twenty-one petals.

She was stumped.

Kirsten sat on the corridor deck, back against a wall, staring into the bridge. 3-5-8-13-21. Seven digits. The suspected password field allowed six.

"Sven!" He looked up at her yell. "You said fuchsias have four petals, not five?"

He nodded and went back to his work.

Discard the five as disinformation. 3-8-13-21. Six digits meant 720 permutations. She could *do* that. She climbed back to her feet.

Light-years and generations and centuries . . .

Would the Colonists' secret past finally be revealed through a brute-force search? For all Kirsten's excitement, the aesthetics of that possibility offended her. *Logic* had brought them here. *Logic* should complete their quest.

What else did they know?

Flowers and Fibonacci numbers. Badly rendered flowers. She recognized only some of the flowers, but even she knew real irises grew much taller than real daisies.

Kirsten searched her pocket computer for an image of the ancient needlework. Of the many flower representations, only that one was in color, obviously labored over the longest. Short irises and tall daisies. Might tallest representation denote the most significant digit? "Jeeves, run the last program fragment we found, with the same isolation measures. Into that text box, enter 8 3 21 13."

A trumpet fanfare rang out. A human hologram appeared, seemingly in a cabin of this ship. No, Kirsten thought, it *is* this ship. The needlework she had taken still hung on the wall behind the apparition. Sven's mouth fell open. Omar froze.

The man in the holo had dark eyes, hair, and complexion, and a face of indeterminate age creased with worry lines. His jumpsuit, of a curious plaid pattern, did not disguise a pudgy body build. His eyes were worldly wise and weary, and yet they conveyed a hint of humor. Kirsten could not help but think: I would like to have known this man.

He spoke. "I am the navigator of starship *Long Pass*. I have a story to tell.

"My name is Diego MacMillan."

35

Nike plunged into the murmuring throng that filled a randomly selected outdoor mall. Vesta struggled to keep pace. Sunlight panels shone from arcologies all around. Jets of water shot high into the air from a fountain not otherwise visible through the crowd, the spray cool on Nike's hide. Herd scent embraced him.

"Excellency," Vesta wheezed. "Please wait."

Poor Vesta could not understand the fleeting nature of this moment. Soon, there would be no more opportunity to mingle with the crowd, at least not for Nike.

Voices warbled and chanted, crooned and trilled. The main topic of conversation, today as ever since the recent announcement, was the prospective unity government. The harmonies: acceptance, trust, concurrence. The everyday-fewer discordances: doubt, anxiety, resignation.

Experimentalism obsolescent. Exhilaration and fatalism.

Consensus emergent.

"Excellency," Vesta huffed. "This new government will happen. These harmonies cannot be denied. Accord is crystallizing." His voice quavered with the undertunes that, with no answer expected, asked, "Why?"

"Do not worry." Nike's undertunes rang with confidence. "This partnership cannot last. We do not live at the end to history."

For I am making history.

The Colonist rebels must have grown complacent sharing *Preserver* with Citizens. Trusted guards from Clandestine Directorate were in place aboard *Preserver,* in the guise of technicians. All the robots were refueled, fittingly the same robots that first took over the ramscoop built by Sol's wild humans.

Vesta finally caught up. He lowered his voices questioningly. "I do not understand."

"Patience, my friend." Nike swerved to brush flanks. "All will be well."

The picture grew ever sharper in Nike's mind's eye. All four Colonists would be taken prisoner aboard *Preserver.* *Explorer,* docked alongside *Preserver,* was harmless even if the prisoners never revealed the stepping-disc codes needed to reclaim it. Noisy but ultimately impotent furor among the Colonist rulers on Arcadia. Let the Colonists protest about the secret of *Long Pass* so long denied them—the deeper truths that might bring that unrest to a boil remained hidden.

Soon Eos would be proven wrong. Soon Eos would be proven unfit and unworthy to lead the Experimentalists. And soon a new party Consensus must turn to the one who had stopped a crisis here in the heart of the Fleet.

And, if public disappointment raged loud enough? Might the time be ripe even for a new Hindmost?

Very soon now . . .

36

"I am the navigator of starship *Long Pass.* I have a story to tell.

"My name is Diego MacMillan."

Omar, Sven, Eric, and Kirsten hugged the walls of *Explorer*'s relax room. The holo recording shimmered at the center of the room, projected from a copy downloaded into Kirsten's pocket computer. The message Diego had so elaborately safeguarded could be meant only for Colonist eyes and ears.

"I speak human to human, ancestor to descendant. Despite everything that has gone wrong, I retain hope humans will find this message. I had to hide the key in plain sight, trusting my ability to make the clues meaningful only to humans.

"And yet . . ." Diego scowled. "I cannot depend on that. If our descendants are viewing this, I know how you must yearn for the location of your home, the planet Earth. To leave you *that* information would risk revealing it to the Citizens and leading these murderers to Earth itself. That I will not do."

Eric pounded the wall. Sven and Omar exchanged looks of frustration. Kirsten cursed. No matter that she respected Diego's reasoning: The road could not end here. It must not. She couldn't bear that.

Diego's scowl quickly passed. "On our way to settle a new home—New Terra, we agreed to name it—we encountered something amazing. Something awe-inspiring. We found a world traveling between stars. My observations suggested a steady acceleration for years. Reasoning that intelligence must be moving the Ice World, we signaled it by comm laser.

"Earth is a peaceful place, at least in my day. We believed that peace and prosperity arise naturally with advanced technology. We never considered that the knowledge to move worlds might come without wisdom. None of us, that is, except Jaime."

A lovely blonde woman appeared, a holo within a holo. "This is Jaime, my wife," Diego continued, his voice become ineffably sad. "You'll hear more about Jaime, and why she does not take part in this journal. She is the ship's doctor. Barbara is our captain, Sayeed our engineer.

"When we found the Ice World, Jaime dared to wonder: 'What if the aliens *aren't* friendly?' And because she worried, and because I love her, I took the one precaution I could. I prepared a computer virus that would obliterate all astronomical and astrogational data."

Kirsten slumped further. The way Diego had hidden

this journal was brilliant—in ways, a kindred spirit. She could not imagine recovering a secret he had intentionally expunged from the ramscoop's records.

"We knew how long our signal would take to reach the Ice World. We even threw a party when the planet continued on its extrapolated course long enough to receive our message. Our physics makes no allowance for faster-than-light communication or travel. We expected a long wait for a response.

"How naïve we were!

"Within hours of our celebration, a ship arrived, a whale of a ship, large enough to swallow us. Faster-than-light drive, obviously. Much faster. And so began our slavery to the Concordance." Diego smiled wickedly. "But *not* before I released the virus."

Whale was clear enough from context: something big. "Slavery?" Omar asked. "Anyone know that word?"

"Human beings defined and used as property," Jeeves said. The notion didn't bother him.

The definition and its accompanying shock of recognition further blackened Kirsten's mood. She and all of her kind—too manipulated even to realize the depths to which they had sunk.

Wistfully, Diego admired the image of his wife. "We had shown we could track the Ice World, whose course pointed toward their home. Toward Hearth. We were attacked lest we reveal Hearth's location distantly orbiting a red-giant star. And so we were taken to the Fleet of Worlds, the secret place, the place from which, they tell me, we may never leave.

"There our nightmare became far worse.

"*Long Pass* carried more than ten thousand passengers, mostly frozen embryos. Our masters say their Concordance took pity, that they could not let so many perish. A few Citizens admit—but only to us, the few forever trapped on board—that they intend to turn our helpless passengers into a slave race. I believe they're at least being honest." Tears glimmered in his eyes (and Kirsten felt stinging in her own). "Two of those little ones are Jaime's and mine.

"The Citizens removed our onboard hibernation tanks to the world they call Nature Preserve Three. They lied to those they awakened about a derelict found adrift. Even so, most people had their doubts. When Citizens encouraged them to start their planned colony, the women resisted immediate implantation with embryos.

"*Long Pass* also carried embryos of mammals, cows and sheep and such, we meant to introduce on New Terra. Of course we had artificial placentas for those animal embryos. The Citizens were determined to have their colony. They experimented with implanting human embryos into artificial animal placentas. They 'refused to accept our voluntary extinction.'"

Kirsten squeezed Eric's hand. He had trembled since the reference to NP3.

"There were spontaneous abortions, horrific birth defects, and developmental problems." Remembered tragedies brought Diego to an eye-blinking halt. "To our masters, those were 'experiments.' To us . . . each was someone's child. Several women agreed to be surrogate mothers to stop the 'experiments.'

"Following a few successful pregnancies, our masters demanded that all women be surrogates. None would. The Citizens brainwiped a few. The rest submitted. Citizens saw nothing wrong with men alone rearing the babies, if it came to that. My guess is that Citizen females aren't sentient. The few men who rebelled—ran amok—were reunited with the four crew still imprisoned on this ship. Us. It's from them that I know the NP3 part of this sad history.

"Then one day, Jaime and Barbara were taken." Diego trembled with loss and rage. "Someone decided their uteruses offered more value than their minds. I know they couldn't be allowed to talk about the attack on *Long Pass* to the uninformed adults on NP3. They must have been brainwiped before joining the colony."

Diego got his voice under control. "And the men still aboard this ship? We counsel our masters how to structure a human society. We try through our advice to alleviate a bit of the suffering. We're trying to reduce forced pregnancies, especially by brain wiping. All the men insist that the mother's active role in child rearing is critical. Two centuries of gender equality is a small sacrifice to save women's minds.

"We do what else we can. Sometimes that's in the vocabulary and concepts we try to retain in the sanitized English taught to the children. Sometimes it's undoing the effects of Citizen mistakes." He smiled, almost despite himself. "Citizens are hardly beyond error. They wear no clothing, so they considered Colonist clothing a waste of resources. They learned quickly enough that nudity does not go with their disapproval of birth control *and* their hopes of controlling the bloodlines."

The smile faded. "I fear they suspect our indirect interference. We've been told of a new colony, this one on NP4, started with only children under Citizens' supervision.

"All that remains for me is hope for the children. If you viewing this recording are like me, are human, know this: You descend from an accomplished people. We settled our whole solar system. We planted colonies, *peacefully,* on the worlds of other suns." Diego swallowed hard. "I wish I could give you the way home. Earth is a beautiful world.

"And if you viewing this recording are Citizens, I wish you go straight to hell."

37

Beneath the watchful eyes of Zeus, Nike decided: It is time.

He reached Nessus in his cabin aboard *Preserver,* the moment too auspicious to mind the nearly ten-second round-trip delay. "Nessus, the Directorate will soon release an urgent communiqué. I wanted you to hear about it first from me.

"It announces the seizure by renegade Colonists of a Fleet facility in orbit around NP5. Our self-sacrificing crew, aboard to monitor eco-forming progress, were taken hostage, but a few"—he kept speaking over Nessus' protest, finally arriving after a few seconds at light speed— "a few hostages escaped. They radioed a report to authorities and will attempt to reassert control. Clandestine Directorate has surrounded the facility with ships, so that those responsible cannot escape."

"Nike." Nessus waited to be sure it was his turn to talk. "Nike, we *agreed* to the small Colonist presence aboard. The technicians are not hostages—although I suppose neither are they merely technicians. How can you call the Colonist presence a seizure?"

"How can you *not* understand?" Nike demanded. "Promises we made to the Colonists we made under duress. We owe them nothing. Our paramount duty is recovery of *Explorer,* or at least its removal from Colonist control."

The comm channel fell silent for much longer than light-speed delay could explain. Pawing the deck, Nessus finally asked, "And when the Colonial government protests?"

"Who will believe them when *Long Pass* no longer exists?" With a graceful wave of the neck, Nike dismissed the certain response before it could arrive. "We have learned by now everything that that primitive spacecraft has to tell. It is only a memento, and we have surely seen that keeping it is an unnecessary risk."

Nessus shuffled in his cabin, too confined to pace. "And the four Colonists? I consider them friends."

"I am not cruel," Nike said. The questions began to irritate him. A budding relationship did not excuse the implied criticism. "They will be taken to the NP3 compound." *If* they survive the takeover, Nike admitted to himself.

With a shiver, Nessus got his feelings under control. "I understand, Nike. I would not want to get in the way inadvertently. Can you tell me exactly what will happen when?"

Relieved by the change in attitude, Nike did.

Nessus stepped to one of *Preserver*'s empty cargo holds. There he circled and circled, amid the clop-clop-clopping echoes of his hooves. Music skirled and resonated as Nessus muttered to himself. It sounded like a small herd in here.

Were the Colonists a threat to the Fleet or merely an embarrassment to the government? Or were they—and he—puppets in some play he did not understand?

He could say nothing—but silence would betray his friends. He could warn them—but of what, exactly, and how much? Would he be betraying Nike?

Nessus set aside the troubling question he had no time now to confront: Could he love one so deceitful and manipulative?

Nessus tugged at his mane. So many questions! All he knew for certain was that Nike had lied to him. As *he* had lied, on many an occasion, to his crew.

The assault was imminent. This impotent agonizing would soon become a decision. A decision with likely outcomes Nessus did not believe he could live with.

He stepped back to his cabin. The surveillance system

showed no Colonists aboard *Preserver*. On *Explorer*, then.
He called Kirsten's communicator. Nothing.

Finally, she answered, looking wary. "Yes, Nessus?"

Why wary? he wondered. Could she possibly know?
"I need to speak with you four. Where are you?"

"We're busy right now," Kirsten said. "Can this wait?"

Nessus straightened, wondering if the body language
would make any difference to Colonists, especially skeptical ones. His conscience demanded he try. He had to
convince them. "Go to a secure channel." Her image dissolved to kaleidoscopic writhing, then re-formed. "Kirsten,
we've been betrayed. If you return to *Preserver*, you will
be arrested soon. *Explorer* is completely boxed in by other
ships, so you cannot escape that way.

"If we act immediately, I think I can sneak you back
to NP4 aboard *Aegis*."

"Eric, come on," Kirsten shouted. "What are you doing,
anyway?"

"Almost done," Eric said, his face scrunched in concentration, his fingers flying over a bridge console. "I don't
have time to explain." Eric rapped the console. "Done."

They ran to *Explorer*'s relax room and stepped through
to the dayroom aboard *Long Pass*.

Sven and Omar had stepped ahead to *Long Pass* to admit Nessus through its airlock. The stepping disc aboard
the ramscoop remained secured with codes they were
loath to share with any Citizen. Nessus, looking more unkempt than usual, opened his communicator. "Colonist
translation mode, on. You know Nike. Now watch and
listen."

Kirsten steadied herself against a wall. "Nessus, how
can we trust you? You've lied to us before. You've withheld
information from us. Maybe the trap is aboard *Aegis*."

Nessus plucked at his mane. "You are wise to doubt me.
You are wise to doubt *any* of us. If this is a ruse, I am as

much a dupe as you. You have been restoring this ship. Can it receive vid broadcasts?"

"I'll go to the bridge," Eric said. "What should I look for?"

"News from Hearth. I would hope an interstellar receiver can receive leakage from local transmissions."

Eric left. Minutes later, full-textured warbling burst from the intercom. Nessus' communicator translated.

Hostage crisis. Government crisis. Disgrace of the not-quite-formed unity government. The nearly converged Consensus, dissolved and condemned. Swelling clamor for Nike and his Permanent Emergency faction.

Did she trust Nessus' translator?

Eric shared her doubts. "I'm switching to an independent translation."

"Resources under the authority of Clandestine Directorate expect to recapture the facility soon," boomed Jeeves. And in lower tones, "I was taught to translate over the years."

"We must hurry," Nessus insisted. "This broadcast is real. The assault will be real. You will be attacked by robots such as attacked *Long Pass* long ago."

The translated broadcast cut off. "Nessus is right, at least about that," Eric said. "Hull cameras show a dozen Citizens and many more robots converging on the gangway. I've put an override on the exterior airlock controls. That won't keep them out for long."

"Hurry, please," Nessus pleaded. "Step through to *Aegis,* if it is not already too late. When the security forces realize I am with you, they will take over *Aegis* or block it in as well."

Sven's eyes darted like a trapped animal's. Remembering the old video of robots cutting their way in? "Nike's message to Nessus spoke of *removing* this ship. Is *Long Pass* repaired enough to fly out?"

Omar grunted. "*Preserver*'s hull is sealed. I can't find any trace of cargo doors. Nike must mean to remove *Long*

Pass in tiny pieces. Or maybe they'll drop *Preserver* into a star with this ship still inside."

Kirsten's mind raced, desperately seeking an escape. But even if they were doomed, their report must get out. "Eric! Can we transmit, too? If so, send the Diego MacMillan recording to Hearth and NP4."

"Diego MacMillan?" Nessus' heads pivoted in confusion. "Who is that?"

"Will do, Kirsten," Eric replied. "But I need you on the bridge."

She uploaded a copy of Diego's message to Nessus' pocket computer—he should know they would no longer be taken for fools—and ran for the bridge.

Holos floated all around Eric, some status, some system specs, and a few apparently real-time video. In the largest holo, robots approached the gangway. "What can I do?" she asked.

He asked without looking up, "Do you trust me?"

"You and not much else." They were running out of time. "If you have an idea, try it."

Ruby-red, a laser beam blazed out from near *Long Pass*'s bow. Decking bubbled and steamed at the robots' feet. "Comm laser," Eric explained. "Teach them some caution." The smaller holos flickered and danced all around him. "Jeeves, status check on the ramscoop?"

"Ready on your command," Jeeves said.

Eric opened another holo, real-time video of the day-room. "Nessus." The scout was rapt in Diego's recording. "Nessus! Listen to me." Eric raised the intercom volume and whistled sharply. "Nessus!"

Heads snapped up, startled. "Yes, Eric."

"In two minutes, I'm activating the ramscoop field. Do you know what that will do?"

Kirsten had no idea, but Nessus shook like a leaf. "It will kill everyone within hundreds of miles, except here in the life-support area."

Eric fired the comm laser again, scything a robot in

half. "No, Nessus. Just everyone else within *Preserver*. The GP hull will contain the field. Everyone now has a minute, forty seconds to teleport off this ship. You need to tell them because they won't believe a Colonist. Then get out yourself—unless you trust us and truly want to help. A minute and thirty seconds."

Nessus screamed, like the pulling of a hundred rusty nails. His torso heaved. In seconds he mastered his fear, or anger, or whatever emotion had immobilized him. He warbled rapidly and emphatically into his communicator.

Nike's security team must be somewhat mad, to plot violence against the Colonists aboard *Long Pass,* but they weren't much madder than most Citizens. They pivoted and ran for stepping discs. The robots paused in their tracks— but only briefly. Nike's agents resumed their remote-controlled attack from the safety of their docked ships.

Nessus had not moved.

"Nessus . . ." Kirsten trailed off, at a loss for words.

"Because you do not deserve what has been planned for you," Nessus said. "If nothing else, I offer myself as a witness."

In the composite panorama from the hull cameras, three broad I-beams, one supporting the gangway, converged to support *Long Pass*. All three supports terminated in the massive band that suspended the ramscoop ship in *Preserver*'s vast central cavity, against *Preserver*'s gravity generator. Writhing shadows on the cavity wall hinted at robots scuttling along the hidden undersides of all three approaches. The comm laser could not reach them without severing the support beams and sending *Long Pass* crashing.

Eric called, "Omar, Sven, Nessus. Get aboard *Explorer*. I think you'll get a chance to get away."

Omar's voice snapped, "Then both of you come too!"

"I must be here to give you that chance," Eric said. "Kirsten, you'll be safer with them."

She massaged his shoulders, taut with tension. "I'm staying with you."

"Where will I be most helpful?" Nessus asked.

"Here on *Long Pass*." Eric opened another display. A wire-frame map of *Preserver,* Kirsten thought. A red dot pulsed on the hull, its significance lost on her.

"Sven, Omar, go!" Eric shouted. "In about a minute, all hell will break loose. Your autopilot will kick on. That's your chance."

Kirsten watched them vanish from the dayroom. Nessus remained, pawing at the deck.

"We're hemmed in, all right," Omar reported a moment later. "Right up against *Preserver*'s hull. I don't see how the autopilot can help that."

On the distant, curved wall of the central cavity, the scuttling shadows seemed closer. They would begin carving their way into the hull at any moment.

Eric never looked away from his keyboard. *Long Pass* appeared now inside the wire-frame drawing, with a faint line connecting the ramscoop with the mysterious red dot. "What happens now?" Kirsten asked.

"Now we see if I'm worthy of you." As Eric spoke, the communications laser blazed out from *Long Pass*'s bow, far brighter than before. Bright enough, Kirsten marveled, to reach between the stars. The beam punched through *Preserver*'s cavity wall like tissue paper. Molten metal dripped from the hole. As the beam traced a spiral, the hole grew. Chunks of wall and decking fell inward.

Eric finally looked at Kirsten. "Remember the General Products factory? Remember how unhappy Baedeker was at my questions?"

Through metal vapor and a maelstrom of in-falling debris, she glimpsed a tunnel that gaped to *Preserver*'s hull. There the ruby-red light vanished, the absence of scattering in a vacuum rendering the beam invisible. "Baedeker?" she repeated. "He didn't say anything about light. Anyway, we know the hull is transparent to visible light. How does the laser help us?"

The shadows had almost reached *Long Pass*'s hull.

"Remember what Baedeker refused to explain. Nessus said there's a power plant embedded in the hull. The power plant reinforces the interatomic bonds of the hull supermolecule. I found it. The hull—the supermolecule—is transparent to visible light.

"Kirsten, we know we can't find Earth. We need to concentrate on what we want from the Concordance when we win."

"We're *winning*?"

Terawatts of coherent light poured from *Preserver*'s General Products #4 hull—all but the tiny fraction of the questing beam intersected by a sealed, lifetime-fueled, embedded power plant. A tiny fraction, but still gigawatts of focused power.

The fusion reactor overheated and shut itself down.

Artificially constructed interatomic bonds were suddenly without reinforcement. The super-molecule that was *Preserver*'s hull regressed into ordinary matter. To Kirsten's view, a wave of opaque gray spread across the big ship's hull.

The dust shell around *Long Pass* held, bulged, then blew away like a dandelion puff in a tornado.

Air pressure exploded the flimsy decks and partitions, spewing shrapnel large and small. Lights, gravity, communications—every system died. Kirsten gasped as the floor fell out from under her. Eric didn't twitch.

Explorer, whose autopilot Eric had set to dart *inward* on full thrusters, bulldozed through the debris, away from the ships that had confined it.

Now *Long Pass*'s laser flicked downward, severing the massive support beams. Attitude jets set *Long Pass* spinning, faster and faster, hurling away any robots that still clung to the stubs.

"Jeeves," said Eric steadily, "We're getting too much radiation. Way too much. How are you doing with the ramscoop?"

Kirsten needed a moment to decode that. Orbiting NP5 with neither *Preserver*'s hull nor the planetary force field for protection, radiation induced by the Fleet's own velocity was blasting the old starship. Was blasting *them*. They needed the ramscoop's magnetic field to divert the oncoming muck.

"Working," Jeeves answered. "Working. Hydrogen density is adequate, velocity is adequate. Ramscoop fields in place. Accelerating at point zero zero three gee and rising. Eric, *Long Pass* is surrounded by rubble."

"Use the comm laser on anything that's in our way. Kirsten." Eric's voice shook with tension and exhaustion. "I could really use a good pilot just now."

"You got it," Kirsten said.

Atop a miles-long column of blue-white fusion flame, *Long Pass* set its course for nearby Hearth.

38

Shouting.

Nessus squeezed himself yet more tightly, and the muffled noise faded. Then a rough kneading began, the heads—no, hands—unfamiliar to him. Colonists!

He remembered the gravity dying, then spinning, faster and faster. He'd been flung off his hooves. He had tucked himself into a tight ball just as he hit the dayroom wall.

Nessus cautiously unclenched a bit. A man's voice called his name. Eric's voice. Nessus unclenched a little more. "Where are we? Are we safe?"

"We're on *Long Pass,* on our way to Hearth. As to our safety, the circumstances don't permit an easy answer. Come out so we can talk."

"*Preserver* is going to Hearth? Why?" Nessus asked.

"*Preserver* has been destroyed. It's just *Long Pass*."

With a wail, he compressed as tightly as he could. Eric's voice became unintelligible until suffocation forced him to loosen a bit. Then Nessus heard: "Less than an hour to Hearth."

Shuddering convulsively, Nessus unrolled and stood. He was still in the dayroom. The room's main holo showed a telescopic image: a cloud of debris glittering by sunlight against the stormy backdrop of NP5. Gases faintly aglow, streaming past in primary colors, converged aft: the ancient ship's ramscoop come to life.

"*Preserver* destroyed? That's impossible! It would take large amounts of antimatter." Nessus waited out an involuntary tremor. "Are you bringing antimatter to Hearth? You play with star-fire energies as casually as you put edges on furniture!"

"You've kept many secrets, Nessus." Eric grinned unpleasantly. "I have mine. I suggest you consider more pressing matters. Kirsten"—he raised his voice—"what's our status?"

"I'm here." Her voice over the intercom sounded frighteningly tense. "I've been beaming Diego's final message to Hearth for the past twenty minutes. We arrive in another forty."

Nessus sensed an unarticulated question in her tension: What then?

He nipped and tore at his mane, thoughts churning. Freed of *Preserver,* the Colonists hardly needed antimatter to threaten Hearth. A low orbit while operating the ramscoop field would quickly kill billions on the ground. A drifting hover over almost any populated area would kill mere millions. Lacking hyperwave radio, *Long Pass* carried a comm laser powerful enough to beam across light-years. At short distances, it, too, would be fearsome.

Eric watched silently, appraisingly. Nessus thought: I'm

meant to work through the horrors of this situation. He knows they have a position of strength.

Forty minutes. What could possibly stop this ship? Very few Citizen pilots were insane enough to fly anything other than routine food transfers. That was why the Colonist scouting program began in the first place. Who would be *so* insane as to board a ship now, knowing that it could be dissolved around him?

Hearth was *hidden,* not *protected.* How could a planetary defense be organized in mere minutes?

Shaking violently, Nessus battled his useless instinct to flight. Where could he go? Where could anyone go? "You said I would be most helpful here. What would you have me do?"

"Kirsten?" Eric prompted.

She answered in a firm voice. "Radio the Concordance. Persuade the authorities that the price of Hearth's safety is immediate freedom for all Colonists, publicly promised."

"We arrive in minutes!" Nessus said. "The government is in chaos. You cannot expect—"

"We do expect," Eric interrupted. "Time changes nothing except their ability to conspire against us."

"Call Nike," Kirsten said. "Do it now. Convince him we're serious, so that we do not have to show *how* serious. However chaotic the government, Nike will know whom to contact."

"Freedom from what? What do you want?"

Kirsten said, "I think we want NP4."

Nessus whistled a wordless query.

"I can't think of a safe way to claim just the continent of Arcadia," Kirsten said. "We'll have to take the whole planet. Does NP4 still have its motor? Of course it does, we've been accelerating for years. Nessus, you wouldn't still want us as neighbors, would you? After this is over, we'll have to be gone, one way or another. We're too dangerous."

Nessus' thoughts raced. Less than forty minutes until the end of the world. "I'm coming to the bridge, if that's satisfactory."

Eric shook his head. "You can talk from here."

Did they think him insane enough to attempt to retake the ship from them? Perhaps so: Eric now held a flashlight laser. Nessus shook with fear and rage. "I'll stay." He plunged a head into a belt pocket to tongue communications codes. "This will get us through to Nike."

The holo broadcast was ubiquitous: in millions of stores and dining halls, in billions of homes, and, magnified to many times life-size, in public spaces around the globe.

Even here in the remote island retreat of the Hindmost.

Everywhere, Diego MacMillan glared at his oppressors. Nothing short of a Fleet-wide network shutdown might interrupt the damning recitation. Nothing short of a Fleet-wide network restart might purge all the copies. Even then, countless billions would remember it.

I do not believe in ghosts, thought Nike, and yet here one is.

Nike did his best to ignore the dissonant clamoring that filled the room. The Hindmost let his ministers, Eos newly among them, prattle on, obsessing illogically on how best to explain or excuse or resuppress centuries-old tragedies. Did no one wonder why the Colonists had released this history?

Maybe a few did. The more practical among the ministers had succumbed already to the dubious safety of their underbellies.

Unexpected trilling released Nike from his futile musings. Only Vesta held the access code that could reach him now. Nessus had known it too, Nike thought sadly. There had been no word from Nessus since the destruction of *Preserver*.

Nike took the call, wondering: What new catastrophe has occurred?

Nessus appeared in a small holo, and Nike felt a glow of relief. "You're alive!"

"For now," Nessus said. He stepped backward to reveal a hard-faced Colonist with flashlight laser in hand. "You remember Eric. He and Kirsten now control *Long Pass*."

The Hindmost extended a neck at the unexpected holo. "You dare to take calls at this time?" he roared.

Nike did not flinch. "The Colonists now command a weapon of frightening potency. Clandestine Directorate has an agent aboard, and he is our best source of information. Report, Nessus."

Voices quavering, Nessus spoke: Of the dissolution of *Preserver*. Of Citizen ships fleeing from NP5. Of *Long Pass*, a fearful engine of death now rushing to Hearth. Of Colonist demands and dire threats.

Incomprehensible but nonetheless familiar English translation droned in the background.

"And they have antimatter?" the Hindmost asked, focused finally on a real problem.

Nessus plucked at his mane. "How else can one dissolve a General Products hull?"

Antimatter or fusion flame? Did the precise mechanism of megadeath truly matter? Nike whistled over the swelling fear of the ministers. "Describe their demands."

Nessus moaned. "Ceding all of NP4 to the Colonists. The right to withdraw NP4 from the Fleet, if and when they choose, and our cooperation in doing so."

"We're humans, not your colonists. Not any longer." Eric bared his teeth in a feral snarl. "We also require the repatriation of all humans to NP4—regardless of the world on which you now hold them."

"These are extraordinary demands," the Hindmost said with undertunes of fear and dread. "It is impossible to meet them before your arrival. Impossible."

"In a few minutes," Kirsten said flatly, "you will receive a demonstration. It may make you reconsider what is achievable." Her disembodied voice made the warning all the more chilling. "An arcology or two seared in the fire of suns."

With a howl of despair, the Hindmost collapsed. He rolled into a tight ball.

A few ministers remained on their hooves. They turned as one to Nike, and an eerie calm came over him. This was *his* moment. "Kirsten and Eric, I have a proposal. Reverse course immediately and return control of your ship to authorities. In exchange, the government will publicly pledge to honor your demands."

"Trust you?" Eric laughed humorlessly. "We tried that before, Nike."

"Then what would you suggest?" Nike asked.

"You publicly commit the Concordance to our freedom," Kirsten said. "We keep *Long Pass,* but promise not to use it against the Fleet." Unless you renege, she did not bother to add.

"Five minutes," Eric reminded.

The attempt on the Colonists' lives had failed. So had his more recent and elaborate betrayal. Perhaps, Nike mused, it was time to consider a new approach toward the Colonists.

Respect.

Assuming a confident, wide-legged stance, necks extended high, Nike said, "The Concordance accepts."

ODYSSEY

Earth date: 2652

39

Transfer-booth abduction still worked.

"Welcome back," Nessus said to the woman trembling before him. Unobservable behind a one-way mirror, he yanked at his mane. Hull material enclosed his guest—which was not the comfort it once had been.

He scarcely recognized Sangeeta Kudrin. Only in part was that due to the skimpy black evening dress in which he had found her. Her facial piercings were gone; the bold blue dye job he remembered had been exchanged for muted greens; and new muscle hung on her petite frame.

"Two years," she finally said. "I had dared to hope you were gone for good. It's Nessus, isn't it?"

"Correct." On his exterior views, Mojave Spaceport was emptier and seedier than on his last visit. "I hope to make this brief."

Sangeeta said nothing.

"You prospered during my absence," Nessus continued. Public databases now listed her as a UN undersecretary, no longer a mere deputy.

She sighed. "You kidnapped me before for information. Is that why you've taken me now?"

"It is." Nessus shifted in his nest of cushions. "Information about Sigmund Ausfaller."

Sangeeta stiffened. "Him again. He's still away chasing pirates."

That was too cryptic for Nessus. He queried through the spaceport network for a definition. Armed thieves operating on a water surface? "Go on."

"Back when you first contacted me, Ausfaller was obsessed with distant ship disappearances. Then starships much nearer began disappearing."

"Where?" Nessus asked.

The question surprised her. "On the fringes of Sol system. Around the third disappearance, other systems started shunning us. Ship captains here began refusing to leave. Ausfaller declared the situation a threat to the state, and launched an investigation."

Her hands wandered, vainly seeking pockets in which to hide. "In a few months, eight ships vanished. The last communication with any of them was from the Oort Cloud, which the newsies took to calling 'The Borderland of Sol.' Then Ausfaller himself went after suspected pirates, using his own ship as bait."

Ausfaller diverted from the scent of the Fleet by pirates. It seemed much too convenient. Nessus disbelieved in coincidences, especially those that worked to his advantage. "Continue."

"How can you not know about this?" Sangeeta asked incredulously.

"I was busy. Tell me more."

"Ausfaller's reports are highly classified. No administrator, even a full undersecretary, has access."

"So he reported pirates." A suspicion came over Nessus. Yes, the Oort Cloud was an immense region. It was still odd that he could not contact Julian Forward. It was odder still that public databases made no mention of Forward Station since shortly after Nessus' hasty return to the Fleet. Nessus ventured a guess. "Pirates operating out of Forward Station?"

Her eyes widened. "How did you know?"

"Then you *do* know something more," Nessus said.

"Nothing certain. You have to understand." She swallowed hard. "There were rumors everywhere about conspiracies and cover-ups. One of the most prominent scientists in Human Space, gone without a trace. Ausfaller was suddenly questioning gravity theorists, cosmologists, every manner of esoteric physicist. Interstellar commerce shut down for months. People feared to leave the inner system. Surely you remember how confusing everything was."

Behind the mirror, Nessus twitched. He knew all about conspiracy and confusion.

Sangeeta babbled on about witch hunts. "And the Jinx government is still demanding answers about Julian Forward, information Ausfaller refuses to give." She leaned forward to whisper, "I believe Forward is dead, that Ausfaller killed him."

Nessus did not believe in coincidences. Sangeeta's account suggested he did not need to. "So Ausfaller is obsessed now, wondering how Forward made neutronium," he summarized.

"Yes, damn you! Haven't you been listening? No one knows much more. Ausfaller simply won't talk. After he ended the pirate attacks, no one, not even the ARM director, would dare challenge Ausfaller to reveal more than he chooses."

Nessus shut his eyes in thought. It was suddenly clear. After he lost his grant from the Institute of Knowledge, Julian had fixated about money for his research. Forward must have managed to produce enough neutronium to make a tiny hyperspace singularity, a mini black hole. Any ship passing close enough to it would be dropped precipitously from hyperspace, to be looted by Julian's lurking henchmen. Probably the looted ships and their crews were now but a bit more mass added to the singularity.

"Very good. You may go." Nessus transferred Sangeeta to a remote booth before she could comment.

Ausfaller chasing shadows. Julian Forward, and the advanced Concordance technology reluctantly disclosed to him, both gone. The Fleet, once again, safe from prying eyes.

On the other head . . .

Eight starship crews vanished, dead. Earth still in convulsion—in the final analysis, unnecessarily—over

Fertility Board corruption scandals and birthright lotteries. Rather than research and tally those casualties, Nessus turned his attention to ending the mayhem.

Perhaps minions could be put to *good* use.

Glowing streaks of pink cloud alternated with impossibly azure bands of sky. Pink deepened to red, and azure to ever darker shades of blue, as the great crimson ball of Sol sank slowly behind the mountains.

Nessus watched in awe until the sky over the spaceport faded to black. Once, on sunless Hearth, he had described the beauty of a sunrise to Nike. How long ago that seemed!

How distant seemed the time until they might reunite.

An upper atmosphere wind drove the clouds steadily eastward. Stars took their place, glittering like diamonds. Nessus watched until the sun rose.

In his hearts, Nessus knew: If he and Nike were to have ° future, first they needed time apart. Time to come to terms with each other's actions. Time to accept actions that could never be admitted.

When Hearth itself faced imminent catastrophe, what did a *promise* matter? Nessus had had no choice but to urge it. Nike had had no choice but to give it.

Had Nike guessed how overwhelmingly the terrified populace would support that coerced promise? That Kirsten's War, no less than the false emergency Nike had sought to contrive, would crystallize into a new Consensus? Probably, yes. Who but Experimentalists could even *look* at the *Long Pass* crisis, let alone deal with it?

But Nike must wonder whether Nessus had acted under duress. Far better *that* ambiguity than that Nike ever know Nessus' true beliefs:

The Colonists deserved their freedom.

He had never believed Kirsten capable of fulfilling her threat.

Nessus rose stiffly from his nest of pillows, grateful that his responsibilities would keep him in Sol system for a while. He still looked forward, in the fullness of time, to returning to Hearth. To never again leaving Hearth.

And just possibly, to life there as the mate of the new Hindmost.

40

Boldly striped in yellows and browns, its unbroken clouds aswirl with storms, the mighty world, ninety thousand miles wide, dominated the sky. From the Ice Moon's orbit the gas giant spanned six degrees—a dozen times the apparent size of nearest neighbors within the Fleet.

The Ice Moon itself glowed, on one side from the light of the distant sun, and on the other side, far more brightly, from the sunlight reflected by its primary. Large structures snaked across the ice, many erected since *Explorer*'s previous visit.

From the comparative comfort of her crash couch, Kirsten pointed into the holo. The incomplete ice-and-metal space station glittered like jewels. "They did it, Omar. Crewed spaceflight."

"I can almost understand a Citizen's instinctive reaction," Omar said. "The Gw'oth rate of development is astonishing." He waved off her objection faster than she could get it out. "I said *almost,* Kirsten. The galaxy would be a poorer place without the little guys. I'm happy to find them faring so well."

She was gladdest to have found and disarmed the comet bomb Nessus had insisted they rig. The recovered and reprogrammed GP #1 probe would forever orbit this solar system, reporting by hyperwave radio any abrupt change in radio chatter—such as would occur if the Concordance should ever drop a comet on them.

"They must be protected." Omar grunted agreement, but Kirsten knew she spoke mostly to herself. "We owe the Gw'oth a *lot*. Appreciating their accomplishments taught us to appreciate our own. Questioning Citizen intentions toward the Gw'oth taught us to question Concordance policy toward Colonists."

Habits died hard. She corrected herself: "I mean toward humans."

Omar stood and yawned. "I'm going for coffee. Can I bring you anything?"

"Ice cream. Strawberry," she said. One of the first changes made to *Explorer* after the crisis was new choices in the synthesizer's repertoire.

"Kirsten."

She looked up, and Omar handed her a bowl. How long had she been contemplating the holo? Omar said, "We're done here, Kirsten. The Gw'oth are as safe as we can make them. Our place now is at home."

Omar was right, of course, and yet . . . "There is one thing more we can do. A message for them. A way to thank them properly."

He shook his head. "Everyone agreed, Kirsten, before we set out. Science and technology are very new to the Gw'oth. We can't know how they would respond to alien contact."

"That isn't what I meant." She explained, and he went off to translate her words.

And so they departed—but first they left a message.

The Ice Moon's closest neighbor was a rocky, cloud-shrouded moon. It was tidally locked to its more distant primary, keeping one face forever hidden from the Ice Moon.

But not, if they continued to advance, from the Gw'oth.

A miles-long X, etched by laser, now marked the far side of that moon. A cubic structure of laser-carved stone slabs stood at the X's center. Inside that cube, sealed within a clear plasteel container, in an inert atmosphere of pure nitrogen, the Gw'oth would someday find the powerful radio buoy for which the guardian hyperwave buoy would forever listen. In every common pictographic script of the Gw'oth, ahead of instructions on operating the radio, the accompanying note began:

"Call if you ever find yourselves in need. The Gw'oth are not without friends in the galaxy."

Kirsten shifted positions yet again, wondering how she had ever considered crash couches comfortable. More likely, the General Products couches were yet another evil device designed by Baedeker. She stood, circled the tiny bridge several times, then settled back down with a groan. The mass pointer remained empty.

Omar walked onto the bridge and handed her a bowl. Vanilla. "I'm ready for home, too. New Terra."

Kirsten patted her swelling belly. "We both are."

41

Jeeves had described the long delay as necessary to get their ducks in a row. Eric had neither the patience nor the passivity of an AI. For him, this was personal. For that matter, Eric didn't know what a duck was.

Metaphor aside, Jeeves's meaning was clear. Many milestones necessarily preceded this mission. Repatriation of Colonists from the secret facility on NP3. The vote whether to withdraw NP4 from the Fleet. Instruction on operating and maintaining the world-moving drive. Accumulating new deuterium and tritium reserves. Acceleration of NP4—New Terra—away from the Fleet of Worlds. Learning to stealth the few starships retained by the former colony.

The painful recovery of long repressed memories.

Sharing the tiny bridge of *Long Pass Two*, Sven fidgeted with his gear and pretended to ignore the blind spot that lurked just beyond the covered view port. "How much longer?" he asked yet again.

Minutes matter when using hyperdrive. Exit a minute earlier than necessary and you had an extra billion miles of normal space to cross. Of course waiting a minute too long could drop you into a singularity, beyond the knowledge of even Citizen science. "It's all right, Sven. No one likes being in hyperspace." Eric canted his head and assessed the mass pointer one more time. Five scarcely distinguishable lines pointed toward them. "A few more minutes."

Shadowy figures darkened Eric's own thoughts. NP3 repatriates shared too many irrational dreads to doubt a common cause. It had taken extensive painful therapy to reconstruct their—and his—repressed memories of another human facility somewhere on NP3. Neither psychotherapy nor data mining had located that other place, the compound whose existence the Concordance indignantly denied.

Traumatic amnesia, Jeeves had called the condition, and recovering the lost childhood memories was painful. As an adult, Eric understood: The coerced cooperation of *Long Pass*'s women had not ended Citizens' experimentation with human breeding.

The successes, their memories suppressed, were relocated to the main NP3 colony, or even, as in Eric's case, to NP4. The failures, those beyond the ability of autodocs to help, remained behind: crippled and scarred in ways not even therapy could force Eric to face.

What he no longer forgot, he would never forgive.

They would find out soon enough whether the pain of recovering those memories had been worth it.

Sven squirmed in his crash couch. In the mass pointer, singularities reached out to devour them. It's time, Eric thought. "Ten seconds. Five. Now." He uncovered the view port.

Five dull lights in a pentagon lay directly ahead.

* * *

Moments later, Eric received a radio burst: *Courageous*. After final confirmation of details, Eric took *Long Pass Two* ahead on an arcing course.

They approached the Fleet from within the plane of the pentagon, waiting until NP3 hid the other worlds before reversing thrusters to hover. Chance observation by a Citizen ship could be disastrous. In free flight, the embedded power plant of another ship would be an impossible target. The credible threat of antimatter encouraged the Concordance to honor its commitments to Arcadia—and, of course, Arcadia had only the illusion of antimatter.

Ice caps glittered in the suns. Extensive snow cover appeared on northern and southern continents. One more duck they had waited for, Eric thought. Winter, and with it the evacuation of most Citizens from the compound. Hearth with its unavoidable waste heat, like NP4 with its polar-orbiting suns, had a temperate climate worldwide. Citizens hated the cold.

Despite himself, Eric smiled. Romping in the snow was a *good* recovered memory; he savored it while waiting for the suns to set.

Preserving samples of all Hearthian life required reproducing all Hearthian climates and seasons. NP3's equatorial suns heated higher latitudes less. In full "winter," a few suns at the end of the orbiting string went dark, for the shorter and cooler days some life forms required.

The last sun finally disappeared around the horizon. "Ready?" Eric asked.

"Ready," Sven agreed.

Viewed in infrared, the night side cooled rapidly. Scattered areas continued to glow hot. A few glowed *too* hot: hot springs and volcanoes. Other anomalies took study to identify: factories and power plants.

By process of elimination, Eric narrowed the possibilities to five heat sources. Two were at latitudes too low to fit the consensus recovered memory of long winters at the compound. High-resolution thermal sensing eliminated two more locations—

And revealed unmistakably human shapes at the last site. Sven said, "That must be it."

At some level, Eric had dared to hope the traumatic memories false. He breathed slowly and deeply until he trusted himself to speak. "Agreed. We're going in."

Hearthian forest surrounded the compound. He set *Long Pass Two* down in the closest clearing, ten miles away, trying not to remember the hike through woods to the Human Studies Institute—or Kirsten. Better to remain focused. "Let's unload the floaters."

Stepping discs had eliminated most ground transportation. The floaters they rode from the cargo bay were essentially miniaturized but full-powered tractors. Snow swirled all around. Despite heating elements woven into his nanofabric garment, Eric shivered.

They slipped into the woods, guided by inertial navigation units in the floaters. Infrared goggles made the view bright as day. Only wind whistling through the branches and the soft hum of the floater motors broke the silence.

These woods were far denser than on Elysium or in the Hearthian park. Thickets and hedges far outnumbered single-trunk trees. Their route grew circuitous as the dense growth stymied their passage. Glancing at his wrist Sven said, "This is taking too long,"

"Agreed." Eric dialed a flashlight-laser down to a narrow beam that scythed through the undergrowth. Snow on the forest floor flashed to steam, enveloping them. Sap sizzled and popped, and scattered plants burst into flame. Things screamed in dismay from the winter-bare limbs of the forest canopy. "Let's go."

Seventy minutes later, with several smoldering thickets in their wake, they reached a sprawl of buildings within a tall fence. The sky remained dark. They circled the facility on foot, scanning with infrared as they went.

The only Citizen IR signatures came from a single building. Unmoving: asleep. The human signatures were concentrated in a second building. A dormitory and hospital, Eric guessed. Dispersed quarters would have made their task that much harder.

Their breath hung before them in the cold. "Let's do this," Sven finally said. Without waiting for an answer, he sent his floater soaring over the fence. Eric followed.

A few faces peered out of dormitory windows. Within moments, the windows filled. Eric bypassed the alarm on the dormitory door, then stepped back. "Your turn, Sven."

Eric followed Sven inside and jammed the door latch behind them. Sven spoke soothingly, about nothing specific at first, as Eric reset stepping discs to send-only mode. He tried to ignore the people he glimpsed as he worked. Shriveled adults, unlike anyone he had ever encountered. Short people who must be children, whose eyes revealed sad truths no child should ever have to bear. Crippled and wasted bodies. Terrified faces.

And a few faces that awakened memories in a terrifying rush.

"We have come to take you home," Sven was saying. "To where *our* kind, not Citizens, make the laws. I promise you will be cared for if you come. It is your choice, but I urge you, I implore you, to join us. You must decide now, and quickly.

"I bring you something of our past to help you decide." Sven activated his pocket computer.

The image of Diego MacMillan appeared. "I am the navigator of starship *Long Pass*. I have a story to tell."

As people wept and moaned, and the younger children stared with incomprehension, Eric radioed *Courageous*. "Loading to commence within minutes," he said.

"Copy that," replied Terrence, the pilot. "We're standing by, burning fuel like mad to hover ten thousand miles over your heads."

In other words: hurry.

"There were spontaneous abortions, horrific birth defects, and developmental problems," Diego said. Tears streamed down the faces of the inmates. They understood all too well.

When the recording ended Sven added, quite simply, "These reprogrammed stepping discs will bring you to our ship, for a short flight to a better world. A *human* world."

A bent and wizened woman stepped forward and disappeared. An emaciated man with horribly gnarled limbs followed. Parents gathered their weeping children. With a shuffling gait, people formed lines. The lines shortened. Shortened. Disappeared.

"Time to go," Eric said. He had never felt so drained. He retrieved the stepping-disc address that would return them to *Long Pass Two*.

Sven was gone.

"Over here!" Sven's voice echoed down a long corridor. Eric followed. He found Sven gazing through a massive plasteel window into a lab. Shiny metal cabinets covered in gauges and buttons lined the walls.

"Look at those corners and edges!" Sven gestured at the cabinets. "Humans built those. And from old records I've seen, I'm sure I know what they are! Embryo banks. Egg banks. Incubators and placentas. They must be from *Long Pass*." Sven pounded on the window in frustration. "Is there a way to deduce the stepping-disc address for inside?"

Embryo banks! Eric shook with rage, unable to speak. He sliced a door-sized opening with his laser. The slab teetered, then toppled inward with a crash.

Sven rushed to the cabinets. "This one has sea life: sea turtles, squid, all kinds of fish. Some names I've encountered, more I haven't." He looked at the next case. "Big mammals: lions, polar bears, elephants." And the next case. "Dozens of bird species, including ducks."

"*Courageous*," Eric called. "We've sent all the people. Now we have cargo for you." He ignored Sven's oblivious excitement at some seed findings.

"Copy that, Eric. Standing by."

Sven's computer clattered to the floor. His face was ashen. "More human embryos. Almost a thousand."

He'd found what Eric feared—and somehow knew—they would.

They did not step back onto *Long Pass Two* until they had teleported every earthly seed, egg, and embryo to the cargo ship hovering overhead.

Once more the nothingness lay in wait, inches away.

Eric scarcely noticed. Maybe, he thought, he was getting used to hyperspace. Or maybe he had not realized just how many emotional scabs the mission to NP3 would rip open.

He only knew that he could not wait to get home to New Terra.

Sven also ignored what lay outside, lost in data he had recovered from the lab. Every few minutes he would murmur or nod or exclaim cryptically.

"Take over for a while. I'm going for some soup. Anything for you?" Eric took the shrug he got to mean, who has time for food?

He returned to the bridge to find Sven smiling strangely. "What now?" Eric asked.

"One of my uploads is a genealogical database. Breeding records—for NP3 and also from Arcadian hospitals."

Eric couldn't understand why that made Sven smile. Then Sven showed Eric an excerpt from the database, and Eric grinned, too.

He and Kirsten had decided to name their baby Diego or Jaime. They meant it as a token of respect.

It was a far more fitting choice than they had known. Diego and Jaime, Eric now read, were Kirsten's great-to-the-sixteenth grandparents.

42

Sudden murmuring among his aides, the words indistinct but the significance unmistakably familiar. Nike sighed. Another problematical state of affairs, about which those in the next room debated whether to disturb him.

They already had.

The universe was strange, Nike thought. The most significant changes could manifest themselves in the subtlest ways. Only two NP worlds presently hung overhead, and yet their slightly increased spacing shouted that another world was set free to wander.

He would be happier when it had wandered farther. A fraction of a light-year still made the rebels close neighbors.

He stood alone on the grand balcony of his favorite mountainside estate. The view down to the sea was as spectacular as ever. The wind, blowing now from just the wrong direction, carried a hint of something rank—another of those small but essential reminders. Removing a world from the Fleet had complications. Ocean surges had washed ashore great piles of still-rotting sea life.

So many changes, Nike mused. Nessus would adjust quickly—when he returned to the Fleet, that was. It was best for them both that Nessus stay away for a while.

When would his doubts, anger, and loss finally sort themselves out? Nike stared upward, determined to consider anything other than his feelings toward Nessus.

Five worlds, not six—surely a small thing. Within his grandfathers' lifetimes, the Fleet had comprised but five worlds. Within his grandfathers' lifetimes, those worlds had coped without human servants.

The exquisite irony delighted Nike. Everything returning to so recent a norm had swept *out* the Conservatives and brought *in* the Experimentalists. Of course it was a Conservative government that had allowed the Colonists to get antimatter. His security forces had yet to determine how, but Nessus had had it right: How else could *Preserver*'s GP hull have been destroyed?

No wonder the people had rebelled.

Still the aides murmured inside. Nike pressed through the weather-resistant force field into their room. "What now?" he warbled impatiently.

"Apologies, Hindmost," one of them offered. "Vesta insists on speaking with you now."

"Then bring him!" Nike blasted enough harmonics to make a point. To *this* Hindmost, foreign affairs mattered. Vesta was now the Deputy Minister directing Clandestine Affairs.

Permitted access, Vesta arrived immediately. They brushed heads, and Nike led Vesta back to the balcony. "What has happened?"

"We have a problem on NP3," Vesta said. He bowed heads submissively. "A Colonist raid. The breeding compound was evidently not so secret. They removed everyone and everything."

Overhead on NP5, cyclones raged worse than ever. Energy from the recent ocean surges must have strengthened the storms. Nike listened to the report. "Are our people safe?"

"Yes, Hindmost."

At the base of the mountain, great combers washed in. The tide: now one of eight daily, not ten. Another reminder to embrace change. "Perhaps it is for the best," Nike decided. "If we still had the ability, we would surely be tempted to create new servants. Recent events suggest we are better off without them."

Vesta pawed at the marble tiled floor. "We should punish the Colonists."

"No," Nike said adamantly. "And it would be best, my friend, if you stopped thinking of them as Colonists. The humans reclaimed their own. I think I respect them for that."

"Understood, Hindmost."

"And of your human agents on New Terra?" Nike asked.

Vesta straightened. "They radio according to schedule, Hindmost. Our hyperwave buoy just beyond their planetary singularity continues to relay. I expect regular updates to continue."

"Excellent." Citizens could also play tricks with hyperwave radio buoys. Would Baedeker appreciate that? Probably not, Nike decided. Hard labor in the fields of NP1 left little time or energy for such abstract musings.

In a few hundred years, the Fleet would rise above the crowded galactic disk. A consensus no longer existed as to which way to turn next.

Of course, that was a decision the "liberated" humans would now have to make first.

Perhaps, according to planted hints, they would turn toward the galactic center. Inward, to where they could at least hope to encounter their ancestors. Inward, to where myriads of newly sterilized worlds lay fallow. Inward, and away from the now-hated Fleet.

But *inward* was exactly where Nike meant for the Fleet to go. How much better, then, if an unwitting world of scouts could first draw the attention of any intelligent races that still survived in the core.

These Colonists were quite mistaken to believe their fate and the Concordance's fate could be so easily disentwined.